# THE BLOODSTAINED THRONE

# THE BLOODSTAINED THRONE

## Simon Beaufort

This first world edition published 2010
in Great Britain and in the USA by
SEVERN HOUSE PUBLISHERS LTD of
9–15 High Street, Sutton, Surrey, England, SM1 1DF.
Trade paperback edition first published
in Great Britain and the USA 2011 by
SEVERN HOUSE PUBLISHERS LTD.

British Library Cataloguing in Publication Data

Beaufort, Simon.
  The Bloodstained Throne. – (A Sir Geoffrey Mappestone
  mystery)
  1. Mappestone, Geoffrey, Sir (Fictitious character) –
  Fiction. 2. Shipwreck victims – Fiction. 3. Great Britain –
  History – Norman period, 1066–1154 – Fiction. 4. Detective
  and mystery stories.
  I. Title II. Series
  823.9'14–dc22

ISBN-13: 978-0-7278-6917-3   (cased)
ISBN-13: 978-1-84751-264-2   (trade paper)

*All Severn House titles are printed on acid-free paper.*

Severn House Publishers support The Forest Stewardship Council [FSC],
the leading international forest certification organisation. All our titles that
are printed on Greenpeace-approved FSC-certified paper carry the FSC logo.

**Mixed Sources**
Product group from well-managed
forests and other controlled sources
www.fsc.org  Cert no. SA-COC-1565
© 1996 Forest Stewardship Council
FSC

Typeset by Palimpsest Book Production Ltd.,
Falkirk, Stirlingshire, Scotland.
Printed and bound in Great Britain by the
MPG Books Group, Bodmin, Cornwall.

*For Ken and Janie Thomas,
the dearest of friends*

# One

The groans of the dying ship were terrible to hear. The tearing of her hull and the snap of her spars and masts were audible even above the crashing of waves and the manic shriek of wind. The sails were reduced to tattered rags, and the ship's carved bow was little more than splinters. Planking and stores ripped from her were thrown ashore by waves twice the height of a man.

Overhead, the afternoon sky was dark, although rent now and then by slashes of lightning. Thunder growled, but in the distance now, indicating that the storm was finally moving west. Miraculously, some passengers and crew had survived. A few were still flailing in the breakers, while others were in small groups ashore, huddled around the scanty possessions they had managed to salvage.

It was thanks to Captain Fingar's skill and experience that anyone had survived at all. When the ship's hold had flooded suddenly, Fingar had known she was lost, so he had driven her towards shore to give everyone a better chance. But within moments of scraping the bottom, the ship began to disintegrate.

Sir Geoffrey Mappestone was among the lucky ones. He had guessed as soon as he had heard the roar of breakers that the ship was doomed, and he had managed to warn his companions, seize his saddlebag and unleash his dog. The horses, however, had been tethered aft, and although he had tried his best to reach them, the task was impossible. It was a sickening wrench to lose his warhorse: the animal had carried him into battle when Jerusalem had fallen to the Crusading army three years before, and he could not imagine life without it. Geoffrey was a knight, trained from an early age to fight on horseback. Now he had no horse he was unable to suppress the sense that he was less of a man because of it.

'I told you we should never have sailed in this weather,' said his friend accusingly, spitting to remove the taste of salty water from his mouth.

Sir Roger of Durham was a massive, powerful man with a thick black beard and long raven curls, both cultivated in accordance with latest fashions at Court. Geoffrey preferred to keep his light-brown hair short, military fashion, and was clean-shaven, indicating Roger had adapted far more readily to civilian life than had Geoffrey. Both wore surcoats that proclaimed them *Jerosolimitani* – those who had rallied to the Pope's call to wrest the Holy City from the infidel. Their surcoats, armour and small arsenal of weapons had been the first items they had bundled up to save from the wreck.

The two made unlikely companions. Roger was blunt, transparent and suspicious of anything he did not understand – and since he was illiterate and deeply superstitious, this meant there was a great deal he deemed heretical or sinister. By contrast, Geoffrey had occasionally considered dedicating his life to scholarship. Unusually for a knight, he could read and write, and he owned a deep love of books and scrolls.

'The weather was fine when we left Bristol,' he said, watching the dying ship writhe in the waves. It was ugly to behold, and when a shrill cry sounded, he hoped it was a gull, not a horse.

'But there were omens,' countered Roger. 'And you ignored them. Your wife *and* your sister urged you to remain at Goodrich, and I said the same. But you knew better, and now look where it has landed us.'

'At least we *are* landed,' said Geoffrey's squire, Bale, loyally defending his master, although he had not approved of the journey either, when celestial phenomenon had warned against it. He nodded towards the churning sea. 'We might still be out there.'

Geoffrey glanced at the other survivors, noting that many were missing – Vitalis, an old man with whom he had quarrelled, and his two female companions; there had been a monk and a pair of Saxons, too . . .

'Vitalis will not be missed,' said Roger, reading his thoughts. He glanced at Geoffrey, a hard look in his dark-brown eyes. 'I do not take kindly to men who make accusations, then use their age as an excuse to avoid a duel.'

'He was not in his right wits,' said Geoffrey.

'He deserved to drown,' Bale declared harshly. 'No man should accuse Sir Geoffrey of cowardice and live to tell the tale.'

'He did not accuse me of cowardice!' objected Geoffrey, startled by the way Bale had interpreted the argument from two days before.

'It does not matter exactly what he said,' stated Roger, his abrupt tone indicating he thought his friend was quibbling. 'He insulted your family, and you should have fought him for it. Now he is drowned you will not have the chance to kill him.'

'Perhaps *God* took Vitalis's life because he spoke unjustly,' suggested Bale. 'The wicked are often struck down for their sins, and Sir Geoffrey is a *Jerosolimitanus*, so He will disapprove of people saying nasty things to him. Father Adrian *loved* talking about holy vengeance.'

His eyes took on a curiously pious expression, although Geoffrey strongly suspected that Goodrich's gentle parish priest had actually been trying to warn Bale to curb his violent instincts. Bale was a huge hulk of a man, larger even than Roger, with a bald, shiny head and uncannily expressive eyes. His immense strength, combined with a passion for sharp implements, made him a sinister and unnerving figure. The people on Geoffrey's estates had been delighted when he had agreed to take the man as his squire, and it was clear they hoped he would never return. Geoffrey understood their unease; he was wary of Bale himself.

'There are still men in the water,' Geoffrey said, scanning the tossing sea. 'Vitalis may yet come ashore.'

'Those are sailors,' said Roger. 'They went back to see what they could salvage before the ship is lost completely. Fingar is one of them; I recognize his orange hair.'

Geoffrey set off towards them. 'If they have gone back, then perhaps we can do something for the horses—'

Roger's heavy hand clamped around his arm to prevent him from going farther, although his voice was gentle when he spoke. 'It is too late, lad. The stern went under first, and they were drowned long before we reached the shore. The sailors are used to the sea and know how to rescue stuff from it, but we are not. It would be madness to attempt it.'

'That is true,' agreed Roger's squire, a sturdy Saxon youth by the name of Ulfrith, whose thick yellow locks were a mad tangle from their time in the water. 'I grew up on the coast, and the sea is treacherous at this time of year.' Tears filled his eyes. 'Poor Lady Philippa! I cannot . . .'

He trailed off, and Geoffrey rested a sympathetic hand on his shoulder. Ulfrith had been smitten with one of the female passengers and had been grieving for her ever since Geoffrey had pulled him from the waves. Ulfrith had loved the horses, too, but their loss seemed nothing compared to that of the woman he had idolized.

'Vitalis was stupid,' said Bale, studiously looking in the opposite direction to Ulfrith's unmanly display. 'You told him to take off his armour before we swam for the shore, because it would drag him under, but he refused.'

'Worse yet, he accused you of wanting to steal it,' said Roger, indignant on Geoffrey's behalf. 'The man was insane! What could you do with a tiny mail tunic and a blunt old sword? You tried to help him and he repaid you with nastiness.'

Roger patted his own armour – knee-length mail tunic with gauntlets and hood, boiled leather leggings, surcoat and a conical helmet with a distinctive Norman nosepiece. He had donned it all the moment he was on firm ground, in anticipation of an attack by locals, who might kill survivors so they could claim salvage.

'It was a good idea, Sir Geoffrey, to put our equipment in a barrel and tow it ashore,' said Bale. 'But it is a shame you could not devise a way to save the horses, too.'

'Of course,' said Roger, turning accusing eyes on his friend, 'they would not have died had you listened to the heavenly portents ordering you to stay in England.'

Geoffrey winced. He did not share his companions' belief that the omens were aimed at his intended journey to Jerusalem, but he hated the fact that *he* was responsible for the horses' deaths.

'Not one beast has come ashore,' elaborated Bale. 'Poor things! It would have been better to have cut their throats than for them to drown.'

There had been a number of passengers aboard the ship – Captain Fingar was quite happy to accept paying fares for a journey he was making anyway. His ship *Patrick* traded between Dublin and Ribe in Denmark, carrying hides and linen one way, and timber and furs the other. It did not sound especially lucrative, but Fingar was clearly wealthy, and Geoffrey suspected that the large crew and abundance of weapons were not just for defence: *Patrick* was owned by pirates.

Autumn was normally a good time for sea-travel, and most of the ships Geoffrey had approached in the port of Bristol had been full. He was beginning to think they might have to go home again, when *Patrick* had put in, ostensibly for repairs, although she docked in a quiet backwater that was the haunt of those who preferred to unload their cargos away from the King's taxors. Whether her goods were smuggled or stolen from another ship was impossible to say, but the number of guards and their furtive demeanour indicated it was one or the other.

Geoffrey was not the only one desperate enough to accept a berth on a ship operating outside the law. So had Sir Vitalis and his two women, a monk, and their servants. Vitalis, a crusty old knight from Falaise, owned lands in the ancient Danish diocese of Ribe, and he and his ladies were going to visit them. Meanwhile, Brother Lucian maintained he was on official Benedictine business. With his shiny black hair and ready smile for the ladies, everything about Lucian said he hailed from wealth. He was too young and handsome to be trusted out alone by any sensible abbot, and Geoffrey had not believed him when he said he had been carrying important documents.

When they had embarked, they discovered Fingar already had four other paying passengers, who had joined *Patrick* in Dublin. These comprised an uncommunicative Saxon and his servant who were secretive to the point of rudeness; a loquacious Breton named Juhel; and a Norman called Paisnel who had been lost overboard several days before.

During his career as a soldier, Geoffrey had spent a fair amount of time on ships, mostly in the Mediterranean Sea, travelling at the command of his liege lord, Prince Tancred. *Patrick*, however, was like no other. Normally, tents were rigged on deck for passengers, but Fingar claimed such clutter would interfere with safety. His fares had the choice of eating and sleeping on the open deck or crawling on top of the Irish leathers in the holds.

Geoffrey was blessed with a strong stomach, although even he had been sick in the monstrous seas in the Channel. His fellow passengers fared worse. Vitalis, the silent Saxons and the servants spent most of their time in the hold, vomiting what little they managed to eat. Geoffrey suggested they might feel better away from the odoriferous hides, but they groaned they were too ill to move. The longest conversation he had had with the Saxons – the squire was called Simon, but he had no idea of the master's name – comprised them ordering him away when he tried to help them.

Vitalis's women – each separately introduced as his wife – were more robust and made regular forays to the deck, where they stood clutching the rails and screeching at the size of the waves. They were often joined by Brother Lucian, who flirted outrageously despite the fact that he appeared at times when he should have been reciting his holy offices. It had not escaped Geoffrey's attention that Lucian had not prayed when they were in danger, although every other soul on board had done so with increasing desperation.

Paisnel and Juhel had also been largely unaffected by the elements. Paisnel was the more likeable, a serious, sober senior clerk in the service of the Bishop of Ribe. His friend Juhel was a parchment merchant, and when he was not chatting to his fellow passengers, he talked to his pet chicken, a pale-brown bird with wicked eyes.

But, Geoffrey reflected sadly as he huddled with his companions in the biting wind and stinging rain, trying to regain his strength after the desperate struggle ashore, he could see none of them on the beach.

'What shall we do?' asked Bale eventually. 'We cannot sit here all day. It is too cold.'

'We should wait for the captain to say something,' said Ulfrith. 'He is in charge.'

'Not any more,' argued Bale. 'Besides, all he is interested in is rescuing what he can from the waves before *they* move in.'

Geoffrey looked to where Bale pointed and saw a tremor in the vegetation behind the shore. People were gathering, watching the survivors but making no attempt to help.

'Locals,' said Ulfrith uneasily. 'They are hoping we will all die, so they can claim what is washed ashore. Folk like them killed shipwrecked mariners when I was a boy.'

'They had better not try anything with us,' said Roger grimly, fingering his sword.

Geoffrey was glad they had all donned their armour. Mail was not total protection against arrows, but it would give them a chance to fight back, should the villagers be rash enough to attack two fully armed Norman knights and their squires.

'They will,' predicted Ulfrith. 'But not yet – they are not stupid. They will wait for nightfall, when we fall asleep from exhaustion.'

Roger scowled. 'They are already growing bold. Look at that fellow with the green hat there. He has been watching us from behind that tree since we first reached the shore.'

'We should offer to help Fingar deploy sentries,' said Geoffrey. It would not be easy to protect themselves in the dark, but it would be foolishness itself not to try.

The captain, however, was unreceptive to Geoffrey's suggestion to move inland and find shelter. Fingar was a short, powerful man with red hair and a scar that ran from the centre of his forehead, down his nose and across his lips, to end at the cleft in his chin. It was perfectly symmetrical, and Geoffrey wondered how it had happened.

'I am not playing milksop to passengers,' Fingar growled, his attention on the seething waves and those of his men who still floundered in them. The rest sat in deflated, sullen groups around their salvage. 'I am busy.'

'Busy doing what?' asked Geoffrey. 'Nothing is coming ashore in one piece, and smashed planking and soaking pelts cannot be of value to you. We should make our way to the nearest settlement for—'

Fingar rounded on him with a fury that would have made most men take a step back. 'You do not know what you are talking about! We need to gather every scrap of timber or leather that washes ashore if we want a chance of buying a new ship. And my obligations to you finished when you reached the shore, so you can make your own way.'

'We do not need your protection,' said Geoffrey irritably. 'But you can see from here that the locals have arrived and are just waiting for the right time to attack. None of us will be safe once night falls, so it is better to pool our—'

'No one will dare attack me,' said Fingar with great finality. 'Now bugger off.'

Without waiting for a reply, he turned and strode towards the thundering surf, where two of his men were struggling with a barrel. Its side was stoved in and its contents lost, and Geoffrey wondered why they were so determined to have it. Disgusted and bemused, he headed back to where Bale and Ulfrith were packing sodden belongings into the saddlebags, aware that the silent locals had edged much closer.

'No!' howled Bale, whipping around suddenly, knife in hand. 'Get away!'

By the time Geoffrey reached his companions, the hapless villager was staggering to safety, trailing blood behind him. The other villagers, clutching a haphazard array of cudgels and pikes, watched tensely, ready to flee if anyone should give chase.

'That will warn them to keep their distance,' said Roger, watching Bale wipe the blood from his blade with a handful of seaweed.

'It will warn them to be careful,' countered Geoffrey. 'The fellow in the green hat is now even closer – so is that large man by him. Fingar will be in trouble tonight if he does not post guards.'

'There is still no sign of our fellow passengers,' said Roger, again scanning the turbulent sea. 'I can only see crew.'

'What a pity Lucian is dead,' said Ulfrith with undisguised malice. Normally affable, Ulfrith had taken strongly against Lucian, whose courtly manners had made him feel gauche and loutish in front of Lady Philippa. He heaved a melancholy sigh. 'Poor ladies! They were so lovely. I cannot imagine why either married Vitalis. He was old enough to be their grandfather.'

'Perhaps he *was* their grandfather,' suggested Bale. 'I did not see him demanding his conjugal rights the whole time we were aboard.'

Carefully, he began to pack away the ink pots, pens and parchment that had been in the bag Geoffrey had saved, although his disapproving expression indicated he thought his master should have taken the other one – containing clothes and a small store of gold coins.

'He was seasick,' explained Ulfrith. 'Although I suspect an hour or two with Philippa would have cured any sickness of *mine*.'

'And I could have managed a bout with the other one – that Edith,' said Roger salaciously. 'She was a fine, strapping wench, with plenty of meat for a man to—'

'There is Juhel!' exclaimed Geoffrey, pointing suddenly along the beach.

'So it is,' said Ulfrith, squinting. 'An undertow must have pulled him away from the rest of us. He is lucky – few men live once undertows get them.'

Bale stood to wave and catch the parchmenter's attention. 'He has the cage that held his pet chicken, although I cannot imagine the bird is in it.'

Geoffrey glanced down at his dog, glad it had survived, but thinking again with sadness about his horse. He wondered if *Patrick* had floundered because Fingar's greed had led him to pile her with more cargo than was safe, or if she had simply been poorly loaded.

Juhel arrived, breathlessly relating his brush with death. He was stocky, with a wide, smiling mouth and prominent eyes reminiscent of a frog. Geoffrey wavered between liking him for his readiness to laugh and distrusting him because he had caught him out in several lies. The knight was amused to note that not only was the chicken in the cage but it was alive, albeit bedraggled.

Geoffrey tuned out the parchmenter's gabbling and stared pensively across the heaving waves. Another casket, badly smashed and with its lid missing, rolled on to the shingle, where it was seized by crewmen. He looked up at the sky, gauging how much daylight was left. A glance behind showed that the villagers were inching forward again, all clutching weapons. Was there time for him and his companions to reach a friendly settlement with them before dark? And how easy would it be to find another ship that was eastward-bound? He realized he must have spoken aloud, because the others were gazing at him aghast.

'You intend to try again?' whispered Ulfrith. 'After we narrowly escaped with our lives? God is telling us *not* to travel east, and only a fool would disobey His wishes!'

'Only a fool would have gone in the first place,' muttered Roger. 'And we are bigger fools for going with him.'

'Then stay,' said Geoffrey shortly. There were often violent storms in the English Channel, and he did not imagine for a moment that God had engineered one for his benefit. 'I will go alone.'

'How?' demanded Roger. He nodded to the saddlebag in Bale's hand. 'You did not bother to save your gold, and you have no horse. *How* do you propose to reach the Holy Land?'

He had a point. Geoffrey's little manor on the Welsh borders was experiencing a lean period, but his sister – who managed the estate in his absence – had managed to scrape enough together for his journey. He could hardly go back and ask for more, especially since Joan had not wanted him to go in the first place. Neither had his wife – Geoffrey had recently been forced into a political marriage in the interests of peace. But he had a burning desire to travel east again, and it had not taken many weeks of life in the country before the yearning had become too strong to ignore.

'You should return to Lady Hilde, sir,' recommended Bale tentatively, when he saw Geoffrey had no reply to Roger's remarks. 'She is not yet with child.'

Geoffrey gaped at the effrontery, but Bale suddenly lowered his bald head and vomited a gush of seawater, and the knight supposed he had spoken out of turn because he was not himself: Bale was normally diffident to the point of obsequiousness. Meanwhile, Roger was more concerned about their current predicament than his friend's obligations in the marriage bed.

'Fingar is incompetent,' he declared. 'His ship was a paltry, leaking basin, not fit to bob down a river. I could tell just by looking that it would sink in the first puff of wind.'

'Then why did you not say so in Bristol?' asked Geoffrey. 'You were happy when we sailed – especially when you learned he might be a pirate. You entertained high hopes of joining him in his work, so you might share the spoils.'

'Pirates!' spat Roger. 'He and his crew are no more pirates than my mother.'

Geoffrey glanced at him. Roger had some very odd relations, so it was entirely possible that Roger's mother – long-term Saxon mistress to the corrupt and treacherous Bishop of Durham – might take to the high seas for booty.

'*Irish* pirates,' said Bale, looking evilly at the seamen and fingering his favourite dagger. His weapons were his most prized possessions, lovingly honed to a vicious sharpness on a daily basis. 'And not even a Christian part of Ireland. They are infidels who worship graven images and drink the blood of babies.'

'Oh, really, Bale!' exclaimed Geoffrey irritably. 'They are just—'

'I want them to pay for my horse,' interrupted Roger, working himself into a temper. 'I know they have gold, because I saw it.'

'Where?' asked Bale eagerly.

Roger pointed with a thick finger, indicating a sturdy, heavily secured box about the length of his forearm. It stood in the middle of one of the salvaged piles. 'I saw them counting what was in it just this morning. If they had been watching their sails instead, we would still be afloat.'

'It is thanks to Fingar's fine seamanship that we survived at all,' argued Geoffrey. 'A lesser sailor would have lost the ship out at sea, where we would all have drowned.'

'Regardless, they will pay for my horse,' vowed Roger.

Meanwhile, a small sailor with a pinched, mean face became aware that Roger was eyeing the chest. Donan was Fingar's second-in-command, and he muttered something to his companions as he pushed it out of sight. Geoffrey did not like the looks that were exchanged and was about to tell Roger to be careful when Juhel suddenly cried out, jabbing his finger towards someone struggling through the waves.

'It is that rude Saxon,' said Ulfrith. 'The one who never bothered to tell us his name.'

'His servant is with him,' said Bale. 'Simon.'

But the Saxons were in difficulty. Geoffrey tore down the beach and into the churning waves, fighting to stay upright as the water surged around his legs. Too late, he realized he should have removed his armour and surcoat first. Then a crashing breaker tossed the pair within reaching distance.

The Saxon was swimming strongly, so Geoffrey flailed towards Simon, but the Saxon grabbed Geoffrey around the neck as he passed. Geoffrey tried to push him away, but the Saxon's grip was a powerful one. He glanced at the man's face, expecting to see panic or terror, and was startled to see it calm and determined.

'Bear me to the shore,' the fellow ordered imperiously. 'I cannot swim another stroke.'

Geoffrey struggled to be free of him. 'Your servant needs help.'

'Take me to the shore first,' the man snarled.

Angrily, Geoffrey prised his hands away, but when he looked to where Simon had been, there was only water.

For the second time that afternoon, Geoffrey was forced to strip off his clothes so Bale could wring them out. It was not pleasant to replace them, chilled as he was, but even sodden garments were better than none in the biting wind. He jumped up and down in an attempt to warm himself, at the same time listening to Juhel regale the Saxon with details of how the current had dragged him miles along the beach before he could break free of it. The Saxon remained haughtily aloof, although he did not object when Juhel helped him remove his clothes for wringing – now the hapless Simon was dead he seemed unsure how to make himself more comfortable.

'You cannot go to the Holy Land, Sir Geoffrey,' said Bale, resuming their earlier conversation as though it had never been interrupted. 'God wants you to stay here, see.'

Roger agreed. 'He wants us in England, and I dare not risk His wrath again. I am staying and I urge you to do the same.'

Geoffrey was relieved. Since he had no money, taking companions was out of the question anyway. He would miss Roger's ready sword and cheerful friendship, but it could not be helped.

'We are lucky,' said Bale. 'Not only are we still alive, but we are still in England. We might have ended up in Normandy.' He crossed himself vigorously, shooting the others meaningful looks.

Ulfrith nodded sagely. 'And with Robert de Bellême rampaging there we would have been killed within a week.'

'Do not be ridiculous!' said Roger. 'How would he have known we had arrived? Bellême does not rule *all* Normandy, and he does not know *everything* that happens.'

Bale and Ulfrith exchanged a glance that said they thought differently. Geoffrey was wary of the wicked Earl of Shrewsbury's network of informants, too. Bellême had been banished from England the previous year and was currently venting his spleen on his Norman domains, leaving behind death and destruction.

Geoffrey's decision to travel to the Holy Land the longer way through Denmark and Franconia said a good deal about his reluctance to venture into the hellish maelstrom of Bellême's sphere of influence.

The light was fading, but with the end of the day came a respite from the storm. The wind lessened and the stinging slash of rain gave way to drizzle. The waves still crashed on to the shore, however, thrusting pieces of wreckage before them. As the locals resumed their relentless advance, Geoffrey suggested that he and his companions find somewhere safe to spend the night.

'Which way?' asked Roger, gathering up his possessions. Besides his armour and weapons, he had somehow contrived to save all his better clothes and a heavy pouch stuffed with coins and jewellery. Geoffrey might be penniless, but Roger remained wealthy.

Geoffrey considered. 'Just before we left the ship I saw a tower. It was probably a church, but it looked to be made of stone, so it must belong to a settlement of some substance – not like the hamlets of these fishermen.'

'Then why did no one come to help us?' demanded Roger. 'It is unchristian to sit in warm houses while we shiver out here.'

'*All* the villages around here consider wrecks their personal property,' stated Ulfrith.

Geoffrey grimaced. Ulfrith spoke with conviction, but he was miles from where he grew up, so could not know what 'all the villages around here' believed. Still, Geoffrey was sure about one thing: the sullen fishermen who fingered their knives and cudgels were Saxon and would certainly be happy to strike a blow against two Norman knights. The conquest thirty-seven years before was still raw in the minds of many, and Normans had done little to make themselves popular with the nation they had so ruthlessly subjugated.

'We had better make a move before it is too dark,' he said.

'I think that headland we passed – the one with the beacon – lies a few miles from Pevenesel,' said Ulfrith tentatively. 'We cannot be very far from the castle there.'

'Good,' said Roger fervently. 'I would rather lie in a cramped hall full of snoring Norman soldiers than on a Saxon feather mattress.'

'Look!' cried Bale suddenly. 'Someone else is coming our way!'

Ulfrith gave a grin of unadulterated delight. 'It is Lady Philippa and Lady Edith! They must have been washed farther down the coast, like Juhel.'

With a happy whoop, he raced away to greet them.

# Two

Philippa and Edith were elegant ladies, but chalk and cheese. Edith was a tall, golden-haired beauty with a long neck, large blue eyes and haughty Norman manners; Philippa was small, dark, lively and full of opinions. Edith was older and the more dominant of the pair.

Geoffrey had spent little time in their company on *Patrick* due to their husband's vehement accusations. However, what he *had* seen of them convinced him there was not an intelligent thought in the head of either.

'Vitalis is dead!' wept Philippa as Ulfrith ushered them forward. 'He was alive when we reached the shore, but water must have swelled inside his lungs and choked him, even as he gave thanks for his deliverance. What shall I do now? He was all I had!'

'There, there, sister,' crooned Edith. 'We shall look after each other. *I* will never leave you.'

'Thank you,' said Philippa, forcing a wan smile. 'And I suppose we have two knights to protect us now. Thank God! I thought we might have to throw ourselves on the mercy of a rabble.'

She gazed distastefully at the pirates and then at Ulfrith and Bale, who, as mere squires, were too lowly to be considered genteel company. Ulfrith did not notice and continued to beam. His happy grin faded at the next comment, however.

'Have you seen dear Brother Lucian?' asked Edith. 'We looked for him on the beach but saw only two drowned sailors. And Lucian's manservant. He was dead, too.'

'Poor man,' said Juhel with gentle compassion.

Philippa barely glanced at him, clearly considering a mere parchmenter beneath her. Then she started to cry. 'Actually, it is poor Vitalis! And poor Lucian!'

'Vitalis was a good man,' Edith agreed, also tearful. 'We shall have masses said for his soul when we reach a place of safety.' After a moment, she inclined her head towards the villagers. 'Do they mean to attack us? They seem very menacing.'

'They frighten me,' added Philippa. 'I do not want to stay here.'

Edith agreed. 'No one else will come ashore alive now, and we should consider our own safety. It distresses me to leave without knowing poor Brother Lucian's fate, but he would have understood our need to protect ourselves.'

'He certainly would,' muttered Ulfrith. 'He was a selfish brute, who put himself above everyone. He was the first overboard when Fingar gave the order to abandon ship.'

'We must stay together,' said Juhel to Geoffrey and Roger, apparently deciding that two knights represented his best chance of staying alive. 'At least until we reach civilization.'

'Do you have money?' asked Roger bluntly. 'Or just that chicken?'

Juhel smiled and raised the cage so everyone could see the disconsolate bundle within. Geoffrey saw his dog lick its lips and leaned down to grab it before it did anything irreversible.

'My bird is worth more than all the treasure in Jerusalem,' Juhel declared. 'But I have enough gold to pay my way. I saved my dagger, too, so I am not completely helpless. But the ladies are right: we should not linger here with daylight fading.'

'A knight with a sword is better than a merchant with a dagger,' said Philippa, simpering at Geoffrey. 'We are fortunate to have found *you*.'

'I agree,' said Edith. She rested a hand on Roger's arm and beamed. 'I know you will find us somewhere warm tonight.'

'Aye, lass,' said Roger with a leer that suggested he might supply some of the heat personally.

'Then we should go,' said Geoffrey promptly. 'We will walk towards that tower I saw.'

'And tomorrow?' asked the Saxon haughtily. 'What happens tomorrow?'

Geoffrey shrugged. 'If we do not find shelter, there may not be a tomorrow for us.'

'Aye,' agreed Roger. 'The fellow with the green hat is still watching us. The others are concentrating on Fingar's salvage, but not him. Look! There he is among those trees.'

'So he is,' muttered Geoffrey, following Roger's gaze. 'And his large friend is with him. Is he interested in us because he thinks we will be easier to rob? Or is there another reason?'

★   ★   ★

Unsettled by the peculiar interest of the green-hatted man and his hulking friend, Geoffrey began to walk towards the tower. Roger marched behind him, Edith clinging to his arm, followed by the other passengers, with Bale bringing up the rear. Philippa ran to catch up with Geoffrey, but so did Ulfrith, taking her hand in a powerful grip to support her over the uneven surface. She grimaced, loath to settle for a squire when her friend had a knight, but she made the best of it and began to chatter gaily about herself – the subject she seemed to like best.

She had some serious competition, though, because Juhel was also determined to hear his own voice. He rattled on about some perfumed oil he had sold to Bellême. Geoffrey was dubious: he could not imagine that ruthless tyrant being interested in fripperies. As they babbled, Geoffrey glanced behind him to ensure Bale was carrying out his duties as vanguard.

He need not have worried. Bale took seriously any order issued by his master and was assiduously looking backwards every two or three steps to ensure no one was in pursuit. He had Geoffrey's dog on a piece of rope, knowing the animal would growl if any villager came too close. Geoffrey had a feeling the would-be looters would be disappointed if they did intend to attack after dark: about thirty sailors had survived, and such a large group would present a formidable challenge.

'Have you noticed that Saxon has attached himself to us?' asked Ulfrith of Geoffrey, rather indignantly. 'He has been very unfriendly, so I do not know how he dares!'

'Because we are a better proposition than Fingar and his rabble,' said Juhel, overhearing. '*We* will not slit his throat in the night and make off with his belongings.'

'Life will be difficult for me now,' said Philippa, bringing the discussion back to herself. 'I am a young widow, whose husband has been ripped away in untimely fashion.'

'Vitalis was rather old,' remarked Ulfrith tactlessly. 'But now you can choose a younger man.' He glanced hopefully at her out of the corner of his eye.

'I *should* like a younger man,' said Philippa, smiling at Geoffrey.

But Geoffrey was not paying attention to her; he was concentrating on the curious movements of the green-hatted man and his friend, who had started to follow the party. Besides, Hilde had aroused in him an odd sense of affection and loyalty he had rarely felt towards women. If he did break his marriage vows, it would not be with a simpering girl.

'Sir Geoffrey is married,' said Ulfrith with a hint of triumph. 'However, *I* am unattached. And I have fair prospects, being a fighting man – loot, you understand.'

'But you are only a squire,' said Philippa in distaste. 'I am used to being wed to a knight.'

'I understand Edith was wed to him, too,' said Ulfrith sanctimoniously. 'Such situations are frowned upon in England. It is called bigamy, and we Saxons disapprove. Of course, Denmark is different.'

'Not *that* different,' said Juhel, laughing. 'The only countries that countenance multiple wives are those that follow the teachings of Mohammed – and then only if they can be afforded.'

'Well, Sir Vitalis could afford me *and* Edith,' said Philippa sulkily. 'I cannot imagine what I will do now he is dead. Edith has wealthy kin, but I am friendless and alone. Who will care for me?'

'*I* will,' called Edith from where she walked with Roger. 'As I keep telling you. You need have no fears for your future, Philippa.'

Philippa smiled back at her, then tripped over a stone. Ulfrith's clumsy attempt to catch her resulted in the inadvertent grabbing of a breast, and her squeals of outrage were loud enough to draw the attention of several villagers. Growing exasperated, Geoffrey took her hand and set a cracking pace that had the others running to keep up. After a while, the villagers lost interest and turned back towards Fingar's salvage. When he next glanced around, the green-hatted man was also moving in the opposite direction.

'The Church dictates that a man may not have more than one wife,' said Edith, when Geoffrey slowed a little, allowing breath for conversation again. 'But the Church is full of celibates, who are hardly in a position to appreciate the needs of normal men. A knight should be allowed to take more than one wife if he feels like it. And a woman should be allowed more than one husband, too.'

'I have been happier than I ever thought possible with Vitalis and Edith,' said Philippa wistfully. 'Damn those wretched pirates! They have lost me more than they could ever imagine.' When she saw Geoffrey glance behind again, she misunderstood the object of his wary attention and lowered her voice conspiratorially. 'You do not approve of that nasty man coming with us. Neither do I. He is a killer!'

'I know,' said Geoffrey, recalling how the Saxon had sacrificed his servant to save himself.

'And he talks *all* the time,' said Philippa.

'You refer to Juhel?' asked Geoffrey in surprise. 'I thought you meant the Saxon.'

'No,' said Philippa in disdain. 'I would not waste my breath talking about an arrogant stick of a man who would not even tell my husband his name. I meant that garrulous Juhel. He might be witty and clever, but he is a *murderer!*'

'Is he now?' said Geoffrey, paying her scant attention.

'I saw him kill his friend,' Philippa chatted on. 'Do you remember how distressed he was, rushing all over the ship the morning Paisnel disappeared?'

'*I* remember,' said Ulfrith, keen to show he was interested in her tale, even if Geoffrey was not. 'He wept bitterly when we realized Paisnel must have gone overboard during the night.'

Philippa continued to address Geoffrey. 'Well, his tears were not of grief, but of guilt. I saw him throw Paisnel overboard with my own eyes, and I heard the splash as his body hit the water.'

Geoffrey did not believe a word Philippa said, and assumed she was telling spiteful tales to win the sympathy of the men who were most likely to care for her. He smiled at that notion: Philippa was a poor judge of character if she imagined she would be safe from Roger. The big knight already had her companion in an inappropriate 'protective' embrace, but would shift his attentions to Philippa once Edith had fallen to his charms.

'We will see you settled in a convent,' Geoffrey said, planning to be rid of them both as soon as possible. 'And I will write to Edith's kinsmen, so they will know to come and fetch you.'

'I do not want to stay with nuns!' cried Philippa, aghast. 'I want to be left with some rich nobleman. Preferably one in need of a wife.'

'Did you really see Juhel throw Paisnel overboard?' asked Ulfrith, whose slow wits were still coming to terms with her accusations.

'I did,' said Philippa, still looking at Geoffrey. 'But I see you do not believe me.'

'I do!' declared Ulfrith. 'I believe anything *you* tell me, dear lady.'

'Your master does not,' said Philippa sulkily. 'He thinks I am lying to gain his attention.'

'I am merely curious as to why you have waited so long to tell anyone,' said Geoffrey with a noncommittal shrug. 'Why not when Paisnel first went missing?'

He glanced behind and saw that Juhel had abandoned Roger and Edith to take advantage of the Saxon's taciturn nature and natter at him. Geoffrey wondered whether Philippa had only made her accusations because Juhel was safely out of earshot.

'Because Vitalis told me not to,' replied Philippa. 'I was obliged to get up in the night, you see. For natural purposes.' She lowered her voice and pursed her lips prudishly.

'You mean to take fresh air?' asked Ulfrith innocently.

This drew a reluctant smile. 'You could say that. It was a night when the seas were too rough for the deck, so everyone was sleeping in the hold. I finished my business and was making my way down the ladder again when I heard voices. I thought it was sailors at first, but then I realized they were speaking Norman-French.'

'And it was Juhel and Paisnel?' asked Ulfrith politely.

Philippa nodded. 'Juhel was doing all the talking, of course. They were huddled at the back of the ship, where they thought they would not be seen or overheard. I was bored, so I made my way towards them – for company.' Her eyes filled with tears, and Geoffrey could not decide whether it was genuine distress, a ploy for sympathy or the effects of the cold wind.

Ulfrith was less cynical. 'Poor lady,' he said kindly.

'There was blood,' Philippa whispered brokenly. 'A lot of it. Paisnel had been stabbed in the chest, or perhaps the neck. Juhel was sobbing when he tossed him overboard. I ran away at that point, but when Juhel returned to the hold, he was wet: he had washed off the blood.'

Geoffrey regarded her sharply as something jarred in his mind. He had also noticed that the parchmenter's tunic had been wet the morning after Paisnel's disappearance. Philippa continued when she saw she had his attention at last.

'But the truly vile thing is that Paisnel was not dead. I saw him raise one arm as the ship sailed on and left him to his horrible fate.'

'They were friends,' said Geoffrey, not sure what to believe. 'They had travelled together from Dublin, and Juhel was going to stay with Paisnel's family in Ribe. Why would he kill a friend?'

Philippa shrugged. 'Not every man can be as gentle as poor, dear Vitalis. There are some dreadful brutes around, and Juhel is one of them.'

'Vitalis was not always gentle – he accused Sir Geoffrey of some awful things,' said Ulfrith, clearly unsure where his loyalties should lie. 'Truly wicked things.'

'He did not,' objected Geoffrey. 'He said—'

'Everything he said was true,' interrupted Philippa. 'He whispered them again as he lay dying on the beach, his lungs all gurgling and full of water. You will have to do penance for them, Sir Geoffrey, perhaps in the nunnery where you plan to leave me.'

'I cannot believe Juhel killed Paisnel,' said Geoffrey, preferring to discuss her story than the old man's accusations. 'They never even had a cross word . . .'

But that was not true, he recalled. He had caught them quarrelling the day before Paisnel went missing. They had kept their voices low, so he had not heard the nature of the disagreement, but there was no mistaking the angry gestures. But did it mean anything? Geoffrey frequently argued with Roger, and *their* friendship was as robust as any. Companions often fought, and surely there was nothing significant in Paisnel squabbling with Juhel?

'He threw Paisnel's bag overboard, too,' said Philippa, seeing the doubt in his face and pressing her point. 'I saw the poor man flap towards it, probably hoping it would keep him afloat. But Vitalis told me not to tell anyone, because he was too seasick to protect me from Juhel's inevitable anger. You are not seasick, though, and—'

'But why would Juhel do such a thing?' interrupted Ulfrith, bewildered. 'Paisnel was so nice and polite. He even tried to make friends with that rude Saxon. Of course, even Juhel's chicken detested *him* – she scratched him cruelly, if you recall. Animals are seldom wrong when they take against people. But why did Juhel throw Paisnel's pack overboard?'

Philippa shook her head. 'I do not know! It made no sense, because, as his friend, Juhel would have been entitled to keep it. But he threw it in the sea with great haste. Perhaps it contained something he did not want to see again.'

'Such as what?' pressed Ulfrith.

Philippa was becoming exasperated with him. 'I do not *know*! Perhaps those documents that were tied up with red ribbon. That braid would have looked rather well with my best kirtle; I asked Paisnel if he would exchange it for a green one, but he refused.'

'Sir Geoffrey uses red ribbon when he writes to his wife and sister,' said Ulfrith. 'I am sure I can persuade him to give you a little.'

'I shall persuade him myself, thank you,' said Philippa with a sultry smile.

'Paisnel had a medallion,' said Ulfrith thoughtfully. He was thinking about Philippa's story and did not notice the smouldering look she shot Geoffrey. 'It was a large gold one. Perhaps Juhel wanted to get rid of that, although I cannot imagine why. You would think he would keep it, especially if it was valuable.'

'What kind of medallion?' asked Geoffrey.

Ulfrith shrugged. 'A big gold one, with writing on it. You know: a medallion.'

Geoffrey's thoughts were in turmoil. He had noticed Paisnel's bag was missing the day after the man had disappeared; he had thought it odd at the time that Juhel had failed to mention it. And then there were the ribbon-bound documents. Geoffrey had seen Paisnel reading them once and had passed close enough to see they were official deeds of some kind. And the day *after* it had been decided that Paisnel must have fallen overboard, Geoffrey had seen Juhel with them. Had Juhel thrown away the pack so no one would notice the documents were no longer in it? But that made no sense, because, as Philippa pointed out, Juhel was Paisnel's companion and would have come into possession of them anyway. Or was he afraid Fingar might have his own views on the distribution of a dead man's property?

Geoffrey shook himself impatiently. It was not his concern. Nevertheless, he decided he could not be rid of his travelling companions quickly enough and began to look forward keenly to the time when he would be alone.

They had not gone far before Edith, unbalanced by the weight of Roger's arm about her shoulders, took a tumble and twisted her knee. She wept piteously but declined to allow Geoffrey to inspect it, claiming it would be improper for a married man to see her bare flesh. Roger offered his services instead, pointing out that *he* had no wife, but Edith was angry with him for making her stumble in the first place, and his offer was repelled with equal iciness. Philippa obliged in the end, and the men were ordered to move a respectable distance away.

'She is irked with me,' said Roger, dismayed. 'I was only trying to help.'

'I would be careful, if I were you,' advised Geoffrey. 'Their relationship with Vitalis was odd, and Philippa has been making accusations of murder against Juhel.'

'Be careful of what?' demanded Ulfrith, leaping to defend the woman who had captured his heart. 'They are decent ladies who will not even reveal a knee to a man.'

Usually, Geoffrey would have boxed the lad's ears for his impudence, but the previous month Ulfrith had saved Geoffrey's sister by killing a wild boar that was about to attack her. Ulfrith could do no wrong in Joan's eyes, and she had extracted a promise from Geoffrey to be gentle with the lad. *Jerosolimitani* took vows seriously, and Ulfrith had been permitted to overstep the mark on several occasions.

'They are lucky they have you to watch over them,' was all Geoffrey said.

Ulfrith nodded stiffly. 'I will protect them.'

'So will I,' said Roger with a leer. 'I will protect Philippa next, as Edith seems out of sorts.'

'No!' cried Ulfrith, who was not so naïve that he did not know where that would lead. 'She should walk with me.'

Roger gazed at him in astonishment, amazed that a squire should presume to argue with him. Then he saw the fiercely ardent expression, and his face creased into a grin of understanding.

'Very well – you go for her, lad, and good luck to you! It is about time you cut your teeth on a decent wench. I shall persist with Edith. We were getting along famously until she took her tumble.'

'Vitalis was lucky to have *two* such women,' said Bale sadly. 'I would like a wife, but ladies do not seem to find me very attractive. Perhaps they will like me more when I have some money.'

'It is the bald head, man,' said Roger bluntly. 'They do not like the way you shave it. You would do better if you had a bit of hair.'

'If I had hair, it would only be at the back and sides, and it would be grey,' said Bale mournfully. 'I would look like a monk, and no woman wants to bed one of those.'

Geoffrey tried to imagine what his squire might look like with a tonsure, but found he could not do it. However, he certainly did not think patchy grey locks would make Bale resemble a cleric – unless it was a very debauched and violent one.

'Lady Hilde cried bitterly when you left,' Bale went on, still thinking of female companions. 'I wish a lady would weep for me.'

Geoffrey regarded him in surprise. 'She did not! She had no interest in marrying me, and I imagine she is only too pleased to be left on her own. My estates will do well under her and my sister, and they were both relieved when I said I was leaving.'

'They were not,' contradicted Roger immediately. 'Joan was furious, and Hilde was hurt. They like you better than you think, lad. They will be pleased when you return so soon – and you have to go home now, because you cannot travel without money.'

'Perhaps Lord Baderon will give you some,' suggested Ulfrith. 'Your father-in-law is a wealthy man. You can offer to pray for his soul when you reach the Holy City. In fact, you can persuade him while Sir Roger and I deliver Philippa and Edith to their home.'

Geoffrey smiled at Ulfrith's transparency. He was also amused by the notion that Baderon would pay for his visit to the Holy Land: his kinsman had been dead set against the journey in the first place. Geoffrey's sole duty, Baderon had claimed angrily, was in the marriage bed until he had produced a son to ensure the succession. Geoffrey had done his best, but Hilde was old to be a first-time mother. Moreover, he could tell from their time together that he was not the first man to enjoy her favours, but she had not conceived before. It was entirely possible that their union was destined to be childless.

'You were not married a month before you mentioned travelling east,' said Roger. 'What is wrong with Hilde? She is a nice, big lass – better than the other weaklings that were on offer.'

Geoffrey had not taken to any of the local heiresses presented to him, and that had included Hilde at first. Almost as tall and broad as Geoffrey – and he was taller and broader than most – Hilde could wield a variety of weapons with devastating effect and was not afraid to practise her military skills in the skirmishes that often broke out in the volatile Marches. Roger admired her greatly, but Geoffrey wished she was gentler. He was still pondering her idiosyncrasies when his dog growled. The aloof Saxon was approaching.

'It is too dangerous to linger here,' he declared. 'If the women cannot continue, we shall abandon them. It is imperative that you convey me to a place of safety.'

'Is it indeed?' asked Geoffrey, as Roger gaped at the presumption.

'Yes,' stated the Saxon with finality. 'And do not tell me you plan to continue your journey east instead, because you barely have enough to take you to Hastinges, let alone Jerusalem.'

'How do you know?' demanded Roger. Geoffrey might be penniless, but he himself had enough to travel to the Holy Land and back several times in comparative luxury.

'Because I overheard you talking. You were right: it *was* folly to have undertaken your journey when there were double moons portending disaster and blood bubbling from the ground in lieu of springs. God's message to you is clear: stay in England. Now we must find the church you saw from the ship. It cannot be far, and I want to reach it before it is completely dark.'

'I shall go when it pleases me,' said Roger dangerously. 'It is not for you to tell a *Jerosolimitanus* what to do.'

'Ah, but it is,' replied the Saxon enigmatically. 'Your father is only a Norman bishop, but your mother was a true Saxon lady, and you have a fine Saxon lad as your squire. You are a Saxon at heart, and *that* is why I have decided to trust you.'

'Trust him for what?' asked Geoffrey suspiciously, knowing that

Roger was far more Norman than Saxon, especially in his love of other people's property.

'To help me in my quest. But I do not need *you*. I am only interested in recruiting Saxons. Now, if we walk along this beach for just a little longer, we should reach that church.'

'Who *are* you?' asked Geoffrey. 'And how do you know this coast? You joined the ship in Ireland, and it is only by chance that we landed here.'

The man pulled himself up to his full height, which was considerable: he towered over Roger. 'I am Magnus, eldest son of King Harold and England's rightful monarch.'

Despite Ulfrith carrying Edith, and Geoffrey setting a pace that had them all gasping for breath, it was pitch black by the time they reached the tower. It was not a church at all – which made him sceptical of Magnus's local knowledge – but a fortress glowering across the heaving waves.

'What place is this?' asked Roger, studying the stalwart earthworks and ancient but powerful stone wall that ran in a massive oval around a substantial bailey. A stone keep dominated the buildings inside, standing atop a motte.

'It must have been built by Romans,' said Geoffrey, admiringly. 'The walls have been repaired in places, but they still stand tall and strong.'

'Never mind that,' said Edith irritably. 'My leg hurts. Tell them to admit us at once.'

'God help us!' breathed Magnus in sudden alarm, once he had come close enough to see the place through the darkness. 'It is Pevenesel Castle! We must have fetched up farther west than I thought. It is a Norman stronghold, in the care of a nobleman named Richer de Laigle.'

'You seem to know a lot about it,' said Roger suspiciously.

Magnus regarded him pityingly. 'Yes. What sort of king would I be if I were unfamiliar with the defences of my enemies? But we cannot stay here. If they learn who I am, they will kill me.'

'Then do not tell them,' suggested Juhel. 'As I always say to the Duke of Normandy, if you—'

'You must find somewhere else,' said Magnus to Roger. 'This is unacceptable.'

'Any ideas where?' asked Geoffrey archly, gesturing around him. 'The castle is the only thing here — except for those houses outside the bailey, and they will be inhabited by people who work for de Laigle. We have no choice but to beg his hospitality.'

'And I am staying with *him*,' said Roger, pointing at Geoffrey. 'So you can stop giving me orders. I may have Saxon blood, but I do not serve any master who demands my loyalty. I only honour leaders who can pay.'

'*I* will pay you,' insisted Magnus. 'As soon as I am king. But you must conduct me to a Saxon haven first — tonight. It is imperative that I do not fall into enemy hands.'

'I doubt de Laigle will see you as an enemy,' said Geoffrey, suspecting the man would probably deem Magnus insane.

He was not sure he believed the tale himself, because Magnus did not look like the son of a great warrior, although embroidery and gold thread on his clothes indicated that he had some wealth. Tall and painfully thin, he had straggly grey hair tied in a meagre tail at the back of his head, and an enormous silver moustache — an odd fashion in England, where most men were bearded. His bony face — which still bore the scars of its spat with Juhel's chicken — was dominated by a wedge-shaped nose and bloodless lips. Geoffrey's father had fought at Hastinges and had often talked about King Harold's strength of body and character. If Magnus was indeed his son, then he had not inherited his sire's looks or his commanding personality.

'I cannot take that chance,' said Magnus curtly. 'Lead on, Sir Roger.'

'No,' said Roger firmly. 'I have been shipwrecked, man. All I want is meat, wine and a wench to warm my bed.' He winked at Edith, who ignored him.

'Well, I cannot walk any further,' declared Philippa. 'So I shall throw myself on their mercy.'

Before anyone could stop her, she strode up to the gatehouse and thumped on the door.

'What?' came an irritable voice after she had hammered for some time.

'I demand to see de Laigle,' she shouted. 'My . . . *sister* and I are shipwrecked gentlewomen in distress. Open the gate immediately.'

There was a short silence and then a lot of coarse laughter.

'Nice try, Mabel! You *almost* had us convinced. But Lord de Laigle said we were not to let you in any more – not after that trick with the onion and the candle. You will have to ply your trade elsewhere.'

'I am not Mabel!' cried Philippa, outraged. 'Open the gate, before I tell de Laigle what a dreadful gaggle of oafs he has in his service.'

'Bugger off,' came the reply.

'Open up!' yelled Roger in a furious bellow. 'My name is Sir Roger of Durham, *Jerosolimitanus*, and I demand entry.'

This time a grille was unfastened, followed by a hasty, urgent debate inside. Some soldiers were won over by Roger's fierce demeanour and the bright Crusader's cross on his surcoat; others were sceptical. When Roger made some colourful threats, the gate was hastily pulled open. Geoffrey was unimpressed: they should have asked more questions before admitting strangers after dark. He saw Magnus watching in silence and wondered what they would say if they knew they had revealed their weakness to a Saxon pretender to the crown.

Once inside, a soldier led them across the bailey to a long hall. Although it was late and snores emanated from some of the huts they passed, the hall itself was ablaze with light, and the guard opened the door to reveal a throng of people who did not look at all as though they were ready for bed. Most were brightly clad nobles who raised brimming goblets in sloppy salutes or grabbed clumsily at the serving girls, while perspiring minstrels strove valiantly to make their music heard over the racket. The chamber smelled of roasted meat, spilt wine, stale rushes and damp dogs.

The soldier hurried to a young, jauntily dressed man who sat at a table on a dais. The fellow's eyebrows shot up at the whispered message, and he tottered towards his unexpected guests. Several of his companions followed, including a woman dressed entirely in white. This was a poor choice of colours, since it revealed exactly where she had spilled her victuals, while manly fingermarks showed in inappropriate places.

'Shipwrecked mariners?' asked the man with supercilious amusement. 'You do not look like sailors. And what do these women do aboard ship? Furl your sails? Or are they put to the oars?'

His friends howled with laughter, and Geoffrey felt Roger

tense beside him. Philippa and Edith seemed bewildered, and Juhel startled into silence; Magnus kept to the shadows.

'I should never be able to row a ship,' declared the woman in white. 'So you must protect me, husband. I would not like to be carried off by pirates.'

More laughter followed, and Geoffrey decided they were too intoxicated for sensible conversation. Explanations could wait until the next day. He had reckoned without Ulfrith, though.

'Ladies Philippa and Edith are the wives of a knight, so treat them with respect,' he said coldly.

'Saxon dog,' sneered the man contemptuously. 'Who are you to address me, Richer de Laigle, so familiarly? Remember your place, boy, before I have you run through.'

'We are sorry to interrupt your entertainment,' said Geoffrey, before the argument could escalate. 'We ask only for food and shelter – for which we can pay. Tomorrow we will be gone.'

De Laigle regarded him blearily. 'You are a *Jerosolimitanus*, I see. I have heard they are a vile, unmannerly breed, and now I see for myself that the rumours are true.'

'Now look here,' hissed Roger, stepping forward in a way that had de Laigle staggering back in alarm. 'I did not come here to be insulted by some cockerel—'

'Cockerel, am I?' asked de Laigle from behind the guard. 'Well, *you* are a brute.'

He folded his arms and pursed his lips, as though he had scored some kind of point. Roger regarded him uncertainly, taken off guard by the peculiar response.

'Oh, leave them, Richer,' said Lady de Laigle, draining the contents of her cup. Another purple stain was added to her kirtle. 'I would rather dance than exchange obscenities with ruffians.'

'My guard will find you a stable,' said de Laigle to Roger. He grabbed his wife and hauled her towards him for a long, passionate kiss that almost made her pass out. 'I cannot be bothered to banter with you tonight.'

Lady de Laigle managed to claw herself more or less upright by using Geoffrey as a prop. 'I hate England – there are too many Saxons scurrying about with their heads down and glints of malice in their eyes. They still think the country should be theirs, you know.'

'It should,' snarled Magnus, galled into imprudence.

De Laigle waved a finger at him, and it was only the guard's timely lunge that prevented him from dropping into the startled Saxon's arms like a lover.

'It should be Norman, because Saxons are debauched drunkards who cannot hold their wine. But who are you, anyway? You are no *Jerosolimitanus.* You are too skinny to wield a sword. I, of course, leave that sort of thing to brutal fellows I employ.'

Geoffrey hoped Magnus would be discreet, but the Saxon was buoyed up with a sense of moral advantage. 'I am King Magnus,' he declared. 'Rightful monarch of England.'

De Laigle regarded him open-mouthed for a moment and then burst into derisive laughter. His wife lurched to the nearest table, grabbed someone else's wine and raised it in a salute before downing it in a series of determined gulps. Geoffrey watched in fascination, waiting for her to fall flat on her face. He had never seen a woman drink with quite so much indomitable resolve.

'The stable,' prompted Juhel, prudently drawing an end to the encounter.

'This way,' said the guard, stepping aside smartly as Lady de Laigle pitched towards him, landing in a way that would have hurt had she been sober. 'Follow me.'

'Stable?' whispered Roger indignantly in Geoffrey's ear. 'I am the son of the Bishop of Durham, and they put me in a stable?'

'It does not matter,' said Geoffrey quietly. 'We leave at dawn – I have no intention of being around when de Laigle wakes. Especially if he recalls what Magnus said.'

Roger nodded slowly. 'You are right. We do not want him telling King Henry that there is a Saxon claimant for his throne on the loose, and that I am his chief henchman.'

'No,' agreed Geoffrey vehemently. 'We do not!'

# Three

Geoffrey followed the guard across the bailey to a dilapidated building with a sod roof, and thought Magnus had been right in his reluctance to accept Pevenesel's hospitality. He did not like its drunken constable, slack guards and unruly merrymaking. Or was marriage ruining his sense of fun, and he was becoming a withered old prude who frowned on the gaiety of others?

'Lord!' exclaimed Philippa, impressed. '*They* know how to entertain themselves!'

The guard grimaced. 'Yes, and Lord de Laigle will not like it one bit.'

'But he *was* liking it,' Roger pointed out.

'I mean the senior Lord de Laigle, who owns this castle. Richer is his son – the youngest and most useless of his brood. The *real* Lord de Laigle is with the King in Winchester, discussing how the coastal castles might be strengthened.'

'Is there talk of an invasion, then?' asked Geoffrey uneasily.

'There is always talk of invasion,' said the guard with a dismissive wave. 'But the Duke of Normandy is in St Valery at the moment – the place where the Conqueror sailed from when he snatched the English throne. Lord de Laigle wants to be prepared.'

'Then he had better hope the Duke does not invade while he is away,' said Roger. 'Because his son will do little to repel him – except perhaps shock him with his disgraceful manners.'

'He writes,' said the guard with considerable disapproval. 'Young Richer, I mean. He was supposed to enter the Church, so they taught him his letters. Perhaps that is what sent him sour.'

'It is often the case,' agreed Magnus, as Geoffrey rolled his eyes. 'No good ever comes from learning. Paisnel was a clerk, and look what happened to him.'

'What do you mean?' asked Juhel, his voice tight.

'I mean he was always poring over documents and they sent him insane,' explained Magnus. 'Then he fell over the side of the ship.'

'I suspect he was a spy,' said Philippa in a transparent effort to provoke Juhel into saying something incriminating. 'It would explain why he took his bag when he *jumped overboard*.'

If she was expecting Juhel to confess to his friend's murder, she was disappointed. Juhel only looked away, as if he found Paisnel's death too painful to discuss. Philippa, seeing she was not to be satisfied, turned to the guard.

'The locals were not very hospitable when our ship floundered in the storm,' she said.

'Well, you *are* Normans,' said the guard. 'And they recall what happened when the Conqueror arrived – how he destroyed all manner of villages before having himself crowned. People around here have long memories. You may think your welcome was unfriendly here at Pevenesel, but at least no one will cut your throat while you sleep.'

With that, he opened the door to the shabby building, handed her a candle and left. A number of men were already snoring inside, so Geoffrey took two blankets from a pile near the door, passed them to Philippa and Edith and suggested they sleep in the loft. Roger and Ulfrith volunteered to accompany them there, but, wisely, Edith declined their offer.

Philippa shot Geoffrey a smile full of invitation as she left, which had Ulfrith gaping in dismay. To allay his distress, Geoffrey suggested that he sleep at the foot of the ladder, to prevent anyone from following them. Pleased to serve Philippa, Ulfrith promptly curled around the bottom rung.

'The rest of you will sleep in a circle around me,' said Magnus. 'It is your duty to protect me.'

'I do not think so,' said Roger, selecting a place as far away as possible. Magnus's confident authority faltered when Geoffrey followed, leaving him with Juhel.

'Have no fear,' said Juhel, laughing when he saw Magnus's distrust. 'My chicken and I will look after you.'

'I am uneasy here,' Roger said to Geoffrey in a low voice, throwing his friend a blanket. 'I distrust de Laigle and his whore wife.'

Geoffrey grimaced in distaste when he found his blanket was damp and stank of urine. He flung it away, and his dog scratched it into a suitable shape before sinking down in abject pleasure.

It rested its head on its paws, but its eyes were open and its ears flicked back and forth. Geoffrey went to fetch a cleaner one, but there were only two left: one so thick with lice that they were visible even in the faint light of the candle, the other with brown stains that looked like blood. He chose the bloody one and went to lie next to Roger and Bale.

'It is freezing, too,' the big knight grumbled. 'And it is only September. Another omen against your plans, Geoff. A sensible man always pays heed to the real meanings behind unseasonable weather.'

The words were no sooner out of his mouth than a distant howl sounded on the wind. The dog whimpered and Juhel's chicken clucked and flapped in agitation.

'That was a wolf!' exclaimed Bale in astonishment. 'I never expected to hear one again. They are all but gone near Goodrich.'

'That was no wolf,' said Roger with considerable conviction. 'That was a fay.'

'A fay?' asked Geoffrey, peering at him in the darkness. 'What is a fay?'

'A fairy,' replied Roger in a hoarse, meaningful whisper. 'You know — a mysterious being. It is odd, is it not, that the moment I mention these omens, a fay should utter her eerie call?'

The animal howled a second time, and Roger and Bale both sat up.

'She did it again,' whispered Bale. 'She is warning him to heed these omens.'

When the creature howled a third time, and Bale began to cross himself, Geoffrey lost patience.

'That is a wolf, not a spirit. And omens can be interpreted in any number of ways. How do you know the signs were not telling me I *should* return to the Holy Land?'

'Because God would not have wrecked your ship if they were,' said Roger with finality. 'He would have seen you safely across the water. I know what I am talking about: my father is a bishop, and your head is stuffed too full of silliness from books and scrolls.'

They were silent for a while, Geoffrey listening to the sounds of other men sleeping. Juhel lay flat on his back, seemingly asleep, but Geoffrey saw his hand edge towards his dagger when someone went to drink from a communal bucket. Juhel's reactions were almost as finely honed as his own, and the knight wondered how a parchmenter came to be so well trained.

'I do not want to travel any farther with our companions,' he whispered to Roger. 'Philippa says Juhel drowned Paisnel, and it would be rash to become involved with would-be Saxon kings.'

'I agree,' murmured Roger. 'If we start early, we can be gone before they are awake.'

'My father described this part of the coast to me – it was where he landed with the Conqueror. It is no great journey to Dover, which has ships leaving every day. I will make my way there.'

'And do what?' asked Roger. 'God's blood, it is cold in here! Move closer to me: there is a savage draught coming under that door and you will block it if you ease over a touch.'

'And see what kind of berth I can buy. I did not want to travel through Normandy while Bellême is there, but I will do if there is no choice.'

Roger gave Geoffrey a hefty shove, to place him in the path of the gale that swept under the door. 'And how do you propose to fund this journey? By selling your dog? He is the only thing you have left, other than your armour, and you will need that.'

'You will lend me some,' said Geoffrey, moving back to his previous position.

Roger sat up. 'Normally you would be right: I would give you my last penny, as long as you promised to pay it back. But not this time. The omens—'

'Omens!' spat Geoffrey. 'There are no omens. And I will not rest easy until I learn why Tancred dismissed me after so many years of faithful service. We were friends, and I do not understand why he—'

'Because you used him badly,' interrupted Roger. 'You ignored his order to return to the Holy Land immediately and served another master instead. What do you expect? Would you accept Bale back after two years, during which he had repeatedly ignored *your* demands?'

'That is not the same.'

'Yes, it is,' insisted Roger. 'At the end of the day, you are Tancred's *servant*, no matter how many times you fought at his side – or saved his life. It is time you forgot him and accepted what God has given you: fertile lands, a good wife and a sister who does all the work.'

'I am still going,' said Geoffrey stubbornly.

Roger sighed and lay back down again, turning on his side and pushing Geoffrey with his back until he had them both in a position where he was comfortable. 'Then you go alone, Geoff, because I will not ignore Heaven's wishes. Ulfrith and I will ride to Durham once we see you to Dover.'

Geoffrey's early escape was thwarted by Roger's fay. Shortly before dawn, it resumed howling, although much closer than before. It woke everyone, and Roger's declaration that it was an evil spirit looking for blood was sufficiently convincing that a consensus was reached that the gate should not be opened. By the time he announced that all fays must have returned to their dark holes, the sun was shining brightly. A bank of clouds in the distance and a nip in the air indicated it would not stay fine for long, however, and even as Geoffrey watched, the waves seemed to swell in size, as if in anticipation of another tempest.

They were served a meagre breakfast of ale, gritty bread and some kind of fish that stank enough to make Geoffrey's eyes water. His dog declined the one he tossed it, so he decided to abstain, too.

'Give the rest to me,' ordered Magnus. 'They are a Saxon delicacy and too good to waste on that revolting creature. This Norman fortress may be a temple to Sodom, but at least *someone* knows how to provide a decent meal.'

'The cows are under the hedge,' said Juhel conversationally, pointing to where four skinny bovines huddled near a straggly line of hawthorn bushes at the far end of the bailey. 'That means rain is in the offing.'

'And the gulls are aiming inland,' agreed Roger. 'That is always a sign of a brewing storm.' He cast a baleful eye at Geoffrey.

'What do you mean?' asked Juhel, intrigued by the meaningful look.

'I mean it is a sign from God,' said Roger. 'He has already sent several, warning against going to the Holy Land. I imagine He thought a shipwreck would have been sufficient to prove His case, but someone continues to be obstinate, so He is obliged to summon yet another tempest.'

'The wreck was your doing, was it?' asked Juhel, humour gleaming in his eyes.

'Yes,' said Roger before Geoffrey could reply. 'And now he is intent on going to Dover, to find another boat that he will lead to its doom.'

'Dover?' asked Magnus. 'That will take you back the way we came yesterday.'

'I suppose it will,' said Geoffrey.

'Then I shall come with you,' determined Magnus. 'I need to travel that direction myself.'

'I thought your destination was Ribe.' Geoffrey was reluctant to have anything to do with him.

'No – Fingar said he would make one or two brief stops en route,' said Magnus. 'One of those was *my* destination.'

Geoffrey frowned. 'He told me he had no intention of stopping anywhere.'

Juhel laughed. 'It would have been foolish in the extreme for him to put in along the English coast, given the amount of contraband he collected in Bristol. The King's agents would have been after him in a trice.'

Geoffrey raised his eyebrows. 'I knew he was smuggling, but I did not know it was on the scale you are suggesting. That answers why his crew was gathering up all the wreckage.'

'Evidence,' explained Juhel when Roger looked puzzled. 'They can hardly wander off leaving barrels of contraband strewn across the beach. They must destroy it first.'

'Is that what they were doing?' mused Roger. 'I thought they were hoping to sell it.'

'Pepper and sugar mixed with sea water will not fetch much,' said Juhel. 'And that was what was under all those Irish pelts: spices – the gold of the East.'

'It is a good thing Lord de Laigle is away,' said Magnus. 'He is an efficient taxor and would have arrested the lot of us. I doubt he would have believed we were innocent.'

'But I had no idea there were spices aboard,' cried Roger indignantly.

'Neither did I until we were underway,' said Juhel. 'Although the cheap berth did arouse my suspicions. But that is immaterial – we all would have hanged at Fingar's side had we been caught.'

'I thought you dealt in parchment – a lucrative commodity,' said Geoffrey. 'Why should you seek out a cheap berth?'

Juhel winced. 'Business was poor this year, and I am short of funds. Paisnel was able to pay for my passage, as well as his own, by opting for Fingar's ship. What about you? Are you trying to evade justice?'

'No!' exclaimed Geoffrey, startled. 'We just wanted a route that would not involve journeying through Bellême's territory.'

Juhel nodded understanding. 'He is a bad enemy, and I am fortunate that he likes me. But I may accompany you to Dover, too. Now poor Paisnel is dead I have two reasons for reaching Ribe: to make arrangements with Danish leather sellers *and* to deliver Paisnel's dispatches to the Bishop. Paisnel was devoted to his prelate and would have wanted me to complete his work.'

'I am leaving today,' said Geoffrey. 'But I am used to travelling quickly in unfavourable conditions. You should wait for better weather, then join a larger party.'

'*I* cannot wait,' objected Magnus. 'I want Sir Roger to escort me to an abbey that stands nearby. It is no more than ten miles from here.'

'Do you mean the abbey that was built after the battle?' asked Geoffrey. His father had told him how the Conqueror had ordered a fine monastery to be founded on the spot where so many men had died. It had been a decision rooted in self-interest: the shocked Church was appeased over the terrible bloodshed, and it meant there were plenty of monks to pray for the souls of those who had died, lest the battle was held against the instigator on Judgement Day.

Magnus nodded. 'There are a number of Saxon villages surrounding the abbey, and I will be safe there until I decide my next move. You will appreciate that, as the true claimant to the crown, I did not intend to be washed up in England with little more than my clothes.'

'I shall come with you,' said Juhel. 'It would be prudent to pay for a mass, to give thanks for our deliverance. I do not want to experience another violent storm.'

'I shall do the same,' said Edith, coming to join them. 'We are lucky to be alive, and I want God to know I am grateful. Philippa and I will travel with you to the abbey.'

'We are not going there,' said Geoffrey. 'Roger is going home, and I am going to Dover.'

'Actually, Geoff, I think we should, so we can purchase masses, too,' said Roger. 'And if you want to borrow money for your journey to the Holy Land, you must come with us – it is my condition for lending it to you.'

Geoffrey was unimpressed by Roger's stipulation, although he did appreciate that they had had a narrow escape. He just wished Roger would simply let him say a few prayers in a church along the way instead.

However, his displeasure was nothing compared to that of Philippa and Edith when they learned that Lord de Laigle's wife – somewhat fragile that morning – had offered to keep them at Pevenesel until their kin could collect them. Geoffrey accepted the offer with alacrity. Ulfrith was distraught, and Roger disappointed, especially as Edith's irritation from the previous day seemed to have dissipated. She appealed to him to persuade Geoffrey to allow them to go to the abbey instead.

'They will be no trouble, Geoff,' wheedled Roger. 'And it will please Ulfrith. He is like a moonstruck calf with Philippa.'

'She will never submit to the charms of a squire, and they will have to be parted sooner or later,' said Geoffrey, unmoved. 'It is better to do it before matters get out of hand.'

'Then I will make it a condition of your loan,' countered Roger craftily. 'Either we take the ladies or I will not lend you the money.'

'Then I will manage without it,' said Geoffrey, suspecting there would be an ongoing set of provisos if he did not take a stand.

Roger glared. 'You will find that difficult.'

'But not impossible. There will be some merchant or pilgrim who will accept me as a guide or protector. It is a long and dangerous journey, and I have made it several times. Someone will pay my passage in return for my skills.'

'Unlikely,' said Juhel with one of his cheery grins. 'You look far too disreputable. We all know what kind of men went on the Crusade, and you appear to be one of the rougher ones. Your surcoat is stained with blood, and your armour has clearly seen too much use to be respectable.'

Geoffrey stared at him. 'I am a soldier – of course it has seen plenty of use. And these stains are not blood, but rust. Bale left my shield lying on top of it.'

'I think you are very handsome,' said Philippa, sidling up to him. 'You have beautiful eyes and you are not badly scarred like many warriors. All you need is a good wash and some clean clothes, and you will be an Adonis.'

Ulfrith's eyes narrowed. 'Who is Adonis? And where do you know him from?'

'If you accept payment for that sort of commission, you will be a common mercenary,' said Roger, conveniently forgetting that he often sold his talents to anyone who had enough gold. 'And is it so much to ask that you let me take these women to the abbey?'

Fortunately, Juhel began to chat to the women about the perfumes Adonis was alleged to have used, so Geoffrey took the opportunity to haul Roger away. There was no point in trying to reason with the big knight while Edith had him fixed with great, piteous eyes.

'We cannot, Roger. Their fathers and brothers will assume we abducted them – and I am a married man. They must stay here, where women of their own status are willing to look after them.'

'I could look after them,' said Roger with a meaningful wink.

'Quite, and it will not do. Besides, what happens if we arrive at this abbey and find it has no facilities for women? It is a community of Benedictine monks, so there is no reason to suppose they can accommodate females. You may be obliged to take them as far as Dover.'

'I would not mind.'

'You would, because then you will be forced to stay there until their relatives decide to fetch them. You could be waiting months, and it will be expensive to feed and house them.'

'Are you ready?' bawled Roger to the squires, thoughts of extra costs quickly bringing him in line with Geoffrey's position. He made a perfunctory bow to the women. 'I am sorry, ladies: my friend is right. We cannot expose you to unnecessary danger.'

He strode out of the bailey, his possessions wrapped in one of the castle's blankets and slung over his shoulder. Magnus shot after him, determined to walk next to the man he considered his protector. With considerable reluctance, Ulfrith followed, Bale murmuring sympathetically in his ear. Geoffrey went last with Juhel at his side, chicken swinging in the cage next to him.

Juhel chattered incessantly, and since his monologue did not require much response, Geoffrey's mind wandered. He was brought back to the present when Ulfrith suddenly stopped at an oddly shaped tree that had grown twisted in the coastal winds.

'This is where Philippa came ashore,' he said. 'We should make sure the tide has not washed Vitalis out of his grave. It is a small service, but she may be grateful when she learns I suggested it.'

'No, we should press on,' argued Magnus. 'We do not have time for the dead.'

'I agree,' said Juhel. 'Those black clouds are coming up fast. Can you not feel the tingle in the air as thunder gathers?'

'No,' said Ulfrith shortly. 'But I can manage alone. You go ahead. I will catch up.'

'I will stay with him,' said Geoffrey to Roger, suspecting that the lad might take the opportunity to return to Philippa if he was allowed to linger on his own.

'You want to claim the credit for a good deed that was *my* idea,' said Ulfrith accusingly.

Geoffrey fought down his irritation. 'I am offering to help you, boy. I am not interested in your lady. I am married, remember?'

'But only to big old Hilde Baderon,' Ulfrith muttered in a sufficiently low voice that Geoffrey could not be absolutely certain he had heard him right. He decided to overlook the remark in the interests of harmony, hoping Ulfrith would soon forget about Philippa and be back to his normal ebullient self.

'Come,' he said shortly. 'We will not have so far to run if we hurry.'

Ulfrith followed him down the beach, Bale trailing behind.

'I see no grave,' said Ulfrith, looking around with his hands on his hips.

Geoffrey pointed to a knot of squawking, flapping gulls a short distance away. 'I imagine it is over there.'

Ulfrith gaped. 'What are they doing?'

'I thought you grew up near the sea,' said Geoffrey, advancing cautiously. The birds took to the air, although they did not go far. 'You must have seen this sort of thing before.'

'You mean they are *eating* him?' exclaimed Ulfrith, appalled. 'But he was a man!'

Geoffrey did not reply but stared at the body in the sand. Vitalis's wives had made a poor job of burying him. They had interred him below the high-water mark, so the next tide had scoured him out. Their hole had been too shallow, and they had not protected the grave with stones. Moreover, the birds were not the only ones to have ravaged Vitalis; it appeared that the villagers had been at him, too.

Geoffrey indicated that Bale was to help him carry the corpse to the boggy meadow behind the beach. He then set the squires to scooping out a decent hole with pieces of driftwood, while he gathered rocks to make a cairn. Fortunately, the soil was soft, and it was not long before they were able to roll Vitalis into his new final resting place.

'He has a nice cloak,' said Bale, fingering it. 'And I like that ring.'

'No,' said Geoffrey sharply. He and Bale had had this discussion before. 'We do not steal from the dead. Besides, clothes harvested from cadavers carry diseases.'

'Only after they begin to rot, sir,' countered Bale. 'Vitalis is relatively fresh. And the ring—'

'The ring belongs to Vitalis,' said Geoffrey firmly. 'And with Vitalis it will stay.'

'But he will not be needing it where he is going,' reasoned Bale. 'And you are about to embark for the Holy Land without so much as a spare shirt. The ring would mean you would not have to borrow funds from Sir Roger. Besides, if we do not take it, those greedy villagers will.'

'That is why we are burying him deep,' replied Geoffrey. He looked around uneasily, suddenly assailed with the sense that they might be being watched. 'Put the ring back, Bale. We are not corpse robbers.'

Bale looked sorry but did as he was told. Geoffrey gazed out to sea, wondering what it was about corpses that Bale so liked. He was one of the least greedy men Geoffrey had ever known, but he seemed unable to resist items belonging to the dead.

'You should say something, sir,' said Ulfrith. He was pale, and Geoffrey supposed he had not buried many men who had been half-eaten by birds. 'We cannot just leave. It would not be right.'

'Say something in Latin,' suggested Bale helpfully. 'That always sounds nice.'

'Oh, yes!' agreed Ulfrith keenly, removing his hat in anticipation. 'Like a priest. Lady Philippa will like that when I tell her.'

'I wish my horse had not died in this wretched place,' said Geoffrey in Latin, staring down at the dead, sand-brushed features of the old knight but thinking of the animal he had lost. '*Should I have listened to Roger about the omens? But that is odd! What is that line on Vitalis's neck?*'

'Amen,' said Ulfrith and Bale in unison as Geoffrey dropped to one knee to inspect the mark more closely. It lay under Vitalis's cloak, which Bale's rummaging had disturbed.

'Something is tied around his neck,' said Geoffrey, turning the dead man's pecked head in his hands. 'A piece of twine.'

'It is tight,' said Bale, squatting next to him and touching it with his forefinger. He took one of his sharp little knives and cut through it, showing where it had bitten deeply into the skin below. Then he leaned all his weight on Vitalis's chest. Nothing happened. 'There,' he said in satisfaction.

'There what?' asked Ulfrith, bemused.

'He did not drown,' explained Geoffrey. 'Or Bale would have been able to squeeze water from his lungs. No, he was strangled with that piece of twine.'

'Not twine,' said Bale, handing it to Geoffrey. 'Ribbon. Fine red ribbon.'

'I have seen its like before,' said Ulfrith, staring at it. 'But I cannot remember where.'

Geoffrey frowned. 'Paisnel used red ribbon to keep his documents in order.'

The documents that had been in Paisnel's bag, he thought, but that he himself had seen Juhel inspecting the day after Paisnel's mysterious disappearance.

'Then Juhel killed Vitalis!' exclaimed Ulfrith, wide-eyed. 'Philippa said he killed Paisnel, so he must have strangled Vitalis, too.'

'There is no evidence to suggest that,' said Geoffrey, his thoughts whirling. He had red ribbon of his own in the saddlebag he had saved from *Patrick*, but his was coarser. He looked at the stuff in Bale's hand and tried to assess whether it was the same kind that Paisnel had owned. But ribbons were often used by clerks, and it could belong to anyone.

'It *was* a long time before Juhel rejoined us yesterday,' Bale pointed out. 'He could have been off throttling Vitalis. And Lady Philippa was right to accuse him of dispatching Paisnel, because they were *always* squabbling. Men get a taste for killing, see, and they cannot help themselves.'

'Well, this is definitely Juhel's ribbon,' declared Ulfrith, as Geoffrey wondered uneasily whether Bale had a taste for killing, too.

'You seem very sure of that. How?'

Ulfrith shrugged. 'I saw Paisnel reading documents with important-looking seals one night, and I saw Juhel glancing through similar ones after Paisnel went missing. Red ribbon kept them in a neat bundle. It is obvious what happened: Juhel used Paisnel's ribbon to strangle Vitalis.'

'Not necessarily,' said Geoffrey. 'Even if Juhel did take Paisnel's documents, we do not know if he salvaged them when the ship sank. And you cannot prove this particular piece of ribbon belonged to Juhel. The stuff is not exactly rare – I have some myself.'

'You did not kill Vitalis, though,' said Bale loyally.

'Then who else could it have been?' asked Ulfrith. 'The pirates?'

'Possibly,' said Geoffrey. 'But they were not with Vitalis when he died. Nor did they try to bury his corpse.'

'Philippa and Edith dug the grave,' said Ulfrith. 'And they were with him when he died. Philippa told us herself that Vitalis's last words were that he had spoken the truth when he accused you of . . .' He trailed off when the implications of what he was saying dawned on him.

'Yes,' said Geoffrey soberly. 'It very much looks as though Philippa and Edith are the prime candidates for their husband's murder.'

'This is monstrous!' yelled Ulfrith, tears of rage and distress rolling down his flushed cheeks as he followed Geoffrey and Bale along the beach. 'You have no right to make such accusations.'

'I accused no one,' said Geoffrey calmly. 'I merely outlined the evidence.'

'You will see Philippa hanged,' shouted Ulfrith. 'How could you? I thought you liked her.'

'I do like her.' Geoffrey saw that was the wrong thing to say, because Ulfrith's eyes narrowed.

'You intend to hold it over her,' he said, white-faced. 'To force her to lie with you.'

If it had not been for the promise Geoffrey had made to his sister, Ulfrith would have been flat on his back with a blade at his throat. Seeing his master's hand twitch towards his dagger, Bale turned quickly and rested a warning hand on the younger man's shoulder. Ulfrith shrugged it off.

'I am going back to her,' he said. 'I want to be at her side if she is accused of terrible crimes.'

'No one will accuse her,' said Geoffrey, struggling to be patient. 'The only people who know Vitalis did not drown are us and his killer – who may or may not be Philippa.'

'Or Edith,' added Bale helpfully.

'And we will say nothing, so they have nothing to worry about,' Geoffrey went on. 'But you cannot ignore the facts. We all saw Vitalis alive as we abandoned ship, and Bale has just proved he did not drown. *Ergo*, he was strangled on the shore.'

'But not by Philippa,' persisted Ulfrith.

Geoffrey continued with his analysis. 'Philippa said Vitalis reiterated his accusations about my family before he died. She also said there was water in his lungs and that he gurgled as he spoke. We know that was not true, because we just saw for ourselves that his lungs were dry. She lied.'

'She was mistaken!' cried Ulfrith. 'She must have heard the gurgle of waves in the pebbles and assumed it was her husband.'

That was highly unlikely, even with Philippa's dim intellect. 'You explain what happened, then,' suggested Geoffrey.

'Juhel was late in joining the rest of us,' began Bale when Ulfrith could not rise to the challenge. 'And some of the pirates wandered off to look for their contraband. Any of them could have killed Vitalis.'

'How?' demanded Geoffrey. 'Philippa stated quite clearly that she was with him when he died – which means she was with him when he was *strangled*. As I imagine she would have noticed someone else choking the life out of him, the only logical explanation is that she and Edith did it.'

'Perhaps they *thought* he was dead when they buried him, but someone else came along, dug him up and strangled him later,' suggested Bale, doing his best for Ulfrith.

Geoffrey shook his head. 'The truth is that Philippa and Edith either killed him or were complicit in his death. The facts simply do not allow any other conclusion.'

Unwilling to debate the matter further, he turned away and began to walk again. But he had underestimated the intensity of Ulfrith's feelings, and, with no warning, the squire attacked. Geoffrey had never been assaulted by a servant before and was taken off guard by Ulfrith's ferocity. Ulfrith was a powerful lad, and the weight of his body knocked Geoffrey from his feet. He began to pummel the knight with his fists, the dog racing around them, barking frantically. The battering did not even stop when Geoffrey pressed his dagger against Ulfrith's throat: the lad was in such a rage that he was oblivious to everything.

'No!' Geoffrey yelled as Bale jumped forward with one of his knives. Bale might be Ulfrith's friend, but protecting Geoffrey came first.

Bale hesitated, giving Geoffrey just enough time to drop his dagger and scrabble for a rock, which he brought up sharply against the side of Ulfrith's head. Ulfrith slumped, dazed, and Geoffrey struggled out from underneath him.

'God's teeth!' he muttered, not sure which had unnerved him more: Ulfrith's blind fury or Bale's readiness to kill a comrade. He ran his hand over his face and found Ulfrith had scored a scratch on his cheek, which would soon probably be joined by bruises. He grimaced in annoyance, thinking he would hardly be hired by a pilgrim if he looked like a man who brawled. He prodded the squire with the toe of his boot, watching impassively as he regained his senses.

'Get up,' he ordered coldly. 'I did not hit you that hard.' *And certainly not as hard as I wanted to*, he added inwardly.

'Oh, God!' groaned Ulfrith. He looked up at Geoffrey, his face ashen. 'Will you tell Sir Roger what I . . . He will dismiss me. Or worse.'

'It is no more than you deserve,' said Geoffrey, regarding him dispassionately. 'You should be thankful you did not attack *him*, or you would be dead now.'

'That is true,' agreed Bale. 'His knife would have been through your throat in an instant.'

'That is enough, Bale,' said Geoffrey, wondering what he had done to be saddled with such a pair. 'Rinse your face in the sea, Ulfrith. You look as though you have been crying, and *that* will not impress Roger.'

'I will fetch you some water,' said Bale when Ulfrith was slow to obey. He glanced at Geoffrey. 'I will get some for you too, sir. For the blood.'

'You are a fool,' said Geoffrey when Bale had gone. 'All this for a woman who has not even noticed you. And a lying one at that, who may have murdered her husband.'

Ulfrith shot him a bleak look, but his fury was spent. When Bale returned, he rinsed the cut on Ulfrith's head, then did the same for Geoffrey, humming all the while. He was never so content as when he was up to his elbows in gore.

'There,' he said, standing back to inspect his handiwork. 'That is better. You are lucky he did not knock out one of your teeth, sir.'

'No, *he* is lucky he did not knock out one of my teeth. And now we had better catch up with Roger; he will be wondering what we have been doing.'

'He will not be pleased when he hears what happened,' said Bale in a wicked understatement. 'So could we say Sir Vitalis's corpse jumped out of its grave and set about us – and you were obliged to strangle it? That would explain why Vitalis was throttled, why you two are battered – *and* it would exonerate Philippa and Edith. Everyone will be happy.'

Geoffrey regarded him uncertainly. 'Everyone except me. I would earn a reputation as a corpse throttler.'

'Do you intend to look into it, sir?' asked Bale. 'The murder, I mean? You have investigated similar crimes, and there is nothing to stop you from exploring this one.'

'Other than the fact that I have no authority to start poking about in such affairs. But this is the second murder to occur among *Patrick*'s passengers, if Philippa is to be believed. They are far too dangerous company for me, and all I want is to be away from them all.' *And from Bale and Ulfrith, too*, Geoffrey thought acidly.

# Four

Roger, Juhel and Magnus had not gone far. They had reached the place where *Patrick* had foundered the previous day and were watching the sailors gather the remaining flotsam and set it alight. Roger had found a low bush on a rise above the beach and was spying on them. Magnus sat with him, fretting about the passing time, while Juhel lay on his back next to them, fast asleep.

'Get down!' hissed Magnus when Geoffrey approached. 'They will see you.'

'They must have been here all night,' said Roger, not taking his eyes off the beach. 'Burning everything, lest taxors come to investigate.'

'Perhaps,' said Geoffrey, resisting Magnus's attempts to pull him down. 'But we have no need to hide from them.'

'I disagree,' said Roger, reaching out a powerful hand to haul on Geoffrey's surcoat. Puzzled, Geoffrey crouched next to him. 'They look dangerous to me – and desperate. They have already killed some of the scavengers, and, much as I like a fight, I do not think we should risk an encounter with thirty smugglers and murderers.'

Geoffrey looked to where he pointed and saw several bodies – villagers, judging by their clothes. Then he glanced at the marshy vegetation behind the beach and saw that although most of the locals had gone, two shadows still loitered. The distinctive green hat identified one; the other was the heavyset man. Eventually, Roger climbed to his feet, taking care to stay out of sight.

'God's blood!' he swore when he noticed Geoffrey's face. 'What happened to you?'

'We found Vitalis,' said Geoffrey. 'But he was strangled, not drowned.'

He showed Roger the ribbon. Meanwhile, Juhel's rest had been disturbed by their voices, and he was waking up. Geoffrey watched his reaction to the news intently, but Juhel revealed nothing other than the astonished dismay that any innocent man would have expressed.

'It looks like something a woman might own,' said Roger, handing it back. Then his jaw dropped. 'Do not tell me that Philippa and Edith did it?'

'They were very distressed by his death,' said Ulfrith stiffly. 'You saw how bitterly they wept.'

Geoffrey thought, but did not say, that if Edith and Philippa *had* dispatched Vitalis, they would hardly celebrate the deed with smiles and laughter. He held up the ribbon for Magnus and Juhel to see, watching for any flicker of recognition. He was not surprised when there was nothing.

'It is the kind of cord used for binding documents,' remarked Magnus. 'Paisnel owned some, because he dabbled in sinister clerkly activities.'

'He could write, yes,' acknowledged Geoffrey. 'But so can I.'

'Quite,' agreed Magnus acidly. 'And that is why I trust Sir Roger over you. Literate types cannot help but dissemble and lie.'

'You speak like a peasant,' said Juhel in distaste, the twinkle fading from his eyes. 'There was no dishonesty in Paisnel, and there is none in Sir Geoffrey. You should watch your tongue, man, or you will find yourself abandoned – you do not win protectors with insults.'

Magnus glowered. 'I was speaking my mind, and if honesty offends you, then you have no place in my kingdom. I was pointing out that this kind of ribbon is favoured by men who possess documents: if Vitalis was strangled with some, then it means his killer can write.'

'No, it means he owned some ribbon,' corrected Geoffrey. 'Or that there was some to hand when he – or she – decided that Vitalis should die.'

'This debate will get us nowhere,' said Roger impatiently. 'That sort of cord is common – Geoff owns some, I saw a bit in Juhel's bag, and Magnus used a piece on the ship to tie his hair.'

Juhel regarded him uneasily. 'You looked in my bag? Why?'

Roger shrugged nonchalantly. 'Because you left it unguarded. It was an open invitation to any man with any enquiring mind, such as my own.'

'Vitalis's death is very sad,' said Magnus, cutting across Juhel's spluttering indignation. 'But we have been here far too long. Your battered faces show you have already endured one encounter with those damned pirates, and even ruffians like you must want to avoid another.'

'Is it true?' asked Roger. 'You met a stray sailor? They have been wandering everywhere, hunting for wreckage, so it does not surprise me. I take it the scoundrel will be no further trouble?'

'No,' said Geoffrey evenly. 'The scoundrel most certainly will not.'

'Good,' said Roger, slinging his blanket of possessions over his shoulder. 'Then I suggest we leave before we are obliged to dispatch any more. So who killed Vitalis? Tell me as we walk.'

Geoffrey followed him to the path that ran behind the beach, where everyone ducked and weaved in an effort to stay out of sight. He glanced at Juhel, who was walking behind him.

'I have no idea who would want Vitalis dead,' he said. 'Do *you*?'

'Me?' Juhel seemed startled by the question. 'Why ask me?'

Geoffrey shrugged. 'You spent more time with him than the rest of us. Why should I not ask your opinion?'

'I *did* spend time with him, but I found him very bitter, and he said horrible things about your family. If I had to choose a suspect, I am afraid *you* would be top of my list.'

'I have been with Roger, Ulfrith and Bale ever since we abandoned ship – when we all saw Vitalis alive. Besides, I would not be telling people he was murdered if I were the culprit, would I?'

'True,' acknowledged Juhel. 'But I thought we were speaking hypothetically. And you did argue with him.'

'It was hardly an argument,' said Geoffrey wryly. 'It was more a case of him railing at me.'

'*You* have no alibi, though,' said Ulfrith, looking hard at Juhel. 'Sir Geoffrey has one, but you were gone a long time before you joined us.'

'Yes,' agreed Juhel with a shudder. 'Because I was in the sea, fighting for my life. I came to you the moment I could stand – but I certainly had no spare strength for murder. You must look for another culprit. Magnus – what do you have to say for yourself?'

'Vitalis was a Norman,' said Magnus in disdain. 'One who fought at the battle that saw my father slain. It is beneath my dignity to soil my hands with his blood.'

'Down!' hissed Roger sharply, dropping to his belly on the damp, sandy path. Geoffrey was beside him almost before he had finished speaking; long years of campaigning had taught him that instant obedience could mean the difference between life and death. The squires were not far behind, although Magnus and Juhel stood stupidly before they were dragged from their feet.

'How dare you!' snarled Magnus, trying to free himself.

'Hush!' snapped Roger. 'The sailors are coming! Do you *want* to be killed?'

The crew were indeed making their way to the path, carrying all they deemed portable. It would be only a matter of moments before they stumbled across their hiding passengers.

'They will see us!' squeaked Magnus in terror, indignation forgotten. 'What shall we do?'

'Perhaps they will leave us alone when they see we will fight,' said Roger, drawing his sword.

'We cannot win against so many.' Geoffrey glanced around urgently. 'We should hide.'

'Too late!' whispered Juhel. 'They are here!'

Just as the first sailors reached the path, there was a yell from their captain, and they turned and trotted obediently back to him. They gathered in a circle, where Fingar was announcing something in a furious howl. Whatever news he imparted seemed to incense them, too, because there was a good deal of yelling. Although Geoffrey could hear them quite clearly, they spoke a language he did not understand.

'It looks as though they have lost something,' said Juhel. 'My God!'

This last exclamation was in response to an action of Fingar's. One of his crew had been edging towards the path again. The captain's weapon flashed and the man fell.

'That is a bad sign,' muttered Bale. 'We would do better to avoid them.'

'He is right,' said Magnus, addressing Roger. 'We should slip away now, while they are busy with each other. Hurry! You must not dally when your king has commanded you.'

'If I am to be in your service, I should be paid,' said Roger, following him along the path at a rapid lick. The others were not far behind. 'Did you save any gold or jewellery from the ship?'

'I might have a little gold,' hedged Magnus evasively.

'How little?' demanded Roger. He was not easily deceived where money was concerned. '*Jerosolimitani* do not come cheap.'

'Well, I do not have a lot *with* me,' admitted Magnus. 'But it will not be long before I can give you whatever you like – treasure, land, even a see.'

'A see?' asked Roger, intrigued. 'You mean to make me a bishop? Like my father?'

'Yes. Then you will have tithes to enjoy, and manors and woodlands in which to hunt – although you will have to give sermons on Sundays. All you have to do is see me safely on my throne. And help me depose Henry the Usurper.'

'No,' said Geoffrey sharply. 'He is not going to become involved in treason.'

'It is treason to back the Usurper against England's rightful king,' flashed Magnus.

'I *might* help you,' said Roger slyly. 'But only if you can pay me appropriately. Ulfrith, too. He is a good Saxon lad.'

'And me,' said Bale. 'But I do not want gold. I want a wife – one who likes me.'

'I will see what I can do,' said Magnus, looking as though he thought finding a loving wife for Bale might be considerably more difficult than providing a bishopric for Roger.

Geoffrey did not waste his breath pointing out that assisting rebels against a powerful king like Henry was suicide – especially a rebel like Magnus, who was either an impostor or a madman with illusions of grandeur. He only walked faster, wanting as much distance between him and the sailors as possible. They had not gone far before they reached a junction.

'Here is the path to the abbey,' said Magnus, pointing to the track that wound inland. 'It becomes a causeway that runs across the marshes, before rising to higher ground. We can be there by this afternoon.'

'Then we should hurry,' said Juhel. He nodded to where the thunderheads were now a good deal closer. 'I am not keen on meeting Fingar's crew; nor do I want to sit out here while the heavens open.'

Geoffrey would have preferred to continue along the coast, but suspected that was the route the sailors would take – no mariner liked to be too far from the sea, and they would be looking for another ship. Reluctantly, he conceded that wasting a day or two at the abbey was preferable to taking the coastal path with Fingar on his heels. Without a word, he took the abbey track, ignoring Roger's victorious smirk as he assumed Geoffrey had yielded to the conditions of his loan.

'The sailors are coming this way, too,' blurted Ulfrith after a while. 'They are following us!'

'Not necessarily,' said Geoffrey. 'Perhaps they just want to be a little distance inland when the storm breaks.'

'Damn this path,' muttered Roger, glancing around uneasily. 'We can be seen for miles! There are few trees and the bushes are low. And the mud! You can tell it is dangerous – if we leave the path, we will be sucked under.'

'Yes,' agreed Magnus. 'But I know these marshes like the back of my hand. If the sailors gain on us, we shall hide in a channel. Of course, that might be a mistake if the tide comes in . . .'

'Then we should stay well ahead,' said Geoffrey, breaking into the steady trot that he could maintain for hours, even in full armour. 'Although they have no reason to attack us.'

The others seemed to think differently, but they were struggling to keep up and made no reply. Roger was breathing hard under the weight of his possessions, while Juhel's chicken cackled her displeasure at the way she was being jostled. Bale began to lag behind, and Ulfrith was obliged to mutter encouragement to keep him going. Magnus was the only one who seemed happy running, and Geoffrey wondered how much of it the Saxon pretender had done in his life.

'So,' said Magnus, using the opportunity to talk, 'you do not believe I have a right to my throne?'

'I do not believe you can take it from Henry,' corrected Geoffrey. 'Bellême tried it last summer and failed – and he had troops and castles.'

'I do not intend to fight him in open warfare,' said Magnus contemptuously. 'There are other ways to topple a tyrant. I shall—'

'No,' interrupted Geoffrey. 'I do not want to know. And you can leave Roger out of it, too. I will not allow him to become embroiled in something so dangerous. We will travel with you to the abbey, but after that you are on your own.'

Magnus smiled under his silver moustache. 'We shall see. But let us talk of other matters, since we are the only ones with the breath to do so. You have not said who you think killed Vitalis.'

'That is because I do not know.'

'Well, he was an aggressive Norman fool, and you should not waste your time. He had the temerity to say that I look nothing like my father.'

'Did he?' asked Geoffrey, uninterested.

'He said he fought at Hastinges. So did I – well, perhaps I did not *fight* exactly, but I was there, at my mother's side. However, I know what my father looked like, and I am his very image.'

'*My* father said he was sturdy and strong,' said Geoffrey pointedly.

'Quite,' said Magnus, preening. 'And he had thick yellow hair, just like me.'

'Yours is grey.'

Magnus sighed impatiently. 'Yes, but it was yellow once. It is the sign of a true Saxon.'

He glanced behind and increased his pace when he saw one of the sailors had gained ground. Then he ducked down a smaller path, muttering something about a shortcut. Bale blundered after him, too winded to care what he was doing, and Ulfrith followed Bale. Juhel slogged along behind them, short legs pumping furiously. Geoffrey waited for Roger.

'Magnus seems very eager to avoid meeting Fingar,' he said. 'Should we be suspicious?'

Roger shrugged, one hand to his side to ease a stitch. 'God knows. But I do not want to be out here when the storm comes. He seems to know this area, so I am willing to stay with him for now.'

'I am not sure it is wise to keep company with a man who claims to be England's rightful heir. Henry has spies everywhere, and it will not be long before Magnus's presence is discovered.

Anyone who has consorted with him may be considered a traitor.'

'Even Henry cannot blame us for taking the same road away from a shipwreck,' said Roger. He shot a furtive glance behind. 'I do not like those pirates being behind us. They may blame us for their ship sinking, and I am not in the mood for a brawl.'

'Why would they think that? And why are you not in the mood for a brawl? Are you ill?'

'I do not want *my* good looks marred by cuts and bruises,' retorted Roger curtly. 'It does not go down well with the ladies.'

'What ladies? We left Philippa and Edith behind.'

'Philippa,' growled Roger in distaste, changing the subject. 'Is *she* the reason Ulfrith hit you? Because you accused her of murder?'

'You know?' Geoffrey was astonished. Roger was not normally astute.

'I can tell by his sheepish manner. He has gone for me in the past, too, although I did not come off as badly as you seem to have done.'

'And I thought I was the one with the dangerous squire!'

Roger grinned. 'I do not mind him displaying the odd flare of temper. Indeed, I encourage it, because otherwise he is too gentle for his own good. But he should not have tried it on you.'

'No, and he only got away with it because of my promise to Joan.'

Roger began running to catch up with the others. Before he followed, Geoffrey glanced back to see the seamen streaming along in their wake. Then he saw Fingar point directly at him. Several whoops sounded as the crew put on a spurt of speed.

Magnus's shortcut led in an almost straight line across the marshes, but it was sodden from recent storms. In places it had sunk below the surrounding land and was virtually indistinguishable from the matted, boggy vegetation that lay in all directions. Progress was agonizingly slow, and the only consolation was that it was slow for their pursuers, too.

'This is near where the Conqueror's first troops landed,' Ulfrith announced brightly. He either did not see or did not understand Magnus's malevolent glare – he was trying to inveigle his way back into the knights' good graces and was oblivious to the reactions of everyone except them.

'Is it?' asked Roger keenly. 'I would like to see the place where the battle was fought.'

'You will,' said Ulfrith, transparently obsequious. 'Because the abbey we are heading for is La Batailge – *Battle* Abbey. The Conqueror built it on the exact spot to atone for all the slaughter.'

'I hope the buildings have not obscured the site, then,' said Roger disapprovingly. 'Or we shall never understand and appreciate the Conqueror's tactics.'

Ulfrith shrugged. 'Apparently, he thought founding an abbey would save him doing penance for starting a war – he was not thinking about preserving the field in its original condition.'

'*I* do not need to do penance for starting fights *or* for my sins,' declared Roger grandly. 'I am a *Jerosolimitanus*, which means all that sort of thing is taken care of.'

'All the abbeys in the world will not atone for what happened that day,' said Magnus in a cold voice. 'Saxon blood still screams out for vengeance. And I shall see it done.'

'How?' asked Roger curiously. 'By raising an army? By shooting Henry when he is off guard? By urging Bellême or the Duke of Normandy to invade and help you?'

'I have not decided yet,' said Magnus.

Roger laughed, then began a lively debate with Ulfrith about the best way to topple a king. Bale and Juhel were lagging behind, gasping like old nags, although Bale was not so breathless that he could not speak: he was regaling Juhel with a bloody account of the battle that he had heard from Geoffrey's father. Godric Mappestone had often entertained his villagers with tales of his military prowess, and Bale had been one of the few who had actually listened.

'I thought King Harold's sons were named Harold and Ulf,' Geoffrey said to Magnus, noting that the sailors, unused to travelling long distances on foot, were falling behind.

At his side, the dog growled, so he slipped his belt around its neck. He knew from the wild look in its eyes that it did not like Magnus, and it would only be a matter of time before blood was spilled. As the dog was cowardly and never attacked unless it was sure of success, the spillage was unlikely to be canine.

'They were the offspring of his union with Queen Ealdgyth,'
explained Magnus. 'Twins, born after he died. But *my* mother
was his handfast wife, Edith Swannehals.'

'You are illegitimate?' asked Geoffrey, realizing as he spoke that
it was not a question to pose to such a proud man. He was right.
Magnus stopped abruptly to glare at him.

'You impertinent dog! Still, I expect no better from Norman
scum. They are incapable of decency, and having been on the
Crusade makes you even more of a villain.'

Geoffrey blinked, unused to men insulting him quite so brazenly.
Most took one look at his surcoat and weapons and opted for
politeness. He could only suppose that Magnus was more of a
lunatic than he had imagined.

'I met a man in Flanders who went on the Crusade,' Magnus
went on icily. 'He was a brute before he went, but he returned
a monster. He told me the venture took three years because the
Normans fought among themselves, rather than uniting against
the infidel.'

'Different factions did bicker,' acknowledged Geoffrey. 'But it
was not confined to Normans.'

'But Normans were the worst – they always are. However, I was
talking about my mother, Edith Swannehals – "Swan Neck" to you.
She bore Harold five children, and I am the eldest surviving son.'

'I see,' said Geoffrey, even more convinced the man was insane.
'But reclaiming your throne from Henry will not be easy. I can
tell you from personal experience that he is very attached to it.'

'You know him?' asked Magnus in astonishment. He looked
the knight up and down. 'You do not seem the kind of man with
whom a king would consort.'

'I have met him several times,' said Geoffrey, amazed by the
steady flow of insults. He considered challenging him, but there
would be small satisfaction in besting a scrawny wretch.

'You have sworn loyalty to him?' asked Magnus keenly.

'I hold my manor at Goodrich from him,' Geoffrey replied,
wondering where the discussion was going. 'So of course he has
my loyalty.'

'But you do not like him,' stated Magnus. 'He does not have
your respect. You are unwilling to serve such a serpent, and *that*
is why you were fleeing England in an unseaworthy vessel.'

'My liege lord is Tancred, Prince of Galilee,' said Geoffrey, seeing Magnus was more astute than he had appreciated. 'He—'

'He is not,' interrupted Roger, overhearing. 'Tancred dismissed him, because he spent too long here, helping King Henry. But Geoffrey wants to hear it from Tancred's own lips. Of course, it is a journey God does not want him to make.'

'I do not believe Tancred would release me without explanation,' said Geoffrey doggedly.

'He *did* explain,' said Roger wearily. 'He said you are insolent and disloyal, and that he will have you executed if he ever sees you again. Still, I do not blame you for hoping there was a mistake. Tancred is ten times finer than Henry.'

'Amen to that,' agreed Magnus as Geoffrey winced, still unable to accept that a man he had loved like a brother would have written such things. 'There is only one man who should be sitting on that throne: me. I tried to overthrow the Bastard in the years following Hastinges – I invaded with my brothers, but something always went wrong. I even begged help from my Norwegian kin, but they declined, and time passed. Now I am ready to try again.'

'So, you have invaded England alone?' asked Geoffrey caustically. 'That was brave.'

Magnus scowled. 'I have a plan. It begins at the abbey, at the high altar. It stands on the spot where my father was foully slain, you see, so Henry will never touch me there.'

'Right,' said Geoffrey, wondering whether they had been wise to take a shortcut across treacherous bogs recommended by a man who was so patently out of his wits. 'And how will you take Henry's crown from there?'

'It is not *his*; it is mine,' snapped Magnus. He glared at the knight. 'You said earlier that you did not want to know my intentions, but now you are full of questions. Why?'

'Curiosity, I suppose,' said Geoffrey, wishing he had remained in blissful ignorance.

Magnus pulled himself up to his considerable full height. 'All I will say is that La Batailge will go down in history as the place where Saxon honour was restored. And *you* are the lucky men who will be remembered for helping to bring it about.'

Geoffrey saw the fierce blue light of the fanatic burning in

Magnus's eyes and knew he believed he would succeed. That made him dangerous. Geoffrey stopped walking abruptly.

'I want no part of this,' he said. 'I have seen how the King treats traitors, and I have a wife to consider. You can go to the abbey, but we are going the other direction.'

'I would not do that, if I were you,' said Magnus, a crafty look stealing across his thin face. 'Those sailors are catching up fast and they do not look friendly. Even two *Jerosolimitani* cannot fight thirty seamen, so we shall have to run again – all of us.'

Geoffrey had not fled from many confrontations during his life as a soldier, and it went against the grain. Besides, he saw no reason why the sailors should mean them harm – if anyone should bear a grudge, it was the passengers against Fingar, for losing the ship – and he was keen to talk to them. Roger was unwilling to let him try.

'You put too much faith in your negotiating skills,' he said. 'Pirates are not reasonable beings, anyway. I am not staying here to be cut down, and Magnus knows somewhere we can hide.'

Just then there was a furious yell from behind, and Geoffrey saw the mariners coming closer, rage etched into every movement. He stared in puzzlement. They had been on the beach together the previous day, and there had been no trouble then. So what had changed?

'I do not like this,' gasped Juhel, bending double to catch his breath. 'They are so determined to get us that they have abandoned their salvage. Why do that, with those scavengers still at large?'

'Where is this refuge?' Roger demanded of Magnus, his face red from exertion. 'If we do not reach it soon, it will be too late.'

Magnus began flailing furiously with a stick at the side of the causeway. He stopped for a moment, closed his eyes in intense concentration, then began prodding a little farther on. He gave a triumphant yell. 'Here!'

Geoffrey regarded the narrow track he had exposed. It looked like something made by birds, cutting raggedly between two treacherous-looking bogs. 'I still do not understand why—'

'Come,' ordered Magnus urgently. 'They will never follow us down there. Hurry!'

Geoffrey glanced behind and saw the seamen drawing steadily closer. He frowned. There was definitely something odd about their determination to catch their former passengers. Magnus seemed keen to evade them, and so did Roger. Had one of them done something to antagonize them?

'Run!' urged Magnus, plucking at his sleeve. 'Stealing is a hanging crime among pirates.'

Geoffrey was puzzled. 'We have not stolen anything.'

Roger looked defiant. 'No, we have not. We took only what is rightfully ours.'

Geoffrey regarded him in horror. 'What have you done?'

Roger scowled, then unclenched one of his big fists to reveal three gold coins. 'They paid for the loss of our horses.'

'That does not explain why they are chasing us,' said Geoffrey. He narrowed his eyes. 'Or did you take it without their permission?'

'These were lying on the beach,' said Roger defiantly. He sighed when Geoffrey looked sceptical. 'All right – they were in that chest. But when they left it unattended, it seemed a good opportunity to claim what was our due.'

Geoffrey was disgusted. 'No wonder they are angry! Give the money to me. I will return—'

'No,' said Roger shortly. 'Those damned villains owe me a horse, so the only way they are getting this back from me is if they take it from my corpse.'

'They will not be content with its return now anyway,' Magnus pointed out. 'They will kill us regardless. I have been forced to associate with Fingar for years, and he is deadly when crossed – even his own men are terrified of him.'

Geoffrey stole a glance over his shoulder and saw the captain was leading the chase. Even from a distance, Fingar's face was slashed with a savage fury, and he suspected Magnus was right: Roger's actions had crossed some irreversible line.

'Your only hope for avoiding death is to come with me, but I will not wait,' said Magnus, moving away. 'Come now or die.'

Reluctantly, Geoffrey followed him along a narrow path that soon had them out of sight from the main track. Then he was stumbling along a barely visible trail that snaked past quicksands, through alder thickets and across muddy channels. It jigged and twisted, and Geoffrey quickly lost all sense of direction. They had not gone far when Roger, bringing up the rear, released a yell that brought Geoffrey to an abrupt standstill. Then came the sound of clashing weapons.

Ignoring Magnus, who declared that thieves should be left to their fate, Geoffrey raced back along the path. But when he reached Roger, it was to find his friend wiping the blade of his sword on the grass, two bodies lying nearby.

'*They* will not be hoodwinking hapless travellers into sailing with them again,' he said grimly. 'I have saved countless lives by dispatching such wicked fellows.'

'Come on,' said Geoffrey urgently. It was no time for Roger's contorted logic and twisted morals – the slapping of feet on mud indicated more sailors were catching up. He turned and ran, Roger's lumbering footsteps behind him.

It was easy to retrace his steps at first – his rush to Roger's aid had left a trail of broken twigs and bruised leaves – but then the path disappeared. Geoffrey had the uneasy sense that Magnus had abandoned them, but he blundered on, breath coming in short gasps and sweat drenching his shirt under his heavy mail. Roger was already slowing, and Geoffrey knew they could not keep up such a rapid pace for much longer.

'Here!' Juhel suddenly hissed from one side. 'This way.'

He rearranged the bushes after the knights went by, to disguise their passage. It was not a moment too soon, because one of the ship's boys appeared, carrying a dagger and clearly intending to use it. He raced past, eyes fixed on the more obvious track ahead. Four or five others followed, and then there was silence.

'Hurry,' said Juhel, pushing past Geoffrey so he could be in front. 'Magnus said he would post Ulfrith at the next junction, but I do not trust him.'

'I do,' panted Roger. 'He needs us as much as we need him – more, probably. And besides, there he is.'

'Where have you been?' demanded Magnus furiously. 'I ordered you to stay with me, not go haring off. Here is the next junction, and we turn right. No, left.' He reconsidered. 'No, it *is* right. Hide our tracks, Ulfrith.'

'You must have been very young when William fought Harold,'

said Geoffrey to Magnus, watching Ulfrith jump to obey. 'When were you last here?'

Magnus started to jog along the path he had chosen. 'I was eight when I fought at my father's side at Hastinges, and eleven when I last tried to wrest my throne from the Normans, so it has been some thirty years . . . but I know these paths well—'

The rest of the sentence was lost as he plunged head-first into a boggy pool. With some trepidation, and aware that the sounds of pursuit were coming closer again, Geoffrey tugged him out, recalling that earlier Magnus had admitted to being with his mother during the battle. The Saxons' great hope was liberal with the truth.

'I was just seeing how deep it was,' snapped Magnus in embarrassment, once he was on dry land. He looked around quickly, then headed for a mud bank that stood the height of a man. Its sides were slippery with algae, and trees grew along its crest, roots twisting downwards. He scrabbled towards a dense patch of brambles. 'This is it. Help me.'

To his surprise, Geoffrey saw a cunningly hidden refuge – a screen of woven twigs concealing a small door that led to a dank cavern. Magnus dived inside, leaving the others to follow. Ulfrith, Juhel and Bale were next, then Roger; Geoffrey brought up the rear, dragging the screen back into position as he did so.

The cave was a marvel. Not only was it so well concealed that it was invisible from outside, but it was surprisingly spacious. It comprised a single chamber, high enough at the front to allow a man to stand without stooping, and tapering off to shadowy recesses at the back. It was wide enough for several men to stand side by side without touching, and there were pots and containers attached to the walls, suggesting it was sometimes used for extended periods.

However, it was pitch black once the door was shut, and it felt close and airless. Geoffrey detested underground places of any kind, and ones that had slippery walls and water on the floor were among the worst. He felt his chest tighten when the stench of old mud clogged his nostrils, and he was sure there was not enough air for everyone to breathe. He began to cough, trying desperately to muffle the sound, which made it worse. The urge to run outside again was intense.

Roger reached past him and cracked open the door. The gap was no more than the width of a finger, but it allowed light and air to filter inside and was enough to let the panic recede. Roger clapped a gruffly comforting hand on his shoulder. Geoffrey had once been in charge of a countermine under a castle Tancred was besieging, and it had been several days before they had excavated him after its collapse. Although years had passed, the terror of his ordeal remained. He focussed his attention on the sliver of light, forcing himself not to think about where he was.

Meanwhile, the pirates had discovered the path and had reached the mud bank. It began to rain hard, so that the whole marsh seemed to hiss and sway with the force of it, and somewhere nearby a bird issued a low, undulating cry. Donan, Fingar's rodent-faced second-in-command, muttered a prayer to ward off evil spirits.

'Fays,' he said. 'They haunt bogs and come out to grab unwary souls. Unless you cross yourself and say the name of your favourite saint three times, they will get you.'

Immediately, a variety of saints were invoked in a mixture of Irish and English, some of whom Geoffrey had never heard of.

Fingar bent to inspect some footprints, and the dog began to growl. Sensing rather than seeing a movement behind him, Geoffrey became aware of Magnus holding a knife – he intended to kill the animal, to shut it up. Geoffrey crouched down and put his arm around it, reassuring it into silence.

Just when Geoffrey was sure they were going to be caught, Donan pointed across the marshes.

'There!' he hissed. 'I saw a flash of movement. It must be them. Come on!'

Most of the men followed, although Fingar stood uncertainly, squinting into the rain and clearly not convinced that Donan was right. But Donan shouted something else, and, with an impatient grunt, Fingar followed. And then they were gone.

# Five

Inside the cave, a collective sigh of relief was heaved. Roger sheathed his sword, and Geoffrey opened the door a little wider. The shelter might be cleverly constructed, but it stank, for some reason, of garlic, and he preferred the odour of wet vegetation from outside.

'We have given them the slip,' said Bale in satisfaction. He sat on a platform that was obviously intended to serve as a bed, and glanced up at Roger. 'How much are those coins worth?'

Roger tossed him one, accompanying it with a grin that oozed wicked greed. Bale hefted it in his hand and whistled under his breath before handing it to Geoffrey, who was also astonished by its weight. He had never seen such a thick, heavy coin and was certain each would be worth a small fortune – more than ample to buy horses and travel to the Holy Land. He was not surprised Fingar was keen to have them back.

'How many did you take?' he asked. 'Just three?'

'A handful,' replied Roger evasively. 'I did not have time to count.'

'How many?' repeated Geoffrey coldly.

With considerable reluctance, Roger emptied the pouch on his belt. A dozen or so gold coins dropped out, along with a huge number of silver ones of lesser value. Geoffrey was horrified.

'There is a king's ransom here!' he cried. 'Fingar and his men will follow us to the ends of the world to get this back.'

'You are right,' said Juhel. He was pale, and Geoffrey saw he was equally shocked by Roger's crime. 'Men are willing to risk anything for this kind of money.'

'It is paltry,' said Roger dismissively. 'They were lucky I did not demand their salvage, too.'

'If I had such a fortune, England would be mine in a week,' said Magnus, eyeing it lustfully. 'I do not suppose you would care to donate it to the cause? I will repay it with interest when I am king. And I will make you Bishop of Ely.'

'Not Ely,' said Roger in distaste. 'It is surrounded by bogs. I want Salisbury.'

'You may be waiting some time,' warned Juhel. 'For your gold *and* your title.'

Magnus glared. 'I will repay him tenfold before the end of summer.'

'I shall not part with it just yet,' said Roger, although Geoffrey was alarmed to see he was giving the offer consideration. Roger was a man for whom 'tenfold' was a tempting word.

'You are wise,' said Juhel. 'King Henry would not be pleased to hear that the funding for a Saxon revolt came from Norman knights.'

'How would he hear that?' demanded Magnus, rounding on him. 'Will *you* tell?'

Juhel laughed. 'Of course I will! He and I often dine in his private chambers, and he frequently asks my advice. I shall mention it the very next time I see him.'

'Enough,' said Geoffrey. Magnus's visions of Saxon rebellion were no better than smoke in the wind. 'I am more concerned with Fingar. None of us will be safe until you give that money back.'

'Rubbish,' declared Roger. 'For all Fingar knows, these are coins I carried in my personal baggage, and he will never be able to prove otherwise. Besides, he is a pirate, so this is almost certainly gold he stole from someone else.'

'Then it is probably cursed,' said Juhel. 'The original owners may have asked God to avenge the crime by making dreadful things happen to the thieves. I always do, when villains wrong me.'

'We should give it back,' said Bale, crossing himself hurriedly. 'I have heard that pirates are rather free and easy with curses, too.'

'They are not,' said Roger, with completely unwarranted confidence. 'My father is Bishop of Durham, so you can trust that I know about such things.'

Geoffrey was disinclined to argue. Like many Normans, Roger was highly partial to gold, and Geoffrey knew from long and bitter experience that nothing would induce him to part with it.

'Very well,' he said. 'But I want no part of it.'

'He is right,' came an unfamiliar voice from the depths of the hole. Geoffrey and the others raised their weapons in alarm.

'Nothing good ever comes from theft – as that usurper Henry is about to discover.'

'Who are you?' demanded Geoffrey, as a short, chubby man emerged from the darkness. His bright yellow hair and flowing moustache indicated he was in his thirties, like Geoffrey himself, but his skin had a reddish, debauched look, and the broken veins on his round nose indicated a fondness for good living. His clothes were fine, although mud-stained, and, like Magnus's, were adorned with a good deal of expensive thread and intricate Saxon embroidery.

'I am King Harold,' replied the man grandly.

'Lord,' muttered Geoffrey in the startled silence that followed. '*Another* monarch?'

'A number of us have claims,' said Magnus stiffly. 'Some stronger than others.'

'Are you eating garlic?' asked Juhel, sniffing. 'The smell is suddenly a good deal stronger.'

'I like garlic,' said Harold defensively. 'It thickens the blood, protects against evil and inspires courage. I have a few cloves here, ready peeled. Would you like one?'

When he stretched out his hand to present his offering, Geoffrey saw faint scars around the man's wrists and wondered what had caused them.

'No, thank you,' said Juhel. 'But I was under the impression that King Harold had died more than thirty years ago – on the battlefield.'

'Hacked to pieces,' added Roger rather ghoulishly, 'with axes.'

'Actually,' said Magnus curtly, 'my father was killed by an arrow in the face. I was not on the field when he died – a battleground is no place for a child of eight – but I saw his body afterwards.'

'But *my* father said he was hacked to death by swords,' said Geoffrey doubtfully. 'He claimed to have witnessed it.'

Of course, Godric Mappestone had not been the most truthful of men, and his memories of the battle had grown more elaborate as he had aged. Further, Geoffrey's mother, famous for her own martial skills, had once confided that she had fought at Hastinges herself, and she had told a different story – one of confusion and panic as the long day of fighting drew to a close, and encroaching darkness, blood and thick mud had rendered one man much like another. Herleve Mappestone had maintained that it was impossible to tell what had happened to King Harold. His corpse had certainly been mutilated, but it would never be known whether he had died at the point of a sword, an axe or an arrow.

'All this is immaterial,' said Roger to the newcomer. 'The point is that you *cannot* be King Harold, because he is dead. Unless you are his ghost?'

He smirked, but, at that moment, a marsh bird released an eerie, whooping call, and the grin faded. He took a step away and crossed himself. Ulfrith and Bale did the same.

Harold did not seem affected by their superstitious unease and addressed Roger slowly, as if speaking to a simpleton. 'I am his son – his *legitimate* son. He had twins from his marriage to Queen Ealdgyth, and I am one of them.'

'You mean there is another, just like you?' asked Roger rather stupidly.

Harold nodded. 'Poor Ulf was kept prisoner after our father's murder, but the Bastard released him on his deathbed. I suppose he thought it would lessen his time in Purgatory. But it will take a good deal more than the release of a few hostages to open the gates of Heaven to *him*. He is destined for the Other Place, because his soul is so deeply stained with Saxon blood.'

'Too right,' agreed Magnus fervently. 'When I am king, I shall invade France, snatch the Bastard's bones from his tomb and toss them in the nearest river.'

Harold regarded him admonishingly, his chubby face grave. 'We agreed that we would not discuss this yet, that we would consult our Saxon vassals about—'

'They will want *me*,' stated Magnus confidently. 'I am King Harold's eldest surviving son and, according to Saxon law, his rightful heir. Your claim is based on the fact that he married Queen Ealdgyth in a church, which I deem irrelevant.'

Harold sighed in a long-suffering manner. 'We are *both* irrelevant until we overthrow the Usurper. Then we shall ask our vassals to decide whom they want as king.'

'A democracy to elect a king?' asked Geoffrey, amused. 'What an odd notion!'

'Not at all,' said Harold, smiling at him. 'Once our subjects have made their choice, I shall revert to the autocracy that works so well.'

'They will not choose you,' said Magnus disdainfully. 'You are too short.'

'You mentioned a twin brother,' said Juhel, as Harold looked hurt. 'Is he to participate in this election, too? Or perhaps there are yet more siblings who would like a chance to win a crown?'

'My two older brothers are dead, and the younger ones are happy in Norway,' replied Magnus. 'Ulf intends to put himself forward, but no one will choose *him* – he is violent and would be a tyrant. Indeed, I forbade him to come anywhere near my uprising – he will put people off.'

'Not so,' cried Harold, stung. 'My brother is just misunderstood and has no patience with fools. He spent the best years of his life as the Bastard's prisoner, so it is not surprising he is bitter.'

'Whichever of you it is will have to dispatch England's current king first,' said Juhel. He was struggling to conceal his amusement at the notion that the likes of Harold and Magnus could best Henry.

'We have a nation full of bold Saxon warriors,' declared Magnus haughtily. 'And when they see I have returned, they will rally to my call.'

Harold crunched loudly on a clove of garlic. Geoffrey wondered whether he had strayed into a community of madmen, because he had never heard a more ridiculous collection of claims and aspirations.

'And when will this grand summoning take place?' asked Juhel, smothering a smile.

'In a while,' said Harold, waving an airy hand. 'Now Magnus is here we can get on with it. That is why I was waiting here for him, as we had agreed. We have signed a formal contract to be brothers-in-arms and to make no moves against each other until the Usurper is deposed.'

Juhel finally lost his self-control and roared with laughter, until Ulfrith pointed out that the sailors might hear. Geoffrey peered out of the door and detected angry voices in the distance. He frowned as something Harold had said jarred in his mind, and he turned to face him.

'You said you were waiting here for Magnus, but *Patrick* was bound for Ribe. So how—'

Magnus was unrepentant. 'I paid Fingar ten pounds to drop me off, but the storm blew up, and he said he would be unable to fulfil our arrangement. I was lucky we happened to founder here.'

'I have been waiting here for the best part of a week,' said Harold, looking at his surroundings in distaste. 'A mud-hole is scarcely a suitable haunt for a future king!'

'It was not chance that we sank here, was it?' said Geoffrey, looking hard at Magnus. '*That* is why the sailors were inspecting the wreckage – they suspect foul play. It also explains why you were so keen to escape. It is not just the theft of their gold that drives them after us, but the sabotage of their ship.'

Magnus shrugged. 'What choice did I have? England awaits, and I have a destiny to fulfil. Simon took an axe to some vital timber, so we would put ashore as near to Hastinges as possible.'

Geoffrey was disgusted. 'Is that why you let him drown? You hoped his death would appease the crew, and they would not blame you for the disaster?'

'It did not work,' said Magnus ruefully. 'But I am here now, and my work can begin.'

The storm that had been approaching all day hit with breathtaking ferocity. Even from their mud refuge, Geoffrey could hear the surf pounding the beach, while the wind that screamed across the marshes ripped branches from trees and uprooted bushes. Travel was impossible, so Roger, who hated long periods of enforced inactivity, probed the Saxons relentlessly about their plans. It was not long before the whole tale emerged.

Magnus had been a child and Harold unborn when their father had been defeated near Hastinges. There had followed a few sporadic rebellions, but the Normans were efficient and ruthless and soon stamped out revolts. The Bastard was succeeded by two of his sons – first William Rufus and then Henry. The latter had been obliged to quell an uprising by his barons, led by Bellême, but had put it down with comparative ease.

Harold's offspring had watched from afar, and when Bellême was routed, they decided to act, on the grounds that Henry's troops would be battle-weary and the royal coffers drained. Geoffrey thought they were wrong on both counts: Henry's soldiers were professionals who did not tire of fighting, and Henry had seized the property of the exiled barons, so was actually rather well off. He had the resources to finance a war on a scale unimagined by the dreamers in the mud cave.

'So,' concluded Roger, 'you agreed to meet in this hole a week ago . . .'

'I am a little late,' acknowledged Magnus. 'But how was I to know the journey from Ireland would take so long?'

'And you bribed Fingar to drop you off,' Roger continued, 'because you decided it was better not to disembark at a proper port, lest King Henry got wind of it.'

Magnus nodded. 'But I sense you are not fond of the Usurper, either; my instinct is never wrong about these things. Did you fight for Bellême last summer?'

'Certainly not,' said Roger, offended. 'I would never demean myself by fighting for a tyrant − well, I might, if he paid well enough. Geoff and I were engaged on important business for the King, and Henry was so grateful that he offered us posts in his household.'

'But you did not accept?' asked Harold. 'That was wise. The Usurper often forgets to pay and has a nasty habit of sending his retainers on very dangerous missions.'

Geoffrey gazed at him in surprise, wondering how an exile would know. Magnus saw the look and gave a self-satisfied smile.

'We have our spies. You think we are unprepared, but we have been watching and waiting for more than thirty years.'

'Do you prefer Tancred to Henry, Geoffrey?' asked Juhel, sitting on the bed next to Bale and opening the chicken's cage.

'I prefer the Holy Land to England,' he replied evasively. 'It rains too much here.'

Juhel laughed. 'So the weather determines your allegiances? Well, why not? It is as good a reason as any.'

The chicken emerged from its cage and fixed Magnus with sharp eyes. He edged away, sitting with his long legs folded in front of him and his bony arms ready to fend off an airborne attack.

'Keep that thing away from me, Juhel,' he ordered. 'I do not like it.'

'She is not overly enamoured of you, either,' said Juhel, laughing again. 'What strange company I find myself in today! Two princelings who intend to start a civil war, and two knights and their squires who prefer the Holy Land to the country where they were born.'

'Not true,' said Roger. 'I do not care where I am, as long as I am well paid. And I am not going to the Holy Land. I shall head north as soon as I see him safely on a ship.'

'You will serve *us*, then?' asked Harold eagerly. 'A knight would be a good start to our army.'

'I might,' replied Roger. 'But I will wait and see what happens.'

Geoffrey was relieved, thinking that if Roger was their first recruit, then the rest of their force would take a long time to assemble – by which time Roger would have grown bored and deserted.

'Come, my love,' said Juhel, pursing his lips and blowing a smacking kiss at his hen. 'Show these hot rebels and tepid loyalists your beautiful feathers.'

The chicken, having satisfied herself that the cave was safe, began to preen. Unable to resist the sight of a plump hen ready for the taking, Geoffrey's dog wrenched itself from his grasp and hurtled towards her, leaving the horrified knight holding a few stray hairs. The chicken did not issue the terrified squawks that invariably preceded a kill, but fixed the dog with a pale eye. For a short moment, neither animal moved: they stood facing each other, slathering muzzle within inches of an avian dinner. Then the hen clucked. The dog released an abrupt yelp, turned tail and shot towards the door. When it found it could not squeeze through, it cowered behind Geoffrey. Proudly, Juhel stroked the hen's soft brown feathers.

'I do not think much of your hound,' said Harold in disbelief. 'Afraid of a chicken! If this is the quality of Norman courage, then our victory is going to come sooner that we anticipated!'

'Like master, like dog,' said Magnus contemptuously. 'Thank God Roger has Saxon courage in his veins, or I might never reach the abbey! Perhaps Vitalis's accusations were valid after all.'

'Delilah *is* remarkable,' said Juhel, ruffling her feathers with doting affection as Geoffrey stifled an irritable sigh at the reminder of the old man's claims. 'No mere dog will get the better of *her*. They try, of course, but she has no trouble in seeing them off.'

'Delilah?' asked Roger warily.

'After the lady in the Bible who had the upper hand over manly suitors.'

Delilah flapped off his lap and began to strut around, pecking and scratching. When she approached the dog, she clucked challengingly, and it released a low whine. She fluffed herself up and moved away, and, had he believed in such things, Geoffrey would have sworn she was laughing.

Outside, the storm increased in intensity. The walls of the cave were thick and afforded good protection, but even they were beginning to be overwhelmed by the onslaught, and water was running freely down the walls.

'This is no ordinary tempest,' whispered Bale. 'It is another omen. The moment we started talking about Sir Geoffrey travelling to the Holy Land, it became more violent.'

'The day he told his wife of his plans, blood bubbled from a spring near the castle,' Ulfrith told the Saxons. 'And the night before we left, two moons were seen in the sky. Sir Roger said these were messages from God, advising us all to stay in England.'

'And I am the son of a bishop,' announced Roger. 'So there is nothing you can tell *me* about such matters. And Bale is right: here is another warning. Since I have already decided to obey Him, this particular storm must be aimed at Geoff alone. *He* is the reason we are stuck here.'

While the others discussed omens, rebellion and the superiority of chickens, Geoffrey stared at the sodden marshes through the crack in the door. He touched the scratch on his cheek, which made his mind turn to Ulfrith. He had been astonished to learn that the lad had attacked Roger – *and* had lived to tell the tale. Ulfrith was normally gentle and amiable, and Geoffrey did not like the notion that Roger was corroding his decent nature. He supposed encouraging Ulfrith's dormant temper might serve him well in battle, but, equally, blind rage might drive him into situations where he could be killed – as he might have been earlier that day, had Geoffrey been less tolerant.

And why had they fought? Because Ulfrith did not like the

evidence that suggested Philippa had killed her husband. Geoffrey supposed Edith might be the murderer, acting without Philippa's knowledge, but that did not fit well with Philippa claiming she had been with their husband when he had died and that his lungs had been full of water. Even if Edith had been responsible for the throttling, Philippa's lie meant she was complicit in the crime. Or had the women found Vitalis already strangled, then fabricated the 'death scene' to arouse sympathy, so they could claim protection? But if that were the case, then who *had* throttled the old man?

Magnus? He was so determined to succeed in his ridiculous rebellion that he had allowed his servant to drown. That was murder in Geoffrey's book. But had Magnus had the opportunity to dispatch Vitalis? Geoffrey had deduced that the murder had occurred on the beach, and he himself was Magnus's alibi for that time. Or was his assumption wrong, given that he had based his conclusions on Philippa's dubious testimony? But why would Magnus kill a half-senile old warrior? Because Vitalis had guessed his plans and threatened to expose him?

Or was Juhel the culprit? He had had plenty of opportunity, having been missing for several hours. Philippa claimed to have seen him murder Paisnel and had told her husband. Had Juhel strangled Vitalis to prevent him from blabbing? Did that mean Philippa was in danger, too? Geoffrey had not noticed any hostility towards the women the previous day, but Juhel was a complex man, and Geoffrey still did not have his measure.

Or had Vitalis been strangled by the pirates? Geoffrey had witnessed Fingar dispatching one of his own men, so they were certainly killers. Had they suspected early on that a passenger had damaged their ship, and taken instant revenge against Vitalis? Perhaps they had wanted to see what Vitalis had managed to bring ashore: he was a man of wealth, after all. A sailor seemed the most likely culprit.

And what about the odd business of Paisnel? If Philippa was a liar, should Geoffrey discount her tale about Juhel throwing him overboard? However, the details suggested there was some truth in her tale; her story explained the disappearance of Paisnel's bag and accounted for Juhel's inexplicable dampness afterwards.

Geoffrey found he could answer none of his questions with certainty, but he did not intend to remain with his suspects much longer anyway. He had decided to leave everyone, including Roger and the squires, before reaching the abbey, then travel alone to Dover. He did not want to accept a loan laden with inconvenient conditions, and Bale and Ulfrith were liabilities. He would do better with just his cowardly dog for company.

But he was no longer a bachelor with unlimited freedom. He was a married man with estates, and he was fond of his sister. He did not know his wife well enough for love, but he liked her. So where *did* his duty lie? Should he return to them and accept the yoke of lord of the manor? Should he leave England, so there could be no question of his having associated with Saxon rebels? Or should he ride to King Henry and warn him that there were men who intended to have his crown? But he looked at Magnus's thin, eager face and Harold's fat, smiling one, and he knew he could not sentence these inept dreamers to death. To take his mind off his questions and quandaries, he turned his attention to the discussion among his companions.

'I saw Simon in the lower hold,' Roger was saying to Magnus. 'But when I asked why he was holding an axe, he said Fingar had ordered him to adjust the cargo, to reset *Patrick*'s balance.'

Geoffrey was unimpressed that Roger had not questioned such an explanation: Fingar would never have entrusted such a task to passengers. He wished Roger had mentioned it sooner, because he would never have contemplated reasoning with the pirates if he had understood the magnitude of his companions' crimes against them.

Outside, the storm abated suddenly. The rain stopped, and the wind dropped with peculiar abruptness. Geoffrey glanced out of the door again, wondering whether it was his imagination or if he had heard voices carried on the remaining breeze.

'I thought you had brought the Usurper's men with you when you burst in with Norman knights at your heels,' Harold was saying to Magnus, as Geoffrey turned his attention to the cave again. 'I hid, quaking like a leaf. It might have been amusing, had you not given me such an awful fright!'

'I hid here when I was a child,' said Magnus. 'After the battle, when the Bastard was looking for Saxons to slaughter. It seems an appropriate place from which to launch our glorious—'

Voices outside silenced him abruptly, and Geoffrey shot to his feet. Fingar sounded as though he might be standing on their roof as he hailed his men. They had taken advantage of the lull in the weather to resume their search.

'He is calling his men over here, because this is the last place he saw footprints,' said Magnus, cocking his head. 'I know a little Irish, you see – I learned it when I was exiled there.'

At that moment, Delilah laid an egg, and her delighted clucks were answered by a peevish yap from the dog. No one needed to know Irish to understand Fingar's next statement.

'Hah! Now we have them!'

Silently, Geoffrey drew his sword and waited, Roger next to him similarly alert. Through the crack in the door they could see the sailors milling outside, and Geoffrey reviewed their options. He and Roger could not fight inside the shelter: there was no room to wield their weapons. But almost all Fingar's men had gathered, and he and Roger were unlikely to defeat them all, even with Bale and Ulfrith. He dismissed the Saxons and Juhel as of no consequence – Magnus, for one, had always borrowed Simon's knife when he had needed to cut his meat, and was never armed.

The pirates were arguing. Fingar was convinced their quarry was nearby – he tapped his nose to indicate he could smell something, and Geoffrey wondered if it was garlic – but his crew were pointing deeper into the marshes. Fingar was angry, his face a dangerous red. Kale, an unkempt, ugly man who had spent most of his time onboard trimming the sail, was the most vocal. The debate became heated, and although Geoffrey understood few of the words, the gist was clear.

Kale thrust a finger towards the sky, almost screaming in frustration: the sound the captain had heard was a bird, and they should not be wasting time in an area they had already searched. Most of the crew nodded agreement. Fingar roared something in return, perhaps that birds did not sound like dogs. Kale said something in a sneering voice that made the others snigger. Fingar moved quickly, and Kale was suddenly on his knees, gasping as blood gushed between his fingers. There was a deathly silence as he toppled forward.

Fingar's eyebrows were raised in a question: did anyone else think he could not tell the difference between a bird and a dog? Then a flock of waterfowl flapped overheard, and one uttered a low honk – a sound that could easily have passed for a bark. There were a lot of carefully impassive faces as Fingar glared at his people. Clearly, no one wanted to say that Kale had told him so, and there was a sullen silence before Fingar gestured that Donan should lead them back the way they had come. Without a word, Donan obliged, Fingar and the others trailing.

When he was sure they had gone, Roger released a pent-up sigh. 'Thank God for geese! I shall never eat one again.'

'We cannot leave while they are rampaging around,' said Geoffrey. 'It is safer to wait here.'

He expected someone to disagree, but no one did. Magnus, Harold and Juhel clearly had no intention of challenging such ferocious adversaries, and Roger was too experienced a warrior to argue with sound military advice. They settled as comfortably as they could, Geoffrey keeping watch by the door.

It was not long before the wind began to pick up again. Then came the rain, brought by dark clouds that scudded in from the west. Lightning forked once or twice, and thunder rebounded across the marshes. Again, Geoffrey watched the grass outside go from a moderate sway to a violent flap, and then to lying flat against the ground.

'What will you do next?' Geoffrey asked after a while. He was bored, and even conversation with the Saxons was better than nothing, although common sense told him it might be wiser to remain in ignorance. 'Now that you two are together and your plan is underway?'

'As soon as it is safe to leave, you will escort us to the abbey,' said Magnus.

'I am travelling directly to Dover,' said Geoffrey. 'Nowhere near the abbey.'

'It is only a few miles out of your way,' said Magnus, wheedlingly. 'And no ships can put to sea as long as the weather remains wild. You can stay in the abbey until the storms subside, and then your moral duty to me will have been fulfilled into the bargain.'

'He has a point, Geoff,' said Roger. 'About the weather, I mean, not the moral duty. There is no point in travelling anywhere during storms. Besides, we *should* give thanks for our deliverance.'

It galled him, but Geoffrey knew they were right. All ships would be port-bound until the wind subsided, and he had no money for an inn. An abbey, however, would provide free food and shelter. And while he was at La Batailge, he could ask about the accusations Vitalis had made.

'Your father fought at Hastinges,' said Roger when he did not reply. 'You should visit the abbey and pay the monks to say a mass for his soul – and for the souls of the men he killed.'

'It might shorten his time in Purgatory,' agreed Harold, taking another clove of garlic from his pouch and biting it in half. He offered the other to Geoffrey, who declined. 'Of course, the slaughter of innocent Saxons was a dreadful thing, so I am fairly certain he will be condemned to Hell.'

He spoke without rancour, and Geoffrey had the feeling that he said such things because he was expected to, rather than from a deep conviction that they were right.

'Tell me about the abbey,' said Geoffrey, supposing that if there was no way to avoid the place, he might as well make the best of it. He was fascinated by architecture and reluctantly conceded that the excursion might be interesting.

'It has a big church,' said Harold with a shrug. 'And it is full of Norman monks.'

Juhel laughed. 'That description applies to virtually every religious foundation in England! *How many* monks are there?'

'Forty, perhaps,' said Harold vaguely. 'Or fifty. Or sixty. But there are more than twice as many lay-brothers in the kitchens, stables, alehouse, bakery and gardens. And there are others still who tend the crops and the livestock. The abbey would be nothing without its Saxon helpers.'

'Do you know if a monk called Wardard lives there?' asked Geoffrey. 'I am told he also fought at Hastinges.'

Harold nodded. 'He is the fellow who looks after my father's shrine – the abbey church's high altar is on the spot where he died. Why do you ask?'

'Do not pay any heed to what Vitalis said,' advised Roger, who saw the direction in which the conversation was going. 'You will probably have no truth from this Brother Wardard, just as you had none from Vitalis.'

'Yes, but I may as well see Wardard and find out for certain,' said Geoffrey.

'Find out what?' said Harold. 'Perhaps I can help.'

'I want to know about something that happened a long time ago,' said Geoffrey, deliberately vague. 'It concerns my father and his conduct at the battle at Hastinges.'

'Vitalis cursed him for being lily-livered,' elaborated Roger, ignoring Geoffrey's wince. 'He said it was Godric Mappestone's cowardice that brought about the deaths of so many soldiers – that the fight would have ended hours sooner if Godric had done what he was ordered.'

# Six

'You should not heed Vitalis's claims,' said Roger, seeing the matter still bothered his friend. 'He spoke to hurt you. As soon as he learned your name, he was after blood. And because he knew he could never defeat you in a fair fight with swords, he resorted to striking at your dead father.'

Geoffrey nodded. The old man's eyes *had* gleamed with spite the moment he had learned that Geoffrey was Godric's son. He looked out of the crack again, watching the wind whip some large pieces of vegetation past.

'My father was many things, but I do not think he was a coward. He fought our Welsh neighbours for years, and I never saw him flinch.'

'Well, there you are,' said Roger. 'I know you, and I know your sister. Neither is a coward, and I do not believe you sprang from the loins of one.'

'Yet he always refused to visit the abbey raised to commemorate the battle's dead,' said Geoffrey, thinking back to his childhood. Hastings had been a frequent topic of conversation – all of it tales that highlighted his father's honour, courage and daring. If Godric were to be believed, the Conqueror would have been defeated if he had not been there. Yet Geoffrey's mother, who had also played her part, had said very little.

Geoffrey rubbed his head. Would the Conqueror have given Godric an estate if he had behaved dishonourably? Or had he not known, and the truth of Godric's shabby conduct lay only with a few? Godric had been with the Norman army's left flank, many of whom had been killed. Godric and Vitalis had agreed on that point: Godric *had* fought on the left.

'Brother Wardard told me *he* became a monk to atone for the slaughter,' said Harold helpfully. 'He said the deaths of so many brave warriors weighed heavily on his conscience until he took the cowl. I expect your father felt the same, Sir Geoffrey.'

'Not really,' replied Geoffrey, recalling his father's pride at the number of Saxons he had sent to their graves. The count of his victims had, of course, risen steadily through the years.

Geoffrey had once sarcastically remarked to one of his brothers that the Conqueror had not needed an army at Hastinges, because Godric had managed the victory single-handed. When the comment had been repeated to Godric, Geoffrey had expected retribution to be immediate and severe, but Godric had only fixed his defiant son with an unreadable expression, then marched away. It had been the last time they had discussed the battle, however, because the following week Geoffrey had been sent to Normandy to begin his knightly training.

'Was your father proud of his conduct, then?' pressed Harold.

'He saw the battle as his sacred duty. He never regretted what he did.'

'He did not visit shrines and churches, to beg forgiveness?' asked Harold uneasily.

'Not that I recall. But I did not see him for twenty years once I left for Normandy.'

But asking forgiveness for *anything* would have been anathema to Godric. Of course, if Vitalis was right, he would have had no need – because he had not fought at all, but had skulked in the woods, causing the battle to go on far longer than it should have done and bringing about the deaths of hundreds.

Geoffrey sighed, not sure what to think. Vitalis had certainly known Godric, because he related details that only his family shared. He had also known Geoffrey's mother and had confessed to being more afraid of her than her husband. Geoffrey understood that perfectly: he had been wary of the formidable Herleve himself. He had often wondered why, with such parents, he had not grown into a brutal tyrant; he could only suppose that being sent away at an early age had removed him from their malign influence.

'Well, perhaps you should ask Wardard to intercede on your father's behalf,' suggested Harold.

'He *does* need prayers, sir,' added Bale, who had spent most of his life on Godric's manor. 'And not only for those he killed in battle. There are also those he hanged for poaching, even though they were innocent; the families he evicted for not paying rent – they *had* paid, but he demanded the money again; the people of that Welsh village he burned for stealing his cattle, although it turned out he had taken the cows to the high byre himself—'

'Enough, Bale,' interrupted Geoffrey tiredly.

'It does sound as if you should see this monk,' said Magnus. 'You will want to put your mind at ease about your father's doings. And you can escort me at the same time.'

At that moment, the wind caught a tree outside, and its contorted trunk issued a low, moaning, keening sound that made Ulfrith and Bale start up in alarm.

'It is only marsh fays,' said Roger, which did little to allay their unease. 'Or perhaps the soul of murdered Vitalis, howling for vengeance. Restless spirits will not like this gale, either.'

'Then perhaps we should invite them in,' said Geoffrey, his temper sour from the preceding discussion. 'I am sure we can find them a corner.'

'Do not jest about such matters,' said Roger sternly. 'This storm is *your* doing for ignoring God's will. And you do not want marsh fays and ghosts angry with you as well.'

'Marsh fays are terrible beings, and I should not like to see Vitalis here, either,' said Bale fearfully. 'But I would rather do that than meet the ghost of Sir Godric Mappestone. In fact, I would sooner meet the Devil than *him*!'

The storm lasted a good deal longer than any of them anticipated. It raged all night and well into the following evening. They ate the rations in the knights' saddlebags – dried meat past its best and a packet of old peas – and the corn that Juhel carried for Delilah, boiling them into a stew with some of Harold's garlic. Roger, who could make a fire in almost any conditions, soon had a blaze going. The smoke threatened to suffocate them, but at least it kept them warm and provided a hot meal.

Water they had in abundance. It battered the door, dripped through the roof and was soon calf-deep on the floor. They took it in turns to sit on the bed. But it was the wind that kept them pinned down. At times it reached deafening proportions, and Geoffrey was certain the top would be torn from the shelter. He had seen many storms, but none compared to the ferocity of this.

Towards the end of the second day, there was an ominous crack above their heads.

'The rain is making the mud too heavy for these wooden supports,' said Harold, poking the structure with a podgy forefinger. 'It may collapse and crush us all.'

Manfully, Geoffrey resisted the urge to run outside.

'It is because God knows *he* still plans to go to the Holy Land,' murmured Ulfrith, glaring.

'Do not be ridiculous,' snapped Geoffrey curtly. 'It has nothing to do with me.'

Ulfrith started to argue, but Geoffrey rounded on him with such a dangerous expression that the squire's mouth closed with a snap. The knight was not often angry, but his companions had learned that once he had been provoked into an outburst, it was wise to leave him alone.

Geoffrey turned his attention to the crack in the door again, noting that the rainclouds were so thick that it was dark, even though the sun had not yet set. The wind's howl rose another octave, and he was sure that if the door had faced directly into the wind, instead of to the lee, they would not have survived.

The squires huddled together, making no attempt to disguise their fear, while Harold wedged himself at the very back of the shelter, as if he thought it might be safer. Juhel hugged his bird to his chest and attempted to comfort her with a handful of seed. She pecked the treats from his hand, but when he rummaged for more, his bag fell, spilling some of its contents into the water. He swore as he retrieved them, and Geoffrey saw that the bundle of documents was the first thing he saved. A flash of yellow indicated that something gold was the second.

Geoffrey stared at him. The parchments were still bound together with red ribbon. Did it mean Juhel had not strangled Vitalis, because the ribbon was still in place? He fingered the piece Bale had recovered from Vitalis's neck, noting that it was the same thickness and quality as that on Juhel's package.

'You should leave those out to dry,' he advised. 'The ink will run otherwise, and you will not be able to read them later.'

Alarmed, Juhel unpicked the knotted ribbon, allowing Geoffrey to see the same seal he had observed on the letters Paisnel had owned. So, he thought, Juhel *had* managed to secure them before

Paisnel and his bag had gone missing. But did it mean Philippa was right: that Juhel had murdered his friend, first ensuring that he had taken anything of value from his pack? He watched Juhel peer at the writing, then give it a rub, nodding in satisfaction when the ink stayed firm.

'It is all right,' he said, smiling. 'I caught them in time.'

'The Bishop of Ribe,' said Geoffrey, reading the name on the top one. The second, addressed to Juhel himself, was upside down. Was that because Juhel could not read and up or down made no difference to him? He also seemed to know remarkably little about parchment for a man who sold it: it needed more than a rub to dry it out. 'Paisnel said he was one of the bishop's clerks.'

'His best clerk,' corrected Juhel sadly. 'A man who was invaluable to him in many ways.'

'You mean he was a spy?' asked Magnus baldly.

'No,' said Juhel. His expression was cold, with no trace of its customary humour. 'He was not a spy.'

The words were hardly out of his mouth when the wind suddenly veered to the south, and a tremendous gust blasted the door inwards so it smashed against the wall, splinters flying in all directions. Geoffrey was hurled sideways, and feathers, splinters and pieces of vegetation billowed furiously around the shelter.

The maelstrom of debris continued to whirl until Geoffrey and Roger used their combined strength to close the door. Fortunately, it was sturdy, and although it had been damaged, it still shut out the weather. Once closed – and this time Roger permitted no cracks – the shelter's shaken occupants began to pull themselves together. Only Delilah seemed unperturbed: she had flown up to a rafter, where she settled down to roost. It was pitch black until Roger lit a candle, and Geoffrey looked around in dismay, not liking the notion of spending the night sealed in so tightly.

'I have never known such a tempest,' said Harold.

'We might never get out of it alive,' said Ulfrith unsteadily. 'And it will be *his* fault.' He glared at Geoffrey.

'He is right, Geoff,' said Roger quietly. 'This storm has gone on too long to be natural. Do you really want to be in this cave for the next week – all dark and airless, with the sea whipping about outside and threatening to flood in and drown us? You must promise God that you will do what He wants and stay in England.'

Using Geoffrey's dislike of enclosed places was sly but effective. He did not want to spend another hour inside, and the thought of being there for days made his stomach churn.

'I am going to the Holy Land,' he said, defiantly but unsteadily. 'This storm is not—'

'Do you remember what happened to Job when *he* defied God during a storm?' interrupted Roger, pressing his point relentlessly. 'He was eaten alive by a great sea serpent and spent the rest of his life in its belly – in the *dark*, with *no clean air*, and up to his neck in water. I imagine it was much like this cave.'

'It was Jonah, and he was inside a whale, not a serpent,' said Geoffrey, wondering who had taught Roger his theology. 'And he was only there for three days.'

'Three days!' echoed Roger, looking around meaningfully. 'Do you want to be *here* for another three days? Look at how the water is rising. We will drown, just like Jonah almost did.'

'Do you think these sea serpents will reach us here?' asked Bale fearfully. 'They have no legs, so cannot travel far, but . . .'

'There are channels,' said Ulfrith darkly, wincing as a particularly fierce gust rattled the door. 'They can swim along those, so they do not need legs.'

The wooden supports in the roof gave another ominous crack, and a clod of mud dropped on to Magnus, who gave a frightened yelp.

'This place cannot take much more,' said Juhel worriedly. 'We should take the bed and turn it on its end, so when the roof does collapse, it will give us at least a chance of survival. Unless Sir Geoffrey appeases God, of course.'

Geoffrey was beginning to feel sick, and he crawled towards the door, groping for the bar that secured it. Roger came to stand next to him, to make sure he did nothing foolish, although Geoffrey was somewhat calmed by the blasts of wind shooting through the gaps on to his hands.

'You promised to show me a cathedral being built, sir,' whispered Bale. 'It is a pity I shall die without seeing one.'

He was on the verge of tears, and Geoffrey was startled. In most situations, Bale was fearless enough to be a liability, yet he was frightened now. And Roger, one of the bravest men he had ever met, was reverting to underhand tactics to make him swear vows he did not want to take. The dog whined, and Juhel shot it a reassuring smile that failed to conceal the terror that lay beneath it.

Then Roger dropped to his knees, hands clasped together. The big knight only ever prayed in churches, and then only in a very indifferent manner. The overt piety unsettled Geoffrey.

'You *must* make the vow, sir,' said Ulfrith in a low voice. 'You *must* agree to bide by God's wishes and not travel to the Holy Land.'

'Please!' squeaked Magnus. 'It is unfair to kill us all for your own selfish ends.'

'God, deliver us from small, dark, cramped, water-filled places,' intoned Roger, one eye open to gauge his friend's reaction. 'Do not allow your faithful servants to perish in airless holes—'

'All right,' cried Geoffrey, yielding to the intolerable pressure. 'I will not go.'

Lightning forked outside, followed by a clap of thunder so loud that Magnus flung his hands over his ears and began to wail in terror. Harold dropped to his knees, as Roger shot up from his. Bale and Ulfrith clutched each other for support, and Juhel scrambled to grab his agitated chicken.

'You have to do it properly,' shouted Roger. 'Kneel and put your hands together, like King Harold, and say the words in a clear, loud voice, to make sure the Almighty can hear. You have to *mean* them, too. He knew you were insincere just now, which is why He sent the lightning.'

Geoffrey dropped to one knee in the icy water and placed his hands as Roger had instructed.

'I will not go to the Holy City,' he said, although the thunder was so loud that his voice was barely audible. 'I will remain in England until God instructs me otherwise.'

The thunder finished its roll and died away.

'It is easing off already,' said Bale, relieved. 'We are all saved. Thanks be to God!'

'Amen,' chorused the others, and even the hen clucked.

It did not sound as though it was easing to Geoffrey, although he supposed the next rumble might be a little farther away.

His companions began an impromptu celebration, and Bale was so convinced the danger was over that he curled into a ball and fell asleep.

The storm did fizzle out eventually, and Geoffrey stood to leave, itching to be away from the cave. But Harold said the marshes were likely to have been re-sculpted, and it would be a pity to survive the gale only to drown in a newly created bog in the dark. Geoffrey spent what was left of the night outside, sleeping peacefully, if damply, under an alder, while the others stayed in the comparative comfort of the shelter.

Shortly after dawn, which was bright and clear, Geoffrey climbed to the top of the shelter to take stock of their surroundings. The marshes behind the coast were ruggedly beautiful and, now the storm was over, full of birds. But everywhere were signs of the storm: wood, branches and other debris lay thick on the ground, and Geoffrey could see at least six trees on their sides, roots clawing upwards. Nearby were two smashed boats and the sodden carcass of a sheep.

It did not take long to locate a causeway that led roughly north, although parts had been washed away or were so covered in mud that it was difficult to follow. It was a grimy, dishevelled group that finally emerged from the squelching flatlands to climb a low, oak-clad hill. Geoffrey looked back at the land they had traversed. It was dissected by channels and streams, some fringed by trees and shrubs, but most bare, and everywhere were pools of water. To his surprise, the grey walls of Pevenesel Castle were startlingly near, and they were not in the direction he had expected. Thus, it was with reservations that he followed Harold and Magnus, both of whom claimed to know where they were going.

'I have horses nearby,' said Harold to his half-brother, taking a bulb of garlic from his pack. 'Well, for you and me. You did not tell me you would bring supporters, so I only arranged for two.'

'We are not supporters,' said Roger. 'You should stop saying that.'

'You should be proud to serve your rightful king,' asserted Magnus. 'Many men would give their right arms to be in your position.'

'Men with no right arms would be of no use to you,' Bale

pointed out helpfully. 'They would be unable to put up a fight, and warriors like me would slaughter them.'

'I have decided not to accept your offer of a see, Magnus,' said Roger. 'On reflection, I do not think life as a bishop would suit me. So we will travel with you as far as this abbey, but there our association finishes.'

'We shall see,' said Magnus in a voice that made Geoffrey look at him sharply. The sense that things were not all they seemed, which had been with him since Magnus had grabbed him in the frothing waves, returned more strongly than ever, and when he saw Juhel listening carefully to the exchange, his unease intensified. He trusted none of the little party.

'We will say prayers of deliverance in the abbey,' determined Roger. 'And Geoff can talk to Brother Wardard. But none of it will take long, and we shall be on the road today.'

'The road to where?' asked Ulfrith. He glanced uneasily at Geoffrey. 'Not Dover, I hope.'

'I swore a vow,' said Geoffrey tartly, annoyed that the squire should question his integrity. 'You are going to Durham, and I will travel west. Joan will not mind seeing me again so soon.'

'Neither will Hilde,' said Roger with a leering wink. 'Unless you have put her with child already, in which case she will want you gone until it is safely delivered. She will not like you tampering with her when she is carrying – they never do.'

Geoffrey did not reply and concentrated on their surroundings. It would be a pity to be taken by Fingar now, just because they were careless. He listened intently, alert for anything that might suggest an ambush. It would be a perfect place for one – the track was narrow and hemmed in by vegetation. Roger also listened, glaring Juhel into silence when the man started to chatter.

'Is there another way to the abbey?' Like Geoffrey, Roger did not like the look of the path.

Harold shook his head. 'Not from this direction. Why? What is wrong with it?'

'Birds,' replied Roger, looking meaningfully at his friend.

Geoffrey nodded his understanding, and they listened again.

'What about birds?' asked Juhel in a whisper. 'I cannot hear any.'

'Quite,' said Geoffrey. 'We should be able to, but there is nothing.'

'Perhaps it is too early in the morning for them,' suggested Harold, demonstrating an outrageous lack of countryside awareness.

'More likely, they have been disturbed.' Geoffrey drew his sword and advanced cautiously.

He had not gone far before a movement caught his eye. He shot into the undergrowth after it and was astonished to find not battle-hungry seamen or would-be wreckers from the villages, but a man in dark, sodden clothing, who climbed to his feet with an expression of pure relief.

'Sir Geoffrey!' he breathed. 'Thank God! I thought you were a marsh fay!'

It took some time for Brother Lucian to explain how he came to be in the woods, because Roger, Magnus and Harold kept interrupting to give details about their own experiences. Bored, Juhel wandered off to sit alone. Eventually, though, Geoffrey understood what had happened.

Lucian had been the first to leave *Patrick* – even before the captain had given the order to abandon ship – because, he said, he knew it was doomed. Thus he had come ashore a considerable distance from everyone else and had wandered for hours looking for survivors. All he had found were Donan and Kale, who had promptly relieved him of his purse and pectoral cross, and would have relieved him of his life, too, had he not pointed out that it was a mortal sin to kill a monk. He had then fled inland, spending the first night sheltering in a shepherd's hut. However, the next night, the shepherd had returned and evicted him, obliging him to shelter among the trees.

'But God punished him for his lack of charity,' Lucian concluded, 'because He caused a tree to fall on the hut and crush it.'

He pointed towards a venerable old beech that was lying on its side, remnants of a thatch and timber structure all but invisible among the mess of branches.

'Was the shepherd in it at the time?' asked Bale, regarding it with round eyes.

Lucian nodded. 'I am afraid so.'

'We do not want to see,' said Geoffrey, grabbing Bale, who most certainly did. 'Have you seen the sailors since you left the beach?'

Lucian nodded. 'Several times, but I do not know where they are now. What are your plans? I asked some locals for help, but their only response was to pelt me with stones. If you intend to rely on their assistance, you will be disappointed.'

'They were probably afraid of you,' explained Magnus. 'The Bastard's invasion forty years ago has rendered folk in these parts wary of strangers. He destroyed any number of villages.'

'But not Werlinges,' said Harold, nodding to farther along the path. 'He spared Werlinges, although he destroyed several settlements that lay in a circle around it.'

'Why?' asked Geoffrey. 'Did Werlinges offer him help? Provide information or swear fealty?'

'Not that I know,' said Harold. 'But it stands on a hill, so perhaps the Normans could not be bothered to climb up it in their armour.'

Lucian nodded at the cut on Geoffrey's face. 'It looks as though you have had trouble, too. Of course, you are a soldier, whereas I am a monk, and people are usually generous to those.'

'Not around here,' said Harold. 'Because of La Batailge. The Conqueror gifted the abbey a lot of Saxon land, and tithes and rents are ruthlessly gathered. It means Benedictines are unpopular. If you had been from another order, you probably would have had a warmer reception.'

'Oh,' said Lucian, swallowing hard. 'That is unfortunate.'

'Very,' agreed Magnus. 'I shall take all these lands away from La Batailge when I am king.'

'I meant it is unfortunate that *I* happened to land here,' said Lucian. Then his eyes narrowed and he regarded Magnus askance. 'You plan to be king? Of England?'

'I am your rightful monarch,' declared Magnus. He gestured to Harold. 'So is he.'

'I see,' said Lucian, bemused. 'Does Henry know?'

'He will, soon enough,' replied Magnus. 'We are the sons of King Harold, who was viciously murdered near here by Norman invaders.'

'Are you?' asked Lucian, startled. 'Lord!'

'Yes, you may address me as lord,' said Magnus. 'It is a fitting title until I claim my throne. Then you can call me Your Majesty. But we should not linger. We must make our way to the abbey without further delay.'

'Do you know what happened to Philippa and Edith?' asked Lucian of Geoffrey and Roger. He turned his back on the Saxons, and it was clear he did not believe their claims. 'And their husband?'

'The ladies are alive and well at Pevenesel,' replied Geoffrey, aware of Ulfrith's immediate jealousy at the question. 'But Vitalis is dead.'

'At Pevenesel?' asked Lucian uneasily. 'But Richer de Laigle the younger lives there! Their virtue will not be safe with him.'

'I said they would be better off with us!' cried Ulfrith, regarding Geoffrey accusingly.

'Not with that terrible storm and vicious pirates on the loose,' said Lucian. 'But the situation is easily remedied: we shall ask the abbey to send for them. De Laigle is a slothful, indolent sort of man and has probably not got around to seducing them yet anyway.'

'You told me on the ship that you had never visited this part of the coast before,' said Geoffrey suspiciously. 'So how do you know de Laigle?'

'I do not *know* him,' replied Lucian shortly. 'I have *heard* of him. His father is a different man altogether – conscientious and loyal. So are his older brothers. However, I shall arrange for Philippa and Edith to be removed from young Richer's pawing hands as soon as we reach La Batailge. They will be better off with me.'

'You are a monk,' said Ulfrith coldly. 'You took oaths to practise chastity and have nothing to do with women.'

Lucian smirked. 'I never vowed to have "nothing to do with women". They comprise half the population, and it would be wicked to ignore so many of God's creatures. That sort of thing is for bigots, which I am not. I am just a simple man, who takes pleasure in simple things.'

Ulfrith knew there were hidden meanings in the monk's words, but he was not clever enough to understand them. He opened his mouth to press his point, but Geoffrey, suddenly aware that his squire had slipped away and was prodding about in the remains of the shepherd's hut, spoke before he could think of a suitable remark.

'Fetch Bale back, Ulfrith,' he ordered. 'I do not want him over there.'

'Damn the man! It is not right to be doing that,' cried Lucian in dismay.

Geoffrey regarded him curiously, puzzled by the vehement objection. Meanwhile, Magnus had had enough of talking and began to walk. The dog, which had been ill-tempered and nervous since the storm, took the opportunity to make a flying snap at the Saxon's ankles. Magnus yelped in pain and anger, dropping the bag he had been carrying, and began hopping around on one leg. Guiltily, Geoffrey went to his assistance.

'Leave that sack – it belongs to me,' yelled Magnus, trying unsuccessfully to shove Geoffrey away with his scrawny arms. 'Keep your greedy Norman paws off my possessions!'

'He was trying to help you,' said Roger coldly. 'And if you want us to escort you to the abbey, you had better learn some manners. You are not king yet, you know.'

'How dare you berate me!' cried Magnus, quivering with anger. 'You overstep the mark!'

'And so do you,' retorted Roger angrily. 'Now shut up. I do not want an arrow in *me* because we cannot hear archers in the trees for all your noise.'

Magnus went quiet, although he was still seething. Geoffrey led the way along the track before he could begin another diatribe, glancing behind to make sure the others were following. He saw Ulfrith was obliged to apply considerable force to extricate Bale from the hut, but the squire came eventually and they brought up the rear. Bale shoved something in his purse as they went, and Geoffrey grimaced: his lectures on corpse-robbing had clearly fallen on deaf ears.

'Magnus will never be king,' said Roger to Geoffrey, when they were some distance ahead. 'He is an oaf compared to Henry.'

'Right,' said Geoffrey shortly.

Roger glanced at him askance. 'Is that all you have to say on the matter?'

Geoffrey lowered his voice. 'My dog took a dislike to Magnus from the first, and I should have paid heed. He is nearly always right: he had the same reaction to Bellême, and he does not like Henry, either. I should learn to trust his instincts.'

'Magnus is a silly man, although Harold is charming – like a fat whore, all smiles and cuddles. But Magnus is nothing. He did not even think to bring a sword to aid him in his invasion!'

'He is *not* nothing. He wrecked *Patrick* to ensure we landed here, and he does not care that men died because of it. He is ruthless and fanatical, and his lack of a weapon only means that he practises his viciousness in slyer ways. I wish we had never met him. Or the others, for that matter.'

Roger was watching the surrounding trees, alert for signs that something was amiss. 'Is it because we have no horses and are vulnerable on foot? Is that what makes you uneasy?'

'I am uneasy because something is wrong. Magnus let Simon drown, and Paisnel *and* Vitalis are dead in odd circumstances. The rebellion has not yet started, but it is already claiming victims.'

'This is not a rebellion, lad,' laughed Roger. 'It is Magnus and Harold deluding themselves.'

'That is what I thought,' said Geoffrey. 'Until just now, when I saw what Magnus has in his bag. It fell open when my dog bit him.'

'I went through it at Pevenesel,' said Roger, still scanning the trees. They could hear birds now, and Geoffrey supposed it had been Lucian's lurking presence that had silenced them earlier. 'And Juhel had a rummage during the storm – he thought we were all asleep, but I watched him. He did not take anything, though, and neither did I. There was nothing worth having.'

'There was a list,' said Geoffrey.

As Roger could not read, he was unlikely to have appreciated its significance. And Juhel? Had he declined to take it because he *could* read and knew it might be dangerous, or because he could *not* read and did not understand its value? Or had he simply been looking for money? But Geoffrey had glimpsed the gleam of gold in Juhel's bag when it had fallen in the water the previous night – the parchmenter was already rich, despite his claim that business was poor and he could only afford the cheaper berths supplied by pirates.

'A list of what?' asked Roger, bemused.

'Of Saxon names, with figures next to them. I imagine they indicate the number of men each will provide for this revolt. Harold and Magnus give the impression that they are disorganized and unsupported, but I cannot help but wonder whether they have deliberately misled us and their preparations are actually further along than they would have us believe.'

Roger glanced at him. 'Any such list will be wishful thinking.

It will not be *promises*, but the men they *hope* will come. They have been in exile for four decades and probably had nothing else to do but make plans. Do not read too much into it.'

'There was a letter against each name, representing "yes" or "no". Most were "yes".'

'Are you saying their rebellion might succeed?' Roger was astonished.

'No. But we should not keep company with them, regardless. When we reach La Batailge, I shall ask the abbot for a horse and ride to warn Henry of what is afoot. This uprising must be quashed before more men die. Besides, Henry will learn we were shipwrecked with Magnus, and I do not want my family to suffer because I failed to mention it to him.'

Roger sighed. 'If you are sure that is the right thing to do, then I will come with you. We have no idea where Henry is, and it might take a while to find him.'

'There was something else in Magnus's bag,' said Geoffrey. 'Red ribbon.'

# Seven

Geoffrey was thoughtful as he followed the track deeper into the woods. Could a vain, shallow man like Magnus really initiate a rebellion? It was no secret that many Saxons still itched to take their country back, although Geoffrey was certain they would never succeed. And were the names on Magnus's list truly men who had agreed to provide troops and supplies? Even a glimpse had shown it ran to several pages.

Did Magnus's supercilious airs conceal a mind that could set a country afire? Or did that honour go to Harold? Surely Harold was exactly what he seemed: foolish, genial and gentle? In that case, *should* Geoffrey warn the King? If he did, and Henry sent soldiers only to discover the 'revolt' comprised Magnus, Harold and a handful of Saxons with hoes and pitchforks, Geoffrey would look like an idiot.

And what of Vitalis's murder? Magnus used red ribbon to tie back his hair, and Geoffrey had seen a roll of it when his bag had fallen open. Was he the culprit? Or had someone chosen the stuff deliberately so Magnus *would* be blamed? Of course, the sailors made far more likely suspects, especially as Geoffrey reasoned that Magnus had not had the opportunity to kill Vitalis on the beach. And the women? Philippa certainly knew something about her husband's death, because she had lied about it.

Geoffrey's glance strayed towards Lucian. He had had plenty of opportunity, too, although Geoffrey could not imagine why a monk would want to dispatch a feeble old man. And what about Juhel? He searched other people's bags as they slept, and he may have stabbed a friend and thrown him overboard. Did he have a store of red ribbon? Or had he borrowed some from Magnus? If he had searched Magnus's bag in the cave when he thought no one was looking, there was no reason to suppose he had not done it on other occasions, too.

'I detest that man,' growled Roger suddenly. 'I do not want him with us.'

'Juhel?' asked Geoffrey, startled out of his thoughts. 'We will be rid of him soon.'

'No. Lucian. Ulfrith does not like him, either. And Lucian is no more a monk than I am – he is brazenly irreligious, and I doubt he knows one end of a psalter from another.'

Geoffrey laughed. 'A damning indictment indeed, when it comes from the Bishop Elect of Salisbury! Ulfrith does not like me, either, because Philippa prefers us to him. It is jealousy.'

'I should have looked at that shepherd's corpse,' said Roger sullenly. 'I should have checked he was crushed and not strangled. You may have seen red ribbon in Magnus's bag, but I wager Lucian owns a supply, too.'

'But a tree *had* fallen on the hut,' Geoffrey pointed out. 'Lucian could not possibly have engineered that. What *is* odd is that a shepherd refused a monk shelter.'

'It *is* strange, but so is this revolt, and the sooner we report it to Henry, the better.'

'I am having second thoughts about that,' said Geoffrey. 'We have so few hard facts that it might be better to report it to the nearest baron and let him investigate.'

'That is de Laigle. And as the father is away, you will have to speak to the son. Is that wise?'

'He must have some merit, or his father would not have left him in charge. So we shall make our report to him, and if he fails to act, that is his prerogative – and his responsibility.'

'I feel quite bereft without my purse,' announced Lucian suddenly, speaking to Harold, Juhel and Magnus. His voice was loud, and Roger scowled at him to lower it. The monk complied, but he was still audible. 'We will not be able to go anywhere without gold, and Donan took all mine. Did you salvage any, Magnus? You had a lovely gold pendant on the ship.'

'I did not,' said Magnus curtly. 'But even if I had, I would not sell it to finance *your* travels.'

'That is unchristian,' admonished Lucian. 'We have all been washed ashore together, and it is churlish to refuse each other help.'

'Lucian thinks we should pool our possessions because he has none himself,' murmured Roger. 'Of course, Magnus is a liar. I, too, saw him with a gold medallion on the ship. He may have lost it in the wreck, but to say he never owned one is downright dishonest.'

'Save your morality for your own brethren,' Magnus sneered. 'If you have any.'

'What do you mean by that?' demanded Lucian, his voice rising again.

'I do not believe you are a monk,' snapped Magnus. 'You are too worldly and know too little about your devotions.'

'I am bursar at Bath Abbey,' said Lucian indignantly. 'And, being from a good family, I have been appointed Bishop de Villula's envoy, carrying important missives to the Diocese of Ribe.'

'Then where are they?' interrupted Juhel curiously. 'I managed to salvage my important missives – or, rather, Paisnel's. But you are empty-handed.'

'I lost them,' replied Lucian shortly. 'I shall have to go home for copies, then start the journey all over again. Perhaps next time I should travel most of the way by road instead.'

'You can take him with you when you go to Goodrich,' whispered Roger wickedly. 'Bath will not be far out of your way – assuming he is not making it all up, of course. We have met John de Villula, and he is not the sort of man to employ the likes of Lucian as his envoy.'

'If Lucian really is from a prominent family,' Geoffrey replied, 'then perhaps his appointment came with a large benefaction. De Villula may have had no choice.'

'Speaking of Paisnel, are you *sure* it was wise to salvage his documents?' Lucian was asking Juhel. 'I would not want those on *my* person.'

'Why not?' asked Juhel. He sounded startled. 'They are only property deeds and reports from the Bishop of Ribe's distant outposts.'

'So Paisnel said,' retorted Lucian. 'But have you inspected them?'

'I have no reason to,' said Juhel, puzzled. 'They all bear a seal depicting a legged fish, which is the Bishop's personal symbol.'

'All except the couple that are addressed to him,' whispered Geoffrey to Roger. 'I wonder if he can read. If not, he may have no idea that "Paisnel's" bundle contains some of his own property. If he can, then he is lying.'

'I told you there was something odd about Paisnel,' said Magnus spitefully. 'The man *was* a damned spy!'

'They are property deeds,' insisted Juhel, becoming annoyed. 'He was *not* a spy. And it is none of your concern anyway.'

A loud crunch punctuated the end of the sentence as Harold bit into one of his cloves. 'Garlic, anyone? It is very good for cooling hot tempers.'

The track twisted through several copses, then reached land that had been cleared for fields. Directly ahead were more trees with a hamlet nestling among them, comprising four or five pretty houses and an attractive church. A short distance away was an unusual building, which looked as though it had just been hit by a snowstorm. Geoffrey regarded it curiously.

'Ah! Werlinges,' said Harold in satisfaction. He pointed at the building that had caught Geoffrey's attention. 'And that is one of its salt-houses.'

Geoffrey frowned. The village was strangely deserted at a time when men should have been tending fields or livestock. And someone certainly should have been in the salt-house. Salt was an expensive commodity and usually well guarded. Meanwhile, the door to the chapel was ajar, moving slightly in the breeze. The dog sniffed, then growled, a deep and long rumble that made up Geoffrey's mind.

'Stop,' he said softly. 'There is something wrong.'

'Wrong?' demanded Magnus. His voice was loud and rang off the nearest houses, and they seemed even emptier. 'What do you mean? Are you afraid? Like father, like son?'

The scorn in his voice was more galling than his words, and Roger bristled on his friend's behalf. But Geoffrey was more concerned with the village. Bale gripped a long hunting knife and started to move forward, but Geoffrey stopped him. He had not survived three gruelling years on the Crusade by being reckless, and all his senses clamoured that something was badly amiss.

'I do not want to go through this place,' he said. 'We will walk around it.'

'But what about the horses Harold arranged?' demanded Magnus angrily. 'You cannot expect kings to arrive at La Batailge on foot, like common serfs.'

'Then we will wait here,' said Roger. 'Go and collect your beasts.'

'Alone?' asked Magnus, immediately uneasy. 'When you think it is dangerous?'

'It is all right,' said Harold in relief. 'I can see the horses in the field over there. I asked Wennec the priest to hire me good ones, and he has! I confess I was concerned he might renege.'

'Why?' asked Geoffrey, scanning the trees. There was no birdsong again, and the entire area was eerily silent. 'Is he dishonest? Or just loath to have anything to do with a rebellion?'

'Werlinges has always expressed a preference for Normans,' admitted Harold. 'I imagine that was what prompted the Bastard to spare it.'

'So why ask its priest to find your horses?' asked Geoffrey suspiciously. 'Why not go elsewhere for help?'

'Harold has just told you why,' said Magnus impatiently. 'All the other settlements were laid to waste. Werlinges is the only village available, so he had no choice but to approach Wennec.'

'Then that is even more reason to leave,' said Geoffrey. 'Surely you can sense something oddly awry here? There are no people, but there are the horses, flaunted in an open field. It is a trap.'

'Nonsense,' declared Magnus. 'Everyone left because of the storm. But enough of this blathering – go and fetch the nags at once.'

Neither knights nor squires moved. Then, casually, Roger drew his sword, testing the keenness of its blade by running the ball of his thumb along it. Geoffrey stood next to him, his senses on full alert.

'If you want the horses, get them,' said Roger to the Saxons. 'If not, we shall be on our way.'

'All right,' said Harold, moving forward. 'We shall show you Saxon courage.'

'I will come with you,' said Lucian. 'I do not fancy walking all the way to La Batailge, so I will borrow a pony if there is one to be had.'

'Do not make your selection before your monarch,' ordered Magnus, hurrying after him.

He broke into a trot. So did Lucian, until they both made an unseemly dash towards the field, like children afraid of losing out on treats. Juhel chortled at the spectacle, although Geoffrey was too uneasy to think there was anything remotely humorous in it.

'Perhaps I had better ensure our noble king does not lose out to a "Benedictine"', said the parchmenter. 'Because I suspect he is incapable of selecting a good horse.'

Geoffrey regarded him sharply. 'You are sceptical of Lucian's vocation, too?' he asked.

Juhel gave one of his unreadable smiles. 'Well, I have never seen him pray. Of course, it may just be youthful exuberance that makes him forget his vows.'

'He is certainly not bound to chastity,' said Roger. 'I am sure he and Edith lay together on the ship. And that gold pectoral cross he wore speaks volumes about his adherence to poverty, too. If he is a monk, then he is not a very obedient one.'

'His worldliness makes him an inappropriate choice for such a long, lonely mission,' said Juhel. 'So either Bishop de Villula *had* to choose him for reasons we will probably never know, or Lucian is using a religious habit to disguise his true identity.'

'And why might that be?' asked Geoffrey, regarding Juhel warily, aware that these were probably observations that had been fermenting for some time. But why was the man so interested in his fellow passengers? Geoffrey thought about Paisnel, who Magnus believed was a spy. Was it true, and had Juhel been sent to dispatch him? But who would order such a thing?

'Lord knows,' said Juhel. 'An escape from an unhappy marriage, perhaps? He was the first to abandon ship, and, although he claims he took nothing, I saw him towing a small bundle. And I am sure it did not contain a psalter!'

He ambled away, leaving Geoffrey confused and uncertain. Was Juhel casting aspersions on Lucian to deflect suspicion from himself? Or was he just a man who liked to watch the foibles of others?

'This village has a smell,' said Bale, his whisper hot on Geoffrey's ear. The knight eased away, not liking the hulking figure quite so close. 'A metallic smell, and one I know well.'

'Something to do with the salt-house?'

'Blood,' drooled Bale. 'I smell blood.'

'You do not,' said Geoffrey firmly. 'But we are leaving as soon as Harold has his horses, so go and make sure the road north is clear. Take Ulfrith with you. And be careful.'

'You were right: there *is* something wrong about this place,' said Roger as Bale slipped away. 'And Bale might be right: I think I can smell blood, too. The sooner we are gone, the better.'

Geoffrey's reply was drowned out by a monstrous shriek, and he saw men running from the woods wielding weapons. At their head was Donan, his face a savage grimace of hatred. In the distance, Geoffrey was aware of the Saxons, Juhel and Lucian swivelling around in alarm. They scattered immediately. Magnus ran awkwardly, all knees and flailing arms, while Juhel tipped himself forward and trotted like an overweight bull. Harold and Lucian were less ungainly, and Geoffrey did not think he had ever seen a faster sprinter than the monk.

'Death to thieves and saboteurs,' Donan howled, sword whirling. 'Now you will pay!'

Geoffrey's weapon was drawn long before Donan's cry had faded, and he stood calmly next to Roger, waiting for the onslaught. Not all the pirates were there, but Donan's contingent numbered about a dozen, all carrying swords, daggers or cudgels.

If Geoffrey and Roger had been mounted, twelve sailors would not have caused them much trouble. The additional height, and the length of their swords, meant they could have hacked at their attackers without much risk to themselves. It was more difficult for a knight to fight on foot, but, even so, Geoffrey was not unduly worried by a dozen undisciplined mariners. He and Roger fought back to back, making it difficult for more than a few opponents to attack at a time. Roger's long reach was especially devastating – he killed one and injured another in the first few moments.

'That contains something of ours,' yelled Donan when the first savage encounter was over and the surviving crew had fallen back to regroup. He pointed at the bundle near Roger's feet. 'Give it to me, and I shall kill you quickly. Refuse, and you will regret it.'

'You drowned my horse,' said Roger through clenched teeth. 'And I took compensation. If you have any sense, you will leave while you are still in one piece.'

Geoffrey stole a quick look beyond their attackers. Ulfrith was tackling a single opponent, the two slashing at each other in a highly predictable pattern, and Bale was chasing a cabin boy around one of the houses, doggedly determined to make a kill. Their fellow passengers were nowhere to be seen.

Roger glanced at Geoffrey, passing a silent message, then, before the sailors understood what was happening, both knights launched simultaneous attacks, swords whistling in a series of vicious swipes and thrusts. The ferociousness of the offensive allowed for no rejoinder. Geoffrey dropped one man with a thrust through the chest, then twisted around and sent the dagger skittering from the grasp of another. Fingerless, the man fled, ignoring Donan's screech to stand fast. Out of the corner of his eye, Geoffrey saw another man fall to Roger's onslaught.

Donan faced him, spitting his fury at what was becoming a rout. Geoffrey feinted to his left, then chopped at a man's shoulder, but before he could follow up, he felt a burning pain as a dagger slid under the mail on his right side. He whipped around and saw off the attacker with a thrust that penetrated the man's thigh, but the sharp sting of his own cut did not encourage him to press his advantage. Swearing vilely, the sailor limped after his retreating fellows, Donan among them.

'We should finish this,' said Roger grimly. 'We shall have no peace as long as they are alive.'

'If you want peace, then give them back their gold,' snapped Geoffrey, hand to his side.

'I will not! It is mine, and I will kill anyone who tries to take it.'

As the sounds of the pirates' flight receded, Geoffrey leaned against a tree to catch his breath. Roger took Ulfrith to check there were no lingerers, and Bale hurried to take his sword and clean it – a task he always enjoyed. The knight could see from the squire's bloody hands that Bale had triumphed in his own skirmish.

'Did you kill the cabin boy?' he asked, disapprovingly.

'Unfortunately, he was too nimble for me,' said Bale unhappily. 'I am not the hare I once was. But I slipped up behind one villain and slit his throat before he knew I was there.'

Geoffrey did a quick survey. The encounter had left six dead and several seriously wounded, and he suspected Donan would not attack again until Fingar and the remaining seamen were there to reinforce him. Then he saw the gleam in Bale's face that always shone when there was violence.

'Do not gloat over your victims,' he said sharply. 'It is not seemly.'

'Why not, sir?' asked Bale with genuine curiosity. 'He would have killed me – and you. Why should I not be pleased I got him first?'

'We treat our dead enemies with respect.' Geoffrey's side was burning, and he was in no mood to discuss battle etiquette with a man who was incapable of understanding.

Bale's face was a picture of confusion. 'William the Bastard did not treat the Saxon dead at Hastinges with respect. He left them for carrion and made no attempt to bury them.'

'Perhaps so, but no one went around pawing their corpses and stealing their jewellery.' Geoffrey looked pointedly at the gold earrings Bale held in one bloody paw.

'Sir Roger took a dagger from the man he killed in Bristol last year,' argued Bale. 'He said the corpse no longer needed it, so it should go to a good home. I was following his example.'

Geoffrey sensed he was losing the debate and did not have the energy to regain the initiative. 'I cannot make it any clearer except to say that you should not steal from corpses or take pleasure in your opponents' deaths,' he said shortly.

'But I *do* enjoy it, sir,' protested Bale. 'There is something satisfying about dispatching a man who would have killed me, and to pretend otherwise would be dishonest.'

Geoffrey gave up. He shook his head in weary defeat and heaved himself upright as Roger and Ulfrith returned.

'Is that a serious wound, Geoff?' asked Roger. 'Shall I see to it?'

Geoffrey shook his head, not wanting to be subjected to Roger's rough and clumsy ministrations. 'We should leave before they come back. Where are the others?'

'Well, poor Harold is over there,' said Roger with a vague wave. 'He is dead.'

Geoffrey walked to where he indicated, aware of a sinking sensation in his stomach when he saw the slashed throat. Bright yellow hair tumbled across the cheerful, once-smiling face, and he crouched down to push it back.

'Damn you, Bale,' he said softly. 'You have just killed a contender for the English throne.'

'*Bale* killed King Harold?' asked Roger, gaping in horror. 'God's blood! Now we shall have Saxon rebels baying for our blood, as well as pirates!'

'But he was racing towards you with a sword, sir,' objected Bale. 'I acted from instinct.'

'He did look fearsome,' said Ulfrith loyally. 'I saw him dash towards you while I was fighting that helmsman – the one I defeated.'

'How did you know he was not aiming for the pirates?' asked Geoffrey. 'That he did not intend to join the fight on our side?'

Bale thought carefully before replying. 'Well, I did *not* know, not for certain. But he came out of that church, and everyone else in there is dead. Obviously, *he* killed them all, so I thought I had better cut his throat before he slaughtered you, too.'

'What are you talking about?' snapped Geoffrey impatiently. 'Who is dead in the chapel?'

'The villagers, I suppose,' replied Bale with a shrug. 'Ask King Magnus.'

'Where *is* Magnus?' asked Roger.

'Over there, being sick.' Bale's voice took on a note of defiant pride. '*He* does not have the stomach for massacres. You would never see *me* vomiting at such sights. And I *told* you I could smell blood. I was right – the church is drenched in it. I peeped inside it after that boy ran away.'

Ulfrith was listening to the discussion with growing horror. He gazed at Bale with wide eyes. 'Are you saying King Harold murdered the villagers while we were fighting pirates?'

Ulfrith's sword was stained, indicating he had inflicted some sort of harm on his opponent. The same could not be said of Juhel and Lucian, who came to join them, cool and unmarked. Geoffrey was not surprised Lucian had declined to fight – he was supposed to be in holy orders, after all – but he was disappointed in Juhel.

'Well, Harold's sword is bloody,' Bale was saying, pointing at the stained weapon that lay in the grass next to the body. 'Of course, he was not the only one who went inside the place where the slaughter took place. *Others* did, too.' His accusing gaze encompassed the vomiting Magnus, Juhel and Lucian.

'*I* do not kill,' said Lucian indignantly. 'I am a monk. Besides, I am not ashamed to admit that such situations terrify the wits out of me. I fled when I saw Donan coming, and, although one sailor pursued me, I ran fast enough to lose him.'

'Well, *I* certainly did not kill anyone,' said Magnus, white-faced and shaking as he approached. 'I do not even own a weapon. I am afraid I hid *behind* the church when you were skirmishing.'

'And where were *you*?' Roger demanded of Juhel.

The parchmenter held up the cage containing Delilah. 'I was making sure the sounds of battle did not distress her, but I did not succeed. What should I do to calm her, do you think?'

'Cover the cage and leave her to settle,' advised Ulfrith. 'She will soon forget it.'

'I wish that would work for me,' said Magnus miserably. 'I shall remember this day for the rest of my life. Did Harold really kill all these poor people?'

'They were dead when we arrived,' said Geoffrey, recalling the eerie silence.

'And Harold could not have killed them before that, because he was with us,' added Roger. Then he frowned. 'He could have killed them before he went to the mud shelter, I suppose.'

Bale disagreed. 'These villagers are fresh dead; the blood is still wet and bright.'

Geoffrey supposed he should not be surprised that such a gruesome detail had stuck in Bale's mind.

'Then how did he do it?' asked Ulfrith. 'If they were dead when we arrived, and he did not have the chance to do it before . . .'

Geoffrey felt blood oozing from his own cut and was aware of a sense of unreality. It was a reaction he often experienced after fierce fighting, but he knew he could not afford to give in to it — at least, not until they were safe in the abbey. Wincing, he knelt to inspect the corpse more closely.

'This is not Harold,' he said. 'He is wearing different clothes and his face is thinner. And he does not have scars on his wrists. Unless I am mistaken, this must be Ulf. Harold's twin.'

'But why would *he* want to kill villagers?' asked Roger. 'Because he asked them to side with his revolt, and they refused? Magnus and Harold said this was a place loyal to Normans.'

'But Magnus also said Ulf was violent,' said Juhel. 'So *he* must have killed these people.'

'Yes,' agreed Magnus. 'This must be Ulf, although I have not seen him in years. I was not exaggerating when I described his evil character, though: destroying an entire village is exactly the kind of thing he would enjoy. Yet even so, he had no cause to attack Werlinges. *Ergo*, I do not believe he had anything to do with this.'

'Perhaps,' said Geoffrey. 'Of course, pirates are hardened killers, too. It is possible they dispatched these people, so that they would not warn us against walking into an ambush.'

Magnus wiped his mouth on the back of his hand. 'I agree. One man could not have done this. It is the work of a violent horde.'

Reluctantly, Geoffrey supposed he had better inspect the church for himself. It contained at least thirty people, all lying in twisted heaps or sprawled in a chaotic jumble of limbs. There was not a weapon in sight, and injuries to their arms suggested they had tried to defend themselves with their bare hands. A child near the altar was huddled with his knees drawn up to his chin, as if he had hoped he might not be noticed. It was a massacre, and although Geoffrey had seen its like many times on the Crusade, he had never thought to do so in England.

He forced himself to move among the bodies, to see whether any had survived, but he knew none had. The killers had done their work too well, and most corpses had multiple injuries.

'Christ God!' breathed Roger, appalled. 'They sliced the priest's head clean from his body.'

He pointed to the altar, where an old man with a tonsure had evidently been praying as he had been struck down. There was a tiny room to one side, which had served as a vestry. Harold was in it, sitting on a bench. His head was bowed, his eyes glazed with shock.

'I cannot find Father Wennec,' he said dazedly, looking up when Geoffrey entered. 'Perhaps he escaped. He is an elderly fellow with a tonsure . . .'

'Come outside,' said Geoffrey gently. 'There is nothing you can do here.'

'What evil, wicked monster could do such a thing?' asked Harold, stumbling slightly as Geoffrey pulled him to his feet. 'There are children . . .'

'I do not know. But I do not think we should wait here to find out.'

'They process salt here,' said Harold as Geoffrey escorted him from the chapel. He was burbling irrelevancies, and Geoffrey supposed it was his way of dealing with what he had seen. 'Werlinges is famous for its lovely salt, and it made the place wealthy. I suppose that is why it was attacked.'

'No doubt,' said Geoffrey. There was no point saying more: Harold was incapable of listening.

'I saw them all alive before I went to meet Magnus,' Harold went on. 'And they told me all about their salt. They were proud of it, you see. And Wennec promised to hire me two good horses.'

Geoffrey stood with him while Roger led the squires in a search of the village's outbuildings, hoping to find someone who had escaped and might be able to tell de Laigle what had happened. The brutal execution of an entire village was sure to trigger an official enquiry, and it was important to secure eye-witnesses before they disappeared.

'I am sorry I did not help you fight the pirates,' said Harold dully. 'But I did not have a sword. I ran to the chapel to see whether someone might have left a weapon in the porch that I might use – a pike or something. But when I saw . . . I must have swooned . . . And then you came . . .'

'You were quite right not to have joined the skirmish, Harold,' said Magnus, coming to stand with them. 'And so was I. What would happen to England if we were killed or injured?'

'*Ulf* would not have acted like a stupid coward,' said Harold, full of self-loathing. 'But I am not him. To tell you the truth, I prefer playing the horn to fighting and the like.'

'You play like an angel,' said Magnus comfortingly. 'Do you think Donan did this alone, Sir Geoffrey, or did Fingar help?'

Geoffrey shrugged, thinking that Fingar and his men would have needed a place to stay when the storms struck and might well have imposed themselves on Werlinges. And then, to ensure no one reported pirates at large, they had killed any witnesses. He frowned. But would they really resort to such extremes? Or was it the work of Ulf, the violent marauder? Geoffrey knew that one man with a sword could do a lot of damage to unarmed people in a confined space.

'The massacre was recent, just as Bale says,' said Roger, coming to report. Ulfrith was white-faced at his side and making a valiant but futile attempt to conceal his shock, whereas Bale seemed energized. 'This morning, probably.'

'Then it *must* have been the pirates,' said Magnus. 'When I am king, I will see *them* chopped into pieces for this outrage! That evil Donan—'

'No,' said Geoffrey, taking a deep breath and forcing his wits to work. 'You saw how much blood was spilled. The killers would have been drenched in it, but Donan and his men were not.'

'Perhaps they washed before we came,' suggested Bale.

'Their clothes were those they wore when they escaped the wreck, and they were not wet. They are not the culprits. However, that is not to say Fingar and the rest of the crew are innocent.'

'They may be wandering along some path even now, all red and splattered with gore,' added Bale, eyes gleaming.

'They *are*,' declared Magnus firmly. 'And anyone who thinks otherwise is a fool.'

Harold scrubbed his cheeks; he was beginning to pull himself together. 'Ulf said he would meet me here, so I suppose I should see if he is among the dead . . .' He faltered, then looked at Geoffrey. 'I do not suppose you would oblige, would you? He looks like me.'

# Eight

Harold dropped to his knees in horror when he saw Ulf's body, and it was some time before the round-faced pretender to the crown was able to speak. He staggered to his feet, and the others came to stand next to him in mute sympathy.

'He is covered in blood,' he said hoarsely. 'How did it happen?'

'His throat was cut,' said Geoffrey. He did not look at Bale. 'By a madman.'

'Some of this blood is dry,' said Juhel, kneeling to inspect the corpse's clothes, 'and some is wet. What can be deduced from that?'

'He is a disinherited Saxon in a land inhabited by Normans,' said Magnus harshly. 'He was probably obliged to fight for his life at some point.'

Geoffrey looked to where Juhel pointed. Ulf must have been fighting over a prolonged period, if the stains were anything to go by. However, there were no splatters or sprays, which Geoffrey would have expected had he been involved in killing the villagers. So, if Ulf was innocent of the massacre, then it made sense to assume Fingar was responsible – Geoffrey had seen him kill two of his own men without hesitation, so villagers would present no problem. Magnus was right: the atrocity was the work of ruth-less pirates furious at being deprived of their ship and gold.

'I will ask my father to say a mass for his soul if you like,' said Roger kindly to Harold. 'From what I heard, Ulf will need it, and prayers from a bishop go a long way.'

'Thank you,' said Harold weakly. 'We did not know each other well – fate meant we have been separated most of our lives – but he is still my brother, and I loved him.'

'His death may be a blessing in disguise,' said Magnus, rather baldly. 'It means one fewer contender for the throne. And his rough temper and violent reputation might have put people off joining our rebellion. I told you to keep news of our plans away from him, and you ignored me.'

'He has a right to be here,' said Harold tiredly. 'His claim is as valid as yours or mine.'

'Shall we bury them?' asked Bale, breaking into the discussion before Magnus could reply. 'If we should treat corpses with respect, we had better not abandon a Saxon king to the carrion crows.'

Geoffrey saw his earnest expression and knew he was trying to make amends for what he had done.

'Should I say a prayer?' asked Lucian. 'I am a monk, so I know how.'

'Then you should not need to ask whether you should do it,' said Geoffrey. 'Of course you should pray. The church is a good place to start.'

'No,' said Lucian hastily. 'I am not going in there. Not with all those . . . No!'

Geoffrey frowned. There was no way to know exactly when the massacre had occurred, but Lucian had been alone in the woods all night. There was no blood on his habit, but that did not mean he was not involved in some way.

'Have you been here before?' he asked the monk, who was already kneeling.

Lucian opened one eye to look at him. 'You know I have not: I already told you that I hail from Bath and that I have abbey business in Ribe. Why would I ever have been in Werlinges?'

Geoffrey did not know whether to believe him, but it was not the time for an interrogation.

'Take Ulf's body inside the church,' he ordered Bale. 'Then we shall seal the doors. De Laigle may have a better idea about what happened if we leave everything as we found it.'

'Then why seal the doors?' asked Roger. 'He should see them as they are: smashed open.'

'Because he may take some time to arrive, and we do not want dogs and foxes chewing the corpses. Hurry up, Bale! We should aim for the castle as soon as possible.'

'The castle?' echoed Magnus. 'We are going to the abbey.'

'We need to inform de Laigle about this – back the way we came.' And then, Geoffrey thought, de Laigle could deal with the massacre and the rebellion at the same time.

'We will take the horses,' said Roger. 'If we meet the pirates, we can ride straight through them.'

'But those are mine!' exclaimed Magnus indignantly. 'If you take them, what will I ride?'

'No one will take the horses,' said Geoffrey firmly. 'It is possible that the priest did not purchase them for you, and they belong to the village – or to the Crown now all Werlinges is dead. We do not want to be accused of theft, so we will leave them here.'

'In that case, you would do better going to La Batailge,' said Harold. 'And ask Galfridus – the head monk – to send one of his fast messengers to de Laigle.'

'Besides, the tide is coming in and you cannot navigate the marshes alone,' added Magnus. 'And I am not going with you. I am a king, and I have had enough of bogs for a while.'

'They cannot both be king,' muttered Roger under his breath. 'One will be disappointed.'

'Both will be disappointed,' replied Geoffrey. 'However, I am increasingly suspicious of Magnus. I do not like the fact that he says he hid behind the church while we did battle. Not only was it cowardly but it is not true. He was not hiding *behind* the place, but *in* it.'

'Perhaps that is what made him sick – the sight of those poor devils. I cannot condemn him for that, Geoff. Even I find such sights unsettling. And I have seen them all before.'

'His sickness came later, when the battle was over. But when he came out of the chapel, he had something in his hand. I saw him drop it in the well over there.'

'A weapon?' asked Roger.

'No. It was a package – it looked like documents – and he threw it away when he thought we were all preoccupied. And *then* he was sick.'

'Documents? You mean that list of names you saw – tallies of troops?'

'I do not know. It could have been, although I was under the impression it was something he had taken from the church.'

Roger was thoughtful. 'Does he pose a danger to us? Other than the mere fact of our association with him?'

'No,' said Geoffrey. 'I think he will bide his time until he thinks he has a real chance at the throne. But then I think he will kill Harold.'

★    ★    ★

There was a bitter argument when Geoffrey ordered Magnus and Harold to unsaddle the horses. Having met the drunken de Laigle, he knew it would be unwise to remove anything from a village that might later be forfeit to the Crown, even though the Saxons assured him that the nags would be returned. He did not trust them to honour their promises, or de Laigle to appreciate the difference between borrowing and stealing. The reaction of decent men to the massacre would be horror, and he knew from experience that such emotions often led to accusing fingers being pointed at convenient scapegoats. And he had no intention of being hanged because the Saxons were too lazy to walk.

'It is wrong to deprive me of my mount,' muttered Magnus resentfully. 'No one will think I had anything to do with this nasty business.'

'I hope they do not accuse Ulf,' said Harold unhappily. 'He has a reputation for ferocity, but he would never become embroiled in something like this. We must make certain that the blame rests with the sailors. It was hardly Ulf's fault that he happened to be here when they attacked.'

'The evidence is ambiguous,' said Juhel. 'The stains on Ulf's clothes suggest violence on previous occasions, but do not point to him killing the villagers. Of course, he definitely stabbed someone recently, because there was fresh blood on the tip of his sword.'

Geoffrey itched to be away from the village and shaded his eyes against the sun to see whether Ulfrith had finished stabling the horses.

'You have been hurt,' said Juhel, noticing the blood on Geoffrey's side when the knight raised his arm. 'And you are very white. You should rest or you may find yourself weak later. And I doubt we can carry you.'

'That will not be necessary,' said Geoffrey, suspecting the scene in the church was responsible for his pallor. The injury was more an annoyance than an impediment.

'I will give you a paste to smear on it. It contains woundwort, which will close the cut up and bring about clean healing. I always carry some, because I never know when I might need it.'

'If you were a soldier, I would agree,' said Roger, as Juhel removed a pot from his sack. It was a curious thing, with a blue glaze on one side and red on the other. 'But you are not, so you should not need a potion for wounds.'

'It is not a potion, it is a salve, and I carry it for cases like this,' replied Juhel, unruffled. 'Loosen your mail, Sir Geoffrey. I will apply some.'

'You would do better to take a dose of my cure-all,' said Lucian, producing a phial from inside his habit. The pirates had evidently not deprived him of everything. 'Bishop de Villula – a physician as well as a prelate – insists all his monks take some on long journeys. I never leave home without it – it heals pains in the gut, headaches, sniffling noses, aching bones and sore gums.'

'It is useful, then,' remarked Roger dryly.

'Very,' said Lucian, upending the container and swallowing some, before closing his eyes and exhaling slowly. 'I think it may quell tremors after nasty shocks, too, because I feel better already.'

'It cannot do any harm,' said Roger to Geoffrey, 'especially the cure-all, as Lucian has just drunk some himself. Or, if you prefer, I can bind you up.'

Geoffrey had experienced Roger's bandages on previous occasions and knew they were cruelly tight and sometimes did more harm than good, so he opted for Lucian's cure-all. The monk poured a small amount in a cup supplied by Harold, and recommended that it be swallowed in one. Geoffrey gasped at the burning sensation and thought he might be sick.

'What is in it?' he asked suspiciously. His voice was hoarse.

'I have no idea,' replied Lucian airily. 'And I had the same reaction as you when I first tasted it, but you grow to like it in time.'

Magnus stepped forward. 'I shall take some, too. I need a physic if I am to walk to the abbey like a peasant, because I have hurt my arm. However, I want more than you gave Geoffrey.'

'It is a powerful brew,' objected Lucian. 'A sip will be more than enough.'

'Rubbish,' snapped Magnus, jostling Lucian's elbow so more flowed into the beaker. 'There is no point in taking dribbles. Do not be miserly with your monarch. Lord preserve us! It is firewater.'

'I told you so,' said Lucian, watching him gag. 'It is a waste to take more than you need, and I do not have much left. Can you feel it warming your throat, Sir Geoffrey?'

'I can feel it searing my stomach,' said Geoffrey. 'And the taste . . .'

'Drink this,' said Ulfrith, offering Geoffrey his water flask. 'I filled up it this morning.'

The water had a nasty, brackish flavour that made Geoffrey wonder whether it was as fresh as Ulfrith claimed. The squire snatched it away before he had taken more than a mouthful.

'Leave some for me!'

'I will have some, too,' said Magnus, grabbing the flask and taking a tentative sip. He had learned his lesson with the cure-all and was not about to gulp a second time. He took another sip, and was about to go for a third when Ulfrith pulled it away with a scowl.

'It is not wine, lad,' said Roger admonishingly. 'You did not pay for it, so there is no cause to be mean. Now let me smear some of Juhel's grease on you, Geoff. It contains woundwort, and we both know that is a fine substance for cuts.'

'We do not have time,' said Geoffrey, strangely light-headed. It was not an unpleasant feeling – akin to how he felt after a sixth goblet of wine – and with it came a vague sense of well-being. What was an extra moment? Roger was right: woundwort encouraged rapid healing. He hauled up the tunic, and Juhel rubbed the paste into the cut.

'Now me,' said Magnus, raising his sleeve to reveal a gash. 'I was wounded, too.'

'How?' asked Geoffrey. He tried to remember what he had seen: Magnus entering the church and emerging a short while later. Then there was a blank, when the Saxon could have been anywhere. Next, he had slunk to the well and dropped the package down it. And finally he had deposited his breakfast in someone's cabbage patch.

'A pirate came for me,' replied Magnus. 'I am lucky to be alive.'

'How did you escape?' asked Juhel, smearing the oil on the afflicted limb, then bending to wipe his hand on the grass. 'You had no weapon.'

'The villain ran away when I fixed him with an imperial glare,' replied Magnus.

'I do not believe you,' said Roger. 'Why—'

'All right – he ran because all his friends were routed,' snapped Magnus impatiently. 'Can we leave now? I do not want to be here if the pirates come back.'

'Good idea,' said Juhel, heaving the hen coop on his shoulders. 'I have had enough of bloodshed for one day.'

'So have I,' said Geoffrey fervently.


The day wore on as they followed a path that ran through woods, across streams, up and down hills and finally along a wide track that wound through some pretty valleys – Harold had lied: the abbey was considerably farther than the castle would have been. Eventually, Magnus claimed his wound was making him dizzy and demanded that they rest. Geoffrey refused, wanting to reach La Batailge as quickly as possible.

'What you said earlier,' said Roger, walking next to him. 'You really think he will kill Harold?'

'If the unthinkable happens and Henry is ousted, Magnus would be a fool to let other contenders live. Perhaps I spoke wildly, and he does not intend to kill Harold but to lock him away in some remote dungeon. Regardless, the fact is that Magnus will not be a strong ruler and any opposition will be dangerous.'

'Do you believe he fought a pirate?' asked Roger. 'I do not. Ulfrith cornered one, and Bale lumbered after that boy for a long time, but the rest concentrated on us. Still, we know where we stand: not one of our fellow passengers came to our assistance.'

'They would have been killed if they had,' said Geoffrey. He paused to catch his breath at the top of a rise. The sun was baking him inside his armour, and the light-headedness from the cure-all persisted. 'But speaking of Bale, I am worried about him. It is only a matter of time before he kills someone who is innocent.'

'Like Ulf, you mean?'

'No, not like him, because I am not sure he *was* innocent. Juhel was right: there *was* old blood on his clothes, and I wager anything you like it was not his own. He also tried to kill Magnus.'

'Magnus?' exclaimed Roger, glancing behind to see Geoffrey was not the only one finding the rapid walk difficult: the would-be king was wan and held his arm awkwardly. 'How do you know? He did not mention it.'

'No, which is suspicious. Ulf's sword was stained with fresh blood – not much, as there would have been had he killed the villagers, but enough to have scratched Magnus's arm. I suspect he saw an opportunity to rid himself of a rival, but did not reckon with Magnus's speed – he can run very fast. But Ulf was unlucky, because he blundered into Bale.'

'And that was the end of him,' mused Roger. 'Unwittingly, Bale saved Magnus's life.'

Geoffrey nodded. 'So why did Magnus not tell us what had happened? Does he suspect Harold of being complicit in the attack? Or is he just loath to discuss anything about Werlinges? Given that he was sneaking in and out of the church and dumping documents down wells, I suppose his desire for secrecy is understandable.'

They both considered the matter, although neither had a solution.

'Who has the better claim to the throne?' asked Roger eventually. 'Magnus, who is Harold's eldest son, or Harold, who is legitimate? Personally, I would say Magnus. Being a bastard is no bar to kingship – just ask the Conqueror! I am a bastard myself – my father, being a churchman, could scarcely marry my mother – and it has never held *me* back. Marriage is overrated.'

'Is it?' asked Geoffrey absently. They were climbing again, and he was becoming tired.

'Take yours,' Roger went on. 'You only married Hilde because Goodrich needs an heir, but left to your own devices, you could have had a much prettier lass. Perhaps even one you like.'

'I like Hilde,' objected Geoffrey. 'I do not love her, but I am told that is irrelevant. Besides, I was in love once, and that was more than enough.'

'Was she a whore?' Roger was often in love with prostitutes.

'No. She was the loveliest maiden who ever lived, with hair like shimmering gold and eyes so blue they seemed to be part of Heaven.' Geoffrey was not usually poetic, but that particular lady merited such praise.

'I like a blonde wench, too,' agreed Roger. 'As long as she is buxom. There is no point to a woman who is all bones. Of course,

Magnus will need to pick a good one, if he is to rule England. Incidentally, I hope King Henry does not order *you* to look into what happened at Werlinges. He does trust you with that sort of thing.'

'By the time he hears about it, I will be back in Goodrich.' Geoffrey stopped again to catch his breath, blinking to clear the darkness that encroached the edges of his vision.

'We should let Magnus and Harold take the news of Werlinges to La Batailge,' said Roger, watching him. 'You do not look well, and this walking is making it worse. You should rest.'

'No,' said Geoffrey, forcing himself on. 'We do not know what story they will tell, and I do not want to be accused of the crime. I do not trust Magnus.'

'Then we should hurry,' said Roger, grabbing his arm to help him along. 'Besides, there is the abbey now. Can you see the towers?'

Geoffrey nodded and tried to ignore the burning pain in his ribs.

Work had begun at La Batailge within five years of the Norman victory. The Conqueror had wanted it built so the high altar of the church would be in the exact spot where Harold had fallen, but the Benedictines had thought this a bad idea and had selected a site farther west – one that was not plum in the middle of a bog and that had a convenient source of fresh water.

But they had reckoned without William's iron will. He was livid when he heard his instructions had been ignored; he ordered them to tear down what they had finished and start afresh. Funds poured in from the royal treasury, although the place was still not complete fifteen years later.

The church was a handsome building, comprising a nave with seven bays and three chapels radiating off a short apsidal presbytery. There was also an imposing chapter house, and a wooden fence with a lean-to roof marked where the cloister would be. Nearby were large hall-houses with thatched roofs that served as dormitories and refectories. A sturdy palisade punctuated by a stone gatehouse in the north marked off a sizeable tract of land that comprised the actual battlefield.

'Those mounds are the graves of the Normans who fell that day,'

Harold explained, pointing to weathered bumps in the heath. 'Some are marked, as you can see, but most are becoming difficult to identify.'

'What happened to the Saxon dead?' asked Ulfrith, wide-eyed.

'The Bastard did not deign to bury *them*,' replied Magnus with considerable bitterness. 'The local people had to see them laid to rest in ones and twos, wherever they happened to fall.'

'Do you know the abbot, Harold?' asked Geoffrey, not inclined to listen to more Saxon grievances. 'We should speak to him as soon as possible.'

'There is no abbot,' replied Harold. 'The Usurper is currently keeping the office vacant, so he can keep the tithes for himself. It has been empty since Abbot Henry died last year.'

'Then is there a prior?' Geoffrey asked. 'A second-in-command?'

'A simple monk runs the abbey now,' replied Harold. 'A Benedictine named Galfridus de St Carileff. He is a good man, though apt to be greedy.'

'How do you know him?' asked Geoffrey, following the path that led to the stalwart stone gatehouse. He was grateful for Roger's arm, because his head was beginning to ache in time to the throb in his side. Magnus looked little better, and there was a sheen of sweat on his pallid face.

'That is a good question,' said Roger. 'I thought you had been in exile for three decades.'

'I have not been away *all* that time,' replied Harold, smiling at the notion. 'Ulf has been living in this area for the past sixteen years – ever since he was freed on the Bastard's deathbed – and I occasionally come to visit him. Besides, I like it better here than in Ireland.'

'*I* have not been permitted such liberties,' said Magnus resentfully. 'This is the first time *I* have set foot in England since my last invasion more than thirty years ago. Or was it forty? I feel befuddled in my wits.'

'Skirmishes can do that to a man,' said Roger. Geoffrey saw he was about to make a clumsy attempt to force Magnus to admit that he had been attacked by Ulf. 'And so can being savaged by a maniac intent on murder.'

'Then I am grateful it does not happen very often,' Magnus

replied fervently, rubbing his head. 'Lord! There is such an agony in my pate!'

'Of course, King Henry always seemed to know when I was coming,' said Harold ruefully. 'He even sent me a horse once, although it was a poor brute with weak knees. Still, I put on a decent display of gratitude. It does not do to offend a man like Henry.'

'You will offend Henry if you take his throne,' Geoffrey pointed out.

'Yes,' agreed Harold with a twinkling smile. 'But by then it will not matter.'

The gatehouse was a two-storeyed building that housed a portcullis. Arrow slits pierced the walls, and there was a gallery along the top that could be used by lookouts and bowmen. It was more akin to the entrance to a fortress than a monastery: the Saxons had not been exaggerating when they said the Benedictines were unpopular in the region. Traders, pilgrims and visitors formed a queue outside it, waiting patiently to be allowed in.

'This is impressive,' said Lucian appreciatively. 'My Order certainly knows how to build!'

Magnus raked a supercilious gaze across the queue and strutted to the front, shoving more than one person out of the way as he went. 'I have come to see Gerald. Stand aside and let me pass, you miserable wren.'

The guard regarded him askance. 'There is no Gerald here. And, even if there were, *you* would not be allowed in. We try to keep lunatics out.'

'I am your king,' declared Magnus. Geoffrey winced. He had supposed that Magnus would keep his identity quiet until he had gone some way towards arranging his revolt; he had not expected him to announce it to servants.

The guard peered at him. 'You are not Henry. Nor are you the Duke of Normandy, who is the man *I* would like on the throne. England should never have gone to his younger brother.'

'He is reckless,' said Geoffrey to Roger. '*I* would not make wildly treasonous statements to men I do not know.'

He must have spoken louder than he intended, because the guard overheard. 'Actually, I am being prudent. There is a rumour that the Duke is in St Valery at the moment, and you only go there if you intend to cross into England.'

'The Duke means to invade?' asked Geoffrey uneasily.

'He might, although I have heard nothing about him raising an army,' replied the guard. 'Perhaps he will challenge Henry to mortal combat and save the expense. But *you* cannot come in anyway, whoever you are,' he added to Magnus.

'Galfridus will see *me*, though,' said Harold, jostling Magnus aside. He returned the guard's welcoming smile. 'Good afternoon, Jostin. Open up, will you? We have come with terrible news that must be carried to Richer de Laigle as soon as possible.'

The guard continued to beam. 'Lord Harold! I did not see you there. Galfridus will be pleased to see *you*, I am sure. He was saying only yesterday that it has been a great while since you were last here. If you wait a moment, I will summon a novice to take you to him.' He jerked his head at Magnus and lowered his voice. 'Is *he* to be admitted, too?'

'Yes, please, Jostin,' said Harold cheerfully. 'He is my half-brother, believe it or not.'

While they waited for their escort, the guard and Harold began a merry conversation about the service community that was growing up outside the abbey walls. There were smiths to make the nails and braces needed for the buildings, and there were carpenters, masons and stone-cutters and their families. There were also brewers, potters, candle-makers and bakers. Harold seemed to know them all, indicating that he had passed more time in the region than he had led them to believe. Geoffrey wondered what else the smiling Saxon had lied about.

Meanwhile, the waiting people were resentful that Harold's party was to be admitted before them. One threw a small stone that sailed past Magnus. Then a clod of mud struck Roger square in the middle of his forehead with a resounding smack.

'No!' cried Geoffrey, when Roger's sword appeared in his hand and he took several strides towards the culprit, intending to dispense a lesson that was likely to be fatal. Geoffrey staggered when he was suddenly deprived of his support; he had not realized how heavily he had been leaning on his friend. 'Wait!'

The guilty party did not seem at all intimidated by Roger, which meant he was either very brave or a fool. He stood a little straighter under his heavy pack and looked the knight square in the eye. He was a burly fellow with wavy dark hair and a thick beard that had traces of grey. His eyes were dark brown, almost black, and his nose was so round and red that it looked like a plum.

'You do not frighten me,' he declared. 'Crusader knights do not strike down unarmed citizens, so do not bluster and breathe at *me* like an angry bull!'

Roger's advance faltered and he regarded the man in surprise. 'You are very sure of yourself.'

'Roger,' Geoffrey called, painfully aware that most Crusader knights – Roger among them – were more than happy to slaughter unarmed citizens and that the fellow's confidence was sadly misplaced. 'Leave him alone.'

'I have you, sir,' said Bale, grabbing Geoffrey's arm when he began to list heavily to one side.

Geoffrey wondered what was wrong with him. The gash in his side was not serious, and he had suffered a good deal worse in the past without swooning like a virgin.

Harold was next to him. 'Have some garlic,' he suggested solicitously, pressing a ready-peeled clove into the knight's hand. 'It will set you up nicely.'

It was a measure of Geoffrey's muddled wits that the thing was in his mouth before he realized what he was about to crush between his teeth. Repelled, he spat it out.

'What is your name?' Roger was asking the man as he sheathed his sword. 'And how do you know about *Jerosolimitani*? You are right, of course: we are an honourable brotherhood.'

'My name is Breme, and my father told me about the Crusade. He was a skilled archer and fought at the battle here – one of the men the Conqueror said was most invaluable to him.'

'You are the son of a soldier?' asked Roger. 'Why did you not follow in his footsteps?'

Breme shrugged. 'I prefer to be my own master. But that does not make me a lesser man than you, and you should wait your turn. We *all* have important business with the abbey.'

'Not as important as mine,' declared Roger. 'I have come to tell Galfridus about a dreadful massacre. That is more urgent than selling baubles.' He cast a disparaging glance at Breme's pack.

'Pens and ink,' corrected Breme. 'I sell *writing materials*, and my wares are vital to any man who produces deeds and letters. How can your news be more important than providing an abbey with the means to communicate with its King?'

Fortunately, the escort arrived at that point, and the guard ushered Roger's party inside before an argument could break out. The knights, squires, two Saxons, Lucian and Juhel followed the guide to a hall that was filled with benches and tables. It was a pleasant room, and there were goblets and a jug of cool ale set on one table, along with a basket of honey-smeared bread. Gratefully, the travellers ate, drank and sat to rest sore feet. Geoffrey hoped Galfridus would not be long, eager that messengers be sent to de Laigle as soon as possible. His thoughts were interrupted by a high, girlish voice.

'Brother Lucian! You are still alive! What a lovely surprise! It is me, Philippa.'

All Geoffrey wanted to do was deliver his news to Galfridus and lie down. He did not want to make polite conversation with Philippa and Edith, both of whom were sweeping through the hall, clearly intent on enjoying a warm welcome. He felt what little energy he had left drain away at the prospect of their silly, prattling company.

'Lady Philippa!' cried Ulfrith in delight. 'How do you come to be here?'

'More bloody Normans,' muttered Magnus. 'And women, no less, so they can breed others, until they swarm over the Earth like ravenous locals . . . locusts. I am going to sit down. I have no inclination for the empty-headed clatter of benches.'

'The clatter of benches?' asked Juhel, bemused.

'Wenches,' snapped Magnus. 'I said the *chatter of wenches*.'

Philippa ignored the churlish Saxon and fixed her happy grin on the others. Edith was dressed in a splendid cloak made from thick, red wool and adorned with elegant embroidery. By contrast, Philippa wore a simple black gown that looked as if it had been borrowed from a nun. Absently, Geoffrey wondered at the disparity in the standard of clothes they had been lent.

'I came ashore a long way from anyone else,' Lucian was explaining. 'And was obliged to flee inland when the storm struck.

I was lucky I chanced to meet these others, or I might still be
wandering. It is a very dangerous part of the world, with violent
weather, marauding pirates and unfriendly inhabitants. I lost *all*
my gold.'

'Did you?' asked Edith sympathetically. 'Even your cross?'

'Everything,' said Lucian, looking away, as though the loss was
too much to bear. 'I may be able to beg funds from La Batailge,
but I doubt they will be enough to keep me in the style to which
I am accustomed.'

Immediately, Edith removed a ring from her finger and pressed
it into his hand. 'Then you must take this. You can repay me
when you are safely home.'

Lucian accepted it, and there were tears in his eyes when he
spoke. 'You are a dear, kind lady. I shall certainly repay you – and
I shall say masses for your soul every Sunday for a month.'

'I doubt that,' murmured Roger to Geoffrey. 'He would not
know the words.'

'You were very wrong to leave us with Richer de Laigle,' said
Philippa scoldingly, pouting at Geoffrey. 'Our virtue was in grave
peril, and we were in constant fear of seduction.'

'It must have been dreadful,' murmured Juhel. Geoffrey glanced
at him and saw humour gleam in his dark eyes for the first time
since Werlinges.

Edith regarded him coolly. 'I hope you are not being satiric
with us, Master Juhel. That would be shabby after all we have
been through to defend our honour.'

Lucian pressed her hand to his lips. 'God bless you, dear lady.
Juhel meant no offence and, like all of us, has been out of sorts
since we happened across that poor village. I was obliged to pray
for them, and now there is a splinter in my knee.'

'You are a monk,' said Roger, fixing him with an unfriendly
eye. 'You should be used to kneeling and praying. What sort of
abbey is Bath that you are not?'

'A very fine one,' said Lucian coolly. He turned his back on
the knight. 'But, sweet lady, how do *you* come to be here, when
Sir Geoffrey says he left you at Pevenesel?'

'De Laigle is a knave, and his wife is almost as bad,' replied
Edith. 'Still, we managed to learn from a guard that Galfridus de
St Carileff is in charge here. He is my cousin, so it was only right

that I should appeal to *him* for sanctuary. He was delighted to receive me.'

'He was,' agreed Philippa. She turned to Geoffrey with a smile that made Ulfrith bristle. 'I told you I would prefer a nobleman's court to a convent, but I was wrong. De Laigle's household was populated by idle lechers, all far too drunk to know what they were doing. If I am to be ravished, I would at least like my seducer to remember me in the morning.'

'Philippa!' exclaimed Edith. 'You should not say such things! They may believe you.'

Philippa's puzzled expression made it abundantly clear that she had been speaking in earnest.

'I reburied Vitalis in a lovely deep grave,' blurted Ulfrith, eager to join the discussion and be noticed. 'I did it for you, although it was a terrible task.'

'I was going to ask Galfridus to do that, since de Laigle was never sober enough,' said Edith. 'Now you have saved me – and him – the trouble. It was very kind of you, Ulfrith.'

Philippa's eyes filled with tears. 'Poor Vitalis. I miss him so very much.'

'Yes,' said Edith, holding her hand with affectionate sympathy. 'I know you do.'

Her response suggested *she* did not, although Geoffrey could not begin to fathom why he felt the remark was important. The blackness was beginning to seep into his vision again, and he desperately wanted to rest. While Ulfrith beamed his delight at their gratitude, Geoffrey took the squire's flask, hoping water might render him more alert, given that the abbey's ale was a powerful brew. The contents were warm and brackish, but he felt better once he had swallowed it all.

'We both loved him,' said Edith, apparently realizing that she might have said something inappropriate. 'We both made our vows to him in the sight of God, and we kept them well.'

'You both married him at the same time?' asked Juhel, smothering a startled grin.

'I was a year later,' said Philippa, sniffing. 'But in the same church.'

'This is distressing her,' said Edith, watching her friend in concern. 'We must not talk about it any longer. You are as bad as that spy Paisnel with your questions about our home life.'

'Paisnel was not a spy,' said Juhel. The amusement was gone. 'He was a clerk for the Bishop of Ribe.'

'Actually, I am not so sure about that,' said Lucian. 'I have spent a lot of time in that Bishop's court and I never met *or* heard of Paisnel there. If he was a clerk, he was a very junior one.'

'I *knew* he was exaggerating his importance!' exclaimed Philippa. 'Senior clerks' names appear all over the place in legal writs, but Paisnel's never did. And we know that because Vitalis's personal clerk told us so, although the poor man was drowned when *Patrick* went down . . .'

'Paisnel was very familiar with Normandy, though,' said Magnus, rubbing his head. 'So I expect he was a spy for the Duke. He will have heard about *me* and will be eager to capitalize on my imminent victory over his brother the Usurper. But he can hope, because I am not rewarding any Normans – not *ever*.'

'Except me,' said Roger. 'Bishop of Salisbury, remember?'

'Only if you lend us some money,' said Harold pleasantly. 'But you may be right about Paisnel, Magnus. I heard there might be a spy on the ship you were going to take.'

Geoffrey did not know what to think about Paisnel. *Had* he been murdered because he was the Duke's spy? And if Juhel had dispatched him, was it because of Paisnel's dubious occupation or simply an argument between friends? But it was all too complex for him to untangle, and he was grateful it was none of his affair. His attention returned to the discussion.

'But how do you come to be here *before* us, Lady Philippa?' Ulfrith was asking.

Philippa gave a tight smile, evidently wishing someone more important than a squire would show concern for her welfare. 'We left to take refuge with Galfridus the very day you abandoned us with de Laigle. We were surprised when we did not meet you on the highway; our guards said you must have taken the slower and more dangerous route across the marshes.'

Roger shot Magnus a withering look, but the latter merely shrugged. 'We were obliged to go that way to collect the horses. Besides, the pirates might have been watching the other route.'

'Captain Fingar and his crew?' asked Edith. 'We did not see them. But we were escorted by several of de Laigle's knights, all on horseback, and probably represented too formidable a target.'

'Were you much battered by the storm?' asked Ulfrith solicitously. He tried to take Philippa's hand but was immediately pushed away.

'Terribly,' she replied, addressing her comments to Geoffrey. This did not escape Ulfrith's notice, and some of the joy faded from his face. 'But we arrived before it became too violent, and we have been here since Wednesday.'

'Is he?' Geoffrey asked. He sensed that everyone was regarding him oddly, and he struggled to put his question in a form Philippa might understand, wishing his mind was sharper. 'Is Galfridus Edith's cousin?'

'Yes, of course,' replied Edith indignantly. 'And learning of his new post was a great excuse to be away from de Laigle. So now here we all are.'

'But what have *you* been doing?' asked Philippa, reaching out to touch Geoffrey's scratched face. He was aware of Ulfrith's dismay at the gesture, but she had removed her hand before he thought to push it away. 'Did *you* meet Fingar and his men?'

'Yes,' said Lucian. 'They came at us with whirling swords and cudgels. I am no fighting man, so I dropped to my knees and prayed for deliverance. But even so, we were almost killed.'

Philippa released an appalled shriek, a sound that drew admonishing glares from several elderly monks.

Edith wrinkled her nose at them and turned back to Lucian. 'We were very worried about *you*.'

Lucian gave a courtly bow. 'Would you like to hear about my adventures? Then we shall sit over there, where we will not be the object of disapproval by my prudish brethren.'

'How fickle she is,' muttered Roger, as Lucian escorted Edith away. 'She was grabbing at me like a tavern wench not three days ago and now she shifts her amorous attentions to him.'

'You were the one doing the groping, not her,' retorted Geoffrey. 'Will you save me from Philippa, before Ulfrith attacks me again? I do not feel well, and if he tries it, I might not be able to resist the impulse to skewer him.'

Roger tapped the side of his nose. 'Leave it to me, lad. I will put her off you once and for all.'

'Be discreet,' warned Geoffrey. He was seized with the notion that he should not have asked.

'Here,' said Roger loudly, 'did you know that Geoffrey carries a pox caught from whores? His wife says he should abstain from other women until he is cured.'

For a moment, Geoffrey was not sure he had heard correctly, but then he started to laugh. 'You are discretion personified,' he said, though Roger clearly did not see the joke.

'Well,' drawled Juhel, wide-eyed, 'I feel better for knowing that! But Galfridus does not need us all to tell him about Werlinges, so if you will excuse me, I shall go to the guesthouse.'

He bowed and sauntered away.

Philippa's eyes narrowed as she watched Juhel leave the hall. 'He is sly and wicked, and do not forget what I told you, Sir Geoffrey – he is a killer. Moreover, Edith asked him to write her father a letter on the ship, but when she asked one of La Batailge's monks to read it back to her, it was nothing but meaningless symbols. Juhel had deceived her – charged her a penny for a document that was nothing but gibberish.'

'Why did she hire Juhel to write it?' asked Geoffrey. 'Why not Lucian? Or me?'

'Lucian had no pen and parchment to hand and told Juhel to oblige instead – well, he *is* a man who makes his living from the stuff, after all.'

'Do you still have it?' asked Geoffrey, thinking about Paisnel's documents. Did this mean he could *not* read them and had no idea what they contained? Or that he knew they were important, but was unable to decipher them?

'Edith threw it away, but I retrieved it,' said Philippa. 'I am going to show it to her father when he arrives, so he can get the penny back.'

She pulled something from the front of her gown, leaning forward provocatively. By the time his bemused wits had registered that he should look away before Ulfrith noticed, it was too late.

'I was looking at the letter,' he said, before reminding himself that he did not need to justify his actions to a servant. He took another deep breath and wondered why his mind and body were so out of step with each other. Was his injury more serious than he thought? He clumsily took the document Philippa proffered, then turned it this way and that as he attempted to stop it swimming before his eyes.

'Christ's blood!' he muttered to himself, rubbing his eyes hard.

'It looks like a neat hand to me,' said Roger, who would not know a good one from a bad.

'It *is* neat,' agreed Geoffrey. 'But these are random symbols, not letters.' He tried to pass it back, but Philippa moved forward at the same time, and his hand brushed the bare skin of her bosom.

'Stop!' cried Ulfrith, shocked and angry. 'She is a lady, and this is a monastery! Besides, you have a pox. You should not touch her.'

'I am sorry,' said Geoffrey, quite sincere. He realized he was addressing Ulfrith, when he had meant to speak to Philippa. He rubbed his face again. 'Lord! What is wrong with me?'

'Well, the pox, presumably,' said Harold helpfully. 'It is said to make men rave.'

'Keep the letter,' said Philippa, pressing it into Geoffrey's hand. 'Perhaps *you* can demand an explanation and get our penny back.'

'Is it true?' asked Magnus. 'Is there pox among English whores? I shall put an end to *that* when I am king.'

'How?' asked Roger keenly. 'By monitoring brothels? I know a lot about such places and will act as official advisor, if you like.'

'Lord, I am thirsty – it must be all that seawater I swallowed,' said Magnus, drinking more ale. 'But I *shall* appoint you Whoremaster, Sir Roger. It will suit you better than Bishop of Salisbury.'

'No,' said Geoffrey, not wanting Roger to accept posts from an enemy of the King when there were witnesses. 'He will not take it.'

'I might,' said Roger. 'Do not be too eager to refuse tempting offers on my behalf, lad. I may never get another like it.'

'I am sure you will not,' said Harold, laughing. 'I doubt the Usurper has a Whoremaster in his retinue, and I do not think I shall, either.'

Geoffrey's mind was reeling again. He thought he might feel better if he drank more water. 'Did I finish yours, Ulfrith? My own has gone.'

'Your own what?' cried Ulfrith. 'Whore? I assure you *I* do not have any.' He shot Philippa a sanctimonious smile. 'I do not use whores.'

'Water,' said Geoffrey impatiently, wondering whom the lad thought he was fooling. Ulfrith was as willing as the next man to avail himself of the services of ready women.

'It is all gone,' said Ulfrith, upending his flask. 'You finished it all.'

'You have a spare,' said Roger. 'Give it to him.'

With considerable reluctance, Ulfrith withdrew a skin from his bag. 'It is all I have left, so you can only have a sip.'

But Geoffrey wanted more than a sip and was startled when Ulfrith tried to wrest it from him before he was ready.

'There is water aplenty at La Batailge,' said Philippa angrily. 'You are a mean boy, to begrudge a thirsty man a drink when you can easily replenish your supplies. I am ashamed of you!'

Ulfrith's face took on a rigid, sullen look. 'Then let him have it all,' he snapped. 'See if I care.'

But Geoffrey was not interested in a quarrel and pushed the skin back at Ulfrith. It had done nothing to make him better, and he wondered if he was about to be laid low with a fever.

'Brother Galfridus will see you now,' said a monk, appearing just in time to prevent Roger from cuffing Ulfrith for his truculence. 'He will see Harold first, and Lucian after.'

Although the abbot's house was a temporary building, with wooden walls and a thatched roof, it was still grand, as befitted a man who ran a community of fifty monks and a hundred lay-brothers, and who was responsible not only for overseeing the building of a monastery but also for managing its vast estates.

It boasted three floors. The lowest comprised offices, the top was a bedchamber and private chapel, and the middle was a hall dominated by a massive table and a number of benches. There was a fireplace at one end, where a fierce fire threw out a stifling heat. The walls were decorated with religious murals, and the floor was made from polished wood. It smelled of wood smoke, lavender that hung in bunches from the rafters, and cats.

Galfridus was a stooped, anxious man of indeterminate ancestry. His hair was an odd silvery brown, his eyes a bland brown-grey. He had a thin, nervous face, and Geoffrey's first impression was that he was operating at the limits of his abilities – that he had been promoted to a position that did not suit him and was only just managing to cope.

'Good Lord!' he exclaimed as Magnus led the others inside. It was some moments before Geoffrey became aware that Galfridus was not looking at the Saxon, but at him. 'It is Herleve Mappestone's son.'

# Nine

Geoffrey found the heat in the hall oppressive, and sweat began to course down his back. It made his senses reel even more, and he found it a struggle to stay upright. As Galfridus continued to stare, it occurred to him that there was no reason for the monk to have known his mother. Neither she nor Godric had set foot outside Herefordshire once they had received their estates, not even to inspect their lands in Normandy, nor had they made a habit of entertaining churchmen. He studied the man's face, but there was nothing familiar about it.

'Do I detect garlic?' asked Galfridus when Geoffrey did not reply. His expression hardened. 'I thought I told the cooks to go easy on that, and I can smell it from here. Will no one listen to me?'

'I am Magnus. Your king,' declared Magnus, somewhat out of the blue.

'I know,' said Galfridus dryly. 'We have met on previous occasions, if you recall.'

'Where?' asked Geoffrey, his wits not so dimmed that they did not register that Magnus had claimed to have been absent for three decades. 'Here?'

'Here and in the castle at Arundel, when we were guests of Robert de Bellême. Surely you remember, Magnus?'

'Of course,' said Magnus. 'I was telling you *my* name because you did not acknowledge me. You spoke to Geoffrey instead.'

'That is because I am surprised to see *him*, whereas you are expected,' said Galfridus.

Geoffrey struggled to make sense of the information. More than ever he became convinced that there was more to know about Magnus's plans.

Galfridus addressed him again. 'I could tell just by looking that you are Herleve's kin. You have her face and strength of body, although not her fine black eyes. Which son are you? Walter, Stephen or Henry?'

'They are all dead,' replied Roger helpfully. 'This is *Geoffrey*, Godric's youngest son.'

'Henry was the youngest,' said Galfridus. 'He was born here, just after the battle. I know, because I was present.' Geoffrey had a lurid vision of the monk looming over his mother's birthing stool and must have appeared shocked, because Galfridus hastily corrected himself. 'I mean I was with Sir Godric, in the next room.'

'Which battle?' asked Geoffrey numbly. 'The Fall of Jerusalem?'

'The one that took place here, of course,' hissed Roger. 'What is the matter with you?'

'I do not feel well,' Geoffrey whispered back irritably. 'I should never have taken Lucian's cure-all. Is there a statue of a pig on the windowsill?'

'A sheep,' replied Roger. He beamed at Galfridus, who was regarding them uncertainly, bemused by their muttering. 'Geoffrey was just admiring your carving.'

'It is the Lamb of God,' explained Galfridus. 'It is from some benighted kingdom of ice, far to the north, and is made from the tusk of a sea elephant. Exquisite, is it not?'

'It looks like a pig,' said Geoffrey.

Galfridus regarded it with troubled eyes. 'I suppose it does, now you mention it. But we were talking about your brother. Godric never knew, but young Henry's appearance was early, because of the battle. I advised Herleve not to fight, but when I next saw her, she was clad in mail and wielding her axe. Henry was early by three or four weeks – a puny little runt. I did not think he would survive. Did he?'

'Oh, yes,' replied Geoffrey. 'But he died.'

Galfridus blinked, and Geoffrey was vaguely aware of Roger supplying additional details. He went to look more closely at the Lamb of God and picked it up, but it was heavier than he had anticipated and began to slide from his fingers. He moved quickly, so that it landed on the sill rather than the floor, but it did so with a resounding thump. He grinned sheepishly.

'It must have been the sight of so much blood,' said Magnus. 'If I had been pregnant at Hastinges, I would have dropped my brat too.'

Geoffrey stared at him. He knew his own wits were sadly

awry, but he began to wonder whether the others were similarly affected.

'Blood would never upset *her*,' said Galfridus admiringly. 'She fought like a demon. I was just a novice at the time, but the sight of that noble lady waving her axe at the Saxons was a sight to behold.'

'There was blood at Werlinges,' said Geoffrey, recalling that the purpose of the visit was to inform Galfridus about the massacre, so that word could be sent to de Laigle. He rubbed his head and wondered whether it was Lucian's cure-all or Juhel's paste that had adversely affected him. Did one of them contain poison? But why would either want him ill? Was it something to do with Paisnel being a spy? But Geoffrey's reeling wits were wholly incapable of providing answers.

'Werlinges?' asked Galfridus. 'No, that was one of few villages that escaped being laid to waste by the Normans after the battle – the one place in the region where there was *no* blood.'

Geoffrey felt the room begin to tip. His legs were heavy, as if he had walked halfway to Jerusalem, instead of a few miles. And then he knew nothing at all.

When his senses cleared, he was slumped in a chair closer to the fire than was comfortable, and there was a cup of wine in his hand. He had no recollection of how it came to be there, but, judging by the lounging attitudes of Roger and the Saxons, they had been settled at the hearth for some time. He wondered how long he had been insensible, and what Galfridus's reaction had been when he had learned about the massacre. And how had he responded when told that two claimants to the throne intended to take refuge with him? Or was he expecting them? It would certainly explain why they had been so determined to reach La Batailge – they had been meeting a co-conspirator.

'Drink some wine,' advised Galfridus, regarding him sympathetically. 'Or perhaps I should send for a dish of carp. I apologize: I did not appreciate what a shock it must be to learn that your mother had donned armour and taken part in the most violent battle this country has ever known.'

Galfridus's sympathy was misplaced; Geoffrey had known for years that his mother had played a significant role in the fighting.

She had been a fearsome woman, and he would not have been surprised to learn that she had led the first charge herself.

He felt better now he was sitting, but his senses were still oddly unsettled. When he glanced at the floor, it seemed to be undulating, and Galfridus's face was unnaturally elongated. Then a platter was set on his knees.

'Carp,' said Galfridus, as Geoffrey gazed at it in incomprehension. 'The king of fish. It is from my own ponds, and it will settle your stomach.'

Geoffrey had never liked fish, but the pungent smell that emanated from the silvery beast in his lap rendered it less appealing than most. In an attempt to be polite, and because he had not eaten properly in several days, he forced himself to swallow some, but stopped after a few mouthfuls, certain that the round, glazed eye that gazed so balefully at him had winked.

'So, Godric sired more children,' Galfridus was saying. 'Henry was followed by a fourth son and another daughter. And you honoured your family's name by freeing the Holy City from the infidel. Godric must have been very proud.'

'He was,' said Roger, wholly without foundation, since he had never met Godric or heard his views on the Crusade.

A tabby cat, attracted by the smell of fish, rubbed itself around Geoffrey's legs. Trying to be discreet, he slipped a portion off the platter to the floor. The cat sniffed it and stalked away.

'Where is my dog?' he asked.

'Next to you,' said Roger, regarding him with considerable concern.

Geoffrey looked down and saw the animal lying across his feet, making short work of the fish. Its eyes were fixed on the retreating moggy, and he wondered why there had not been a fight.

'Do not worry about your dog,' said Galfridus, reading his thoughts. 'My cat will not harm it here, although you should endeavour to keep them apart outside. Thomas is fierce, and I am told your hound is frightened of chickens.'

There was unease in the dog's eyes, and Geoffrey wondered whether its defeat by Delilah had unnerved it to the point where it was afraid of any encounter. He sighed and gazed out of the window. As he did so, it occurred to him that the pig on the windowsill had grown larger and was blocking out the sun.

'The Lamb of God has been carved with too much wool,' he remarked.

It was Galfridus's turn to look concerned. 'You are not well, Sir Geoffrey, and should visit our infirmary. Brother Aelfwig has excellent leeches.'

'I do not eat leeches,' said Magnus. 'And especially not on a Friday.'

'It is Wednesday,' said Roger, regarding him askance.

'Well, I still will not eat them,' declared Magnus. 'Filthy, vile, wriggling creatures. I would sooner have an egg. Or perhaps a cat.'

'Have you been here long, Father?' asked Roger quickly, to bring the discussion within normal parameters again.

'For about an hour,' replied Galfridus. 'Before that I was in the church.'

'I mean at La Batailge,' said Roger. 'How long have you been abbot?'

'I am not abbot,' said Galfridus resentfully. 'I should be, because I do an abbot's work, but the King does not see fit to appoint me, probably because my mother was Saxon. But I am perfect for this post: the abbey was built to honour the dead of both nations and I have mixed parentage. However, he does not concur, and so I remain simple Galfridus.'

'Is there a monk here called Brother Wardard?' asked Geoffrey. He knew there was a pressing reason to speak to Wardard, but his mind was frustratingly blank as to why. 'He threw a man from the back of a ship and watched him drown.'

'No, that was someone else,' said Roger. He made a pretence of removing the platter, muttering under his breath, so the others would not hear. 'Say no more, Geoff. Lucian's cure-all or Juhel's paste has sent you out of your wits. Galfridus thinks you are a heretic, and Harold believes you are ranting because of the pox.'

Geoffrey struggled to understand. 'I do not have the pox. Why did you tell him I did?'

'Because you told me to be discreet,' hissed Roger obscurely. He offered Geoffrey his goblet. 'Drink some of this.'

Geoffrey complied, but when he looked at Roger again, he was almost indistinguishable from the Lamb of God, black wool framing his face. There was a painful buzzing in his ears. Moreover, the Lamb of God was growling, and he was certain it would attack him if he moved.

Geoffrey was not sure how long the Lamb of God snarled at him, but eventually he became aware that Galfridus was talking about Wardard. Roger's bulk was protecting him from some of the heat from the fire, but he was still bathed in sweat, and the light-headedness persisted.

'Wardard is one of us. He fought in the battle, along with his friend Vitalis, whom I understand you met. Vitalis lived in Normandy and was a vassal of Robert de Bellême, God help him.'

'I was under the impression you liked Bellême,' said Roger. 'You were his guest in Arundel.'

'That was before he was exiled,' explained Galfridus. 'And I only went because I wanted to see his carp ponds.'

'He tried to seduce my sister once,' said Geoffrey, thinking about an incident in Goodrich. Or was he confusing Bellême with someone else? For a short moment, he could not recall what Joan looked like, but then her determined chin and strong face slipped into his mind. Like their mother, she was a formidable woman.

'Juhel is one of his spies,' said Magnus resentfully. 'He is here to gather information, so that Bellême can invade. I do not know whether to let him do it or not. You see, if Bellême attacks the Usurper, it will squander the Usurper's resources. But Bellême might win, and I do not like the notion of *him* being king. He will be worse than the Usurper.'

'Bellême offered to help me, should I ever mount an armed invasion,' said Harold chattily. 'But he would want too many estates and titles, and it would be difficult to rule a vassal like him. So I decided to reject his kind proposal – politely, of course. I would not want to annoy him.'

'I am sorry to hear Vitalis is dead,' said Galfridus to no one in particular. He turned to Geoffrey, clearly bracing himself for an answer he might not understand. 'Why do you ask about Wardard? Did your father ask you to pass his respects to an old comrade before he died?'

'Not exactly,' said Harold, answering when Geoffrey did not.

'He has questions of a personal nature that he would like to ask Wardard.'

In a sudden flash, Geoffrey remembered Vitalis's accusations. He did not understand why he had been so unsettled by them – he had neither respected nor liked Godric, but, for all his faults, Godric had always been the first to ride at enemies near his estates. In fact, he had always been *too* eager to fight, and Geoffrey had often wished he would allow longer for negotiations.

'Vitalis said Godric ran away from Hastinges and hid until it was over,' said Roger. 'And he told Geoff to ask Brother Wardard.'

Galfridus raised his eyebrows. 'Godric a coward? I doubt it! Herleve was very fussy about her men. But ask him anyway – he likes to talk about the battle, even though he took holy orders to atone for the lives he took that day. As warriors, you two did the right thing by undertaking a Crusade – now all your sins have been expiated and your souls are spotless before God.'

'Yes,' agreed Roger proudly. 'It is always good to have a spotless soul.'

'I do not think it was an open-ended expiation, though,' warned Galfridus. 'You cannot continue killing now you are home.'

Roger shrugged. 'I usually pay a monk to recite prayers on my behalf, so *I* shall have no problems come Judgement Day. The arrangement suits everyone, because I do not have time to say them myself, and monks are always pleased to have the money.'

'Does King Henry know you welcome Saxon rebels in your abbey?' asked Geoffrey. His wits seemed to be returning at last.

Galfridus seemed surprised by the question. 'Of course. I often provide hospitality for members of King Harold's family: Harold, Ulf, Magnus, Edith of the Swan Neck. Why should I not?'

'We will speak to Wardard and then leave,' said Geoffrey, trying to stand. He found his legs were unequal to the task and he sank back down.

'You cannot travel so soon after learning the truth about your mother,' said Galfridus kindly. 'Stay a few days – we have a clean, comfortable hospital, and our food is plentiful and wholesome.'

'No,' said Geoffrey. 'King Henry is likely to arrive soon, and I do not want to meet the sly—'

'Why would Henry come here?' interrupted Galfridus, startled.

'To deal with those claiming his throne, for a start,' said Roger, nodding at Magnus and Harold. 'He is not a man to let a challenge go unanswered.'

Galfridus gazed at Magnus. 'You plan to tell him you are here? That is foolish! He does not mind Harold, but he does not like you at all. And although he turns a blind eye to the occasional visit, to flaunt yourself is asking for trouble.'

'The time for skulking in Flanders is over,' said Magnus grandly. 'I have come to claim my rightful inheritance: the land of my Saxon fathers. And mothers.'

'That is my purpose also,' said Harold. 'I am King Harold's legitimate heir, and England belongs to me.'

Galfridus looked from one to the other in consternation. 'Well, you cannot both be king.'

'Our people will choose which of us they want,' said Magnus. 'But for now we stand united – Saxon right against Norman might.'

'I see,' said Galfridus warily. 'What support do you have? Where is your army?'

'We do not have one yet,' admitted Harold. 'But when they hear we are here, our people will rise up from their ploughs and spades and rally to our cause. By Christmas, there will not be a Norman left in England.'

A waddling infirmarian called Brother Aelfwig led Geoffrey and Roger to the House of Pilgrims, or hospital, which adjoined the abbey gate, while the Saxons were escorted to separate lodgings that overlooked the cloisters. The hospital was a stone building that formed part of the outer wall and comprised a single room with a high ceiling and a beaten earth floor. There were no windows in the wall that bordered the road, but there were enormous ones in the wall that faced the abbey, so that pilgrims could see the church.

It was devoid of guests when Aelfwig opened its door, although an empty cage at the foot of one bed indicated Juhel had already claimed a berth. There were eight beds, each furnished with a chest at its foot for guests' belongings, and two neatly folded blankets. Geoffrey's dog made a quick circuit, sniffing each cot before selecting the only one in the shade. Bale and Ulfrith, the latter dragged from the chamber where Philippa and Edith were still chatting to Lucian, did as they had been taught and assessed the place's defensibility – the quality of the window-shutters and the strength of the bar that would seal the door at night.

Aelfwig was a rotund man with short legs and a kindly face. He recited the abbey's rules for hospital guests – mostly that women were not allowed in – and then extended an invitation for them to attend any of the monks' services, day or night.

'The bell will be chiming for vespers soon.' He peered at Geoffrey. 'But you are not well. Perhaps you should come to my infirmary. It is a pleasant place, near the herb garden, and you hardly notice the smell of the sewers once you are used to them.'

Geoffrey's previous experiences in such places had taught him that they were full of old men waiting to die. He shook his head, only to find that the movement made his senses swim again.

'I would rather stay here,' he said, beginning to remove his armour. He was not sure whether he was relieved to be rid of its weight or uneasy to be stripped of his protection.

Aelfwig sighed disapprovingly. 'Very well, but I shall bring you one of my special tinctures made from herbs of Saturn. It will ease your head and promote healing sleep.'

'Where is Brother Lucian?' asked Roger when Aelfwig returned with a large pottery flask and a beaker. 'I do not want to share a chamber with him.'

'He is far too important to stay here,' said Aelfwig, pouring a measure of his tincture into the cup. 'He is a close friend of Bishop de Villula – his bursar, no less – and hails from a very wealthy family. He will reside with Galfridus, who will do all he can to create a good impression. It is always wise to flatter the associates of powerful bishops.'

Geoffrey was feeling a good deal better now he had divested himself of his mail and was cooling down, and he suspected the strange effects of whatever had been in Juhel's balm or Lucian's cure-all were wearing off at last.

Aelfwig handed him the goblet. 'This is mostly a wine of raspberries, with a little woundwort, henbane and comfrey, all herbs of Saturn that have a soothing effect.'

'Henbane?' asked Geoffrey suspiciously. 'That is poisonous.'

'Not in small quantities.' Aelfwig retrieved the cup and drank some himself. 'See? It is perfectly harmless, although I may have trouble staying awake during vespers now. Do not be awkward – I am a highly respected *medicus* in these parts.'

'Do not drink it all,' advised Ulfrith worriedly when he saw Geoffrey prepare to drain the cup. 'Not after Lucian's cure-all and Juhel's salve.'

'You have taken other medicines?' asked Aelfwig in alarm. 'You should have said. What?'

'Something in Lucian's potion made him ill,' said Ulfrith, predictable in his choice of culprit. He lowered his voice to add in a spiteful hiss, 'Poison.'

'What?' cried Bale, outraged. 'Lucian tried to kill you? I will slit his throat!'

Aelfwig jerked away in horror when he saw a dagger appear in Bale's hand.

'Put it away, Bale,' said Geoffrey tiredly. 'Lucian drank some himself and said it came from his Bishop. Magnus swallowed a hefty dose, too – more than I did – and he is well enough.'

'I am not so sure about that,' said Roger thoughtfully. 'Both you and Magnus said some very odd things when we were with Galfridus. I think there *was* something bad in Lucian's cure-all. Or in Juhel's salve. Magnus did avail himself of both, like you. So, we have two suspects: the villainous monk and the secretive Juhel.'

Aelfwig inspected Geoffrey's scratched side. 'There is no sign of poison here, although the wound is inflamed, probably from chafing under your armour.'

'Then it was the cure-all that harmed him?' asked Ulfrith hopefully. 'Lucian is the villain?'

'If Lucian drank this potion himself, and it came from Bishop de Villula, I doubt it contained anything untoward,' replied the herbalist. 'And your master seems lucid enough now, so whatever it was has worked itself out. Still, this should warn you all not to accept medicines from people you do not know.'

Geoffrey sipped the tonic tentatively, recalling the unpleasant burning that had accompanied Lucian's brew that morning. By contrast, Aelfwig's concoction tasted sweet, like summer fruit.

'Do not drink any more, sir,' begged Ulfrith. 'My grandmother was good with healing herbs and she once told me that good medicines can turn bad when mixed.'

'She was very wise,' said Aelfwig. 'But I suppose I had better ask Juhel what his salve contains. Who knows what enthusiastic amateurs add to their poultices?'

Ulfrith smiled fondly. 'She was a witch and knew all about herbs and plants.'

Geoffrey's dog suddenly abandoned the bed and slunk to the far end of the hall, where it hid behind a chest. Geoffrey turned to see that Juhel had arrived, chicken under his arm.

'Aha!' said Aelfwig. 'Pray, sir, what toxin did you employ on Sir Geoffrey and Magnus?'

'Toxin?' asked Juhel, startled.

'There was something nasty in your balm,' said Bale. His face took on a sly expression. 'Would you care to take a walk with me? Outside the abbey's grounds?'

Juhel raised his hands to indicate he was innocent, then rummaged in his pack to produce the curious half-red, half-blue pot. 'There is nothing nasty in my salve, I assure you – I might be obliged to use it on myself one day! Besides, why would I harm Geoffrey or Magnus?'

Aelfwig took the proffered pot and sniffed it. 'All I can smell is hog's grease.'

'To bind the wound,' explained Juhel, taking it back. 'It also contains woundwort and a few crushed daisy leaves. If Geoffrey has been poisoned, it is none of my doing.'

'Well, he would say that,' muttered Bale in Geoffrey's ear. 'Aelfwig might be the best herbalist in the world, but even *he* cannot detect odourless poisons.'

Geoffrey closed his eyes once Juhel had left. The parchmenter had requested to be housed elsewhere, claiming stiffly that he would be open to further accusations if he remained in the same chamber as his alleged victim, and, in the interests of harmony, Aelfwig agreed. In his agitation at being accused of such an unpleasant crime, Juhel had neglected to take his travelling bag with him, and Bale, from sheer spite, hid it inside a chest. Intrigued by visitors who had seen the Holy Land, Aelfwig lingered to chat.

'Do many people come here for pilgrimages?' Roger asked conversationally.

'Hundreds. First, there were veterans of the battle, who came to pray for their comrades, but these have grown fewer with the passing years. Now it is mostly sons and daughters, who petition for their fathers' souls.'

'Saxons or Normans?' asked Ulfrith.

'Both,' replied Aelfwig. 'We do not care about ancestry here and will pray for anyone who lost his life. The short, fat man with the yellow hair who arrived with you is Saxon – a son of King Harold himself. His twin brother is a terribly violent man, although he has not been here for several years – not since the altar incident. But we all like Harold.'

'The altar incident?' probed Roger curiously.

'The high altar stands on the exact spot where King Harold died,' explained the monk. 'But Ulf, wild with drink, claimed it was in the wrong place – although he could not have known, since he was not at the battle. Anyway, he tried to move it with an axe.'

'He is dead,' said Bale without a flicker of remorse.

'Then I hope he found peace before he died,' said Aelfwig sadly. 'His father's fate turned him bitter and cruel, and he was not popular among his fellow Saxons. I am Saxon myself, and—'

'What about Magnus?' interrupted Roger. 'Do folk like him?'

'Not really. He is arrogant and silly. The only man strong enough to lead a Saxon uprising was Ulf. We would sooner have Harold, but a king cannot afford to be nice. Just look at King Henry. No one could ever accuse *him* of being nice, yet how well he governs the country!'

'Magnus comes here a lot?' asked Ulfrith. 'He told us he had not been for years.'

'He often drops in on his travels,' said Aelfwig. 'He must have lost his way in the marshes and pretended he had not been here in order not to look foolish.'

Aelfwig left eventually, and Geoffrey heard a rasping sound that he knew was Roger rubbing his hand across his beard. 'Damn!' he said. 'We forgot to mention the massacre at Werlinges, and *that* was the main reason for us coming.'

Geoffrey sat up, his head swimming. 'You *forgot*?'

'It was *your* fault,' Roger flashed back. 'You distracted me when you kept passing out. But do not worry – I will do it now.'

'God's teeth!' muttered Geoffrey, unimpressed. He tried to stand, not sure Roger could be trusted, but his side gave such a monstrous twinge that he was forced to lie back down.

'Do not fret,' said Roger. 'I will watch what I say. You think me a fool, but I can be as discreet as the next man.'

After the big knight had gone, Geoffrey watched Bale and Ulfrith sit together near the window and realized they had been left to keep guard. It was a kindly thought, but they were noisy. When Ulfrith began a long list of Philippa's virtues, Geoffrey ordered them both outside and waited for Roger's return.

Closing his eyes, he thought about the sickness that assailed him – a man who was rarely ill and possessed the capacity to carry on through all but the most serious wounds. He was certain some noxious substance *had* been fed to him. Was it deliberate? And if so, was he or Magnus the intended victim? He thought for a while and concluded it was not Magnus. The Saxon had demanded the medicines – no one had forced him to take them.

So, was it Juhel, playing some game Geoffrey did not understand that involved killing friends and dropping them overboard in order to claim their documents? Or was it Lucian, an unconvincing monk, who might be using a religious habit to disguise his real business? Geoffrey was not sure why either would consider him a threat. Was it because he was more able than the others and could read? Or was Magnus responsible, taking a dose of the medicines himself to allay suspicion? He had acted oddly at Werlinges, disappearing inside the church and dropping the package down the well. Was that why Ulf had tried to kill him?

It occurred to Geoffrey that documents were a peculiarly recurring theme. Juhel had taken some from Paisnel; Magnus had thrown some down a well; Juhel had 'written' a letter for Edith. Geoffrey pulled the thing from his tunic and looked at it again, but his vision was blurred, and he knew he would be sick if he continued. He put it away, wondering if it was significant.

The headache was beginning to return, so he lay flat and watched the ceiling billow and twist, the beams closing together, then drifting apart again. Eventually, he dozed, aware of buzzing voices around him, some familiar and some not. Then there was silence, and he slept more deeply. But it did not seem many moments before he was awake again, jolted into consciousness by some innate, soldierly sense that something was amiss. He became aware of someone looming over him and opened his eyes to stare into the cold, furious face of Fingar.

Geoffrey's fingers closed around his dagger even as his feverish mind grappled with Fingar having gained access to the abbey. Fingar looked disreputable, and the knight had imagined a monastery would be more particular about whom it admitted. He brought the blade up quickly, so it jabbed into Fingar's throat. He had not intended to stab him, but his movements were unco-ordinated and his hand had not gone quite where he had intended. Fingar yelped and jerked away.

'There is no need for that!' The pirate's expression was one of disgust, as he rubbed the nick. 'I should have known no good would come from mercy.'

'Mercy?' asked Geoffrey uncertainly, feeling Fingar take the dagger from his hand and alarmed that he was unable to stop him.

'You are sick – poisoned, I am told. So I decided, being in sacred confines, I would not kill you. But then I am stabbed for my pains.'

'Sorry,' said Geoffrey. He wondered why he had apologized; Fingar did not merit it.

'Then you can make amends by telling me what you did with my gold.'

'I do not have it.'

'I know,' said Fingar. 'I have searched your belongings. But tell me what Roger did with it, and I shall leave you in peace.'

'I have no idea,' said Geoffrey tiredly.

Fingar snorted his disdain. 'You will tell me eventually, so you may as well do it now and save yourself some discomfort.'

'I really have no idea.' The pain in Geoffrey's side, which had been a niggle, now came in a great wave, and the pounding in his head was almost blinding. He had been wounded many times before, sometimes seriously, but could not remember ever feeling so wretched.

Fingar leaned closer. 'Where is Sir Roger now?'

'Gone to tell Galfridus about the villagers you murdered.'

'That was not our doing.' Fingar sounded offended. '*We* do

not make war on paupers. You must look to the flaxen-haired fellow your squire killed for that.'

'Ulf did not do it alone.' Geoffrey heard his voice losing its strength. 'He had help.'

'Not from us,' said Fingar firmly. 'We do not become embroiled in politics.'

'Politics?'

'Squabbles for thrones – it is not for us. And it would not be for you, either, if you had any sense.'

'Are you talking about Magnus and Harold?'

'I do not know any Harold, but Magnus is a good example. I overheard him on my ship, talking to his servant. He thinks he is the king of England and is gathering an army.'

'He has no army,' said Geoffrey tiredly. 'It is all dreams.'

'Yes and no. He may not have organized troops, but there are men who will give their lives for his cause. *That* is what happened at Werlinges. His Saxon cronies.'

Geoffrey struggled to understand. 'You saw Saxons kill those people?'

Fingar looked furtive. 'Not exactly. But they were in Werlinges when we reached it. We could see from the villagers' faces that they were not welcome, but we did not want a fight, so we left. When we returned, we found the people dead. It was horrible.'

'I thought you would be used to it. You *are* a pirate.'

'Yes, but we do not kill women and children. Donan watched you after you had routed him and he says you were none too impressed, either.'

'He did not *rout* us,' said a loud voice. 'I told you: we were outnumbered, so we withdrew.'

Geoffrey tried to see who was speaking, but could not. The man was lying, but Geoffrey did not blame him for declining to tell Fingar that a dozen sailors had failed to defeat two knights.

'. . . even that was fake,' someone was saying. 'I thought it was real gold, but it was base metal, and the purse was all but empty.'

'I was always wary of him,' said Fingar. 'Too pleased with himself by half.'

'Juhel?' asked Geoffrey. He realized he must have lost consciousness and missed part of the conversation, because it seemed to have moved on without him.

'No, "Brother" Lucian, who wore a cross of fake gold,' someone replied.

'Enough chatter,' snapped Fingar, glancing towards the door. He grabbed Geoffrey by the front of his shirt. 'I will let you live if you help me find my money, although it goes against the grain. You are lucky: being poisoned and lying on holy ground makes you doubly eligible for mercy.'

'Then leave me alone,' said Geoffrey weakly, 'because I cannot help you.'

'Will not, more like,' said the second speaker, and Geoffrey saw Donan's pinched features become a large rat. 'Make him tell us or *I* will kill him.'

'You will not,' said Fingar with considerable force. 'Do you want more storms to batter us at sea because you sinned on holy ground? Do you want the saints hurling lightning at us, as they did after we let that man drown?'

'What man?' Geoffrey mumbled.

'Donan saw Paisnel in the water, but kept on course.' Fingar scowled. 'It is wicked to leave a man to drown, and he should not have done it. When I have my gold, I will pay for masses for his soul, to set matters right.'

'But the day after Paisnel's disappearance, you said you last saw him playing dice with Juhel,' said Geoffrey, fighting to keep his eyes open.

'Like I said, we do not become involved in politics. I knew from the blood on the deck the next day that Paisnel had fought someone, but it was not our affair. However, leaving him to die at sea – that is something else altogether.'

'Who threw him overboard?' asked Geoffrey, wondering if they would confirm Philippa's tale.

'Donan did not see. I assumed it was Juhel, but Donan thinks it was Philippa.'

'Of course it was her,' argued the rat. 'I saw her sneaking around. She had a knife, too.'

'How could she have lifted a man over the rail?' snapped Fingar. 'She is not strong enough. It was Juhel, I tell you. I saw him rifling through Paisnel's bag, too. He took what he wanted and tossed the rest overboard. Why would he have done that, unless he was the killer?'

'He *can* write,' acknowledged the rat, making it sound sinister. 'But Philippa killed Paisnel.'

'Regardless, we should not have let him drown,' said Fingar.

'The gold,' said Donan, who had turned into a weasel. 'We should think of the gold.'

'Sir Roger has it,' said Fingar. 'So we must wait for his return. Move behind the door, and be ready when he comes in, but do not kill him until I say so.'

'I will make him give it back,' said Geoffrey desperately. 'No killing.'

'You will not succeed,' said Fingar. 'When a man steals a chest of gold, he does not give it up easily, and your friend is greedy. Besides, you are in no condition to force him.'

'It was a few coins, not a chest.' Geoffrey flinched as the ceiling began to collapse. 'Look out!'

Fingar glanced upwards with a puzzled expression. 'I would not go to all this trouble for a few coins. He took our entire fortune.'

'I do not believe you.' The ceiling was back in its rightful place.

'Give him more of that medicine,' recommended the weasel. 'He is out of his wits.'

Fingar took a flask and poured something into a cup. He sniffed it and grimaced. 'No wonder he is ailing! What he needs is clean water.'

There was gurgling as liquid was poured. Geoffrey turned away when Fingar brought the cup to his lips, but the man was too strong.

'More,' said Fingar, refilling it. 'Water is good for fevers.'

'Look at this,' said the weasel, holding something in the air. It glittered, and Geoffrey saw it was a pendant, probably gold.

'Is it Roger's?' asked Fingar. He poked Geoffrey to make him answer. The finger grew longer until it appeared to be touching a sheep that was standing at the far end of the room.

'How did you do that?' Geoffrey asked, awed. 'Magic?'

'He is rambling again,' said the weasel in disgust. He shoved something in Geoffrey's face. 'What do these say? I found them with the pendant, and I know you can read.'

Geoffrey tried to push him away. 'That sheep – it must be the Lamb of God.'

'These are holy visions,' said one of the sailors uneasily.

'Where is my dog?' asked Geoffrey. 'I do not want it chasing the Lamb.'

'We ate him,' replied Fingar. 'Roasted with mint. Hush! I hear footsteps.'

'How did you find us?' asked Geoffrey, desperately trying to speak loudly to warn Roger, but his voice was little more than a whisper.

'A fisherman told us you were heading this way, and we just climbed over the wall. There is a gatehouse, but no guards anywhere else. It was easy!'

There was a creak outside. Geoffrey braced himself, then, as the door began to open, he summoned the last of his strength to yell. 'It is a trap! Fingar is—'

A hand clamped over his mouth, and, struggling to breathe, Geoffrey's world went black.

When he opened his eyes again, the chamber was dim, although there was a candle burning next to the bed. It cast an orange glow and there were monstrous shadows playing on the walls. Someone was still looming over him, and his fingers fumbled for his dagger, but it was not there.

'What are you doing?' came Roger's peevish voice. 'Hoping to stab me?'

'Where is Fingar? He was here . . .'

'Who is Fingar?' asked a voice Geoffrey did not recognize.

'I do not know,' replied Roger shiftily.

Geoffrey struggled to understand what had happened, but the pain in his side was draining his strength, and he lapsed into unconsciousness again. When he next awoke, there was daylight flooding through the windows. A dull clinking was coming from one side. He turned his head and caught the gleam of metal. Roger was counting his ill-gotten gains – and there was a lot more than the handful he had shown Geoffrey in the marshes. Fingar had been telling the truth.

'Where is Fingar?' he asked. 'Did you kill him?'

Roger stuffed the gold out of sight. 'You have been raving about Fingar for two days now,' he said testily. 'He is not here and never has been.'

'He was,' objected Geoffrey, trying to sit up. His senses reeled, so he lay back down. 'He was going to ambush you for his gold.'

'*My* gold,' corrected Roger. 'But he cannot have it, because I have given most of it to the abbey. There have been so many tales about your father – first a paragon of virtue, then a traitor; a bold knight, then a coward – that I asked the monks to pray for the truth.'

'You spent your gold to help me?' asked Geoffrey, touched.

'Masses of it. Then Aelfwig said you would not last the night, so I was obliged to buy candles to place on King Harold's altar, too. I asked him to put in a word for a fellow soldier.'

'I doubt Harold would do much to save a Norman. He is probably still irked over the battle.'

'You are wrong: you fell into a natural sleep shortly after Brother Wardard lit them. Then there was Breme. He was more help than that useless herbalist.'

'Breme?'

'Me,' said the voice Geoffrey had heard earlier. It was the peddler with whom Roger had argued. 'I know a thing or two about medicine. I made a charm, which is still around your neck.'

Geoffrey felt the cord that held a small bundle at his throat, then sat up slowly. No dizziness this time. 'Thank you.'

'It is a pleasure – especially as Sir Roger has been so generous.' He saluted the big knight and left, closing the door behind him.

'I have cost you a great deal of money,' said Geoffrey ruefully. 'How shall I ever repay it?'

Roger waved a dismissive hand. 'You can name your firstborn after me. Roger Mappestone has a fine ring to it.'

'Not if it is a girl. But the bells are ringing. Is it Sunday?'

Roger nodded. 'And the monks have put so many flowers in the church that it smells like a brothel. Remember Abdul's Pleasure Palace in Jerusalem? Those were the days! We knew our enemies then and did not have to look over our shoulders all the time. Not like now.'

'What do you mean?'

'Bale, Ulfrith and I have been taking turns to watch you, but Bale fell asleep once and only woke when someone was standing over you with a knife. He reacted with commendable speed and had his blade in the fellow's throat before he could act, but it was a close call.'

Geoffrey stared at him. 'Someone tried to kill me? Who?'

'No one knows. His corpse is in the charnel house.'

'It must have been one of Fingar's men,' said Geoffrey. 'He laid an ambush for you, and that is the last thing I remember.'

'But you have not been left alone,' said Roger. 'You must have seen the fellow with the dagger and assumed it was Fingar in your delirium. It is not a pirate in the charnel house.'

Geoffrey rubbed his head, but the memories were too jumbled to make sense. 'Donan took a gold medallion. Has anyone lost one?'

'I thought Magnus had one on the ship, but he says I am mistaken. And I have no idea what Juhel has — that damned chicken warns him every time I go near his bag.'

'What about Lucian? Was his pectoral cross real gold or imitation?'

'It looked real to me. But you have been dreaming these conversations, Geoff lad. I can understand it: I dream about gold myself.'

Geoffrey remembered something else. 'They ate my dog.'

Roger stared at him. 'I have not seen it for a day or two, but it will show up when it is hungry.'

'He does not wander away for days on end,' said Geoffrey, worried. 'I should find him.'

Roger shook his head. 'Not today. Rest and we will talk again later.' He pulled the blanket up to Geoffrey's chin with a powerful yank.

'But I need answers,' said Geoffrey. 'What happened about Werlinges?'

'I told Galfridus the facts with no embellishment or supposition — you would have been proud. He said the conjunction of pirates and massacre was damning but not conclusive, and he sent for young de Laigle, who arrived the next day. De Laigle listened to our story, then rode off to Werlinges, taking Bale with him to act as a guide.'

'What did he deduce?'

'Nothing, because he did not even try to investigate. He ordered half his men to loot the houses and the rest to set the church alight, to burn the corpses. Bale was alarmed that the matter was not going to be properly explored, and he tried to look for clues before the flames took hold.'

Geoffrey was anxious. 'He should not have done! De Laigle might have misunderstood what he was doing; he may blame us for the massacre, just to be credited with finding a solution.'

'Bale was careful. But I understand de Laigle's reluctance to take time over such a matter: ships seen at sea have the whole coast buzzing with rumours.'

'An invasion by the Duke of Normandy?'

'Possibly, although people are more afraid that it might be Bellême. De Laigle is terrified and refuses to be outside his stronghold now.'

'Did Bale discover anything?' Geoffrey was uneasy, not wishing to imagine what the ghoulish squire had done unsupervised.

'He can tell you himself. But there is something else you should know.' Roger hesitated before continuing. 'Edith is dead. She was strangled with red ribbon.'

# Ten

Geoffrey refused to drink anything except the fresh water Bale fetched from the well, and he ate only what Roger brought from the communal pans in the refectory. At first, Roger thought him overly suspicious, but Geoffrey made a rapid recovery once he had made his stand against medicines and, by the following day, was well enough to get up.

'I told you,' said Ulfrith. 'I said you would grow well again once you stopped taking Aelfwig's tonics.'

Geoffrey could not remember. 'Did you?'

Ulfrith nodded. 'I said water was best, but he said I did not know what I was talking about.'

Geoffrey frowned. Had it been Ulfrith who had made him drink water in the depths of his illness, and his deluded mind had seen Fingar? His recollection of everything after Werlinges was blurred, and he was unable to separate fact from fiction.

That evening, Harold poked an enquiring head around the door. 'Galfridus said you were better,' he said, smiling. 'But I wanted to see for myself. Someone tried to kill you while you slept, I hear. Who was it?'

'No one knows,' said Roger. 'But Bale stopped him.'

Geoffrey wondered why anyone should mean him harm. Was it because he had asked questions about the deaths of Vitalis and Paisnel, and someone was afraid he was heading towards a solution? Or had Fingar added some toxic substance to one of the medicines Geoffrey had swallowed, as revenge for the theft of his money?

Harold peeled a clove of garlic, struggling to hold something under his arm at the same time. It was a musical instrument, carefully wrapped in cloth. He offered Geoffrey the clove.

'It is almost my last one,' he said pensively. 'But I am willing to sacrifice it for a friend.'

'We are friends?' The question was out before Geoffrey could stop it.

Harold took no offence and merely grinned merrily. 'I would like to think our experiences in the marshes and at Werlinges have forged a bond between us. You are patient with Magnus, who is not the easiest of men, and you ordered my brother's poor body put in the chapel when others would have left him for the crows.'

'But my squire was the one who killed him.' Geoffrey winced. Clearly, he was not quite back to normal, because that was hardly something to confess to a grieving brother.

'Bale has already told me,' said Harold sadly. 'It happened during the heat of the battle, and if anyone is to blame, it is me – I should have looked for him the moment we arrived at Werlinges and kept him out of harm's way. He said he might bring the horses there himself, so . . .' He looked out of the window, tears in his eyes. 'But what is done is done, and there is no point in dwelling on what might have been.'

Geoffrey did not know what to say, so they sat in silence for a while. Then the door opened, and Ulfrith and Bale joined them.

'Is that a horn?' asked Bale, pointing eagerly at Harold's bundle. 'I have not heard a horn for years. Will you play it for us, sir?'

'I would, but it is a poor instrument,' said Harold, pulling off its wrappings. 'I do not think it will sound very nice. Galfridus lent it to me.'

'We are not fussy,' said Roger. 'It cannot be worse than that stringed affair Lucian used to seduce Edith on *Patrick*, which sounded like cats being throttled.'

'Have you heard anything else about Edith's death?' asked Geoffrey.

'Just that she was killed some time between Friday night and Saturday morning,' supplied Harold. 'She retired to bed, and Philippa found her the next morning.'

'Philippa cries all the time,' added Ulfrith from the window. 'They were close, like sisters.'

'Were they sleeping in different rooms?' asked Geoffrey.

Roger shot a glance towards Ulfrith and lowered his voice, while Bale was distracting Harold by inspecting the horn. 'They shared, but Philippa was out that particular night.'

'Out?' asked Geoffrey. He saw Roger's sheepish expression and raised his eyebrows. 'With you? God's teeth, man! Take care Ulfrith does not find out. His sulk will know no limits.'

'I left him a clear field, but he failed to take advantage of it,' said Roger defensively. 'Besides, she *offered* herself to me. But nothing happened anyway. We sat at the high altar in the church, and all she wanted to do was play dice.'

'Dice?' asked Geoffrey, not sure that a hot-blooded knight like Roger would have spent his time gaming when there had been promises of a different nature in the offing.

Roger sighed ruefully. 'She declined to lie with me, and I am not a man for rape. We passed the night chastely, although I doubt Ulfrith will believe it. I would much rather have had Edith, if you want the truth – Philippa is a bit skinny for my taste – but Philippa looked at me prettily, and it seemed a shame to disappoint her. She asked about my gold.'

'Did it occur to you that she might be looking for a wealthy husband now Vitalis is dead? And so was Edith probably, hence her friendship with Lucian.'

'Yes, I had worked that out, thank you,' said Roger dryly. 'And, personally, I believe it was Lucian who killed her. I think she invited him to her chamber to make him break his vows of chastity, and Philippa agreed to make herself scarce for the occasion. But Lucian may not want a wife, so, to make sure Edith did not tell his brethren what he had done, he strangled her.'

'With red ribbon,' mused Geoffrey. 'Does he have any?'

Roger waved a dismissive hand. 'There is a scriptorium here, and any number of people have a supply he could have raided.'

'Have you confronted him?'

'No, because I do not want anyone to know about Philippa and me. We would both be in trouble – for breaking the monastery's rules about associating with women at night, and for gambling on the high altar. But it was the best available surface for my dice.'

'You are right! The monks will be furious. What were you thinking?'

Roger was surprised by the question. 'Of getting her in the right mood, of course! Brother Wardard almost caught us. He came early for his offices, but Philippa was able to persuade him that we were praying for you. Unfortunately, I had to donate a lot of gold to make it convincing.'

'And here I was, thinking you had done it for me. But you were only trying to evade a charge of blasphemy!'

Roger ignored the remark. 'Do you remember when we met Lucian by that shepherd's hut? The shepherd was dead under a fallen tree. Well, I think Lucian killed *him*, too. And, for all we know, he might have murdered Vitalis and Paisnel into the bargain. I said from the start that there was something nasty about him.'

'Very well!' snapped Harold loudly, his voice breaking into their discussion. 'I will play if it will make you happy, but do not expect beauty. This instrument is no better than a piece of pipe.'

He put the horn to his lips and began to blow. Geoffrey winced at the raw, rasping sound that emerged, although Roger bobbed his head and tapped his feet in polite appreciation. Bale listened with a sober, intent face, and Ulfrith put his hands over his ears. Eventually, the noise stopped.

'That was "Sumer is a Cumin in",' said Harold in the silence that followed. 'I told you the instrument was not up to my talents.'

'It was very nice,' said Roger, whose idea of good music was anything with a bit of volume. 'Do you know any dances?'

Harold obliged, with Bale hammering a pewter pot on a table and Roger adding his own rich bass to the cacophony. Geoffrey felt his headache return and was relieved when Aelfwig came to say the noise was disturbing the monks at their devotions.

'Oh dear,' said Harold with a conspiratorial grin. 'Now we are in trouble!'

'They are just jealous,' said Roger. 'They would rather be singing pretty songs, too, not chanting those tedious dirges.'

'How much of the pirates' gold did you take, Roger?' asked Geoffrey the following day, as they ate breakfast with the squires on the steps outside the hospital.

He had slept soundly and was well on the road back to full health. His mind was sharp enough to think about the questions that had been plaguing him since the shipwreck, though there were frustrating blanks in his memory that included much of his meeting with Galfridus, and he was uncertain whether some of the discussions he recalled had actually taken place.

Roger pursed his lips. 'I showed you in the marshes – a few coins for horses.'

'You did not make off with the whole chest?'

'If I had, you would have noticed, surely? That box was large and heavy.'

Geoffrey was not so sure. Roger's salvage had been wrapped in the blanket he had taken from Pevenesel, so it was entirely possible that it had included a chest of gold. Roger was certainly strong enough to carry one and make it appear as if it were of no consequence.

'Have the others gone?' he asked, realizing he was unlikely to have the truth. 'Lucian said he wanted to return to Bath, and Juhel was going to continue to Ribe.'

'Galfridus suggested everyone remain here until we are sure there is no invasion,' replied Ulfrith. 'He said it was too dangerous to roam about until then. So everyone is still here. Well, almost everyone. Poor Philippa.'

'Philippa?' asked Geoffrey in confusion. 'I thought it was Edith who died.'

'Murdered,' corrected Ulfrith. 'Philippa is distraught about the loss of her companion. They loved each other like sisters, despite sharing the same husband.'

'Philippa seemed more fond of Vitalis than Edith was,' said Geoffrey, 'although I suspect the security his money offered was a factor. Now she is afraid of being poor.'

'She did say she wanted a husband,' admitted Ulfrith, 'but that she will not begin her search until the proper period of mourning is over. She spent much of yesterday with Brother Lucian, although I do not think *he* will renounce his vows and marry her.'

Geoffrey raised his eyebrows, recalling Roger's contention that the monk was a prime suspect in Edith's murder, and hoped Philippa knew what she was doing.

'I think she is trying to catch him out,' explained Roger in an undertone. 'She is not a fool and doubtless drew the same conclusions I did.'

'Then let us hope we do not have another strangling on our hands.'

'She gave him a necklace,' said Ulfrith, trying to hear what the knights were saying. 'I think it was because Edith lent him a ring, and she did not want to appear mean by comparison.'

'It was not valuable, though,' said Roger, who had an eye for such things. 'It was coloured glass and cheap metal, whereas the ring held a real ruby. Most monks cannot tell the difference, but Lucian can, of course.' He shot Geoffrey a meaningful look, as if this was evidence of the man's dubious claims to monasticism.

'Well, he *is* a bursar,' Geoffrey pointed out. 'I imagine they are very familiar with jewels.'

'I have barely spoken to Philippa in days,' said Ulfrith, looking around wistfully for a glimpse of her. 'But I thought I had better spend my time with you instead.'

'Thank you,' said Geoffrey, sensing that some acknowledgement of the sacrifice was expected.

'I was worried,' said Ulfrith in a small voice. 'I thought you were going to die.'

'He nearly did,' said Roger grimly. 'And when I find the culprit, he will wish he had never been born.'

After breakfast, Aelfwig talked about the ships that had been seen and his fear that they might be Bellême's. Geoffrey pointed out that the Duke of Normandy was rumoured to be in St Valery, so they were more likely his, but Aelfwig countered that the Duke would not dare visit England without an official invitation from his brother.

'I assume de Laigle has sent word to the King, regardless?' Geoffrey asked, shaking his head when the herbalist offered him another draught of his raspberry tonic.

'Who knows?' muttered Aelfwig. 'De Laigle is so addled by wine that it may not even have occurred to him to warn His Majesty. Did you hear what he did in Werlinges, when Galfridus told him to investigate? He gave his men leave to loot the place, then set it on fire.'

'Did Bale tell you that?'

'No – I was there. Galfridus sent me to monitor proceedings. It was disgraceful, and your squire was the only one who did not leave with his arms full of other folks' possessions.'

Geoffrey was relieved by that at least. He watched Aelfwig pour his medicine back into its flask, thinking that if the Duke or Bellême *were* on the brink of invasion, the King should be told. He should also be informed about the simmering revolt. As Geoffrey did not want royal vengeance to descend on his wife and sister for the want of a letter, he decided to write to Henry that very day. Then he would borrow a horse from Galfridus and deliver it in person.

He was sorry to betray Harold and Magnus, but they both knew the risks and should be ready to suffer the consequences. He considered telling them what he intended to do, to give them a chance to escape, but his recent brush with death made him think twice about rash magnanimity.

While Roger and the squires played a quiet game of dice, Geoffrey wrote an account of all he had learned since the shipwreck, although he hesitated when he reached the part about Werlinges, not sure what was fact and what was speculation. Fingar had said that Ulf, not his sailors, was responsible for the massacre, but Geoffrey could not be sure that discussion had actually taken place. In the end, he merely reported that an entire village was dead for reasons unknown.

'You cannot take that today,' said Ulfrith as Geoffrey sealed the letter and stood. 'You are not well enough.'

Geoffrey smiled at his transparency: Ulfrith did not want to leave Philippa, still hopeful he might be in with a chance if her other choices fell through.

'He is right,' agreed Roger, for more altruistic reasons. 'Moreover, it is not wise to let Henry know you were slipping out of the country. He likes you here, at his beck and call.'

'I doubt he will care. Besides, our names will be in de Laigle's account, so it is only prudent to give our version of events.'

'Then send a dispatch – I will even give you a ring to pay a good man – but do not ride yourself. You are still too pale for my liking.'

'And who here is a good man?' asked Geoffrey. 'Not Bale – he is too easily distracted.'

'What about Breme?' suggested Roger, pointing to the peddler of writing materials who was preparing to leave the abbey, pack already on his powerful shoulders.

Geoffrey still wore Breme's charm – a bundle of herbs and an unusual stone, all tightly bound in twine. Breme had recommended that he keep it until the next full moon, and Geoffrey felt compelled to comply because it had cost fourpence.

'I knew topaz would work,' Breme said smugly, reaching out

to ensure it was still in place. 'It is your birthstone and much more powerful than garnet. We were lucky I had it.'

'How do you know when I was born?' asked Geoffrey curiously.

'From Roger. He was ready to do anything to ensure your survival.'

Geoffrey had never told Roger his birth date, which meant the big knight must have picked one out of the blue. It lessened the likelihood that Breme's magic had been responsible for his recovery, but it would have been churlish to point it out.

'Now I am going to Winchester,' said Breme. 'Juhel tells me the monks there are always in need of decent ink, and he has given me a letter of introduction to a clerk. I feel almost guilty.'

Geoffrey was nonplussed. 'About what?'

'About overcharging for the parchment to write it on. Still, he is a merchant and should have haggled more efficiently.'

'Will you carry a letter for me?' asked Geoffrey. 'I do not know whether the King will be at Winchester, but if you deliver it to the abbot, he will see it sent on.'

'The King?' asked Breme keenly. 'I shall be a royal messenger, then? Well, I am pleased to be of service, especially if you mean to pay me with that ring you hold.'

Geoffrey handed it over. 'I will hire a horse, too, so you can travel more quickly.'

Breme raised his eyebrows. 'I do not blame you for not trusting de Laigle to tell the King about these ship sightings *or* about poor Werlinges – the man is a dreadful sot. So choose me a decent nag, Sir Geoffrey, and I shall ride like the wind for you.'

That evening, when the bells chimed for vespers and the sun was setting behind a bank of clouds, Geoffrey prepared to give Roger the slip. He was grateful for the big knight's solicitous protection, but it was beginning to cloy, and he longed for solitude. He borrowed a warm cloak from Aelfwig and reached for Ulfrith's water flask.

'Where are you going?' demanded Roger.

'You cannot have that,' objected Ulfrith at the same time. 'There is wine on the table.'

'I do not want wine,' said Geoffrey. 'I want water.'

'Then use your own, sir,' said Ulfrith. 'I filled your flask an hour ago, whereas mine has not been changed since yesterday.'

'Yes, but you keep yours with you all the time,' said Geoffrey, taking a gulp, 'whereas mine has been lying on the table, where someone might have tampered with it.'

'You are wise to be cautious,' said Roger. 'Are you going out?'

'Just to the church.'

'I will come with you,' offered Roger.

'That is not necessary.' Geoffrey tossed the flask back to Ulfrith and made for the door.

Ulfrith regarded him uneasily. 'Are you going to see Lady Philippa?'

The question annoyed Geoffrey. 'I am going to the church,' he said shortly.

Before they could ask more, he left, closing the door firmly behind him. He walked across a grassy sward, aware that Ulfrith was watching him from the window. He had intended to visit the nearby village to make enquiries about his dog, but he could not do it while Ulfrith was watching. Ulfrith would tell Roger, who would insist on accompanying him.

With no option, he aimed for the church. It was the first time he had been inside, and he was impressed by the tier upon tier of round-headed arches, carved to flaunt the masons' skills. The dominant colours of the ceiling were blue and gold, like the dawn sky, and the pillars and walls were pale green and yellow at the top, darkening to red and purple at the bottom. It made the building seem taller than it was, and he marvelled at the cleverness of the illusion.

Vespers had started, and the monks' voices rose and fell as they chanted a psalm. Geoffrey leaned against a pillar and closed his eyes, finding peace in the music.

'There you are, Sir Geoffrey! Are you better? Poor Sir Roger was convinced you were going to die and hurled gold at anyone who would pray. The only one who refused payment was Brother Wardard, but I am told he is a saintly man. His brethren wanted him to be abbot, but he declined.'

Geoffrey opened his eyes to see Philippa smiling at him in her flirtatious fashion. He stepped away, not wanting the monks to see them standing so close in their church. She inched forward, and they began a curious dance that saw him backing towards the door and her in dogged pursuit.

'Stop!' she ordered in a fierce whisper. 'I want to talk to you without being overheard, but I cannot if you will not stand still.'

He relented when he saw she did not look well. She wore the thick red cloak he had last seen on Edith, but she kept rubbing her hands together, as though they were chilled. Her face was pale, and there were dark rings under eyes that had produced too many tears.

'I am sorry,' he said, contrite. 'You have suffered another loss.'

She looked away, and two heavy drops made silvery trails down her cheeks. 'Poor Edith! It does not seem possible she is gone. Now I am alone and I do not know what will become of me. It should not have been her.'

'What do you mean? That you should have died in her place?'

Philippa nodded unhappily. 'She was wealthy and had kin who loved her, but I have nothing. It would have been better if I had been the one to die.' Her fists clenched tightly. 'If I ever find the loathsome villain who snuffed out her life, I will choke him and dance on his grave!'

'Hush!' said Geoffrey, alarmed that such sentiments were being uttered in a church.

'I do not know what will happen to me if I cannot find a protector.' She reached out and took his hand, the coquettish smile back again. 'Did anyone ever tell you that your eyes are the most beautiful shade of green? They are the hue of ferns.'

'My wife mentioned it once,' said Geoffrey, freeing his hand.

'Vitalis had a wife, too, but the three of us came to an arrangement that made us all happy.'

Geoffrey smiled. 'I doubt Hilde would agree to that.'

Philippa sighed. 'I did love Vitalis. He was old and sometimes awry in the wits, but he was good to me and I miss him.'

'I know,' said Geoffrey gently. 'You probably did take him for love. Edith, I suspect, was forced into the union. But she was his real wife, even so.'

Philippa's eyes blazed. 'I was legally married! In a church – Edith carried the flowers.'

'But she was already wed to him. *Ergo*, the second ceremony was illegal.'

'Are you calling me a whore?'

Geoffrey supposed he was. 'Edith was grateful to you for drawing Vitalis's attentions from her, and, against all odds, you became friends. Of course you were upset when he died – it shattered your safe life.'

'Edith said she would look after me,' said Philippa, tearful again. 'She was the best friend anyone could have – better and more loyal than your Roger. *She* did not steal gold and have me implicated in a crime. And now she is dead and I must fend for myself. You have no idea how hard it is for a woman with no family and no money. I only hope Lucian means what he says when he waxes lyrical about giving up the cowl to enjoy a secular life.'

'Did he meet Edith the night she died?' asked Geoffrey, taking the opportunity to question her, since she seemed of a mind to talk.

She frowned. 'Not that I know of. Why? Is that what Sir Roger told you? That I vacated our chamber so Edith could enter- tain a lover? I might have known *he* would assume something like that! I suppose he told you he and I were here all night?'

Geoffrey nodded. 'Dicing on the high altar.'

She grimaced. 'I told him we should use the floor. But he is a lewd man to think such things of poor Edith! If you must know, I left because sleeping has been difficult for me since the shipwreck, and my restlessness disturbed her. I told her I was going to keep vigil for Vitalis – to give her a chance to sleep. I wish to God that I had stayed.'

'If you had, you might have been strangled, too.'

Philippa pulled the cloak more firmly around her shoulders: the notion seemed not to have occurred to her. More tears fell, and she brushed them away angrily.

'I cannot seem to stop crying. But Ulfrith tells me you have investigated killers. Will you investigate this one? You do not need to denounce him publicly – just tell me his name, and I will slip a piece of ribbon around *his* throat.'

'Then you will be a murderer, too.'

'I do not care! It would be worth eternal damnation. But you will find it is Juhel. He killed Paisnel, and a man who kills once always itches to do it again – or so your man Bale told me.'

'Did he?' asked Geoffrey, wondering what else his squire had said.

Philippa was silent for a while, and when she next spoke, her voice was low and hoarse. 'This is Edith's cloak. Do you think it is wicked to use it, while her body is still unburied?' She clutched it tighter and sobbed.

'I would want Roger to use mine, if I was dead and he needed clothes.' It occurred to Geoffrey that Bale had used similar arguments, and he supposed there was a very fine line between robbing the dead and justifiably making use of someone's possessions.

'Edith was strangled with ribbon,' Philippa went on. 'Who would do such a thing?'

'Just like your husband,' Geoffrey said absently.

Philippa gaped at him. 'What did you say?'

Too late, Geoffrey realized that unless Ulfrith or Bale had told her what they had found, she would be ignorant of the fact that Vitalis had suffered a similar fate. Philippa gazed at him in horror as he described what they had discovered at Vitalis's grave. He watched her closely for a sign that she might have known something about it, but from her shock, he thought that she had not.

'Oh, God!' she whispered. 'Edith had some ribbon that Paisnel gave her, and we planned to use it to secure Vitalis's cloak when we buried him. But a squall came and we ran for shelter. When we came back, it had blown away.'

Geoffrey took the bull by the horns. 'You said you were with Vitalis when he died. That means either *you* strangled him or you are lying.'

'It means neither! He gasped and choked in my arms, and I *saw* the life pass from him. Then the shower came, and Edith and I ran for shelter. We buried him when we returned.'

Geoffrey was not sure whether to believe her. It *was* a plausible explanation, but only just.

'I would never harm him,' she continued when he said nothing. 'Without him I have nothing.'

'Then what about Edith? She was less fond of him than you.'

'But not enough to kill him! And I have changed my mind: you will *not* investigate Edith's death. You will reach entirely the wrong conclusion. I am sure it is Juhel. He saw me leave and decided to chance his hand while my poor friend was alone, strangling her when she refused him.'

There was no more to be said, so Geoffrey took his leave, walking fast down the nearest path to test his strength. When he reached the bottom of the hill, he strode across the boggy area, towards the abbey's carp ponds, hidden from the buildings by trees. He was breathless when he stopped. Roger was right: he needed more time to recover. He leaned against a tree to catch his breath, noting that he had reached the far southern boundary of La Batailge's precinct.

He had not been there long when he heard a snap. He glanced up at the wall and saw a head poking over the top, and in the fellow's hands was a loaded crossbow.

'Do not move,' ordered Fingar. 'Or it will be the last thing you do.'

The captain had a clear shot and could not possibly miss from close range. Geoffrey was disgusted with himself for not wearing his armour. He glanced behind, noting that the ponds were completely screened by trees, so he should expect no rescue from anyone at the abbey.

'We meet again,' said Fingar softly. 'I am pleased to see you recovered.'

'Did you visit me in the hospital?' asked Geoffrey, buying time while he tried to devise a way to escape.

Fingar smiled enigmatically and declined to answer. 'Are you here to catch fish for the monk who is pretending to be the abbot?'

'No, I came for a walk,' replied Geoffrey, flapping away a marsh insect that whined around his face. 'Why are *you* here?'

'Why do you think? We have been watching La Batailge for days now and know how to move through its grounds unseen, especially at night. I have even been in the church, to thank God for delivering us from the storm.' Fingar paused. 'And to ask Him to help us get our gold back.'

'How much did Roger take?' asked Geoffrey. 'Was it a purse, or the entire chest?'

Fingar grimaced. 'You know the answer to that. However, if you can persuade him to give it back, I shall let you both live.

Refuse, and you will die. See reason, Sir Geoffrey. What use is gold, unless you are alive to enjoy it?'

Roger would never part with what he had taken, and Fingar might just as well have asked for the moon. Geoffrey doubted the pirate would keep his end of the bargain anyway – Roger had sentenced them both to look over their shoulders for the rest of their lives. Silently, he cursed his friend's greed.

'I will do my best,' he promised. 'How is Donan?'

'More eager to leave with every passing day. You would be amazed at how many carts and horses start to appear on the roads after dark and how many men skulk in the shadows – it is downright dangerous here! And this abbey is a veritable refuge for thieves and murderers. Besides Roger, there is Philippa. At least, that is what Donan claims.'

'Donan thinks Philippa stole something?'

'No, he thinks she threw Paisnel overboard. I told you this the other night—'

Suddenly, Fingar disappeared from the wall, accompanied by a howl of pain. Geoffrey gazed in surprise, wondering if the abbey guards had dragged him down from the other side.

'Run!' came an urgent voice from behind him.

Geoffrey spun around: it was Ulfrith. He raced after the squire, who did not stop until they were well outside arrow range. Hands on knees to catch his breath, Geoffrey saw Ulfrith held several large stones.

'You have not been well,' said Ulfrith in explanation. 'So I followed you, to make sure you came to no harm. It was good I did.'

But Geoffrey suspected he had been in no danger, because Fingar hoped to use him to retrieve his gold – Ulfrith's well-meant interruption had merely served to end the conversation before Geoffrey had asked all his questions. Still, at least he now knew that Fingar *had* visited him in the hospital – and that Donan's peculiar claim that it was Philippa who had tossed Paisnel overboard was not a figment of a fevered imagination.

'Did Roger tell you to follow me?' he asked. With hardly a pause, he answered his own question. 'No, he would have come himself. You acted on your own initiative, because you were afraid I was going to meet Philippa.'

'Well, I was right,' said Ulfrith sullenly. 'You *did* meet her.'

'Not on purpose – she crept up on me. Do you have any water? All that running . . .'

'Here.' It was Geoffrey's own flask, and Ulfrith gestured impatiently when the knight hesitated to take it. 'I filled it from the well before I followed you to the church, so it is perfectly safe. I thought if I brought your own supply, you might stop taking mine.'

Geoffrey drank and began to feel better.

Ulfrith hesitated, then spoke in a rush. 'Do you feel any . . . do you feel *love* for Lady Philippa? Did you offer her your heart and tell her you would be hers for ever?'

Geoffrey regarded him warily, thinking these were odd questions to be asking a battle-hardened knight. Especially one who was married. 'No,' he replied cautiously. 'Why?'

'You did not feel an urge to take her?'

Geoffrey blinked. 'We were in a church, Ulfrith! What kind of man do you think I am?'

Ulfrith did not look convinced. 'Then what did you talk about so intently?'

Geoffrey's patience was wearing thin. 'That is none of your affair. I am grateful to you for driving off Fingar, but that does not give you the right to question my actions. Not ever.'

Ulfrith regarded him sullenly, then turned on his heel and slouched away. Geoffrey shook his head, heartily wishing he had never made the vow to Joan, because the young man's passions had grown too tiresome.

# Eleven

The following day was grey and drizzly, and there was a tang of salt in the air. Geoffrey woke when the bell sounded for prime, and he reached out to pet his dog before remembering it was not there. He wished he had asked Fingar about it the previous day. As the notion that it was in the man's stomach made further sleep impossible, he went to the church.

When the service was over, he headed to the lady chapel, muttering prayers of thanks for his deliverance from the shipwreck and the return of his health. Seeing Philippa enter, he left before she could waylay him, and sat near a pillar in the south transept. It was not long before Magnus joined him.

'Harold said you were better. Who poisoned us, do you think? I am certain the vile deed was aimed at me, and I was less badly affected because I am stronger.'

Geoffrey generally enjoyed excellent health and doubted the cadaverous Magnus was fitter than him. 'Who do you think wants you dead?' he asked.

Magnus pursed his lips. 'Well, there are a great many Normans, starting with the Usurper. And not all Saxons are enamoured of me. Lord Gyrth is something of a malcontent.'

'Who is Lord Gyrth?'

'The Earl of East Anglia – my cousin. Well, his father was Earl and he would have inherited the title had Gyrth the Elder not died at Hastinges. The Bastard promptly appointed a Norman to the earldom, so Gyrth was disinherited. He is desperate to retrieve his birthright.'

Absently, Geoffrey wondered whether Gyrth's name was on the list of potential rebels.

'Here is Harold,' said Magnus disapprovingly. 'Grinning as usual and arriving on a waft of garlic. *Must* he smile all the time? And must he fraternize with servants? He will never be king by being popular.'

'He might,' Geoffrey pointed out. 'You say the competition

between you will be decided by an election. People will vote for him if they like him.'

'But peasants will not vote,' said Magnus in disdain. 'Only nobles. Men like Gyrth.'

'Gyrth!' said Harold, overhearing as he approached. 'There is a sullen fellow! He once told me that the only music he enjoys is the screams of dying Normans. What sort of man says that?'

'There is Philippa,' said Magnus, pointing as she emerged from the Lady Chapel. Her path crossed that of Lucian, and she took his arm playfully, much to the disapproval of the older monk who was with him. 'And that is Brother Wardard, one of the "heroes" of Hastinges.'

'I should speak to him,' said Geoffrey. But he hung back, lest Philippa made another play for him, thus earning him the old monk's disapproval, too. He wanted the truth about his father, not some tale coloured by what Wardard thought of his association with Philippa.

He waited, but Wardard went with Philippa when she left, apparently deciding she needed a chaperon. Geoffrey lingered by the high altar, in case he returned, but he was to be disappointed.

Eventually, a bell rang to announce breakfast. The monks filed into their refectory, the servants to a hall near the brewery, and the visitors collected bread, boiled eggs and salted fish from the kitchens – there was ale, but Geoffrey opted for Ulfrith's water. He was surprised by the number of pilgrims, mostly Saxons, who were suddenly in evidence. Apparently unwilling to share the hospital with Norman knights, they had established a little tented camp near the gatehouse.

'I am still surprised you recovered, Sir Geoffrey,' said Aelfwig, when their paths crossed after the meal. He was with another monk – a tall man with a facial twitch. 'Indeed, I told Roger to prepare for the worst one night and suggested he put a deposit down on a coffin – we only have one in stock at the moment, you see, and there is a sick villager who might have claimed it first.'

'Oh,' said Geoffrey, unsure of the appropriate response to such a remark.

'You should be more careful in your predictions, Aelfwig,' chided his companion. 'You declared poor Abbot Henry cured from his fever last year, and he died within the hour.' He turned to Geoffrey. 'I am Ralph of Bec, the abbey's sacristan.'

Aelfwig reached out and grabbed the charm Geoffrey wore around his neck before he could acknowledge the sacristan's greeting.

'What is this? A heathen artefact? You should denounce such things and put your faith in God.'

'Just as long as he does not put his faith in you,' murmured Ralph. He changed the subject before Aelfwig could defend himself. 'I heard you were not very impressed by Galfridus's collection of sculptures, Sir Geoffrey. You took a particular dislike to his amethyst horse, I am told.'

Geoffrey remembered nothing about a horse, although he vividly recollected the ivory carving on the windowsill. 'The Lamb of God looks like a pig,' he said.

The monks looked shocked, but before Geoffrey could say he was referring to the artwork, Ralph adopted an expression of concern.

'Brother Wardard hopes to meet you today, but I hope you will not distress *him* with sacrilegious remarks. He is a good, honourable soul and will not appreciate heresy.'

'Very well,' said Geoffrey, suspecting there was no point in trying to rectify the misunderstanding. Thinking it might be a good time to look at the body of the man Bale had killed, he asked where the charnel house was.

'Why?' asked Aelfwig nervously. 'Who told you that several of my other patients lie there?'

'No one,' said Geoffrey, supposing he had been right to refuse the herbalist's raspberry tonic. 'I want to look at the body of the man Bale killed, to see if I recognize him.'

'He is to be buried this morning,' said Ralph, 'so you had better hurry. It is over there.'

He flapped vaguely with his hand, then both monks hurried away. Ralph's directions had encompassed at least three buildings, and the first one Geoffrey tried was a small hut, apparently used as an annex dormitory when the hospital was full. It was dark inside, because the window shutters were closed, and he was surprised to see Juhel inspecting documents by candlelight.

Juhel moved quickly when he saw Geoffrey, but not quickly enough to conceal what he had been doing.

'I see you are better,' said the parchmenter with an unreadable smile. 'I am glad. None of us expected you to survive such a violent fever.'

'I was saved by water, topaz, gold and the good auspices of King Harold,' said Geoffrey, stepping inside the hut, trying to see what the man had been doing. 'They counteracted the poison.'

Juhel regarded him uneasily. 'Poison? Surely not!'

'Magnus suffered, too, although the effects wore off him more quickly.'

'I suspect you swallowed too many medicines in an effort to heal yourself. Some compounds react violently with each other, and you should have taken nothing else with my salve.'

'That is what Bale told me. So did Breme.' Fingar had, too, he thought. Or had he dreamed it?

'I imagine you would have been well sooner if that herbalist had not dosed you with his remedies. I told Roger as much.'

'What are those?' asked Geoffrey, nodding at the documents Juhel had pushed under his blanket. 'The parchments from Paisnel's pack?'

Juhel regarded him with narrowed eyes. 'How do you know what was in his bag? Did you rifle through it?'

'No, but you did, after he died. You were seen.'

'He was my friend. It was my duty to take charge of his belongings.'

'But you hurled most of them into the sea. You were seen doing that, too.'

Juhel came to his feet fast, and Geoffrey saw there was a good deal of power in his squat limbs.

'I have nothing to hide,' said the parchmenter, smiling wryly when Geoffrey's hand dropped to his dagger. 'Come, see for yourself that you have no right to question my actions.'

Alert for hostile moves, Geoffrey pushed aside the blanket with his foot. The documents lay underneath. He hesitated, not wanting to bend and make himself vulnerable to attack. He indicated that Juhel was to pass them to him. Juhel gave one of his unreadable smiles and obliged wordlessly.

There were two bundles of documents. The first comprised

the same gibberish Juhel had written for Edith. Geoffrey looked hard at the symbols in the light of the candle, but they were nonsense, although they would look like writing to an illiterate. They were tied with red ribbon, and the seals convinced him they were the ones he had seen Paisnel studying.

The second batch was slightly damp, with ink that had run. They were far too badly damaged by rain or seawater to be legible; it was impossible even to tell whether they had been real missives or the same meaningless scrawl of the others.

'Can you read these?' Geoffrey asked, indicating the second batch.

'No,' replied Juhel shortly. 'They have been wet too many times. Still, if I dry them, I may be able to reuse the parchment. It is expensive, and I do not have money to waste.'

'What about the dry ones? Can you read those?'

'They are in the language of the Danes. Do you know it?' Juhel looked superior when Geoffrey shook his head. 'I thought not. The Danish alphabet is different from ours, like Arabic and Hebrew.'

Geoffrey was sceptical. He had never seen Danish written, but there was no reason to suppose it was different from Latin or French. 'Are you sure?'

'Yes. These are runes, which are often used to convey Danish in official documents. Would you like me to translate them for you?'

'Please.'

Juhel took a sheet and went to the door, where the light was better. He rested a grubby finger at the top right, then moved it left, as Geoffrey had learned to read Arabic. The knight was mystified; he had believed only the Semitic languages ran counter to Latin.

Juhel began to speak. '*The Bishop of Ribe holds this manor. It was always in the hands of the monastery, and before there were fifty hides, and then it answered for thirty-eight hides; now for twenty-eight. Land for thirty-three ploughs. In lordship, five ploughs and fifty smallholders. There is meadow of fifteen acres, and woodland of forty.* Would you like me to continue, Sir Geoffrey? There is a good deal more, and it gives a detailed account of the entire diocese, if you are interested.'

Geoffrey took the document from him, trying to see a pattern that would allow him to confirm the translation, but he could make neither head nor tail of it. Juhel retrieved it with a smirk.

'Why do you have it?' asked Geoffrey, still not sure Juhel was telling the truth about his literacy. For all he knew, the man was simply reciting something from memory and the so-called 'runes' were exactly what they appeared – gibberish.

'That is none of your business. However, as I do not want you to start spreading tales about me, I shall answer. Paisnel was a clerk, and these are his documents. I took them from his pack after he died, so I can return them to the Bishop of Ribe. It is what he would have wished.'

'Why did Paisnel have them in the first place? It strikes me that these are deeds that should be in Ribe, not being hauled all across Ireland and England.'

'When he left Denmark after his last visit, Paisnel had a great chest of writs with him. But when he arrived in Ireland, he discovered these were included by mistake. He was returning them, in his capacity as the Bishop's counsellor.'

Geoffrey frowned. 'You told me earlier he was a clerk.'

Juhel licked his lips. 'He was, but—'

'If you lie, you must be blessed with a good memory,' interrupted Geoffrey. 'And you are not. Was Paisnel a clerk or a counsellor? Or would it be more accurate to call him a spy?'

'You pay too much attention to those women,' said Juhel, attempting nonchalance as he gathered up the parchments.

'He *was* a spy,' said Geoffrey, sensing his unease. 'I imagine that is why you threw his pack overboard. You wanted to destroy any items that might incriminate him.'

Juhel's face was white, and Geoffrey did not tell him he had been seen heaving Paisnel's body into the sea as well, afraid it might incur a violent reaction – and he was not yet certain of his own strength. The Breton suddenly clapped both hands over his face and scrubbed hard.

'All right,' he said tiredly. 'There is no point in denying it, when even those stupid women saw through Paisnel's clumsy subterfuge. Yes, he was a spy, although not a very good one. I threw his pack in the sea, because *I* did not want to be accused

of treason should his materials be found. I kept only these manorial rolls, which I *know* are innocent. Are you satisfied?'

'Who was his master?'

'Lord Bellême.' Juhel gave a weak grin when he saw
Geoffrey's astonishment. 'Even Philippa guessed that – but you
thought the notion so outrageous that you did not believe her.
Paisnel's father holds his Norman estates from Bellême, who
often calls for favours. This time, Paisnel was charged to look
at England's coastal defences, because Bellême is considering
invading.'

'Is he?' Geoffrey supposed it might be true.

'Yes, but Bellême should never have entrusted him with such
a mission: Paisnel had no idea how to conduct a discreet survey
and asked the most brazen of questions. We argued, because I
was afraid his incompetence would see us both hanged.'

If that were true, then several things made sense: the whispered argument Geoffrey had witnessed on the ship; the other
one observed by Philippa; Juhel's easy familiarity with his friend's
possessions. But had their disagreement led Juhel to kill Paisnel
because he was a liability?

'Then what about this?' he asked, producing the letter Juhel
had written for Edith. 'Is it more information about manorial
rolls?'

Juhel took it from him, and his expression turned to alarm.
'Where did you get this? It was supposed to have been sent to
Edith's family.'

'She was sceptical about its contents and asked the monks to
translate it for her. They told her it was nonsense. Now she is
dead.'

Juhel was aghast at the implicit accusation. 'Her death was
nothing to do with—'

'She was strangled with red ribbon. Just like Vitalis – he did
not drown, as his wives claimed. And red ribbon fastens *your*
documents.'

'I have seen red ribbon on the parchments in *your* bags, too,'
Juhel shot back.

'My cord is thicker and coarser. It was a finer braid that killed
Vitalis and Edith.'

Juhel was appalled by the direction the discussion had taken.

'You cannot accuse me of murder just because of ribbon! If you want to catch Edith's killer, look to the men she encouraged with her fluttering eyelashes and then abandoned when someone better came along. Ask *Roger* about her.'

Geoffrey stared at him. 'What are you saying?'

'You know perfectly well: Edith enjoyed Roger's company – until Lucian reappeared. If you want suspects for her murder, ask *Roger* what he was doing the night she died. He was certainly out and about, because I saw him.'

Of course, Roger had not harmed Edith, because he had been with Philippa. However, the big knight *did* solve problems with violence, and not everyone would believe his innocence. Moreover, Geoffrey did not trust Philippa to confirm his alibi. She was a woman out for her own ends and might well lie if she thought there was a chance she might benefit from it.

Juhel smirked victoriously when Geoffrey had no reply, 'But I do not believe Roger is the culprit. I suspect Lucian, whom I also saw abroad that night. When I asked him the following day what he had been doing, he claimed he had been at a vigil all night. Do you believe such a tale from a man who did not utter a single prayer while we were on *Patrick*?'

Geoffrey admitted it sounded unlikely. 'Read that to me,' he said, indicating Edith's letter. 'What does it say?'

'It relates a woeful tale to her father, all about high seas and unruly sailors. I will translate it if you like, but you will find it dull listening.'

'But as it is written in runes, her father will not be able to decipher it.'

'No,' said Juhel with malicious satisfaction. 'And it will serve her right. She said I would be paid to write it, but once it was done – and it took several hours, because I am not quick with my pen – Vitalis refused to pay. They cheated me, and I am glad I cheated them back.'

Geoffrey left the hut, not sure what to think. He still believed Danish was written in the same alphabet as other Western languages, but he had never seen it and could not be sure. Perhaps Juhel was telling the truth. But had Juhel killed Vitalis? Geoffrey realized that even if he had, it was not his concern. It was probably incautious queries that had seen him poisoned, and it was time to leave the matter to the appropriate authorities.

However, he had one last question. He retraced his steps, and his second unanticipated invasion showed him a heavy medallion under the blanket with the documents. Philippa had mentioned a necklace in Paisnel's pack, and there was another memory of it, too. Geoffrey frowned, trying to pin down the elusive sense that he had seen it before. Then it came to him in a flash – Donan had found one in the hospital. Like Juhel's, it was engraved with Celtic knots on one side and a lily on the other. Was it the same one? But if Donan had taken it, what was it doing with Juhel?

'How did you come by that?' he asked, forgetting his decision not to meddle.

Juhel shrugged. 'It was Paisnel's. I removed it from his pack when I took the documents. It is valuable, so I shall return it to his father.'

'Have you ever been inside the hospital?'

'Not after Roger accused me of poisoning you. That is why I came here, if you recall. I kept well away from you – but obviously not far enough, because you are still hurling accusations.'

'I saw that pendant,' mused Geoffrey, 'in Donan's hands.'

'La Batailge may admit a lot of Saxon peasants to do homage at the battle shrine, but they will draw the line at pirates. I heard you claimed Fingar came when you were ill, but he would have been noticed – and ejected – I assure you.'

'Has that locket been with you the whole time?'

'No, I have not been as careful with it as I should have been. It was stolen, but then returned. I can only surmise that the culprit had second thoughts about stealing on hallowed ground.'

Roger would have had no such scruples – if he had taken the thing, he would still have it – although Bale and Ulfrith might have put it back when conscience began to prick.

'I would be grateful if you would not mention it to anyone,' Juhel continued. 'I do not want other thieves setting greedy eyes on it.'

Geoffrey nodded agreement, although he was not sure whether he believed Juhel's fear of thieves. He recalled that Roger had mentioned a pendant in Magnus's possession, but Magnus had denied owning any such thing. In all, anything to do with medallions was murky, as far as he was concerned, and he knew he would be wise to put the matter from his mind.

'Why did you come back?' asked Juhel, breaking into his thoughts. 'What do you want now?'

'I wondered whether you had seen my dog. He is missing.'

To Geoffrey's profound embarrassment, Juhel started to cry. 'So is Delilah. I have not seen her for several days and I think she is still grieving for Paisnel. Animals feel a death very keenly, you know. When did you last see . . . what is his name?'

'He does not have one,' said Geoffrey, who had once christened the beast Angel, then abandoned the appellation when he became acquainted with its true character.

Juhel was surprised. 'Then how do you call him?'

'By shouting "dog".'

Juhel regarded him askance. 'Does that not bring other mongrels?'

Geoffrey was beginning to feel foolish. He started to leave. 'I am sorry to have bothered you.'

Juhel sniffed, and more tears rolled. 'Call your dog, Sir Geoffrey. It is a terrible thing when a man loses a beloved companion. Call him, and see if it will bring him back.'

'Dog!' yelled Geoffrey, sorry for the man's distress and willing to shout if it made him feel better. He knew the animal would have made itself known to him if it was close – to be fed – so he was startled to hear an answering bark.

'Did you hear that?' cried Juhel, happy for him.

'He is in that building with the thick door,' said Geoffrey, pointing to a hut with a stone roof and no windows. 'He must have been locked in by accident.'

'That is the charnel house,' said Juhel. 'Edith and the man who tried to stab you are inside.'

Geoffrey regarded him uneasily. 'Lord! Are they?'

He did not like to think what he might find, given that the dog had been missing for some time and was not a beast to ignore the demands of its stomach. Meat was meat, after all. He broke into a run, although he knew haste would make no difference now. He reached the door and hesitated, not sure he wanted to see what he might find. Then he recalled that the monks were going to bury the dead man that morning and would discover it anyway. It would be better if they learned it from him. Aware of Juhel behind him, he pushed open the door – a heavy one with a latch.

He expected the dog to explode out, but it simply barked again. Then there was an answering cluck from above his head: Delilah was roosting above the lintel. The dog padded forward to greet Geoffrey, feathery tail wagging, but then there was a flurry of brown feathers and Delilah was flapping around its head. The dog yelped in terror and retreated to the shadows.

'It is *her*!' shrieked Juhel in delight, plucking the bird from Geoffrey's shoulder. 'Delilah! I did not think of looking for her *here*, Sir Geoffrey. I thought she had more taste than to frequent this sort of place.'

Delilah cackled her pleasure at seeing Juhel, and Geoffrey turned his attention to his dog. Its coat was matted and it seemed thinner, although the hen looked in fine fettle. Geoffrey was massively relieved. The dog had clearly not eaten in days, perhaps kept from the unthinkable by the presence of the chicken.

'He must have followed her in here, and the door closed on them,' Juhel said. 'They could not escape, because the latch is on the outside.'

'They could not have escaped if the latch was on the inside, either,' Geoffrey pointed out.

Juhel regarded him in surprise. 'Have you not taught your dog to open doors? Delilah can do it.' He kissed her head and she clucked appreciatively. 'She must have opened the door, but the wind blew it shut, trapping them both. Your dog cannot have had an easy time of it.'

As if to underline his point, the wind gusted suddenly. There was a creak, a slam and a click, and the charnel house was plunged into darkness. The dog whimpered, Delilah made a noise that sounded very much like disgust, and Geoffrey sighed in weary resignation.

'Oh dear,' said Juhel. 'Now what?'

For several moments, Geoffrey could not even see the door, so complete was the darkness, but then he detected a faint rectangle of light. He made his way towards it. It did not take long, however, to realize that the latch was beyond him. He began to grope around for something to use as a battering ram, irritated that Juhel was more interested in crooning to his bird and did nothing to help.

Eventually, he grasped something that was the right shape for battering, but when he tugged at it, he discovered it was a leg. He released it hastily, but the next thing his tentative hands encountered was a face, cold and rigid. Abandoning the search, he returned to the door, swearing under his breath when increasingly violent tugs and thumps failed to make an impact.

'You will not succeed with brute force,' said Juhel. 'Let me try.'

There was a series of scrapes and taps, then the latch clinked and the door swung open. Geoffrey regarded him warily, but Juhel was more interested in removing Delilah than in explaining how he had done it. He waved away Geoffrey's thanks and started back to his hut, muttering sweet nothings to his feathered companion.

When man and bird had gone, the dog darted to Geoffrey's side, winding around his legs and leaping up to rest its forepaws on his chest so it might be petted. It was not normally affectionate, and Geoffrey saw its experience had seriously discomfited it.

'You have had a miserable time,' he said sympathetically, rubbing its head. 'Trapped by a chicken! You always were a cowardly hound, but I never thought to see you sink this low.'

'Sir Geoffrey,' came an uneasy voice that made him jump in alarm. It was Galfridus, with Aelfwig and Ralph behind him. They carried a box and had come for one of the dead. 'Did I hear you chatting to the corpses? Aelfwig told me you were recovered.'

'I have heard tales of men who talk to cadavers,' said Ralph darkly. 'Sometimes they encourage them to walk around. Is that what you have been doing, Sir Geoffrey? It would explain why there are suddenly so many Saxons in La Batailge.'

'None of *them* are corpses,' said Galfridus wryly. 'Corpses do not eat, and these are devouring our stores at a rate of knots. I cannot imagine why the gatekeepers allow so many in.'

'I was talking to my dog,' said Geoffrey. He frowned, thinking they were not the first to comment on the number of Saxons.

Were they men rallying to Magnus and Harold? He did not have time to ponder, however, because Galfridus was regarding him with a shocked expression.

'Dogs are not permitted in here! They have a tendency to . . . to ravage, if you understand me.'

Geoffrey hoped the conclusions he had drawn from the animal's poor condition were correct and watched with considerable anxiety as Aelfwig pulled away the blankets that covered the bodies. There were three of them: Edith and two men. Neither of the men was familiar: one was old and looked as though he had long been ill – Geoffrey assumed it was his rival for the abbey's last coffin – and the other was a hefty, thick-set man. He tried to disguise his relief that all three appeared to be unchewed.

'I owe you an apology,' he said to Galfridus. 'I was not myself when I first arrived and regret any offence I may have given.'

Some of the rigid wariness faded from Galfridus's face. 'Your apology is accepted, although I suspect it was honesty, not illness, that made you refer to my amethyst horse as the work of a baboon. And to say that you had seen better art in brothels.'

'I came to see if I recognize the man who was killed,' said Geoffrey, to disguise his mortification. He wondered what else he had said.

'He died clutching a dagger,' said Galfridus. 'But Sir Roger says he is not one of the pirates.'

Geoffrey went to inspect the body more closely, wincing when he saw Bale's savage slash to its throat. It was a man in his late thirties with a strong, determined face. Its clothes were too tight for its muscular frame, and Geoffrey assumed that either someone had exchanged them after the man had died or he had borrowed them, perhaps as a disguise. When he inspected the fellow's hair, he saw it had been dyed: in places it was black, in others yellow. He turned over one of the hands, which was soft-palmed with traces of ink on the thumb. The face was entirely unfamiliar, and Geoffrey could not imagine why this man should have been looming over his sickbed with a weapon. However, there were certain conclusions he could draw.

'He was not a labourer, but a man who could write. I am not certain, but I saw a burly fellow rather like this on the beach with the villagers. His yellow hair suggests Saxon—'

'Oh, Lord,' said Galfridus, coming to inspect the dead man's face himself. 'It is Gyrth! I had no idea! Move him into the light, Ralph, so I can see better. Yes, it is him. But why is he wearing a peasant's clothes, and where is his habit?'

Geoffrey looked from Galfridus to Ralph to Aelfwig, trying to work out what was happening. 'Are you saying that one of your monks tried to stab me? But Aelfwig said he did not recognize him.'

'I *do* not,' objected Aelfwig. 'I have never seen him before – I am sure of it!'

'He was a novice,' explained Ralph. 'Or he wanted to be.'

Geoffrey was sceptical. 'He is older than me. How could he be a novice?'

Galfridus shrugged. 'Men come when God calls them, and there is no statutory age to serve Him. However, it helps if you bring a little something to smooth the way, and Gyrth offered the abbey a handsome bracelet – solid gold and studded with rubies.'

'Magnus and Harold mentioned a Gyrth,' said Geoffrey. 'He was Earl of East Anglia.'

'Actually he was not,' said Ralph. 'His father held the title, but this Gyrth never did, although he never stopped railing at the injustice of his disinheritance. He was quite tedious about it.'

'Then he came to us six months ago,' elaborated Galfridus, 'and professed to have had a dream in which God ordered him to take the cowl.'

'I was unsure whether his calling was genuine,' finished Ralph, 'so I recommended that he be sent to the chapel at Lullitune, to see how serious he was.'

'Why did no one recognize him when he was killed?' asked Geoffrey.

'Because no one here had ever met him, except Galfridus and me,' explained Ralph. 'We sent him off to Lullitune the day he arrived, and although we heard that a man had been killed in the hospital, it did not occur to either of us to come and inspect the corpse.'

Geoffrey was bemused. 'So why was he here wearing someone else's clothes and with black dye on his hair?'

Galfridus shrugged again. 'He is one of those Saxons for whom the fire of battle still burns. Perhaps he took against you because you are Norman. Do you think he murdered poor Edith, too?'

Geoffrey was surprised Galfridus should think *he* could supply solutions. 'I do not know. I was ill at the time.'

'Sir Roger says you have a way with murders,' said Ralph. 'And we would greatly appreciate any help. In return, we shall charge you nothing for the medicines Aelfwig provided, and, as Sir Roger told us you lost all your money in the shipwreck, this is a good offer. Just look at Edith's body and see whether you can throw any light on her cruel death.'

Geoffrey wished Roger had kept his mouth shut. But the three monks were looking hopefully at him, and he felt a certain need to make amends for his uncharacteristically caustic criticism of Galfridus's sculptures.

'She was strangled,' he said, walking to Edith's body and noting that the red ribbon was still embedded in her neck. Someone had washed her face and dressed her hair, but the cord remained in place. He looked up questioningly, wondering why no one had removed it.

'I did not like to poke her about too much,' explained Aelfwig, embarrassed. 'She is a woman, you see, and I took a vow to stay away from those.'

'Surely you have female patients from time to time?' asked Geoffrey.

'Well, yes, but I am not tempted by those,' replied Aelfwig enigmatically. Geoffrey decided he did not want to know more and applied himself to his task.

Whoever had throttled Edith had done so with considerable force. Broken fingernails showed she had struggled frantically to prise the ribbon loose, and there were corresponding scratches on her throat that she had put there herself. There were no other marks that he could see, and he had no intention of looking under her clothes when he was surrounded by monks. He stepped back with an apologetic shrug. Roger accused Lucian, Philippa accused Juhel, and the monks were suspicious of Gyrth, but there was nothing on Edith's body to incriminate any of them.

'Gyrth was strong,' said Ralph. 'He had a restrained tension that might have exploded.'

But Geoffrey was sceptical. 'That means Gyrth strangled a woman with ribbon and then tried to stab a man. Two different modes of execution.'

'What is the significance of that?' asked Galfridus.

'Most killers confine themselves to one,' began Geoffrey, then stopped abruptly because he did not want the monks to think him overly familiar with such matters. Besides, it was too much of a coincidence that Edith should have been killed in exactly the same way as her husband.

He started to back away, loath to spend more time in the charnel house than necessary, but his dog, which had declined to stray far from his side, tripped him up. He could have saved himself by grabbing Gyrth's bier, but it was unstable, and instinct told him that dragging a corpse to the ground would not be well received by the monastics. So he twisted to one side and landed on his knees. This placed him at eye level with Edith's left hand, which he had not inspected.

Caught under one of her nails, and held there by dried blood, was a tiny thread of red. For a moment, he thought it was a fibre from the ribbon around her neck, but it was darker and made from cloth rather than cord. He was almost certain the fragment had come from her killer and that she had clawed it away during her death throes. He pointed it out to the three monks.

'This means Gyrth is innocent,' said Aelfwig. 'There is nothing red on his corpse.'

'He could have changed,' suggested Ralph. 'Although it makes no sense to remove clothes after one killing if you intend to indulge in another.'

'I fear it means Edith's murderer is still at large,' said Galfridus, crossing himself. 'God help us!'

Geoffrey left the monks to their ruminations. With his dog trailing at his heels, he wandered towards the battlefield, craving time alone to think. A pair of wading birds in the bogs near the fish-ponds released eerie cries that reminded him of Roger's marsh fays. As he walked, he saw part of a sword blade jutting from the grass. He crouched to inspect it and realized the ground held many such relics from the battle, rusty and ancient and gradually being claimed by the earth.

He reached the top of a ridge and sat on a tree stump, considering what he had learned. Gyrth had offered himself as an abbey monk, but when Galfridus sent him to a distant chapel instead, he had returned in disguise. Geoffrey was fairly sure Gyrth was the burly figure he had seen after the shipwreck – with the man in the green hat. However, since *he* had done nothing to warrant an attack from strangers, he could only suppose that it was a case of mistaken identity.

The ink on his fingers showed Gyrth was literate, not someone who worked the land. Had he agreed to rally to Magnus and Harold, perhaps after promises to see him reinstated as Earl of East Anglia? Was *that* why he had tried to pass himself off as a man with a mission to serve God? To infiltrate La Batailge with a view to furthering whatever Magnus and Harold had in mind? If so, then it seemed the plot had been set in motion months ago.

Who had been Gyrth's target? Magnus or Harold, because he thought they were failing to act quickly enough? Or was he acting under Magnus's orders to dispatch Harold as a rival? Magnus had made no effort to disguise his satisfaction that Ulf would no longer be an issue.

And what about Edith? Were her killer and Vitalis's the same? Geoffrey believed so, because of the ribbon. But who could it be? At one point, he had suspected the women, but their circumstances showed it was not in their interests to have killed the old man. Philippa said she had held him in her arms and had believed him dead. He had probably fainted, and the killer had moved in to finish him off when the women had fled from the drenching squall. Geoffrey was sure Philippa had not killed Vitalis – and neither had Edith, assuming the killer was one and the same.

Roger believed Lucian to be guilty, and Geoffrey admitted the monk's behaviour was odd. There was also the pectoral cross Lucian said had been stolen, which the sailors had claimed was base metal. Or had they? Geoffrey could not decide whether that had been a genuine discussion or an imagined one. He frowned impatiently. It was hard enough to make sense of the situation, without being unsure which conversations had actually taken place.

And what about Juhel, whose friend was a spy for Bellême?

Would he strangle a woman? He would according to Philippa, who also saw him as Paisnel's murderer. Geoffrey tried to recall whether Lucian or Juhel had ever worn a garment of scarlet, but nothing sprang to mind. Of course, Edith had owned a red cloak herself, so perhaps the strand came from her own clothes, not the killer's. Philippa had claimed the cloak, but that had been after Edith was dead, and Geoffrey doubted she would have been permitted to don it while her wealthier friend was still alive.

He turned his mind to the ribbon that had killed Vitalis and Edith. He pulled out the piece Bale had taken from the old man's body and turned it over in his hands. Juhel was right to say there was a lot of it around. Edith had owned some, donated by Paisnel, and so had Juhel. Had ribbon been used to kill her because her murderer knew it had dispatched her husband and he was trying to create confusion?

But the deaths of Vitalis and Edith were irrelevant to the brewing Saxon rebellion. Geoffrey wondered how far Breme had travelled. He hoped his message would be taken seriously, because he was becoming increasingly convinced that the danger to Henry was real. He decided he would leave La Batailge the following morning and deliver his own account.

His mind turned to the battle that had raged over the ground in front of him some thirty-seven years before, changing England for ever. The ridge on which he sat was a superb vantage point, and the geography of the area explained why two fairly evenly matched forces had taken the best part of a day to decide the victor.

He was not alone for long. Several monks were strolling on the field, either singly or in groups, and one laboured up the ridge towards him.

'You are Godric Mappestone's son,' said the monk. 'I am Brother Wardard and I understand you want to speak to me.'

Geoffrey stood and bowed, but now the man was in front of him he did not know how to put his questions. He gestured that Wardard should sit on the tree stump and stared across the battle-field, wondering what it had been like when the monk had been a warrior waiting to advance. Wardard fumbled in his pouch and drew out a piece of dried meat, which he flung to the dog.

As the monk watched the animal eat, Geoffrey studied him. He must have been nearing his eighth decade but was still impressive. He was tall, strong and erect, although lines of pain etched around his mouth indicated his health was not all it might have been. He had obviously been a fine specimen in his prime, and confidence, nobilesse and dignity were still present. His eyes were alight with intelligence, and there was something about him that suggested he was still more soldier than monastic. Geoffrey understood why the monks of La Batailge had wanted him as their abbot.

'You wanted to ask about your father,' said Wardard eventually. 'Sir Roger told me that Vitalis discussed Godric's conduct during the battle. He should not have done.'

'Vitalis was losing his wits,' said Geoffrey, then realized he should moderate his tone. Wardard and Vitalis had been friends.

'Illness had turned him self-absorbed and greedy, and the Vitalis you met was not the one who stood here and fought for the Conqueror. Do not think badly of him.'

Geoffrey inclined his head, although he would make up his own mind about Vitalis once he had heard the truth from Wardard.

'It is wicked to denigrate a beloved father to a son,' Wardard went on. 'Dangerous, too – it is not unknown for sons to withdraw masses for their forbears' souls when they learn certain things. I would not like such a fate to befall Godric's beleaguered soul.'

'Did you know him well?'

'Did you?' countered Wardard.

It was not an easy question to answer. Geoffrey had been sent away for knightly training at the age of twelve and had not met Godric again for twenty years. His memories were of an aggressive, brutal tyrant, who had ruled his household with a brooding temper and ready fists. They had never shared confidences, and even when he was dying, Godric had lied and schemed.

'Not really,' he replied eventually.

'King Harold stood where you are now,' said Wardard, after another silence. 'He had come up in the night and chose to fight from this rise. His men stood close-packed, with their shields forming a solid wall. Duke William's troops were down there, just out of range of the Saxon archers, and there was a bog between them. And then the Normans advanced.'

'Up there, first,' said Geoffrey, waving his hand towards the west, as he recalled Godric's descriptions. 'That was where the Bretons were stationed, and my father was with them. The main troops and Duke William were straight ahead.'

'It was the Breton advance that almost saw the battle lost in its first hour,' said Wardard. 'They became mired in the bogs, then were forced to ride up this hill directly into the path of the Saxon archers. Their horses were unprotected, and most who reached the Saxon line were on foot, their mounts shot from under them. The Saxon counter-attack was savage, and it turned into a rout.'

'Vitalis said my father told his men to retreat before they were halfway up this hill,' said Geoffrey. 'On the grounds that the assault was impossible. Once the Breton line was broken, the other invaders might have left the field – and the victory – to Harold. It was only William's leadership that kept them in battle formation.'

Wardard rubbed his chin. 'It was not easy to watch our comrades slaughtered in such terrible numbers. Our archers were supposed to have advanced first, but their arrows ran out. The Breton advance was a total failure – and demoralizing, too.'

'Was my father the first to run?'

Geoffrey found he was afraid of the answer, worried that if Godric *had* been a coward, then cowardice might be in his own blood, and his courage might fail when *he* was faced with impossible odds. Of course, it had not failed at Civitot, Nicea, Antioch, Jerusalem or countless other skirmishes through the years when he had been certain he was going to die.

Wardard studied him. 'What did Godric tell you?'

Geoffrey sighed, not liking the way Wardard answered questions with questions. 'That he led the charge, screamed encouragement to the faint-hearted, killed at least twenty Saxons in the first assault, and was among the last to leave when it became a rout.'

'And what do you believe?'

Geoffrey studied the terrain, noting the steep angle of the ridge and the soft, muddy ground that would need to be traversed before making the laborious ascent. And he saw how easy it would have been to rain arrows down on those who were scrambling up it.

'That the Norman leading the charge was not likely to have lived very long.'

Wardard nodded. 'So, you have unveiled one truth without my help. It was impossible to tell who reached the Saxons first, but the leaders quickly became trapped between Harold's line and the press of Bretons surging behind. Death was inevitable.'

'What else can you tell me?' asked Geoffrey unhappily, seeing how the discussion was going to go. It was not that he was disappointed in Godric, whom he had never respected, but that he failed to understand how he could then have lied about his conduct on such an unrestrained scale.

Wardard's expression was wistful. 'I had an excellent view of the proceedings, although most of the time I wished I had not. But what I recall most vividly was your mother, swinging her axe. There was not a braver woman in Christendom than Lady Herleve. It was a pity she disguised herself, because her courage would have fired the palest of hearts. If she, a woman heavy with child, could fight like a lion, then so could any man.'

'I am sure she was spectacular,' said Geoffrey, recalling how she had always bested him and his brothers at axe work. 'But I would rather hear about my father.'

'He was given fine estates as a reward for his actions that day,' said Wardard evasively.

'I would like to know if he was awarded them on false pretences.'

'No,' said Wardard, standing up. 'It was a long time ago, and no good can come of opening old wounds. Think of him as a great hero, because that is what he wanted you to believe. And your mother certainly was. If you love them, you will do this.'

'But I do not—' Geoffrey was going to say that he did not love Godric or Herleve and never had, but Wardard raised a hand to silence him.

'We shall not speak of this again. Now, I have much to do: the Duke of Normandy is coming.'

Geoffrey had been about to argue, but the last statement jarred. 'You mean he has invaded?'

Wardard smiled. 'I would not go that far, although he is here without an invitation from King Henry. He apparently arrived with a handful of knights and intends to visit the abbey before riding to Winchester.'

'Not an invasion, then,' said Geoffrey relieved.

'Not from him. But who knows about Bellême, who has been thinking of revenge ever since his defeat last year? He might be crazed enough to attempt it, and strange ships have been seen . . .'

Geoffrey lingered on the rainswept battlefield. Had Wardard really refused to tell him the truth because he felt nothing good could come from sullying the memory of a dead warrior? Or was there another reason? It had not escaped Geoffrey's attention how many old men spoke warmly of his mother, and she had certainly been the more popular of the two. Was the tale of Godric's cowardice mere spite from thwarted rivals?

When he eventually returned to the hospital, he found Roger had visited the barber. His hair and beard were neatly trimmed, his face was scrubbed, and the wild, barbaric look he had assumed since the wreck was moderated. His surcoat had been cleaned, his boots polished, and the half-armour he wore as a knight at ease was spotless.

'Is there a brothel nearby?' Geoffrey asked.

'Have you not heard?' asked Roger. 'The Duke of Normandy is coming, and Galfridus intends to honour him with a feast.'

'Galfridus plays a dangerous game,' said Geoffrey. 'How many more of the King's enemies will he house under his roof?'

'The Duke is not Henry's enemy. He is his brother.'

Geoffrey did not bother to point out that family members were usually the most deadly enemies when thrones were at stake. 'Why is he coming?'

'According to Aelfwig, some of the Duke's friends – such as the Earl of Surrey – lost their English estates after helping Bellême last year, and he has come to ask for them to be given back.'

'Why should Henry agree to that when they sided against him – and might again in the future?'

'Such heady affairs are not our concern,' said Roger carelessly. 'But I am hoping it might set a precedent that will bring back my father, who is also in exile for defying Henry. So I thought I should make myself presentable.' He flaunted his finery. 'What do you think?'

Geoffrey shrugged. 'Very fine. Where is Bale?'

'He went with Galfridus's groom to Werlinges, to collect those horses. Apparently, de Laigle decided they were not worth taking and left them. Bale persuaded Galfridus to let him rescue them. Why? Do you want him to wash your clothes? You probably *should* clean up for the feast.'

Brushing the advice away, Geoffrey told him what he had learned from Juhel and from his examination of Gyrth and Edith. As Roger mulled over the new information, the door opened and Bale walked in. His bald head shone with sweat, and he made straight for the wine jug. Finding it empty, he headed for the bucket of water Ulfrith fetched from the well each morning. Without bothering with a cup, he grasped the entire thing, lifted it to his lips and tipped. Most cascaded down his neck and chest, and Geoffrey sighed – he had wanted a drink himself.

'Ulfrith has some spare water,' said Roger, guessing the reason for his friend's disapproval.

'Again?' muttered Ulfrith, glaring at Bale for his greed.

Roger's expression hardened. 'Again. And you will not answer back if you know what is good for you. I am tired of your cheek.'

Ulfrith was no fool and relinquished the flask, albeit reluctantly. Geoffrey took a gulp, but the contents had a bitter, unpleasant flavour. He supposed Ulfrith had added something nasty, in the hope that he would find another source in future.

'Do not drink any more,' said Ulfrith. He sounded concerned, and Geoffrey regarded him coldly, knowing his suspicions were correct.

'Dogs had been in Werlinges church, after the charred corpses,' reported Bale ghoulishly. 'The fire did not burn hot enough, see, and some of them were still whole.'

Geoffrey shuddered. Bale's fascination with such matters really was disagreeable.

'The groom and I dug a pit and buried the larger pieces,' Bale was saying. 'I said a few Latin words, like you did for Vitalis.'

'What did you say, exactly?' asked Geoffrey.

Bale quoted a few of Geoffrey's favourite obscenities, usually employed when he did not want others to know he was insulting them, and he saw he would have to be more careful in the future.

'De Laigle did not wait around after he fired the church,' Bale continued. 'But he should have done, because a lot of it is intact, and so were several houses he put to the torch. I thought looters would have been, but there was no sign of any.'

'You said de Laigle had already stripped the place,' said Roger. 'So there was probably nothing worth having.'

'There were tables, benches and the like. And there was the altar cross, which de Laigle told his men to leave for fear of being damned. But that sort of thing does not usually bother scavengers.'

'True,' agreed Roger. 'So it is odd that they did not take advantage of the situation – the ones who haunted the beach after the ship went down were determined, to say the least.'

'It *was* odd,' agreed Bale. 'And did I tell you that blood had been smeared on all the doors? Like a warning that it could happen again elsewhere.'

Geoffrey frowned. 'I did not notice any.'

'It was not there initially,' said Bale. 'It had appeared by the time I returned with de Laigle. Perhaps that is why he did not linger. I wonder if the pirates did it, to warn folk for the future.'

Geoffrey did not know what to make of it. He handed the water flask back to Ulfrith as he considered the matter.

'Since de Laigle did not explore much, I had a poke around myself,' Bale continued. 'But I have not had a chance to tell you because you were too ill. Would you like to hear now?'

'Not really,' said Geoffrey. Ulfrith's water had disagreed with him, and he felt slightly sick.

Bale forged on. 'De Laigle said it was obvious that the pirates were responsible – that a massacre and rough foreigners in the area could not be unrelated. But you said you were uncertain, so I decided to inspect the corpses for pieces of clothing ripped from their killers in their death throes.' His eyes gleamed strangely.

'Did you find any?' asked Geoffrey, intrigued.

'No,' came the disappointing reply. Then Bale grimaced. 'Moreover, I was so busy looking for clues on your behalf that the soldiers grabbed everything of value before I could get to it. There was nothing left for me.'

'You got that little cross,' said Ulfrith comfortingly. 'And a nice, thick habit to cut up and make into a new tunic.'

Bale reached inside his jerkin and brought out a small wooden cross of the kind worn by novices. 'It is nothing, and Galfridus will probably ask for it back if he finds out I have it.'

Geoffrey took it from him, then told him to fetch the habit. When it arrived, he inspected it carefully, noting the faint spray of blood across the front. He smiled at Bale and clapped him on the shoulder.

'You underestimate yourself. You have found a very important clue indeed. You see these letters carved on the cross? They spell "Gyrth".'

'Gyrth!' breathed Roger. 'The man who tried to kill you.'

'The very same. And Bale has just found his cross, and probably his habit, in a village where every living soul was murdered.'

# Twelve

The following day, the abbey was full of chaos as monks and laymen hurried to make everything perfect for the Duke of Normandy. The other guests were considered a nuisance: they were of no help with the preparations, but still needed to be fed. Magnus was particularly bothersome, complaining vociferously that no such preparations had been made for him.

Bale went to where a scanty breakfast of bread and unripe apples had been left, and swept the lot into a basket, which he then bore away. Realizing they would not eat unless they followed him, Magnus, Harold, Lucian and Juhel trailed him to where Geoffrey and Roger were sitting in the sun on a day as clear and blue as high summer.

Ulfrith was not far behind, carrying a bucket of ale. Geoffrey regarded it with a distinct lack of interest, and since his own water-skin was inside, he deftly unhooked Ulfrith's and took several gulps before he was discovered. He had spent an unsettled night with uncomfortable griping in his innards, and the bitter taste did little to put him in a better mood. With a scowl, Ulfrith stamped inside the building and pointedly retrieved Geoffrey's own, thrusting it into his hands.

Geoffrey declined the bread Bale offered, then rested his elbows on his knees and listened to the argument that broke out when Bale refused to share the food. Roger ordered the squire to accommodate the others, but only after he had taken the best for himself.

'What was in that water, Ulfrith?' asked Geoffrey after a while.

Ulfrith regarded him in alarm. 'Nothing! Why?'

'It tasted bitter. Did you add anything that will make me sick again?'

'Look!' Ulfrith seized his flask and took several large gulps, although he winced as they went down. 'See? The leather is old, so perhaps you can taste the tanning.'

Geoffrey was not convinced but supposed Ulfrith's concoction could not be too deadly if he was prepared to drink it himself. He turned his attention back to Roger and Lucian.

'I did *not* kill Edith!' Lucian was shouting. 'Galfridus believes me or he would have locked me away. *He* accepts that I was praying all night, so why do you not?'

'You did not recite a single office aboard ship, so why would you start now?' snapped Roger. 'Or were you doing it as penance for Edith's murder?'

'Go to Hell,' muttered Lucian through clenched teeth.

At that moment, Philippa arrived. Still scowling furiously at Roger, Lucian offered her his arm and invited her to stroll to the fishponds with him; good manners would not permit him to leave her in the company of rough knights, stupid squires and loutish Saxons.

'Do not go down there,' Harold called after them, cheeks bulging with the best part of a bulb of garlic. 'There have been reports of pirates in the area, and that part of the abbey is a bit remote.'

'Pirates?' asked Philippa in alarm. 'Are you sure?'

'Yes – ask Ulfrith,' replied Harold. 'One of them shot at Sir Geoffrey, who is only alive now due to Ulfrith's remarkable courage and foresight.'

Geoffrey laughed, earning himself a black glare from Ulfrith. The scowl intensified when Philippa declined to ask for details and flounced away at Lucian's side. Appetite gone, Ulfrith tossed his bread back into the basket, where it was seized by Magnus, moving fractionally faster than Harold. Magnus grinned, gratified by the victory over his rival.

'Are you saying these pirates came *inside* the abbey?' Juhel asked uneasily.

'Fingar told me he has been wandering around as he pleases,' replied Geoffrey.

'He had better not wander near me,' growled Roger, 'or he will find a sword in his gizzard.'

'Do you still intend to leave today?' asked Juhel. 'To tell King Henry what is happening here? If so, you will have to watch yourselves, or Fingar and his crew will be after you in a trice.'

'He is still not right,' said Roger, jerking his thumb at Geoffrey. 'And I refuse to let him go until he is. Besides, I do not want to leave without meeting the Duke. What is in that bag around your neck, Bale? It seems to get bigger every time I see it.'

'This?' asked Bale, shooting a nervous glance in Geoffrey's direction. 'Just bits and pieces.'

'Not from Werlinges, I hope,' said Geoffrey. 'I thought the cross and habit were all you took.'

'They were,' said Ulfrith, standing up for his comrade. 'He had the ring from Vitalis on the beach, and he stole money from the dead shepherd in the wood. None of that is from Werlinges.'

Furious, Bale came to his feet fast, a dangerous look in his eyes. Ulfrith was startled, not understanding what he had done wrong. Geoffrey stood, too, and glared at Bale until he subsided.

'What did you tell him that for?' Bale demanded furiously.

'I was defending you,' snapped Ulfrith, angry in his turn. 'I told him what you already had, so he does not assume it was from Werlinges. I was being a good friend to you.'

Geoffrey sat again, grateful Ulfrith's brand of friendship did not extend to him.

Bale pulled a face at him, then turned to Geoffrey. 'I was going to tell you, sir, but then you gave me that lecture at Werlinges, so I thought I had better keep quiet. I *borrowed* this from the shepherd, because I thought it was odd – a shepherd having this much gold.'

Geoffrey took Bale's purse and emptied it into his hand. He was astonished – Bale had found a fortune.

'There are coins here from Flanders and Ireland,' he said, puzzled. 'What was a shepherd doing with them? And how did you take Vitalis's ring when I was watching you?'

'I did it when I wrapped his body in the cloak,' replied Bale, with the grace to look shamefaced. 'Sir Roger taught me a sleight of hand, see.'

Geoffrey sighed, annoyed with Roger as well as Bale. 'My back was turned for a moment, and you flouted my orders?'

'I *tried* to tell you about it, sir, but you would not listen. Here.' Bale passed the ring to Geoffrey, who regarded it in distaste. 'I took it because, although it was on Vitalis's hand at the beach, previously it belonged to *him*.' His accusing finger indicated Magnus.

'Not me!' said Magnus, startled. 'I do not know what you are talking about.'

'Are you sure, Bale?' asked Geoffrey.

The squire nodded with such conviction that Geoffrey was sure he was telling the truth. Magnus obviously sensed he was about to be exposed, because he leaned forward to inspect the bauble and hastily revised his story.

'Oh, yes, that *is* mine. It went missing on *Patrick*, and I assumed a pirate had taken it.'

Geoffrey was puzzled. 'But you said nothing – and it is valuable.'

Magnus was dismissive. 'When I am king, I shall have a hundred such rings.'

'But you are not king yet,' Geoffrey pointed out. 'And until you are, you need all the treasure you can lay your hands on. Why you were so stoic about its loss?'

'It is *not* valuable, actually,' said Roger, examining it closely. 'So it would not have been worth making a fuss. Especially with the likes of those pirates.'

'But it is a pretty bauble even so.' Magnus held out his hand. 'Give it back.'

'No,' said Geoffrey. Even if Magnus *was* its rightful owner, there was a reason why he had not mentioned its loss, and it was all very suspicious. He was not about to hand it over.

Harold gazed at him in astonishment. 'You intend to keep it for yourself? But Bale has admitted to hauling it from a corpse! It cannot be lucky.'

Geoffrey handed it and the purse to Bale. 'I do not want it, but nor should it go to Magnus. Not yet.'

'This is outrageous!' spluttered Magnus furiously. 'And I do not forget such slights.'

He stalked away, his tall, thin body held rigidly erect.

'He bears grudges,' warned Harold unhappily. 'And he can be spiteful – so watch yourselves.'

It was warm in the sun, and Harold began to doze. Ulfrith wandered away, and Geoffrey supposed he was going to torture himself with the sight of Philippa and Lucian.

'The boy is a fool for that woman,' declared Roger, grimacing in exasperation.

'I shall be glad when we leave this place,' said Geoffrey unhappily. 'His infatuation is making him sly and vengeful. He *did* add something to his water flask to stop me from using it, you know. He would never have resorted to such a low trick before.'

'Did he, by God!' exclaimed Roger. 'That *is* low, especially as you have been so sick. If it brings about a relapse, I shall cleave his head from his shoulders. Of course, he is not the only one who likes to tamper with drinks: Lucian poisoned you with his cure-all.'

'But Magnus took it, too, and he was not nearly as ill as I was.'

'But he *was* unwell. And he also used Juhel's balm for his scratched arm. Yes, I know we have been through this before, but think about what Bale said about stealing Vitalis's ring.'

'A trick he learned from you,' said Geoffrey, rather coolly.

'Yes, yes.' Roger's wave of the hand indicated that was irrelevant. 'But *think* about it: he deceived you with a sleight of the hand. And Lucian and Juhel did the same. Lucian must have had *two* phials – he and Magnus drank from one, but he exchanged it for another when it was your turn. And the same goes for Juhel's balm: one part of the pot is for healing and the other is for harm. Remember his jar – red one side and blue the other? It is so he can remember which is which.'

'No,' said Geoffrey. 'I accept that if Bale can deceive me with tricks, then anyone can, but I doubt *two* men had the idea of poisoning me simultaneously. And, besides, why me? You are the one with the gold.'

'But you have wits, and those are dangerous to men like Juhel and Lucian. I bragged about the cases you have solved – obviously, they became worried.'

'What, both of them?'

'They are in it together,' persisted Roger. 'They are involved in something sinister that saw Vitalis, Edith and that shepherd murdered by Lucian, and Paisnel killed by Juhel. Just because you do not know what it is, does not mean it has not happened.'

'I suppose it is possible,' said Geoffrey, although he could not see the two as partners. He looked at Bale, who was regarding him in much the same way as his dog did on occasion: with a certain desperate affection that he was not sure would be reciprocated.

'You have done well, Bale,' he sad, watching the man's face split into a grin of pleasure. 'You uncovered evidence that put

Gyrth at Werlinges during the massacre, and you were probably right to take the ring and the purse – although you should not make a habit of it.'

'No, sir,' said Bale. 'I will not steal from corpses without good cause in future. But how do the cross and habit prove Gyrth responsible for the massacre? I thought they only showed he visited the village.'

'Because of the way the blood is sprayed across the material. In battles, I have seen many such stains when throats have been slashed. There are also marks in the region of the thigh, where he wiped his blade. Gyrth killed someone at Werlinges without question. Then he donned civilian clothes and came here.'

'Where he wanted to kill someone,' mused Roger. 'But why you, Geoff?'

'I doubt Gyrth was after him,' said Harold, sitting up and rubbing his eyes. Geoffrey wondered how long he had been listening. 'It was more likely a monk who had offended him.'

'That is unlikely,' said Geoffrey. 'It seems he was only here for a few hours before Galfridus dispatched him to some distant village, to test his sincerity.'

'Then perhaps *that* is why he went to the hospital,' suggested Harold. 'He thought it was the monks' dormitory, because he had not been here long enough to know better.'

'No,' said Geoffrey. 'There was not enough time for a monk to have annoyed Gyrth to that extent. I suspect his arrival here had something to do with your rebellion – and so did the massacre. Gyrth was not the only one to have been involved in that. Your brother Ulf was there, and dry blood, combined with wet, indicates he had been fighting *before* Bale got him. These stains indicate he did not *kill* the villagers himself, but he may well have ordered Gyrth to do it.'

Harold shook his head, horrified by the suggestion. 'Impossible! We need people alive, not dead. Whatever happened at Werlinges had nothing to do with us.'

'Of course it did. And the fact that Gyrth was involved proves it.'

'Gyrth did support our cause,' acknowledged Harold unhappily. 'But I do not see how he thought to further it by slaughtering villagers and stabbing men in abbeys.'

Geoffrey was sorry for him. Poor Harold was an innocent who

attracted supporters by his smiling manners. But, as soon as he was no longer needed, harder, more ruthless men would step in, and Harold would find his throat cut.

And then something else became clear. Bale had mentioned blood smeared on doors in Werlinges, as though in warning. Geoffrey suspected that was exactly what it was: Werlinges had escaped being laid to waste by King William, and Ulf and Gyrth wanted everyone to know what happened to those who collaborated with the enemy. The hapless priest had tried to make amends by providing horses for Magnus and Harold, but the Saxon rebels had not been appeased.

'So if Gyrth was not after you, and not after a monk, who *was* he trying to kill?' asked Roger.

'You,' replied Geoffrey. 'Rebellions are always hungry for money, and it is common knowledge that you stole a great deal of gold from the pirates.'

'They wanted to use *my* money to topple Henry?' asked Roger indignantly.

Geoffrey nodded.

Roger rubbed his chin. 'Then it is just as well it is in a safe place.'

'Where?' asked Geoffrey.

Roger grinned and tapped the side of his nose. 'Now, that would be telling.'

The Duke did not come that day, and towards the end of the afternoon the atmosphere of excited anticipation faded to anticlimax. Galfridus retired to the church, although no one was sure whether he was praying for the Duke to arrive or to send word that he was *not* coming.

'It will be a delight to host him,' he said morosely, as he and Geoffrey met near the kitchens – the knight to beg a bone for his dog, the monk to snatch a mouthful of carp. 'But I shall remove the Lamb of God, of course. I do not want him making jokes about the Pig of God, which is how the novices now refer to it, thanks to you. But you know the Duke, do you not? Sir Roger said you were in his service.'

'Many years ago, and as a very lowly squire. He will not remember me. But do not be too anxious – he is easily distracted and might not arrive for days if something amuses him on the way.'

'That would be foolish. The last time the Duke visited England, it was as an invader, and if he dallies before making his obeisance to King Henry, he may find himself attacked.' Galfridus's expression turned to alarm. 'And then perhaps Bellême will come to the Duke's aid, God help us!'

'If you dislike fighting, why do you allow Magnus and Harold to stay here? Surely you can see Magnus is plotting?'

'He is a dreamer. His schemes will come to nothing.'

'I am not so sure. Look at how many Saxons have gathered in your precinct – they cannot *all* be pilgrims. Moreover, I saw Harold address a gathering of about fifty men last night.'

Galfridus swallowed hard. 'But Magnus has no funds for a rebellion,' he said weakly.

'I am not so sure. Bale found a considerable quantity of gold on a shepherd, which I am certain was intended to fuel the revolt. I suspect he was not a shepherd at all and was taking the purse to some central fund, but was killed in the storm before he could deliver it.'

'No,' objected Galfridus miserably. 'Surely not!'

'I believe Gyrth intended to steal Roger's gold, too – he mistook us in the dark. And Fingar told me the roads near here are full of carts and horses after dark. It all adds up to a gathering of troops and resources, and suggests a hostile action against the King. You will be deemed their supporter if you do not make a stand.'

Galfridus rubbed a hand across his face. 'I have an awful feeling you are right. But what can *I* do to stop them? I have sent messages to de Laigle, but I am not sure he reads them, let alone passes them to the King. And I can order these assembled Saxons to disperse until I am blue in the face, but they will not obey *me*, a man of mixed parentage.'

'Your monks—'

'Half my monks and all my lay-brothers are Saxon. The only thing I can pray for now is that Magnus makes his stand elsewhere. But do not let me keep you, Sir Geoffrey.'

He shot into the kitchen and made for the roast carp in an effort to calm himself. Through the open door, Geoffrey watched him snatch some and eat it fast, pausing only to complain to the cook that there was glass in it.

'Glass?' demanded the cook. 'There is not!' He appealed to Harold, who was sitting on a table swinging his short legs as he ate a piece of cheese. 'You see? Normans complain endlessly.'

Later that evening, when the light was fading, Geoffrey sat with Bale behind the chapter house, looking over the battlefield. 'What do *you* make of the business at Werlinges?' he asked.

Bale considered the question seriously. He was not often asked for his opinion, and when he was, he tended to take his time to formulate a response.

'Well, you and Roger fought bravely, and I stopped King Ulf from joining the affray. But I was surprised King Magnus and King Harold did not help us. They must have received some weapons training, and I did not expect them to be so useless.'

'True, but perhaps we should be glad that Juhel and Lucian stayed out of the way.'

'Juhel would have been all right,' said Bale. 'On the ship, he fought a pirate and defeated him with ease, even though the fellow had a dagger and Juhel had only his bare hands.'

Geoffrey was surprised. 'You have not mentioned this before.'

'You did not ask. But Juhel *is* a fighting man. Maybe not with a sword, but with a knife or his hands, he would be a match for most men.'

Geoffrey considered the information. 'It seems there is more to Juhel than meets the eye – or more than he is willing to let anyone see.'

'I still think he poisoned you,' said Bale. 'He is a sly bastard.'

When Geoffrey made no reply, Bale took the ring and pouch of gold from his bag and began fiddling with them. Geoffrey took the purse and looked again at the coins, before handing it back.

'You saw the shepherd's body. Roger believes Brother Lucian killed him. What do you think?'

There was another lengthy pause. 'His head was under the tree trunk,' replied Bale eventually. 'Squashed almost flat. But there were no other wounds. Lucian *may* have held him under the tree when it fell, I suppose, but it would not have been easy to manage.'

'Then I imagine it was an accident. Did you notice his clothes? Did he look Saxon?'

'Oh, yes. His hair was long and braided, like Saxons used to wear it. Why?'

'Because it is too much of a coincidence for a shepherd to be loaded with gold near where Saxon princes are gathering. And it is odd that a pauper would oust a monk while a storm raged outside – even the most reclusive of men do not deny shelter under such conditions. But this shepherd did not want witnesses.'

'Witnesses to what?'

'To this rebellion. I am sure there is more to it than we think.'

Geoffrey's plan to leave for Winchester before dawn the following morning was thwarted when he found the stables virtually empty. An unhelpful groom eventually admitted that the abbey's entire stock had been taken to the blacksmith for re-shoeing, and all that remained were Galfridus's personal nags, which he never lent to anyone. Geoffrey strongly suspected the animals had been quartered somewhere nearby, ready to be used by the Saxons.

'I could walk,' said Geoffrey, returning to Roger after a frustrating interview with Galfridus, during which his request to borrow one of the remaining mounts was politely but firmly denied.

'You would make poor time,' said Roger. 'You are not yet strong enough for such a trek. And I am not leaving you here unprotected, so do not think of asking me to go instead. But Galfridus is playing with fire! I am beginning to think he wants this rebellion to succeed. He does nothing to stop it, and now he refuses to help you warn the King.'

'I suspect he simply does not want to be without a means of escape should the situation turn nasty. Damn! Without horses, our only other option is to stay here and see what we can do to thwart this uprising. I hope to God that Breme has delivered that letter.'

Roger patted his shoulder reassuringly. 'Do not fret. He is a reliable fellow.'

Geoffrey went to the church, but the melodic chanting from the chancel did not soothe him this time, and he prowled restlessly along the nave and aisles, looking at the carvings on the pillars without really seeing them. Roger knelt with his hands pressed together, his heavy features arranged in an expression he imagined was devout. Ulfrith stood behind him and stared miserably at the central crossing, where Philippa loitered with Lucian.

Meanwhile, Juhel leaned against a pier near the south transept, eyes fixed unwaveringly on Harold, who was chatting amiably to some lay-brothers. The Saxon said something to make them laugh, and the sounds of their mirth caused Ralph to storm from the chancel to berate them. When the sacristan had gone, Harold said something else that sent them into paroxysms of merriment, although the laughter was quieter this time.

'Ulf was not a fellow for giggles,' remarked Magnus to Geoffrey. 'He was an iron man, who frightened even his closest friends with his cold heart and ruthless determination.'

'Then you must be glad he is dead. He sounds a more formidable rival than Harold.'

Magnus's expression was dismissive. 'Harold is no rival! Look at how he fraternizes with servants. I cannot imagine how he will manage at the head of an army – he will be too busy gossiping with his stable-boys.'

'What about your cousin Gyrth?' asked Geoffrey. 'Would he have made a good general?'

'Yes, and his death is a bitter blow to our cause.' Magnus regarded him thoughtfully. 'Perhaps *you* should join us. There will be great rewards for men involved in our victory – and dire punishments for those who side with the Usurper. You would be wise to consider your future.'

'I will take my chances with Henry.'

Magnus's expression turned to anger. 'You are a fool, and I shall personally see that you regret your decision.'

He turned on his heel and strode away, not caring that he powered through a procession of monks. Several outraged glances followed him, but Geoffrey saw more that were admiring and hopeful. With the end of prime, monastics and visitors alike began to trail towards their breakfasts. Roger was one of the first, Bale hot on his heels.

Harold walked with Geoffrey, breathing in air scented with newly cut grass. 'It is far warmer here than inside that church. Why do builders always make them so cold? When I am king, the first thing I shall do is commission a warm church. Will you accept the challenge? Roger tells me you are interested in architecture.'

Geoffrey laughed. 'Such a project would be wholly beyond my meagre capabilities.'

Harold laid a hand on Geoffrey's shoulder and lowered his voice. 'I heard what Magnus said, and I want you to know that *I* will not let him harm you.'

'I am not worried about Magnus.'

'You should be. Now our time is close, he is becoming unsettled and dangerous. He told me last night that he will not rest until he has eradicated every Norman from England.'

Geoffrey watched Harold waddle away, thinking he had never encountered a less likely horde of rebels. He was jolted from his musings by a yell and watched Bale lumber after the dog, which was racing away with a piece of smoked pork. Not wanting to be blamed for the theft, he ate his breakfast alone outside the refectory, watching sparrows squabble for crumbs at his feet. Suddenly, droppings splattered on to the bread he was lifting towards his mouth.

'That is a sign of good fortune,' said Juhel, who happened to be passing. 'But you are wise to be out here, because Magnus is holding forth again. Do you think his claims have any substance? There is certainly a lot of Saxon coming and going, and the fish ponds are thick with folk.'

'That is because Galfridus told the layfolk to catch as many carp as possible, so there is a good supply for when the Duke arrives.'

Juhel was unconvinced. 'Delilah has the right idea about that Magnus, and so does your dog: they both took an instant dislike to him.'

'What do you think they see in him that we do not?'

'That he is more dangerous than he looks. I am a stranger here, and what is happening is really none of my business, but I do not like to see a country torn asunder with silly plots. Do you think there is anything we can do to stop this before it goes too far?'

'I sent a message to the King,' replied Geoffrey. 'And de Laigle should have dispatched a warning, too. I imagine it will not be long before someone comes to investigate.'

'Good,' said Juhel. 'I wish I had done the same – I count His Majesty among my list of acquaintances, you know. Incidentally, Magnus is a liar. Do you recall that scratch on his arm at Werlinges? Well, I think he received it fighting Ulf. He ran into the church, then raced out a few moments later with Ulf at his heels.'

'You smeared his injury with your balm,' Geoffrey said, thinking it was time he resolved whether Juhel had poisoned him once and for all. 'Do you still have it?'

Juhel looked uncomfortable. 'No. Roger accused me of poisoning you with it, so I threw it away before he could add something toxic, then denounce me as a murderer. I have seen how scapegoats are procured, and I am too easy a target – a lone Breton among Normans and Saxons.'

'Roger was right to accuse you. You do not like Magnus, and it was not me you wanted to harm, but *him*. The pot has two sides – red and blue – but in your excitement at having your victim at your mercy, you confused them.'

Juhel was aghast. 'That is a dreadful thing to say! I would not know the first thing about feeding a man noxious substances.'

'Obviously, as Magnus and I are still alive. I should have listened to Philippa when she told me you were a killer. She saw you throw Paisnel overboard – and saw him wave his arm in a feeble attempt to call the boat back.'

Juhel's jaw dropped. 'She is lying.'

'I thought so, too. But Donan also saw him struggling in the water.'

Juhel began to tremble, his face ivory pale. 'That cannot be true! He was dead.'

'You admit tossing him over the side?' pounced Geoffrey.

Juhel put his head in his hands. 'He was dead! There was no life-beat.'

'The cold water must have shocked him into consciousness. Why did you kill him? I thought you were friends.'

'I did *not* kill him,' whispered Juhel. 'I admit to tipping his body into the sea. But only after someone else had stabbed him.'

Geoffrey did not believe him. 'You probably murdered Vitalis, too,' he said in disgust. 'A frail old man. How could you?'

'He was not as helpless as you think,' said Juhel, some of his fire returning. 'But *I* did not kill him, and I did not kill Paisnel.'

'Right,' said Geoffrey, walking away.

It had not been a pleasant interview, and Geoffrey was disheartened. When he saw Roger sitting on the hospital steps, he flopped down next to him and put his head in his hands.

'I have been thinking,' the big knight said. 'It is beginning to feel very dangerous here, so I recommend we walk to the nearest town, buy horses, then ride to Winchester. I trust Breme to deliver your message, but it occurs to me that Henry may later ask why we did not do it ourselves.'

Geoffrey was relieved. It was a sensible plan. 'Shall we go now?'

'No – tonight is the eve of the Feast of St Columba, and I intend to keep a vigil until dawn. We shall leave tomorrow at dusk, when the darkness will afford us some protection. Besides, you need the additional day to regain more of your strength. You are still too pale for my liking.'

Geoffrey stared at him. 'St Columba? Who is he?'

Roger waved an expansive hand. 'A holy man – Irish, I believe. Or Scottish. God's blood! What is Ulfrith doing to that woman now?'

Philippa's furious voice was audible over most of the abbey as she screeched her outrage. Geoffrey hurried towards them, Roger at his heels, wondering whether the squire had done something that would see them on their way sooner than anticipated. Galfridus would not want female guests to suffer sexual advances while they were under his protection.

'My Lady!' cried Ulfrith, distraught. 'I meant no harm. I love you!'

Geoffrey saw Lucian nearby, watching the scene with a troubled expression. Philippa looked at him out of the corner of her eye while she railed at Ulfrith, who hung his head with shame. Geoffrey frowned, wondering what she was up to.

'I must go to the chapter house,' mumbled Lucian, edging away. 'Brother Ralph is reading from the writings of the Venerable Bede.'

'Do not leave me!' cried Philippa, swinging around fast, so the folds of Edith's cloak billowed. 'Not to the mercy of louts. Why did you not tell Ulfrith that I am already taken? We have an understanding – I gave you my necklace as our troth.'

'You gave me your necklace for my journey to Bath,' corrected Lucian, a little coolly. 'There was no "understanding" between us. How could there be? I am a monk.'

Philippa gaped at him. 'But you said you would renounce your vows for me.'

The flicker of unease that crossed Lucian's face convinced Geoffrey she was telling the truth, but the monk remained firm. 'You are mistaken, madam. My vows are sacred.'

Philippa was furious. 'It is because of what you read in Vitalis's will,' she declared accusingly. 'You had no right to steal it from me and poke through it without my permission.'

Lucian shrugged. 'You do not own it. So how could you, a woman who willingly undertook a bigamous marriage, stop me?'

Geoffrey understood immediately what had happened: Lucian had not known Philippa's 'marriage' was illegal and had expected her to inherit Vitalis's wealth. Now he was in retreat – and Philippa had used the hapless Ulfrith, fooling the boy into molesting her in the hope that Lucian would be forced to declare himself publicly before it was too late.

'So, Aelfwig was right: you *did* only want me for my money,' said Philippa, bitterly accepting the truth. 'Except that now you know I have none.'

'Men of God are not interested in money, lass,' said Roger slyly. He looked hard at Lucian. 'Unless he is an imposter, of course, and no more a monastic than I am.'

The altercation had attracted the attention of several monks, Aelfwig among them.

'Lucian is not an imposter,' said Aelfwig, not altogether happily. 'He may not act like one of us, but I have visited the abbey at Bath, and he *is* the bursar there. He is most certainly a powerful member of our Order.'

'He may be powerful, but he is not rich,' said Geoffrey. 'His "gold" cross was actually painted steel, and he has been inveigling money, rings and necklaces from anyone who will part with them. And I imagine he has no intention of repaying any "loans", either. Anything left over when he reaches Bath will go straight into his abbey's coffers – from which there will be no return.'

Lucian looked angry. 'So I collect funds for my abbey. What of it? There is nothing wrong with vain women parting with baubles for a worthy cause. I keep very little for myself. Ask my Bishop.'

'He knows what you do?' asked Aelfwig, shocked.

Lucian regarded him coldly. 'He sanctions it.'

'You do it to curry his favour, because you have no influential family to help you,' surmised Roger. 'You lied about that. You are—'

'You forget yourself!' snarled Lucian. 'My family owns most of Herefordshire and my father has the ear of the King.'

Geoffrey smiled. 'My own estates are in Herefordshire, and I know the biggest landowners. Your family is not among them. Like me, they may hold a tiny part, but they will not be wealthy.'

'I did my best to warn you,' said Aelfwig to Philippa. 'I told you not to give him anything.'

Philippa scowled at Lucian, who scowled at Aelfwig. 'So I have parted with my necklace,' she said flatly. 'The only thing of value I own – for a man who does not intend to marry me?'

'There is still me,' said Ulfrith generously. '*I* will marry you.'

'But I do not want *you*,' she sneered, making the squire take a step away, stung. 'Boy!'

Geoffrey watched her, amazed at the risks she had taken to secure herself a safe future. He wondered what else had she done in her relentless pursuit of a man who would keep and protect her. And then answers snapped clear in his mind. Carefully, he eased back her cloak, then pointed to the purse that he had seen as she had twirled around. Protruding from the top was a strand of red ribbon.

'You killed your friend,' he said. 'And your husband.'

'I did not!' screeched Philippa furiously. 'Why would I kill Vitalis, when he was my provider? And Edith said she would look after me.'

'But she could not guarantee it,' said Geoffrey. 'The chances are that she would have been forced to marry another wealthy suitor, and then what would have happened to you? Women are seldom allowed to control the money they inherit, and you knew Edith might not have been able to keep her promise. It was safer to kill her and try for Lucian.'

To Geoffrey's surprise, Philippa proved quick-thinking and resourceful, quite unlike the babbling imbecile he had taken her for. She came towards him with a sly smile.

'You are wrong,' she said. 'About everything. I loved Vitalis and I loved Edith. And, anyway, Edith was killed when I was with Roger – with whom I spent the night.'

'Oh, God!' whispered Ulfrith shakily.

'Yes – we were here, in the church,' said Roger, more to the listening monks than Ulfrith. 'So you must be wrong, Geoff. She could not have killed Edith. I still think it was Lucian.'

'Lucian was in the Lady Chapel from vespers until prime,' said Aelfwig, although he regarded his fellow monk with deep distaste. 'And a dozen brothers will tell you the same. *We* were praying that Bellême will not invade England, and *he* was asking God to send him some money.'

But Geoffrey now knew the truth. He continued to address Philippa. 'Edith was strangled *before* you sought out Roger's company. You used him because you knew you might need an alibi.'

'She was alive when I left, and dead when I returned,' said Philippa coldly. 'And *you* cannot prove otherwise. It is dreadful of you to say these things when I am alone and unprotected.'

She shot a rueful glance at Lucian and drew the cloak more closely around her shoulders. As she did so, one of its pleats opened and revealed the lining underneath. The material was scarlet, but there was a corner that had been ripped away. Geoffrey stepped forward to inspect it, recalling what he had seen in Edith's dead hand. Philippa shoved him away with considerable force and stalked out with her head held high, defiance in her every move.

'Was that ripped when she killed Edith?' asked Roger uneasily.

'I imagine there was an argument between them,' replied Geoffrey. 'And the ribbon was to hand. It is not difficult for one woman to throttle another, if her blood is up. Then she was cunning enough to slip out and secure herself an alibi.'

'Unfortunately, throttling Edith did nothing to affect Philippa's situation one way or the other,' said Lucian. 'I read Vitalis's will today. He bequeathed everything to sons from an earlier marriage, and Edith was to have a paltry pension until her next marriage. Philippa was not even mentioned.'

'He is right,' added Aelfwig. 'She brought me the will when she first arrived, and wept bitterly when I read it to her. She snatched it back, and I assumed she intended to destroy it, perhaps with a view to composing one that was more congenial to her.'

'Yet you did nothing to stop her?' asked Lucian. 'And you criticize *my* behaviour! Hypocrite!'

'She is a poor Saxon lass,' flared Aelfwig. 'Abused by greedy Normans. Of course I kept quiet about the will in the hope that it would give her a chance to redress the injustice of her situation. I did not think she would stoop to murder . . .'

'Philippa is not Saxon,' sneered Lucian. 'She said she was kin to my Bihop, John de Villula – and he is as Norman as they come. She said an alliance with her would earn me untold favour in ecclesiastical courts.'

'And you believed her?' demanded Aelfwig archly. 'When she is so patently poor?'

'I am unused to liars,' replied Lucian stiffly. 'So yes, I believed her – until a few moments ago, when she slipped up with some insignificant fact. I might have overlooked it, had she not then promptly tried to distract me from it by screeching that the squire had assaulted her.'

'And I never touched her,' whispered Ulfrith, still shocked.

'It seems we all underestimated her,' said Geoffrey quietly. 'She is far cleverer than we thought.'

'What a merry dance she has led us all!' muttered Roger, half disapproving and half admiring. He addressed Geoffrey. 'So, is that it? Philippa killed Edith? Did she dispatch Vitalis, too?'

Geoffrey shook his head. 'She had far too much to lose. Edith did not kill him, either, because Philippa would have stopped her.'

'So what happens now?' asked Roger. 'Will she hang? It is a pity – she is a pretty wench.'

'Not on the evidence we have,' said Geoffrey. He lowered his voice. 'However, I would recommend you keep Ulfrith away from her. She is bitter and vengeful, and I would not like to think of her striking at us through him.'

# Thirteen

'I shall never understand monks,' said Roger as he packed up his salvaged possessions later that day. Ulfrith sat in the window looking miserable, while Bale sharpened his knives, humming under his breath. Geoffrey sat on the edge of the bed and took sips from Ulfrith's water flask. Nearby, Aelfwig was folding blankets. 'They let themselves be deceived by a pretty face.'

So, too, had Roger, by allowing Philippa to use him as her alibi, but Geoffrey said nothing.

'Monastics *are* a strange breed,' agreed Bale. 'These notions of not bearing arms and living in peace are not normal. And Lucian *is* a monk, because he did not slaughter anyone after all – Philippa strangled Edith, and the shepherd's death was an accident.'

It was peculiar logic, but Geoffrey did not feel inclined to take issue with him.

'So Juhel must have murdered Paisnel and probably Vitalis, too,' mused Roger. 'Which means that all the murders are solved, but not one culprit will pay the price. Juhel will slip away and may well kill again, and Philippa will find herself a rich husband.'

'You are wrong,' said Ulfrith from the window, although his voice lacked conviction. 'She is too beautiful to be a murderess.'

Aelfwig clicked his tongue admonishingly. 'You had a lucky escape, my boy. If I had known the love potion you charged me to make was to be used on her, I would never have sold it to you.'

'What love potion?' asked Roger.

'I needed help,' said Ulfrith, unrepentant. 'Nothing else was working, but now I see why. She was intent on having Lucian because she thought he was rich. And I am not.'

Geoffrey was about to take another gulp of water but paused with the flask in mid-air. 'Is *that* what I have been drinking these past few days? Well, I suppose it explains your odd questions after you rescued me from Fingar – whether I felt the urge to lie with Philippa. You were afraid you had invested in a charm and I had reaped the benefits.'

'It did not work for either of us,' said Ulfrith mournfully.

Geoffrey rubbed his chin. 'But there was an odd taste to the water *before* we met Aelfwig – after the fight at Werlinges, when you urged me to drink it. Magnus also wanted some, but you were reluctant to let him have it. Shortly afterwards, we were both plagued with odd visions. What was in it? A potion of your own that would make me repellent to her?'

Ulfrith's guilty expression indicated Geoffrey was guessing along the right lines. 'You were not supposed to *keep* drinking it, but I could not stop you.'

Roger looked more dangerous than Geoffrey had ever seen him. He advanced on Ulfrith with a gleam in his eye that was distinctly unnerving.

'*You* poisoned Geoffrey? You fed him something you knew would make him ill? And then, when he was laid low, you gave him more?'

'No!' cried Ulfrith, leaping to his feet and backing away. 'It was not like that! My grandmother used to swallow the stuff when she wanted to see into the future. It used to make her jabber nonsense, but she was never ill. All I wanted was for Sir Geoffrey to be unappealing to Lady Philippa, so she might spare a glance for me.'

Roger regarded him furiously. 'But your grandmother probably drank it all her life, and you fed it to Geoff without knowing what might happen. She was a woman, and he is a man. They are different!'

Geoffrey was unable to prevent a smile. 'But no harm was done.'

Roger rounded on him. 'No harm? You would not say that if you could have seen yourself. Aelfwig told me you would not live the night, and I spent a lot of gold making you well again – buying prayers, paying for Breme's charm, making donations to the abbey. He almost killed you!'

'I did *not*!' squeaked Ulfrith, cowering as Roger spun around again. 'I tried to stop him from taking more, but you ordered me not to be mean. There was nothing I could do . . .'

'He tried to make amends,' said Geoffrey to Roger. 'It was

Ulfrith who gave me water instead of medicine. Breme told me it was his idea, but it was probably Ulfrith's.'

'Yes!' insisted Ulfrith. 'The idea came to me after I saw the jug next to his bed. He must have fetched it himself when I left him to watch . . .'

He trailed off, regarding Roger in horror, but the squire's inadvertent confession clarified more issues in Geoffrey's mind. If Ulfrith had left him unattended, it meant Fingar *had* visited, and he had *not* imagined the conversation. And since Geoffrey had been far too weak to fetch the water himself, it must have been Fingar who had given it to him, thus probably saving his life.

'You *left* him?' demanded Roger with icy fury. 'After I gave you strict instructions to stay?'

'I saw Philippa walking alone,' the squire said miserably. 'I had to make sure she was safe.'

'What was in your water, Ulfrith?' asked Aelfwig gravely, cutting across Roger's spluttering rage. 'My potion contained henbane, which does not mix well with other medicines. I asked whether you were giving him remedies after you arrived, but you all said no.'

'I was not *giving* it to him,' quibbled Ulfrith. 'He just took it. And it was a black fungus that grows on wild grasses. My grandmother called it ergot.'

'Well, there you are,' said Aelfwig. 'The combination of ergot and henbane will certainly drive a man from his wits. And if Geoffrey had continued to take both, we would not be talking now.'

'Lord!' muttered Geoffrey. 'I accused Juhel of doing it. I shall have to apologize.'

'I did not hurt you deliberately,' mumbled Ulfrith. 'I was confused. Philippa was so cold—'

At the name of the woman, Roger's temper snapped. He advanced on his squire with a murderous expression in his eyes. Terrified, Ulfrith darted behind a table, but Roger flung it away as though it were made of feathers.

'No,' said Geoffrey, moving to stop the dreadful advance. He had seen that expression before and knew Roger would be sorry once his squire lay dead. 'That is enough.'

'It is enough when I say so,' snarled Roger. 'He almost killed you.'

'I promise I will never do it again!' squealed Ulfrith.

'Damn right, lad,' growled Roger, moving forward, dagger in his hand. 'You will not.'

Geoffrey dived at the big knight's knees, bringing him crashing to the floor just as the knife flashed towards Ulfrith's throat. For a moment, he thought Roger meant to continue the fight and braced himself, but the fall had brought Roger to his senses. He shoved Geoffrey away.

'Damn you, Geoff,' he growled. 'You have just ripped my best shirt.'

Because he did not feel like being in the same room as Ulfrith, Geoffrey wandered across the battlefield, wishing he did not have to wait until the following day to leave La Batailge. He walked to the tree trunk on the ridge, thinking about his father and the warriors of Hastinges. Pondering the scene of such slaughter made him maudlin, so he went to the church, where he spent a long time staring at the high altar. Several monks knelt around it, their whispered prayers hissing softly.

'Roger told me your father died by his own hand,' came a voice. Geoffrey turned to see Wardard. 'You must have been distressed that he should meet such an ignoble end.'

'Goodrich is a happier place without him,' said Geoffrey shortly, thinking of the misery Godric had inflicted on family and tenants during his violent life.

'So I heard from Bale.' Wardard was rueful. 'It seems I was over-hasty when I declined to tell you of Godric's role in the battle. Most men whose fathers fought here revere them as heroes – and some were abject cowards. But Roger tells me you are well aware of Godric's faults.'

'He was flawed. Like all of us.'

'Your mother deserved better,' said Wardard, almost to himself. 'She was a fine woman.'

'So I am told,' remarked Geoffrey dryly.

Wardard grinned suddenly. 'Perhaps I would be wise not to reminisce too freely about her. Well, we shall discuss Godric instead, then. Men fight better when they have friends around them, but Godric was not a man for friends. He was too brutal, too outspoken and too arrogant.'

'Did he run away that day?'

Wardard nodded. 'But he was not the first, nor even the second. And he rallied with the rest when they were given orders to attack again. He was braver than some, less than others.'

'Truly? He did not balk at the first hurdle and call for others to flee?'

Wardard rested his hand over his heart. 'As God is my witness. Godric fell back early, but I did not hear him calling for anyone to go with him. He was not a hero, just a man.'

'Then why did Vitalis tell me such a tale?'

'I told you: his illness confused his memories. There *was* a knight who screamed his terror at the first charge and unnerved others. But it was not Godric. You will find *your* recollections become hazy with age, too. It happens to us all.'

'So why did the Conqueror give him his estates?'

'That was in recognition of your *mother's* contribution,' replied Wardard. 'Herleve really *did* fight valiantly. She was an inspiration to all who saw her. Godric never knew the truth – and would not have acknowledged it if he had.'

Geoffrey was silent for a while, wondering how his mother could have borne listening to Godric's self-aggrandizing lies all those years. He was not generally proud of his family. With the exception of Joan, they had been acquisitive, dishonest, violent and selfish. But, for the first time, he saw his mother might have possessed qualities he could admire.

'Fear not,' said Wardard, seeming to read his thoughts. 'You are more like her than him.'

Geoffrey was relieved and grateful to know Vitalis had been mistaken. He tried to imagine the formidable Herleve at Hastinges with her axe, but he could not recall her face, and the features that came to mind were those of his wife. It was dusk as he stepped outside the church, and, full of thoughts and memories, barely heard Harold, who waylaid him to say again that he would protect him from Magnus once the Saxons had triumphed. Seeing himself ignored, Harold went to talk to some of the lay-brothers instead, all of whom were delighted to see him.

Geoffrey had not gone much farther when he saw Magnus slinking away from the abbey and towards the fishponds. Intrigued by the Saxon's almost comic furtiveness, Geoffrey followed. Magnus glanced behind frequently and stopped to listen on several occasions, but Geoffrey had no trouble staying out of sight, even on the open battle land.

Eventually, Magnus reached the trees that shielded the ponds, and Geoffrey heard him speak, his tone urgent and confidential. Cautiously, Geoffrey eased through the vegetation to see that a number of men – many of them lay-brothers – had gathered around the largest pond. There was a good deal of splashing, some grunts of exertion, the sound of metal against metal, and then a deep plop. Magnus hissed some additional instructions, and the cohort trailed back towards the abbey, chatting happily and making no attempt to disguise where they had been.

When he was sure they had gone, Geoffrey eased forward and knelt where Magnus had crouched. The edge of the pond was thick with churned mud, amid which lay a flat stone. He lifted it and saw a rope underneath. One end disappeared into the water, and he traced the other to where it was securely fastened to a tree. He noted it was carefully concealed under grass the entire distance. Back at the pond, he discovered another two rocks, a rope leading from each.

He sat for a while, thinking, then walked to the hospital to fetch what he needed. Roger was already asleep – his vigil evidently forgotten – and although he stirred when Geoffrey moved about the room, he did not wake. Geoffrey returned to the fishponds and took up station in the undergrowth again. Gradually, daylight faded to dusk and then to night.

He was perfectly relaxed, and for the first time in days his thoughts were clear. He had answers to nearly all his questions – and he understood why he had made mistakes and drawn erroneous conclusions. Perhaps more importantly, he knew how to make amends. But first he had to wait until he heard the telltale scrape of a leather boot on the wall. When the sound came, he eased forward, so that as the dark figure dropped he was ready to meet him.

'Fingar!' he called softly. 'It is Geoffrey.'

The pirate captain looked around wildly, sword in his hand. 'Come out, where we can see you,' he snarled.

More sailors swarmed over the wall, several holding crossbows and all carrying daggers. Geoffrey sincerely hoped his assumptions were right and that he was not about to make a fatal mistake. He stepped into the open. A crescent moon dodged in and out of flimsy clouds, just bright enough to let them see him. An owl hooted nearby, low and eerie, followed by the answering call from a marsh bird that had the pirates glancing around in alarm.

'Fays,' muttered Donan. 'They have not gone far since *Patrick* went down.'

'I have come to offer you some gold,' said Geoffrey. 'I do not know how much. It may be more than you lost to Roger, it may be less. If I tell you where it is, are you prepared to forget what he took and leave us alone?'

'That depends,' said Fingar. 'I do not want to leave with next to nothing, because I make some Devil's pact with you.'

'The Saxons are mustering a rebellion and have been raising money to fund it. I know where they have hidden it. You can have it all. But you must give me your word that you will leave Roger alone.'

'How much gold have they gathered?' asked Fingar.

'I told you: I do not know.'

'Where is it?' demanded Donan. 'Tell us, and we will let you live.'

'No,' said Geoffrey. 'That is not the bargain. I want you to swear – on your lives – that you will never trouble Roger or my squires again. You will forget about your own gold.'

'No,' said Donan suspiciously. 'It sounds like a trick.'

Fingar agreed. 'And how do *you* know you can trust *us* – that we will not take this Saxon gold and hunt Roger anyway?'

'Because I have invoked a curse,' replied Geoffrey calmly. 'With those marsh fays you heard. If you break your word, the curse will follow you until they snatch away your souls.'

At that moment, the bird cried again, piercingly, so that some of the sailors crossed themselves. The moon ducked behind a thicker cloud, and the night was suddenly very dark.

'All right,' said Fingar, unsettled. 'I am of a mind to be generous. Show us.'

'Swear first,' said Geoffrey.

'You will tell us, and then I will thrust my sword into your gizzard, so you can thank God for a quick death!' cried Donan, darting forward with his weapon raised. This time the bird's cry was high and wavering. Fingar jumped forward and grabbed him.

'Fool!' he hissed. 'Can you not see he can summon these creatures? Why do you think I did not kill him in the hospital?'

'Tell me,' said Donan, although the unsteadiness in his voice said he was growing frightened. He was not the only one: the sailors had gathered in a tight knot, finding reassurance in each other's close proximity. 'I did not understand it then, and I do not see why we cannot kill him now.'

'Because the fays protected him when he was poisoned,' snapped Fingar. 'I heard what the herbalist said – that Geoffrey should have died. But he recovered. We cannot kill a man who has the love of fays. Now sheath your sword before you see us cursed.'

'Very well,' said Donan. He tried to sound reluctant, but it was obvious he was relieved to have an excuse to back down.

Fingar turned to Geoffrey. 'We accept your offer, and I swear, by all I hold holy, that I will take this Saxon gold and not trouble you or your friends again.'

His crew muttered similar oaths. Donan was made to repeat his, to ensure it was done properly. When they had finished, Geoffrey showed them the ropes running into the water, then stood aside as they drew them up. The first bundle appeared, and its coverings were eagerly pulled away. Geoffrey held his breath, aware that if he had guessed wrongly, the sailors would certainly turn on him, vows or no vows. But he need not have worried. Inside was an odd but substantial collection of cups, coins and jewellery. The pirates whooped and gasped, and Fingar was obliged to order them to silence.

'I do not understand you,' the captain said, watching Donan retrieve the second haul. 'You could have had this for yourself.'

'Roger will never part with what he took from you, and I do not want him killed.'

'He is lucky to have a friend like you.' Fingar sounded as though *he* would never have contemplated such an exchange.

'Tell me,' said Geoffrey, changing the subject, 'did you and Donan come to the hospital when I was ill? I believe you did, but I would like to hear if from you.'

'Yes – the moment Ulfrith left you unattended. But Donan did not. He was elsewhere.'

'I imagined Donan?' Geoffrey thought about the man's thin face and how it had assumed the appearance of a rat and then a weasel.

Fingar shrugged. 'You must have done. He was not there.'

'Did any of your men find a heavy gold medallion?' asked Geoffrey.

'Kell did, in one of the chests, along with documents I recognized as Juhel's. Apparently, Roger accused Juhel of poisoning you, and he left in a huff. One of your squires hid his belongings for spite – to annoy him.'

Geoffrey was confused. 'Does Kell have this medallion?'

Fingar regarded him in wonder. 'I am truly amazed you do not recall *that* part! Juhel came in and caught us. We outnumbered him, but he fought noisily and threatened to raise the alarm. We did not want that, and the medallion was left behind in the confusion of our escape. We had intended to ambush Roger, but Juhel made that impossible.'

'Did you tell me you had eaten my dog?'

Fingar looked shocked. 'Of course not! What sort of man do you think I am? I do not eat dog!'

Geoffrey saw Kell look decidedly furtive, and supposed that although Fingar had not taunted him, one of his men certainly had.

'Juhel accused us of torturing you,' Fingar went on. 'But we did nothing of the kind. I am not so reckless as to harm a sick man in an abbey – especially one who has fays watching out for him.'

The bird whistled softly, and Geoffrey frowned, wishing it would go away. It unsettled the sailors, too, and they began to hurry. Soon, two more bundles had joined the first, both equally stuffed with treasure.

'This is far more than Roger stole,' said Fingar, regarding it professionally. 'And he *did* take our whole box – do not believe him when he says otherwise. But this is a handsome night's work. Would you like a share?'

Geoffrey shook his head. 'Just take it as far away from here as you can.'

'No problem there,' said Fingar, indicating his men should gather their booty and leave. They hastened to obey. 'Goodbye, Sir Geoffrey. We shall not meet again.'

He vaulted to the top of the wall like a monkey and raised his hand in salute. The marsh bird sang piercingly, making him jump in alarm, and then he was gone.

'Thank you, Ulfrith,' said Geoffrey, as the squire emerged from the shadows. 'But you did not have to overdo it. Your eager bird almost gave us away.'

'I was only trying to help,' said Ulfrith. 'So, what do we do now? Wait to see which of the lay-brothers comes to check this sunken treasure?'

'We go to bed,' replied Geoffrey. 'And, at first light, we shall visit the King's agent – who has been monitoring this business from the start.'

Ulfrith gaped at him. 'The King has an agent watching? Who is it?'

'Come with me tomorrow and you will find out.'

The hours of darkness passed slowly as Geoffrey considered the solutions he had uncovered. Some were so obvious he wondered he had not seen them before, whereas others were more complex and he was not surprised it had taken him so long to find answers. His thoughts were full of Godric, too, and his vainglorious lies. Eventually, the grey light of dawn began to fill the sky, and he slipped out of the hospital, Ulfrith at his side and his dog at his heels, both panting from the brisk pace he set.

'Philippa really did murder Edith,' he said, bracing himself for trouble. 'There is no question.'

'I know,' said Ulfrith softly. 'I followed her after you tackled her yesterday, and eavesdropped on her confession to Brother Wardard. He urged her to give herself up, but she told him she was free of sin now she had made her act of contrition. She is *evil*, Sir Geoffrey.'

'No, just misguided,' said Geoffrey. 'But I am sorry you had to learn—'

'I almost killed you in order to get her,' interrupted the squire. 'I did not mean to, but that does not make it right. I should have thrown my potion away when I saw what was happening, and I am sorry . . . To make amends, I vow never to fall in love again. It is too dangerous and painful.'

'Do not make promises you will not keep. There will be other women – better than Philippa.'

'But love hurts,' moaned Ulfrith.

'I know,' said Geoffrey softly. 'Believe me.'

'I suppose you are in love with Lady Hilde.' Ulfrith shot Geoffrey a puzzled glance, as if he could not imagine why, but wisely changed the subject. 'Where are we going?'

'I owe Juhel an apology.'

As they approached the hut, Juhel was sitting outside in the semi-darkness, watching his chicken scratch in the grass. Geoffrey's dog promptly slunk away. Juhel stood as they approached, and Geoffrey noticed he held a long hunting knife.

'Delilah likes to be up early,' Juhel said, smiling a cautious welcome.

'Have you been here all night?' asked Geoffrey.

Juhel laughed. 'What a curious question! Of course. I woke a few moments ago, when Delilah clucked to say she wanted to be let out.'

'Your boots say otherwise. They are covered in wet mud. Have you been watching Magnus?'

'Why would I do that?' Juhel's expression became far less friendly.

'Because those are your orders. King Henry is too cautious to allow pretenders to his throne to wander freely around his domain. He would set intelligencers to watch them – to follow them from Ireland and to report on them here.'

'And you think I am one of these agents? I am flattered!'

'The story about Paisnel being a spy for Bellême was a lie, designed to lead me astray – which it did, of course. However, it does not make sense. Why would Paisnel travel from Dublin to Ribe, if he was to carry information about England's defences to Bellême?'

'Poor Sir Geoffrey,' said Juhel, gentle and solicitous. 'Your wits are still awry from—'

'You are an excellent agent – as shown by the fact that no one has guessed who you are – but Paisnel was not. He gave himself away almost immediately, and you argued about it on the ship – you were seen quarrelling by most of the passengers and some of the crew. You were friends, but his amateur carelessness was endangering your mission.'

'You give me too much credit,' said Juhel, shaking his head. 'I am just a simple parchmenter.'

'You even declined to leave the sinking ship before Magnus. You watched him go overboard and only then jumped yourself. But a current dragged you away and it was some time before you found him again. And you have been monitoring him ever since, including at Werlinges, when Roger and I could have done with your help.'

'I am no fighter. I would have been in the way.'

'Not so. Bale witnessed your talent with knives, and you fought off Fingar's men single-handed. You also demonstrated a soldier's reactions in the stable at Pevenesel, and there is your skill at picking locks – an odd talent for a merchant. And you know virtually nothing about parchment. I saw you fold letters when they were damp – they will rot – and Breme overcharged you. If you were a real parchmenter, you would know a fair price.'

'This is arrant nonsense—'

'Breme said you wrote him a letter of introduction to a Winchester clerk, but I imagine it was actually a report to the King. So Henry will have two: one from you and one from me, both delivered by Breme.'

'Yes, you told me you had sent one.'

'You were pleased,' said Geoffrey. 'Now I know why: we are on the same side.'

Juhel sighed. 'Damn you, Geoffrey! I thought I had been careful. I even let you accuse me of murdering Paisnel and poisoning you in order to conceal my true work.'

'For which I owe you an apology. *You* did not kill Paisnel – Magnus did.'

Juhel stared at him. 'Yes – but how did you guess?'

'Chicken scratches. They appeared on Magnus's face the day after Paisnel disappeared. Delilah liked Paisnel – perhaps she tried to defend him. Poor Paisnel probably gave himself away, and Magnus dealt with him ruthlessly – just as he dealt ruthlessly with his own servant, Simon. You threw Paisnel's body overboard to make sure your own identity was not exposed.'

Juhel sighed unhappily. 'Magnus caught Paisnel going through his bag. He died in my arms – or I thought he did. I dropped his body into the sea because I could not have Magnus accused of the crime. And any fool would have been able to link a fatal wound in Paisnel to the fact that Magnus was suddenly minus a knife – he lobbed it overboard after the murder, in a panic.'

Geoffrey was puzzled. 'Why did you want him to evade justice?'

'Because my orders were to learn who was helping him and how far the sedition had spread. I could not have done that if Fingar had ordered him hanged.'

'Are you surprised by the scale of the preparations?'

Juhel shook his head. 'Fortunately, these would-be rebels are supremely incompetent. Gyrth bungled stealing Roger's gold and let himself be dispatched by a squire, and the troops and supplies they gather at night are hardly discreet.'

'But what happened at Werlinges? I know Gyrth and other Saxons killed the villagers.'

'That was another mistake on their part. They remembered that Werlinges had collaborated with the Normans after Hastinges. Gyrth offered the village a chance to make amends by giving him everything they owned. But some of the booty went missing, so Gyrth and his men killed the entire settlement, to show what happens to traitors. He was a fool – the incident will attract attention that will threaten his cause.'

'It was stolen by that "shepherd", I suppose?'

'Almost certainly – a greedy Saxon betraying his own people. And despite the evidence you found that suggested Ulf was innocent of the actual killing, he would certainly have been involved, perhaps by giving orders. It is good that Bale killed him, because he was irredeemably wicked. It is hard to believe he was Harold's twin.'

'Did Magnus fight him? Is that how he came by the cut on his arm?'

'Yes – in the church. I was on the brink of dashing in to rescue him, but he managed to escape on his own.'

'Later, I saw Magnus throw a bundle down the well. Did it contain evidence of the rebellion? And was it *those* documents you were drying when I burst in on you?'

'Some words are still legible. It is a list of men and troops promised. He has the original, but I do not blame him for not wanting duplicate copies floating around.'

'And your "Danish" letters were cipher – coded messages to

the King. Paisnel wrote some, and you composed others. You took them before you . . . after he died.'

'Before I condemned him to drown, you mean,' said Juhel bitterly. 'I took a medallion, too – the one that belonged to Magnus, which Paisnel ripped from him as he was murdered.'

'Why take the medallion?'

'Because it was evidence that *he* murdered Paisnel – to be kept safe and produced later, when he will pay for what he did. Of course, he knows it will incriminate him, which is why he never made a fuss about losing it.'

'And the ring Bale took from Vitalis's corpse? It seems that was Magnus's, too.'

'Yes. Ring and medallion were on the same cord around Magnus's neck, which snapped during the struggle. I could not find the ring in the dark, and Vitalis must have happened across it the following morning. Magnus must have been appalled when he saw it on Vitalis's finger, but he could hardly demand it back, lest subsequent questions led to accusations of murder.'

Geoffrey was thoughtful. 'Was the letter you wrote for Edith's father an account of all this?'

'Yes, and it would have been intercepted as soon as she had entrusted it to a messenger,' said Juhel, nodding. 'But since it was not sent, I sincerely hope Breme does not fail. Magnus is ready to act, and you and I cannot stop him alone.'

'I plan to leave La Batailge tonight, to take word to the King.'

Juhel smiled. 'It is refreshing to meet a loyal man. You repeatedly refuse Magnus's offers, and I know what you did with the treasure last night.'

'You do?' asked Geoffrey uneasily.

'It solved several problems – the most immediate of which is getting rid of the distraction Fingar represented. And it has deprived the Saxons of funds in a way that is permanent.' Juhel rubbed his chin. 'Of course, the King will not be pleased. He would have wanted it for himself.'

Geoffrey was sure he was right and suspected it would see him in trouble. To take his mind off it, he thought about what Galfridus had said when they had discussed the dangers of harbouring rebels in the abbey.

'You are the "important man" to whom Galfridus referred? You decided the rebels should remain, rather than being ousted?'

Juhel inclined his head. 'Better here, where I can see what they are doing, than scattered over half of Sussex. But we shall have to trust Breme for deliverance, because you cannot leave me here alone. I shall need your help if we do not want the country in bloody turmoil.'

Geoffrey was troubled when he left Juhel, so he went to the church, seeking the peace of its silent stones. There he found Roger, yawning in the nave, obviously having just prised himself from bed.

'How was your vigil?' he asked archly.

'Kneeling all night is no task for a knight,' Roger replied grimly. 'I managed a few psalms, but then I grew sleepy. But do not fret, lad. We shall leave as soon as I have collected my gold.'

'Leave it hidden: we are going nowhere.' Geoffrey explained what he had done the previous night and outlined his discussion with Juhel. Roger listened without interruption, but his face was indignant when it finished.

'You gave those pirates the Saxons' treasure? Why did you not give it to *me* and let the pirates have their own back? I could have been fabulously rich!'

'I did not know what the Saxons had. It was a gamble. You might have ended up poorer.'

Roger was about to argue, but was distracted by a commotion at the gatehouse. They went outside to see that a party of wealthy men had arrived, resplendent in fine clothes and awash with baggage. Lay-brothers hurried to welcome them, and Geoffrey could tell that they were more of those who intended to stand with Magnus.

'The short fellow in the blue cloak is Osbjorn, one of Magnus's Danish kinsmen,' said Juhel, materializing suddenly. 'The man with him is Eadric; his father was a deacon who fought at King Harold's side. And there is Brother Aelfwig, greeting them like old friends.'

'Well, he *is* a Saxon,' said Roger disgustedly.

'And no herbalist, as Geoffrey discovered to his cost. His father was King Harold's uncle and Bishop of Winchester, which makes Aelfwig Magnus's cousin. Aelfwig the Elder brought twelve monks and a score of soldiers to the battle. The traitors are coming home to roost.'

A good deal of the newcomers' luggage was spirited away, and Geoffrey guessed it contained weapons or more treasure. Harold hurried forward and almost dragged Osbjorn from his horse with the ferocity of his greeting, muttering something in his ear that made him turn white. Geoffrey supposed Osbjorn had just been told the news about the missing treasure. Meanwhile, Magnus merely regarded his kinsman with cool hauteur.

Supplies were not all the party had brought. There was also a body. The lay-brothers cut the ropes that held it to the back of a horse, then laid it on the ground, where Aelfwig covered it with a piece of sacking.

'About half an hour's ride from here,' Osbjorn was saying. 'We thought he might be one of our own, so we brought him here.'

'He was not one of us,' said Aelfwig in a meaningful way. 'He was just a peddler.'

Once the new arrivals had been escorted to the guest hall, Geoffrey went to inspect the body. He crouched down and removed the sack.

'God's blood!' swore Roger. 'It is Breme.'

'Damn!' said Juhel softly. 'Are our letters in his pouch?'

Geoffrey searched the corpse quickly, then shook his head. 'His pack is gone, too. I imagine we are supposed to assume he was attacked by robbers. But he is still wearing the ring we gave him, and thieves would have taken that.'

'I said the rebels are incompetent,' said Juhel in disgust. 'They cannot even stage a fake robbery.'

'Perhaps not, but they have ensured Breme never reached Winchester,' said Geoffrey grimly. 'We are on our own.'

# Fourteen

The arrival of Osbjorn and Eadric caused considerable delight among the Saxons. At the guest hall, they were plied with the dishes that had been prepared for the Duke of Normandy. The Norman monks were astonished at this, but Galfridus raised a hand to silence their indignation. Lay-brothers and 'pilgrims' continued to crowd in, and it quickly became clear what they really were. A kitchen scullion named Thurkill hefted a sword in a way that indicated he had wielded more than filleting knives in the past, and two 'grooms' clapped Osbjorn on the back in a manner that would have been inappropriate had they really been servants.

'I sincerely hope help is on its way,' said Galfridus when Geoffrey approached. 'You *have* sent for some, have you not? The situation is rapidly becoming untenable.'

'I did, but it will not materialize,' replied Geoffrey.

Galfridus stared at him. 'But I can see at least three disinherited earls from here, plus several fanatics who have made careers of insurrection!'

'How many of your monks will stand against them?'

Galfridus regarded him askance. 'None.'

It was Geoffrey's turn to stare. 'There is not a single man here who is loyal to the King?'

'That is not what I meant. All the Normans will be loyal – about thirty men out of fifty-five – but they have forsworn arms. None will raise so much as a stick.'

'I will,' came Wardard's quiet voice from behind them. 'I will fight, as I did before, although I would prefer peace. Perhaps we can persuade them to disband.'

'This is too far advanced to be stopped by speeches,' said Galfridus. 'If help is not coming, then all we can do is lock ourselves in the church and hope they do not set it alight.'

There was a colossal cheer from the Saxons. Osbjorn had just announced that others would soon arrive at La Batailge – good, honest Saxons armed with hoes and pitchforks.

Galfridus closed his eyes in defeat, but Wardard rested a hand on his shoulder.

'Do not pay heed to defiant words. The nobles will fight, but the peasantry will not be blinded by impossible dreams. Most will slink away at the first clash of steel.'

Geoffrey hoped he was right. Nevertheless, he estimated that the abbey already contained at least three hundred would-be warriors. He turned at the sound of running feet. A number of people were converging on the kitchens, where a fight was in progress between Ralph the sacristan and Thurkill the scullion. Ralph was brandishing a ladle, but Thurkill had his sword.

'Norman pig!' Thurkill howled. 'You have no right to order *me* around.'

'I have every right,' screeched Ralph, lunging with his spoon. 'You are a scullion and I am sacristan. Of course you take orders from me, Saxon scum.'

Thurkill moved in for the kill, and Ralph suddenly realized he had bitten off more than he could chew. Panic-stricken, he darted behind a table and began to lob pieces of food. One hit a cook, who, trying to dodge it, inadvertently jostled a scribe. There followed an unseemly melee, as old scores were settled on both sides.

'Stop them, Sir Geoffrey!' shouted Galfridus in horror.

Geoffrey used the flat of his sword to beat a path through the mass of bodies. He caught the sacristan's arm and yanked him away from a wicked stab by Thurkill. The scullion turned his murderous attention to Geoffrey, but the knight quickly had him in retreat. When Thurkill tripped and disappeared under milling feet, Geoffrey dragged Ralph outside.

'God and all His saints!' cried Galfridus, as Wardard casually repelled a dogged attack by a stable boy. 'They will slaughter us! I thought they would leave me alone – my mother was Saxon, and I assumed they would honour my ancestry.'

'If they are willing to attack you, they will have no compunction about assaulting other Norman monks,' said Wardard urgently. 'We must warn them. I will ring the bell – they will assume it is a call to terce and come to the church.'

'Good,' said Geoffrey. 'It has strong doors and thick shutters. We will be able to defend it.'

'I was thinking of saying prayers, actually,' said Wardard.

'We will fight the bastards!' snarled Ralph. 'Smash their skulls and tear out their innards! Our abbey should not be tainted with Saxons clamouring for my King to be overthrown.'

Geoffrey did not wait to hear more. He ran to the hospital, where Roger had already donned full armour and was inspecting the edge of his sword. Bale and Ulfrith wore their tough leather jerkins and hurried to help Geoffrey with his mail.

'What do you intend to do?' asked Roger. 'There are about three hundred Saxons, most more proficient with hoes than with weapons. But even so, there is little we can do against such odds.'

'We will join Galfridus in the church. I hope Magnus will not murder unarmed monks on holy ground, but if he does, we can try to defend them.'

'Try?' asked Ulfrith in alarm. 'You think we might fail? We might *die*?'

'Very likely,' said Roger without emotion. 'If they do not recognize the sanctity of a church, we stand no chance. We will take plenty with us, but with such numbers, defeat is inevitable.'

'I am glad you are looking on the bright side,' said Geoffrey dryly. 'Steal a couple of horses, Ulfrith, and bring them to the church. No one will harm you – you are Saxon and you look it – and if anyone asks, say you are acting under Earl Osbjorn's orders. Bale, come with me.'

Bale was armed to the teeth, and Geoffrey knew it was only a matter of time before he was at someone's throat. He hoped he would not precipitate a fight that might yet be avoided.

Ulfrith hesitated. 'Are you saying I should bring these nags inside the church?'

Geoffrey nodded as he set his helmet on his head. 'And if you see any Normans, tell them to go there, too.'

Ulfrith sped away. Geoffrey, Roger and Bale left the hospital, alert and ready to fight if attacked. They turned at the sound of running feet, but it was only Juhel, chicken at his heels.

'Those documents,' Juhel gasped, fighting to catch his breath. 'The ones Magnus threw in the well and that I have been attempting to salvage.'

'Not now.' Geoffrey was aware that men were pouring out of the guest hall. Some were armed and all were shouting.

Osbjorn and Eadric had fired them up, and he felt vulnerable and exposed.

'Two were stuck together and were only dry enough for me to separate a few moments ago,' said Juhel, thrusting them at him. 'They are smeared, but still legible. I have been wrong! Magnus is not the driving force behind this rebellion – Ulf is.'

Geoffrey paused just long enough to glance at the pact signed by Ulf and Gyrth. It detailed how they would divide England after the Usurper's execution, and stated that the moment the kingdom was in Saxon hands, Gyrth was to dispatch Magnus. There was even an assassin picked for the task: Aelfwig. Geoffrey supposed the plotters were fortunate that Magnus could not read and had thus remained in ignorance of what his 'loyal' supporters had in mind for him.

'What of it?' he demanded impatiently. 'Ulf is dead and so is Gyrth.'

Juhel grabbed his arm, forcing him to stop. 'Think, man! You have heard the tales about Ulf's temper and love of violence. He is a formidable warrior, and there is no way your squire could have overpowered him. I am disgusted with myself for not seeing this sooner. It was not Ulf who was killed in Werlinges: it was Harold.'

Geoffrey was about to take issue with Juhel when he saw a group of lay-brothers coming from the fishponds with furious looks on their faces. It was no time to be chatting, so he grabbed Juhel's arm and hauled him towards the church. The door was already locked, and Geoffrey pounded on it with his fist. At that moment, a gaggle of Saxons headed towards them, and there was no mistaking their intentions. All carried knives and cudgels. Geoffrey hammered again, and Roger yelled for the door to be opened.

'No!' shouted Ralph. 'If we do, those Saxons will come in with you.'

Geoffrey turned to face the mob, sword in hand, as the man in the lead lowered his pike and braced it under his arm. He was going to use it like a couched lance, and Geoffrey was not sure there was enough space to avoid being spitted. His shield was the one piece of armour he had not managed to salvage from the ship.

But there was a clank and the door opened. Juhel was through it in a trice, with Bale and Roger on his heels, but there was no time for Geoffrey to follow. He leapt in the opposite direction, and the pike whistled past him and struck the door with wicked force. The shaft shattered. Its owner was so intent on driving it home that he had overlooked the need to stop, and the collision knocked him senseless. Geoffrey jumped over him and aimed for the door, alarmed when Ralph tried to close it before he was through. With a furious roar, Roger shoved the sacristan away, and Geoffrey shot inside just as cudgels began to fly.

He turned quickly and added his strength to that of Wardard, Bale and Roger, as the rebels began to force the door open, inch by relentless inch. Geoffrey's boots skidded on the flagstones as he tried to gain purchase, but he could see it was only a matter of moments before the first Saxon would be inside. In the nick of time, several monks rushed to help. Slowly, the door closed, and Roger was able to slide a substantial bar across it. The church was secure – for now, at least.

'Fool!' howled Ralph at Wardard. 'What possessed you – opening the door like that?'

'I was saving innocents from being slaughtered,' said Wardard coolly. 'You may be happy to stand meekly by as murder is done, but I am not. Now, go and check the window shutters are secure. Galfridus? Are you sure the cloister door is locked and barred?'

Galfridus nodded, his face white. 'And ten monks set to guard it, as you ordered. With the dozen you have here, no one should be able to get in.'

'Good,' said Wardard. 'I believe the best way to avert violence is to avoid confrontation. If the Saxons see no Normans, their fury may fade. Magnus cannot keep them at fever pitch indefinitely.'

'I put Odo and Peter in the clerestory with bows, too, like you said,' added Galfridus. 'And there are lookouts everywhere. Your troops are deployed.'

Wardard smiled. 'Then it is time to solicit God's help. I want no more deaths on this field – Norman or Saxon. Will you join us, Geoffrey?'

Geoffrey shook his head. He wanted to inspect the defences and reorganize the 'troops' as *he* saw fit. Wardard might have been a professional soldier once, but it was a long time ago.

'Our situation is worse than I thought,' said Juhel worriedly. 'If Magnus were in charge, we might have escaped unscathed, but Ulf is a different matter altogether.'

'Are you saying I killed *Harold*?' asked Bale, bewildered. 'But they were wearing different clothes, and there was no time for them to change.'

'I agree,' said Geoffrey. 'Besides, they were not identical – Harold has scars around his wrists, and the dead man was thinner.'

'That is because we have been misled from the beginning,' said Juhel, pacing back and forth in agitation. 'He *said* he was Harold, and we all believed him. Even Magnus. But he was lying.'

'That is ridiculous,' declared Roger. 'Magnus could tell his half-brothers apart.'

'Why, when they spent most of their lives separated?' countered Juhel.

'But what benefit is there in Ulf pretending to be Harold?' asked Geoffrey.

'Ulf is a bully and a tyrant, who, given power, will become a monster. No Saxon will follow a man with his reputation, and so he has pretended to be gentle, smiling Harold. He is even allowing Magnus to take a certain degree of command, biding his time until the rebellion has sufficient momentum. Then he will take over.'

'I *have* noticed the odd flare of nastiness in Harold,' said Roger thoughtfully. 'He put glass in Galfridus's carp, and I saw him throw stones at Brother Wardard.'

'That was him, was it?' asked Wardard. 'I thought it was Aelfwig, who has never liked me.'

'I should have seen this sooner,' said Juhel bitterly. 'The clues were all there. At Werlinges, Magnus was sick, and even you two battle-hardened knights were shocked, but "Harold" had to fabricate emotions he certainly would not feel. And he did it badly.'

Geoffrey supposed he might be right: Harold *had* recovered fairly quickly from the shock of seeing his twin's throat cut, which suggested a certain resilience to violent death.

'Was it this Ulf who ordered the massacre, then?' asked Bale.

'I imagine so,' replied Juhel. 'When we first discovered the atrocity, we said it was the kind of thing Ulf would do – although "Harold" insisted on his brother's innocence. I suspect he ordered Gyrth to do it, so knew exactly what we would find when we all arrived there.'

'Ulf was held prisoner by the Conqueror,' said Geoffrey thoughtfully. 'Not Harold. Did you notice his wrists? They are scarred.'

'From being kept in chains,' said Roger in understanding. 'If he is the maniac everyone says, his captors would have needed to subdue him.'

'He also claimed Henry had given him a horse,' Geoffrey went on, becoming more convinced Juhel was right as he considered what they knew. 'But Henry is much more likely to have given one to Ulf – who was his father's prisoner for twenty years. Why would he make a gift to Harold, a man to whom he did not need to make amends?'

'True,' agreed Roger.

'And Harold is supposed to be a fine musician,' said Geoffrey. 'But this man could not play the horn properly – and tried very hard to avoid obliging when Bale insisted on a tune.'

'Because he said it was a cheap, nasty instrument,' supplied Ulfrith.

'It is very expensive, actually,' objected Galfridus. 'From the curia in Rome.'

Juhel turned to Galfridus. 'You know them both. What do you think?'

'I am afraid Sir Geoffrey distracted me by insulting my objet d'art, and I paid Harold scant attention. He usually visits me a lot when he is here, but he has not been once this time. I have been busy, so have not thought to question why. But what about Osbjorn? He knows both twins and will be able to tell them apart. He likes Harold, but detests Ulf.'

Geoffrey recalled the way the surviving twin had almost dragged Osbjorn from his horse with the force of his greeting. It had not been an expression of familial affection, but a muttered threat.

'I know how to tell them apart,' said Wardard suddenly. 'Garlic. Harold hates it, but Ulf is well known to chew it constantly.'

\*　\*　\*

Geoffrey had done no more than make a preliminary inspection of the defences – in the process noticing that both Philippa and Lucian had taken refuge in the church – before there was a yell from a lookout. A contingent of Saxons was approaching. Geoffrey stationed Ulfrith and Bale at the cloister entrance, then trotted to the great west door – the only other way in.

'We can hold out for a while,' muttered Roger. 'Some of the monks brought food, water and weapons. And a couple thought to grab some armour.'

'And Ulfrith managed to acquire us seven horses,' said Geoffrey, nodding to where the beasts were tethered. Four were warhorses belonging to the Saxon earls, but the remaining three were only fat mares.

'Wardard and Ralph are ready to fight, but the others will be useless. We are essentially on our own, Geoff.' Roger cocked his head. 'I can hear Ulf, yelling to his men that we are cowards and ripe for the slaughter.'

They walked to the nearest window. Geoffrey poked a hole in the shutter with his dagger, so they could see what was happening outside.

'God above!' exclaimed Galfridus, white-faced as he peered through it. 'Where have all those men come from?'

'Lay-brothers,' said Wardard shortly. 'And supposed pilgrims. They have used our abbey as a rallying point.'

'They are only armed with sticks, for the most part,' said Ralph, eyeing them with disdain. He and Wardard wore mail jerkins and conical helmets. Little of his monastic clothing was visible, and he looked like a knight. Geoffrey hoped he would behave like one. 'Whereas *we* have swords.'

'But what are a few swords compared to three hundred hoes?' whispered Galfridus.

'Normans!' came a stentorian voice from outside. It was Ulf. He had dispensed with civilian clothes and was wearing a knee-length mail tunic, leather leggings, and a helmet that looked to be gold. He was one of a dozen mounted men. 'Come out before we come in.'

His men roared their approval at the challenge.

'No, thank you,' replied Galfridus in a wavering voice. 'We do not want to.'

'God's blood!' breathed Roger, appalled. 'Could you not think of anything more manly to say? They are laughing at us!'

'Who are *you*?' shouted Ralph, belligerence dripping from every syllable. 'I do not recognize you as a man to be giving *me* orders. *I* am the abbey's sacristan.'

The jeers turned to murmurs of anger, and Geoffrey scowled at him.

'I am Ulf,' came the reply. 'King Harold's legitimate heir.'

This caused consternation on both sides. Those monks who knew of Ulf's reputation crossed themselves, and two abandoned their posts and made a dash for the high altar. A ripple of unease passed along the Saxon lines, and Aelfwig and Eadric regarded Ulf in astonishment. Osbjorn's face was impassive, but his unease was clear. Magnus, whose fat nag stood on Ulf's other side, was patently disbelieving.

'Ulf?' he echoed. 'But you are Harold!'

'I am Ulf!' yelled Ulf, raising his sword and standing up in his stirrups. 'And I am here to lead my people in a glorious Saxon victory.'

There was a cheer, although it was decidedly tentative. Ulf apparently thought so, too, because he turned to glare furiously at his army. One or two bolted, clearly having second thoughts about associating with such a leader. Ulf's scowl deepened, and he muttered to Eadric, who wheeled his horse around and rode to prevent more desertions.

'I should have guessed,' said Magnus coldly. 'I should have known that Harold would not suddenly start chewing garlic. You lied when you told me you had acquired a *recent* taste for it.'

'People of England,' yelled Ulf, ignoring him. 'Our day has come. We will avenge the blood of our fathers, spilled on this sacred ground. We will—'

'Do not listen to him,' ordered Magnus imperiously. '*I* am your rightful king. Ulf lied to me and he will lie to you. You will all serve King Magnus!'

The Saxons were confused. 'I thought we were going to kill Normans first and then choose our king,' said Aelfwig. His habit was hitched up to his knees, and he carried a knife from the kitchen.

'We are,' said Magnus angrily. 'Moreover, I sent a letter to Ulf forbidding him to join us. When I heard he was dead in Werlinges,

I was very relieved, because there is certainly no room for him in *my* plans.'

'And there is no room for you in mine,' snarled Ulf, and there was an appalled silence from both sides as he thrust his sword into his half-brother's chest. The silence continued long after Magnus had crashed to the ground.

As soon as Ulf had dispatched his querulous rival, the situation changed. More Saxons dropped their weapons and ran towards the gate, too many for Eadric to stop. He used the flat of his sword to beat some back, then killed two to make his point. The ploy failed – instead of encouraging them, it saw resolve crumbling among those who had been steady. Next to Ulf, Osbjorn raised an unsteady hand to wipe sweat from his pallid face. Geoffrey had seen enough.

'Mount up,' he said to Roger. 'If we make a charge, most will scatter and slink away. They did not mind rallying for Harold, or even Magnus, but they do not want Ulf. Will you ride with us, Brother?'

Wardard climbed into the saddle of one of the better horses. Geoffrey and Roger took two more, and an ancient pilgrim called Hugh d'Ivry claimed the last. Hugh had not been young when he had fought in the original battle, and it took some time to hoist him into the saddle, accompanied by a medley of grunts, groans and gasps. Geoffrey was not sure how much use he would be, but the man had a sword and knew how to ride. The three mares were left for Ralph, Juhel and Galfridus.

Juhel had a sword, although it was clear he was happier fighting with knives. Ralph's blood was up, and Geoffrey suspected he would be difficult to control. Galfridus was openly terrified and had only agreed to join them because Ralph told him he needed to set an example to his monks.

Geoffrey indicated that the door should be opened, and he rode out. He had expected more taunts when the Saxons saw that the Norman 'cavalry' comprised only seven horsemen, but there was only silence as they formed a line.

'Now we shall see Norman blood!' howled Ulf in delight. 'We have waited almost forty years for vengeance and we begin today. We shall start by killing the monks and replacing them with Saxons.

Who will accept the post of abbot of La Batailge, the first monastery to be freed?'

'I would not refuse it,' offered Aelfwig modestly.

'I am sure you would not,' yelled Ralph. 'But you are not worthy, you Saxon pig.'

'I am a damned sight more worthy than you or Galfridus,' retorted Aelfwig angrily. 'At least *I* do not stuff myself with carp every day and spend the abbey's money on bad carvings. Nor do I sneak off at night for secret sessions with sheep.'

There was an uncertain smattering of laughter.

'I was testing the quality of their wool,' said Ralph to Galfridus, flushing scarlet. Mortified, he lashed out at Aelfwig again. 'You are the son of a whore, and you are a terrible herbalist. Our graveyard is full of the people you have killed with your bumbling ministrations.'

'Well, your mother was a witch and your father was a . . . a Norman!' yelled Aelfwig, drawing appreciative cheers from the Saxons.

'Lord!' muttered Roger to Geoffrey, unimpressed. 'Do we sit here all day and trade insults? Is that their idea of a battle?'

'Let us hope so,' said Geoffrey soberly. 'Because these men are not soldiers. What a ridiculous state of affairs! Magnus and Ulf *do* deserve to die for initiating this.'

'Vile, dirty pigs!' yelled Ralph. 'Cowardly, stupid oafs, who cannot even read!'

'We do not want to read,' said Osbjorn, galled into joining in. 'Not if it will make us like you.'

'Lovers of goats!' came Ralph's shrieked response. 'And donkey bug—'

'Ralph!' snapped Galfridus, deeply shocked. 'Please! This is an abbey!'

'All Normans are slugs!' shouted Aelfwig. His comrades regarded him with pained expressions, unimpressed by the quality of the rejoinder, so he added, 'Uncultured ones.'

'Do we ignore this abuse?' demanded Hugh, keen for action now he had gone through the discomfort of loading his ancient bones with armour and being shoved on a horse.

'Yes, we do,' said Geoffrey quietly. 'I do not want to kill such people, and I cannot imagine you do either.'

'I do, actually,' countered Hugh testily. 'One of them just called me a maggot. Charge!'

And he was away, riding hard into the Saxons and slashing with his sword – until it became too heavy for him and he dropped it. Not wanting a seventh of his army to be cut down without support, Geoffrey had no choice but to follow. He drove his horse at the milling mass of humanity, but did not use his sword, which he held above his head. He was vaguely aware of Roger striking out with the flat of his, mostly terrifying his opponents into flight with a series of unnerving battle cries learned from the Saracens.

Geoffrey disarmed Aelfwig, who was causing as much damage to his friends as his enemies, then knocked a pitchfork from the hand of a groom. More Saxons shrank back in alarm when his horse, which had been well trained, reared and flailed with its front hooves. Suddenly, he found himself emerging at the back of the Saxon line, having ridden clean through it with virtually no resistance. Roger and Wardard were not far behind. When Eadric saw them, his jaw dropped in horror and he raced back to Ulf's side.

'I do not like this,' said Roger in distaste. 'It is like fighting nuns.'

Geoffrey saw he had grabbed Osbjorn as he had passed, and had the man slung over his saddle. The Saxon lord screeched his fury, but his struggles were to no avail as long as Roger's powerful hand held him down.

'They barely know how to hold their weapons,' said Wardard, also disgusted.

Geoffrey glanced behind and saw that Galfridus had fallen off his mare and was riding pillion on Juhel's, sketching benedictions in all directions. This threw Ulf's troops into even greater confusion. Some bowed their heads to accept the blessings, while others stood uncertainly.

Ralph and Hugh were doing their best to make up for their comrades' lack of aggression, though. The sacristan slashed wildly with his weapons, occasionally cutting his own mount as well as his opponents, while Hugh jabbed here and there with a dagger.

'Perhaps it is just as well Breme did not deliver your message,' said Wardard softly. 'If royal troops *had* arrived, Werlinges would not have been the only place to suffer a massacre.'

Geoffrey agreed. 'Run!' he yelled, riding the warhorse at the Saxon line again. 'Go home, before you are all in your graves.'

'He is right,' said one man, ducking away from one of Hugh's blows. 'It is too dangerous here.'

He turned and fled, and others joined him. Roger rode at a tight, bewildered pack of lay-brothers, who scattered in all directions, and then it was a case of driving others after them, much as dogs with sheep.

Ulf was livid and tore after his men, catching one a vicious chop between the shoulder blades. It served to drive even more of his followers towards the gate, and when Geoffrey yelled in the Saxon tongue that Ulf was defeated, the rout was complete. Ulf screamed that he was nothing of the kind, but his supporters had lost the stomach for their skirmish and preferred to believe Geoffrey.

Red with fury and frustration, Ulf charged back to a knot of his horsemen, who were milling about in hopeless confusion, and ordered them to take up formation around him. Then he bellowed an order, and the little cavalcade rode at a hard pace, not towards the gate, but to the ponds.

'Who are those men?' Geoffrey demanded of Osbjorn, who was still in an undignified heap over Roger's saddle.

'Seven are his housecarls,' replied the captured Dane miserably. 'And the eighth is Aelfwig – he must have grabbed someone else's horse to join them. All will fight at Ulf's side until they die.'

'They *will* die if they continue to fight,' said Roger grimly. 'Where are they going?'

'To the fishponds,' said Osbjorn, pathetically eager to cooperate. 'There is gold hidden there, and Ulf will claim it before he leaves. The treasure we hid in the water is stolen, but more is buried under a tree. He will use it to rebel again, although he can do it without me. I would have followed Harold or even Magnus. But never him.'

'We must stop him,' said Wardard urgently to Geoffrey and Roger. 'Too many Saxons have died for his foolishness already, and I will not let him destroy more. Will you help me?'

'Me, you and Geoff against eight Saxon warriors and an inept herbalist,' said Roger. Then he grinned. 'The odds are good enough for me!'

Geoffrey, Roger and Wardard thundered towards the marshes, leaving Juhel, Hugh and Ralph to chase away the last of the Saxons and imprison Osbjorn. Aelfwig was already emerging from the trees with a bundle, staggering under its weight.

'We cannot let him take it,' shouted Geoffrey.

Wardard chuckled. 'Ulf will not be financing anything with what is inside *that* sack, Geoffrey. I took the opportunity to exchange it for a few rocks after I saw you had only given half his treasure trove to your pirate friends.'

Geoffrey glanced at him. 'You were not with Juhel, were you?'

Wardard nodded. 'This is my abbey, my home. Do you really think men can come in and hide their loot without me knowing?'

'What did you do with it?' asked Roger, with more than a passing interest.

Wardard smiled. 'It is locked in the crypt and will be used to purchase the services of a decent *medicus*. We were wrong to give Aelfwig the post and we need to make reparation. Do not worry: it will not fall into the hands of rebels.'

'This is your fault!' shrieked Ulf, sword at the ready when he saw the three horsemen. 'We were poised for victory, and *you* snatched it from us.'

Geoffrey reined in his horse and studied the opposition. He, Roger and Wardard were outnumbered three to one, and their opponents were of the same calibre as the men who had fought at Hastinges, then Ulf might yet live to sow more seeds of rebellion.

'My mother could have commanded the situation better than you did today,' jeered Roger. 'If your rout is anyone's fault, it is yours.'

Ulf snatched the sack from Aelfwig and scrambled back into his saddle.

'Finish it,' he ordered his men. 'No survivors and no quarter.'

The housecarls advanced quickly, while he rode a short distance away to inspect his treasure. Aelfwig followed, muttering in his ear. But there was no time to ponder what he might be saying, because Geoffrey, Roger and Wardard were suddenly facing opponents who knew what they were doing.

'If you had fought like this earlier, you might have won,' gasped

Roger, as he fenced with Eadric, forcing the smaller man back with the ferocity of his assault.

Geoffrey urged his horse forward fast as another knight aimed to strike his friend's unprotected back. The resulting clang of the parry rang out like a bell. He recovered more quickly than his opponent, and a left-handed slash with his dagger opened the man's innards, before a hard chop with his sword dropped another from his saddle. Wardard had already dispatched one of his adversaries, and Geoffrey saw that although the housecarls might well have trained hard, they had little experience of real fighting.

'Kill them!' Ulf screamed, flinging off his helmet and hauling a green hat on his head in its place. 'I will meet up with you later!'

'Go!' Eadric yelled back. 'Save yourself. We will keep them occupied.'

Ulf needed no second invitation. He rode between the skirmish and the fishponds, and Geoffrey saw he was going to escape. He spurred forward to stop him, but two housecarls mounted a coordinated attack that forced him to retreat. He wheeled around and swung his sword in a savage arc that dispatched one of them, and there was a howl of pain as Wardard dealt with the second. Leaving Wardard to help Roger with those remaining, Geoffrey tore after the would-be king.

'You strangled Vitalis!' he shouted, as the last mystery became clear. 'You saw us wrecked, and waited to see if there was anything to steal. You were with Gyrth.'

'I killed an old man,' sneered Ulf, turning around to face him. 'But he had nothing worth taking – except a paltry ring that I could not wrench from his finger anyway. Neither do you, but you will be worth killing regardless!'

Geoffrey met his powerful stroke, then thrust back, intending to force Ulf from his saddle. He might have succeeded, had Ulf's horse not skittered backwards. Geoffrey slashed again, and as Ulf ducked away, his horse skidded in the mud at the pond edge. It slipped, then fell, hurling Ulf backwards into the water. His armour caused him to sink like a stone. Aelfwig ran to the edge of the water with a cry of horror.

'Fetch him out!' he screamed. 'He will drown!'

Breaking away from Wardard, the last surviving housecarl leaped off his horse to obey, but the moment his feet touched the ground, Roger knocked him on the head with the pommel of his sword. The fellow dropped, insensible, and Eadric dropped his weapon and raised his hands when he found Wardard's sword at his throat.

Aelfwig was pointing and gibbering, beside himself with anguish. Not far under the surface was Ulf, arms flailing. Geoffrey could see his terrified eyes and the whiteness of his face against the green water.

'Help him!' screeched Aelfwig.

'*You* help him,' said Roger, unmoved. 'He is your king.'

'I am not strong enough,' sobbed Aelfwig. 'He will drown me.'

Geoffrey watched as mud billowed to obscure the agonized face, aware that he was holding his own breath. He closed his eyes tightly, then began to pull the surcoat over his head. Roger grabbed his shoulder.

'What are you doing?' he demanded.

'I cannot see a man die like this,' said Geoffrey, struggling away from him. 'Let me go.'

But Wardard joined Roger with a grip that was impossible to break, and Geoffrey had no choice but to watch the churning pool and the final torments of the man caught there.

Eventually the water became calm and the mud began to settle. No more than the length of an arm under the surface was Ulf, fair curls floating like a halo.

'There they are!' came a voice from farther up the field. It was Juhel, and with him was a stocky, dark-haired horseman whom Geoffrey recognized immediately. It was the Duke of Normandy.

'Where is the battle?' demanded the Duke eagerly.

'Most of the rebels have fled, my Lord,' replied Juhel. 'These were all that remained.'

'Oh,' said the Duke, disappointed. 'I was in the mood for a skirmish. Now, what did you say it was about?'

'A Saxon uprising, Sire,' explained Juhel.

'Against my brother?' asked the Duke keenly.

'Only a very small one,' explained Juhel. 'Just a few peasants and a handful of disinherited Saxon nobles. The sight of you and your retinue was more than enough to end the last skirmishes.'

'So, I helped to thwart a rebellion against Henry, did I?' asked the Duke softly. 'Damn!'

# Epilogue

Henry was none too pleased to learn that his brother had arrived in his kingdom uninvited, and the Duke was sufficiently alarmed by the prospect of a hostile reunion that he asked Henry's queen to intercede on his behalf. In the end, the two met with forced amicability, after which the Duke set off for home. When he heard the news, Roger was bemused.

'Is that it?' he asked as he sat with Geoffrey in the hospital. 'After all that sailing around at sea, terrifying the life out of half of Sussex, he just turns around and goes away?'

'Just be thankful he did,' said Geoffrey. 'For a while, there was a very real possibility that Henry might eliminate the threat he presents by throwing him in prison – and imagine the trouble *that* would have caused!'

Roger blew out his lips in a sigh. 'The Duke is a fellow *Jerosolimitanus*, so I owe him my respect. But the man is a damned fool! You may not like Henry's devious ways, but England is safer with him than it ever could be with the Duke.'

It galled Geoffrey to agree with him.

He had not wanted to linger in Sussex, but Juhel pointed out that to travel to Herefordshire or Durham before explaining themselves to the King might be construed as sympathy for the Saxons. So Geoffrey and Roger kicked their heels at La Batailge, and within a few days the abbey was graced with a royal visit.

Juhel and Henry were sequestered in Galfridus's solar for the best part of an afternoon. Almost immediately, Osbjorn and several Saxon nobles were spirited to distant castles to face lifelong imprisonment, and the abbey began to recruit new staff, all of them Norman. Before he disappeared on his next assignment, Juhel came to speak to the two knights.

'Does the King want to see us?' asked Roger.

Juhel shook his head. 'But I am afraid he had every last detail out of me. He is too clever to be deceived by lies.'

Geoffrey was unimpressed. 'You promised to say nothing about our involvement.'

'I said I would *try* – and I *did*. I went almost an hour before he realized I had more help than Galfridus and Wardard could have supplied, and demanded names. Do not be alarmed. I told him your loyalty was beyond question.'

'What did he say?' asked Roger, pleased. 'Will he reward us?'

Juhel gave a short laugh. 'He said he expected no less of men who hold estates from him, and that you had done no more than your duty. However, I am afraid he was irritated to learn you had been leaving the country when *Patrick* was wrecked.'

Roger glared at Geoffrey. 'And did you tell him it would not be happening again?'

Juhel nodded. 'And that you had tried to warn him, by sending a message with Breme.'

'Poor Breme,' said Geoffrey. 'Did you hear that Aelfwig has confessed to killing him?'

'Yes, so now you have answers to all your questions: Magnus stabbed Paisnel; Ulf choked Vitalis; Philippa strangled Edith; and Gyrth and his men murdered the villagers of Werlinges on Ulf's orders. And I did not kill anyone.'

'No, you did not,' said Geoffrey with a smile. 'Nor are you a spy for Bellême.'

'What will you do now?' asked Juhel, smiling back. 'Hope God sends you a sign saying you are free to journey to the Holy Land?'

Geoffrey shook his head. 'I will go home to my wife.'

'Then what about Tancred?'

'I suppose I will never know why he took against me. And even if he does write to invite me back, I cannot break the oath I made in that damned mud hole.'

Juhel looked sympathetic. 'Well, I have news that may amuse you. Lucian inspected another document Philippa took from Edith, and found a codicil to Vitalis's will. It bequeaths Edith a wealthy manor, so she will not have to take another husband. It also stipulates that if Edith accepts the estates, she must undertake to look after Philippa for the rest of her life.'

Geoffrey shook his head, disgusted. 'In other words, had Edith lived, Philippa would have been taken care of by someone who liked her. Now Edith is dead, she has nothing.'

'Quite,' said Juhel with satisfaction. 'And she will spend the rest of her life regretting the spat of temper that saw her throttle a loving friend with red ribbon.'

Later that morning, Geoffrey went in search of Roger, who had disappeared. He looked in all the likely places, including the local taverns, and it was only towards the end of the afternoon that Bale came to say Roger was in the church. Geoffrey entered its cool, spacious interior, the squire at his heels, and found him at the high altar, kneeling next to Galfridus and Ralph. His expression, however, was far from devout.

'There is the meal bell,' Roger said as a tinny clatter rang out. 'Surely, you both must be hungry – you have been praying here for days.'

'We are not,' replied Galfridus shortly. 'And please be quiet if you want to stay. I cannot concentrate on my devotions with you chattering.'

'I am here as penance,' explained Roger resentfully. 'For the Saxons I was obliged to dispatch on *your* behalf. I am a warrior, trained to fight, but you worried me with all your muttering about the commandments, and I feel the need for prayers.'

'Then say them and be quiet,' retorted Ralph. 'You are disturbing us.'

Roger climbed to his feet, his face angry, and Geoffrey pulled him away before he could say something he might later regret.

'I do not like it here, Geoff,' he grumbled. 'I never have.'

'Then let us go home,' said Geoffrey softly. 'Before Henry thinks of some favour to ask, and we lose the chance.'

'I cannot,' said Roger sullenly. 'Not yet.'

With a flash of understanding, so sudden it was blinding, Geoffrey knew why. 'You should not have hidden it in such a stupid place,' he said, smiling.

Roger regarded him coldly. 'I do not know what you are talking about.'

'You hid Fingar's gold inside the high altar, but the monks have been praying here constantly since the rebellion, and you have been unable to retrieve it.'

Roger gaped at him. 'How did you know?'

'Because you spend a lot of time here and you are not a religious man. Moreover, it was out of character when you said you wanted to delay warning the King about the pending revolt, because you were eager to keep a vigil for St Columba.'

'It is a good thing you are not a thief,' said Roger ruefully, 'or you would be able to rob me blind. You read my mind like one of your books.'

Geoffrey glanced at the praying monks. 'I suspect you will be waiting for a long time yet. They are so grateful the King has not replaced them that they will be on their knees for the next month. Of course, you could leave it and come back later.'

'No,' said Roger sullenly.

'You can have this,' whispered Bale, pressing a purse into Roger's hand. 'It is not worth as much as what you stole from the pirates, but it is better than nothing.'

Roger emptied the coins into his hand. 'This is very generous, Bale. But where is Vitalis's ring?'

Bale looked sheepish. 'I gave it to Brother Wardard.'

'Ah, yes,' said Roger, not altogether approvingly. 'I forgot he and Vitalis were friends.'

'Actually, sir, I gave it to him because . . . well, I told him it belonged to Sir Geoffrey's mother.'

'Why would he want something of hers?' asked Geoffrey, startled. 'I suspect he *was* once enamoured of her, but it was a long time ago, and he is now in holy orders.'

Bale sighed rather wistfully. 'He told me that he never stopped loving her, and that seeing you brought her back to him as if she was alive all over again. Especially when you went into battle.'

'Did he?' asked Geoffrey, feeling this was rather an unsuitable confidence for a celibate monastic to share with a squire.

Bale nodded. 'I was telling him about my own desire for a wife, see. A good woman, who will love me for myself. And he said that if I find her, I should grab her and slit the throat of anyone who tries to stand in my way.'

Geoffrey laughed. 'Did he now?'

'Well, all right – he said I should fight for her and not let a lesser man have her instead of me. But he was pleased with the ring and said he would pray to God to send me a lovely lady.'

'God help her,' muttered Roger.

Geoffrey regarded his squire in mystification. 'You are a strange man, Bale. You give a ring to Wardard, whom you barely know, and you donate your gold to Roger. Why?'

'They came from corpses, sir,' said Bale in a hushed voice. 'And Galfridus gave such a sermon on Sunday about the perils of such goods that I have not felt comfortable since.'

'I do not blame you,' said Roger, tucking his new acquisition inside his surcoat. 'Pillage is not for the tender-hearted.'

'Quick!' hissed Geoffrey urgently, as a commotion broke out in the nave. 'The King is coming – and I do not want to explain what happened to the Saxons' treasure. He is the kind of man who will take my manor in revenge, and Joan would not like that. Nor would Hilde.'

He eased into the shadows as the King approached the high altar. Roger remained nearby, loath to leave his hoard when one of the biggest thieves in Christendom was close. Galfridus and Ralph became aware of the royal presence behind them and did an awkward shuffle on their knees, turning their subservient poses from God to monarch.

'I leave within the hour,' announced Henry, giving the altar a brisk nod that passed for reverence. 'But I thought I had better pay my respects to Harold's death-site first. I do not want it said that I treat past kings with disrespect.'

'Yes, Sire,' said Galfridus.

'I suppose this business has ended well enough,' Henry went on sternly. 'But I am not pleased about the lost treasure. My coffers are always in need of replenishment.'

'Actually, we do have some spare gold, Sire,' said Galfridus brightly. 'God sent it to us, and I see now He must have left it for you.'

'God?' asked Henry warily.

'There can be no other explanation,' agreed Galfridus. 'Brother Wardard said it just appeared one day, all by itself.'

'Appeared where?'

'Inside the high altar.'

'Here!' cried Roger, hurtling forward. 'That is mine! I put it there for safekeeping and I went through a great deal of hardship for it.'

'Then you will be even more honoured to share it with your monarch,' said Henry smoothly.

'Share?' asked Roger weakly.

Henry nodded. 'A little for you. And a little more for me.'

Early the next day, Galfridus saw Geoffrey and Roger on their way, then retired to his solar. Ralph and Wardard had both requested interviews. With a sigh, he indicated to his secretary that his sacristan was to be admitted, and he listened patiently to the man's complaints about there being Saxon scullions in the kitchens already. He agreed to look into the matter, then summoned Wardard, who was a far more serious threat to his peace of mind.

'I saw Brother Aelfwig skulking about this morning,' said Wardard once the door was closed. 'I thought he had been handed to the King's men.'

'He was,' said Galfridus, rising to pour two goblets of wine. 'You must have imagined it. God knows, we have all been horribly unsettled since our peace was so violently shattered.'

Wardard drank politely, although he disliked wine so early in the day. He sighed and shook his head. 'It was no trick of the mind, Galfridus. The rebellion is not dead, is it? Aelfwig escaped and plans to try again.'

There was a soft movement from behind. Wardard tried to twist around, but his muscles were oddly heavy and he found they would not obey him.

'We *will* try again,' said Aelfwig softly. 'And with Galfridus's help, we will succeed. We would be on the path to victory now, had it not been for meddlers like you and those knights.'

Wardard forced a smile. 'But you have no leader. Ulf, Harold and Magnus are dead, and the earls will be guests of His Majesty for years to come.'

'I am not dead,' said another voice. It was difficult for Wardard to look around, but when he finally managed, it was to see Magnus, bandages swathed around his chest.

Struggling to breathe, Wardard turned to Galfridus. 'Why do you encourage them,' he croaked, 'when they have no chance of success?'

Galfridus poured his untouched wine back in the flask and handed it to Aelfwig, who stoppered it with considerable care. 'We will win eventually. I knew this attempt was doomed as soon as I saw Ulf in place of Harold. But we will not fail next time.'

'And here is the first of the treasure that will fund it,' said Magnus, reaching out suddenly and ripping away the ring that was tied on a string around the old monk's neck. His eyes narrowed. 'Strange! It looks very much like the one I lost aboard *Patrick* as I was dispatching the Usurper's spy.'

As Magnus's voice faded into a discordant jumble of words that no longer held any meaning, Wardard closed his eyes. He did not open them again.

# Historical Note

Every schoolchild knows the date 1066, when William the Conqueror defeated King Harold. But, although there are detailed accounts written by near-contemporary chroniclers and a good deal more is known about the Battle of Hastings than other medieval conflicts, many mysteries remain. Historians cannot state unequivocally, for example, that Harold was shot in the eye, and the various accounts of the battle contradict each other in places. The chroniclers generally had their own agendas – they sympathized with the Saxons or wanted to justify the Norman invasion – so cannot be accepted at face value.

Historians are uncertain how many men died that day, because some of the chroniclers' estimates, provided with great conviction, are clearly unrealistic. However, it is known that the first and very brutal attack by William's left flank almost determined the outcome in the Saxons' favour, and that the battle was long, violent, bitter and desperate. It is likely that the death toll was in the thousands. It was said that the Normans buried their own dead, whereas the Saxons were left for their families to collect. With such a very great slaughter, it is likely that the burial mounds and the remnants of smashed weapons would have been visible for decades.

It was not considered a good thing to break the Commandment 'Thou shalt not kill', even in battle – although an exception was made for the Crusades – and it was a sensible move on William's part to found an abbey as an act of penance. Not only did it pacify the Church and honour the dead, it also populated (with Normans) an area that was vulnerable to invasion. Benedictine monks were brought from Marmoutier in France, and building began. Tradition has it that William wanted the high altar on the site of the fiercest fighting, where Harold died. The monks looked with horror at the clay ridge and nearby bogs, and promptly chose a different site. William was not amused and obliged them to abandon the work and start again – where he had ordered.

By the early 1100s, the church and chapter house had been completed, as were a range of temporary wooden buildings for the brethren to use until they were built in stone. Unfortunately, most of the abbey fell victim to the Dissolution.

After the death of Abbot Henry in 1102, there was an interregnum until 1107 when Abbot Ralph was appointed. During this time, the abbey was in the care of clerks or custodians, including one called Geoffrey, who was a monk of St Carileff. He was said to be a competent businessman, although not well educated. The Latin version of his name, Galfridus, has been used in *The Bloodstained Throne* to avoid confusion with Geoffrey Mappestone.

Not a great deal is known about King Harold and his descendants. His first love was Edith Swannehals (Swan-neck), who provided him with at least five, and possibly six, children. He married the high-born Ealdgyth ten months before he died, and their son Harold was born posthumously. There is some suggestion that young Harold had a twin brother called Ulf, but it is also possible that Ulf was another of Edith's children, or perhaps the son of a third liaison. Ulf was a prisoner of William until the Conqueror's death in 1087.

Meanwhile, Harold was used as a focal point for rebellion by his uncles, but fled from England after the Saxon uprising in 1069–70. He probably went to Ireland and then to Norway, and it is known he took part in a battle at Anglesey in 1098, supporting King Magnus Olaffson against the Norman earls of Shrewsbury (Robert de Bellême) and Chester. Then he disappears from the records.

Harold's sons by Edith – Godwine, Edmund and Magnus – were older than Ulf and Harold, and they were desperate to gain back what their father had lost. They were involved in several invasions, mostly in the south-west, but were beaten back each time. They eventually migrated to Flanders, where they made alliances with William's European enemies.

Godwine and Edmund travelled to Denmark to encourage their cousin King Swein to invade England, but Swein died in 1074, and Denmark entered a period of instability. Edmund and Godwine fade from the records at that point. Magnus may have remained in Flanders or even been killed in one of the English battles. The brothers' rebellions and rabble-rousing have been seen as irrelevant and no more than a nuisance to William, but England was unsettled after the invasion, and it is unlikely that an astute ruler like William – or his equally capable son Henry – would have ignored them.

Duke Robert of Normandy did make a brief visit to his brother Henry in the summer of 1103, when he asked King Henry to restore the estates and title of his friend William de Warrene, Earl of Surrey. Henry was not pleased to see him, but acceded to the request, although it cost Robert a good deal of money. So, Warrene gained back his lands and served Henry faithfully for the rest of his life; Henry gained a loyal supporter and a handsome sum of money; and Robert lost out. It was a foolish, magnanimous gesture typical of a man who, although likeable and generous, was not in Henry's class as a leader. Robert and Henry did not meet again until they were on opposite sides at the Battle of Tinchenbrai in 1106.